DINOSAUR KING™

Vol. 1

STORY AND ART BY
YOHEI SAKAI

MEET THE CHARACTERS

Max ▼
An upbeat, determined boy with a fascination for dinosaurs and fossils

Alpha Gang
The evil scientists plotting to use dinosaurs to take over the world

◀ Rex
Max's best friend, who also shares a passion for dinosaurs

▲ Benjamin
Rex's dinosaur partner

King ▶
Max's dinosaur partner

TABLE OF CONTENTS

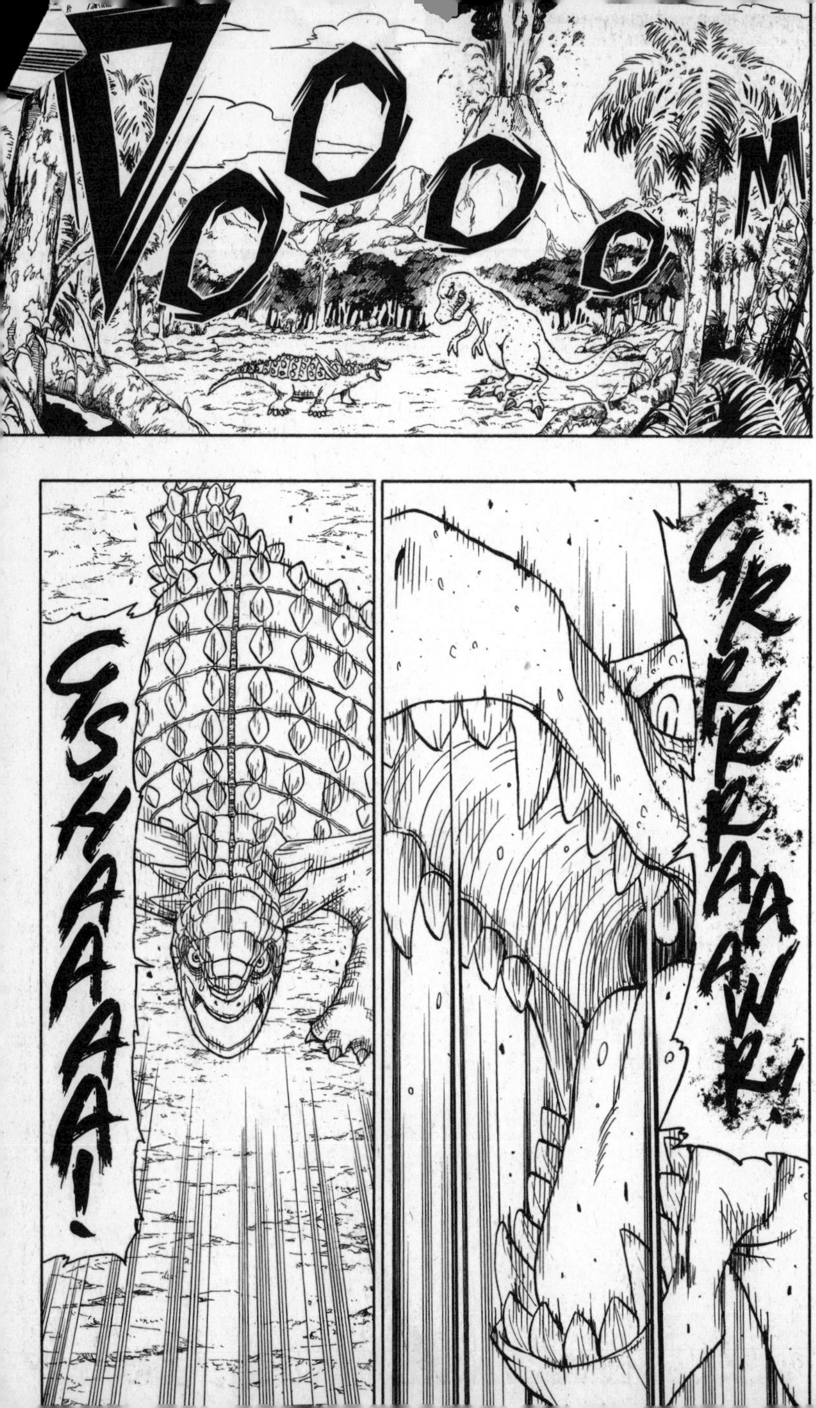
VOOOOOM
GRRRAAWR!
GSHAAAA!

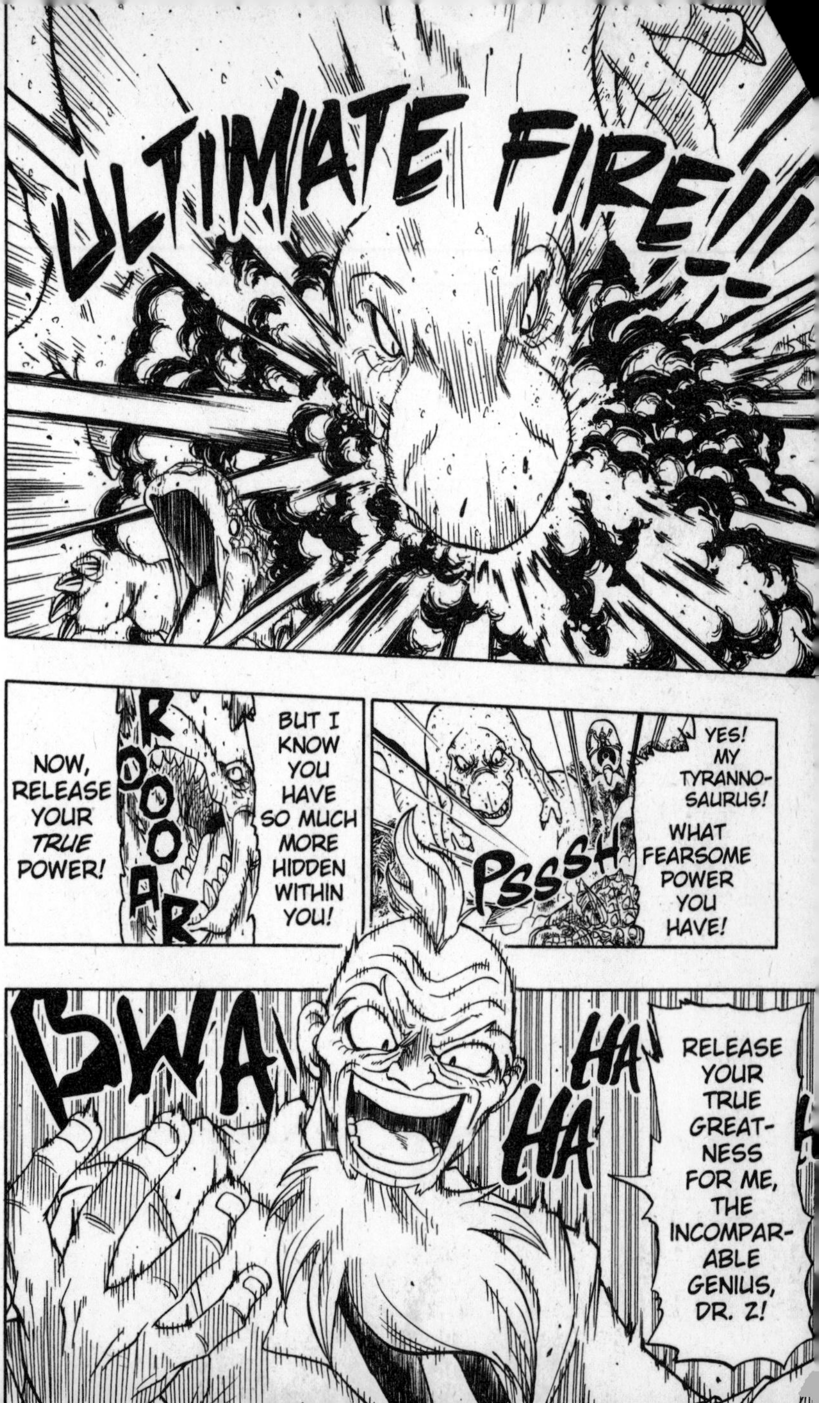
ULTIMATE FIRE!!
YES! MY TYRANNO-SAURUS!
WHAT FEARSOME POWER YOU HAVE!
PSSSH
BUT I KNOW YOU HAVE SO MUCH MORE HIDDEN WITHIN YOU!
ROOOOAR
NOW, RELEASE YOUR TRUE POWER!
RELEASE YOUR TRUE GREAT-NESS FOR ME, THE INCOMPAR-ABLE GENIUS, DR. Z!
BWA HA HA

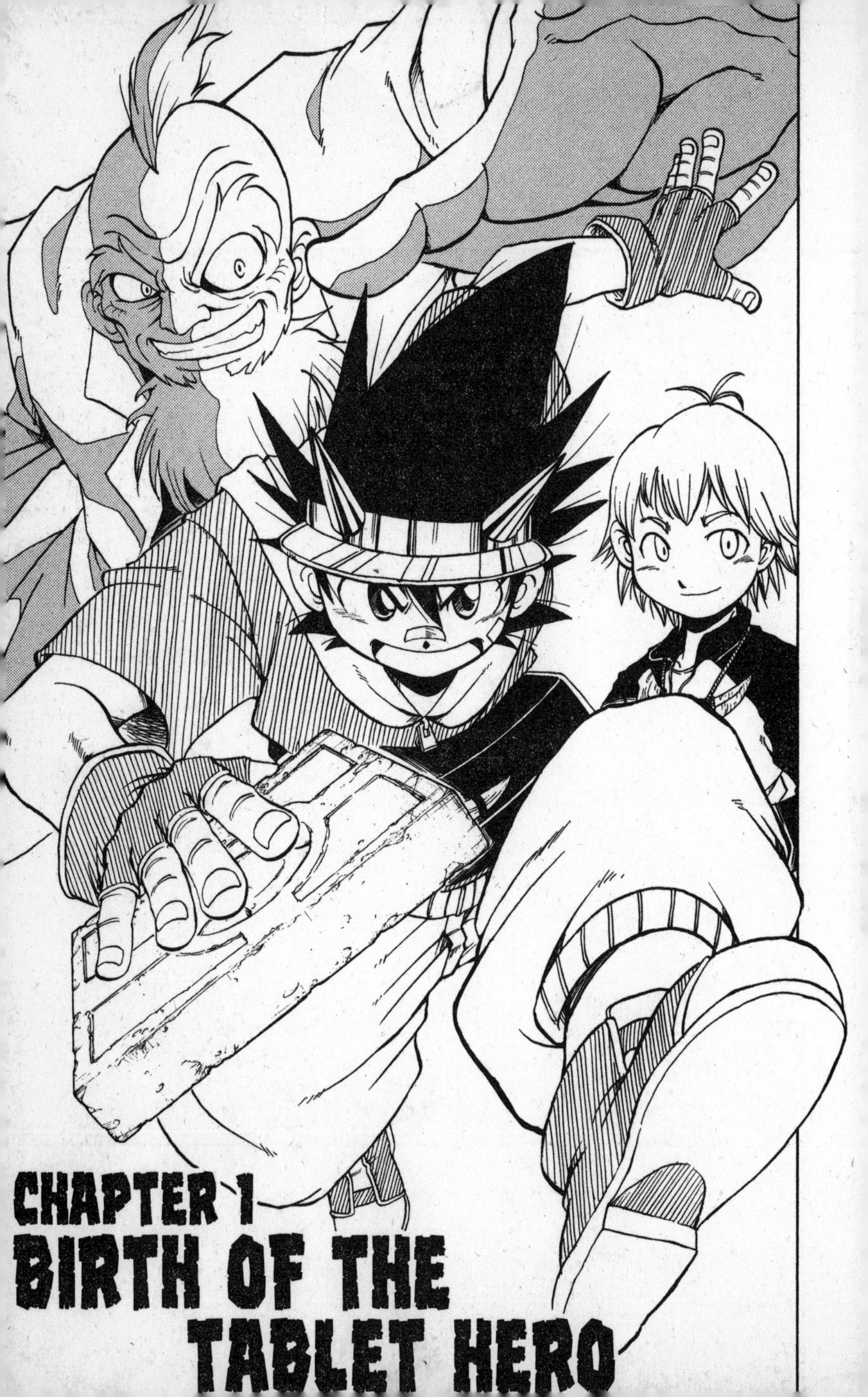
CHAPTER 1
BIRTH OF THE
TABLET HERO

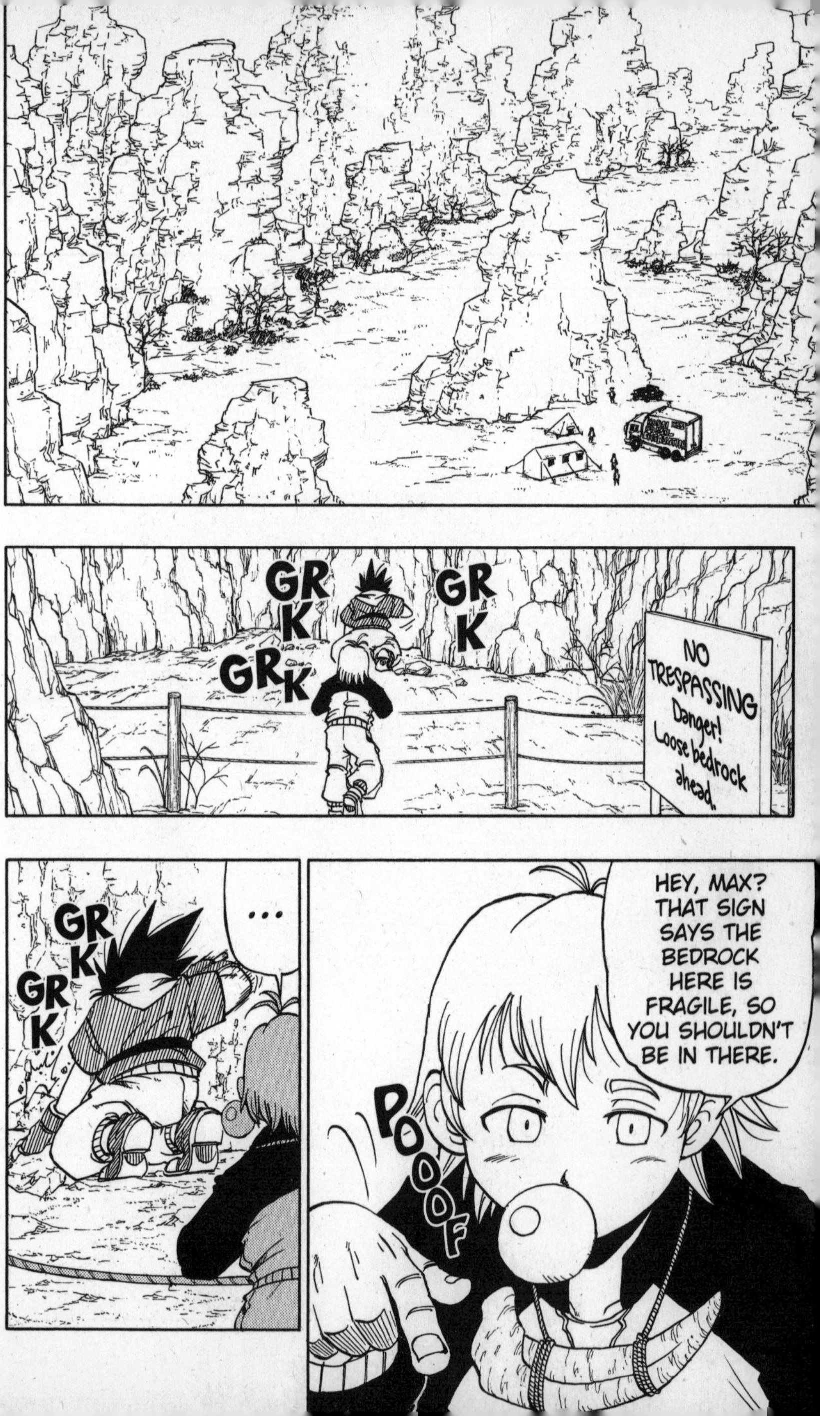
GRK
GRK
GRK
NO TRESPASSING
Danger! Loose bedrock ahead.
HEY, MAX? THAT SIGN SAYS THE BEDROCK HERE IS FRAGILE, SO YOU SHOULDN'T BE IN THERE.
POOOF
...
GRK
GRK

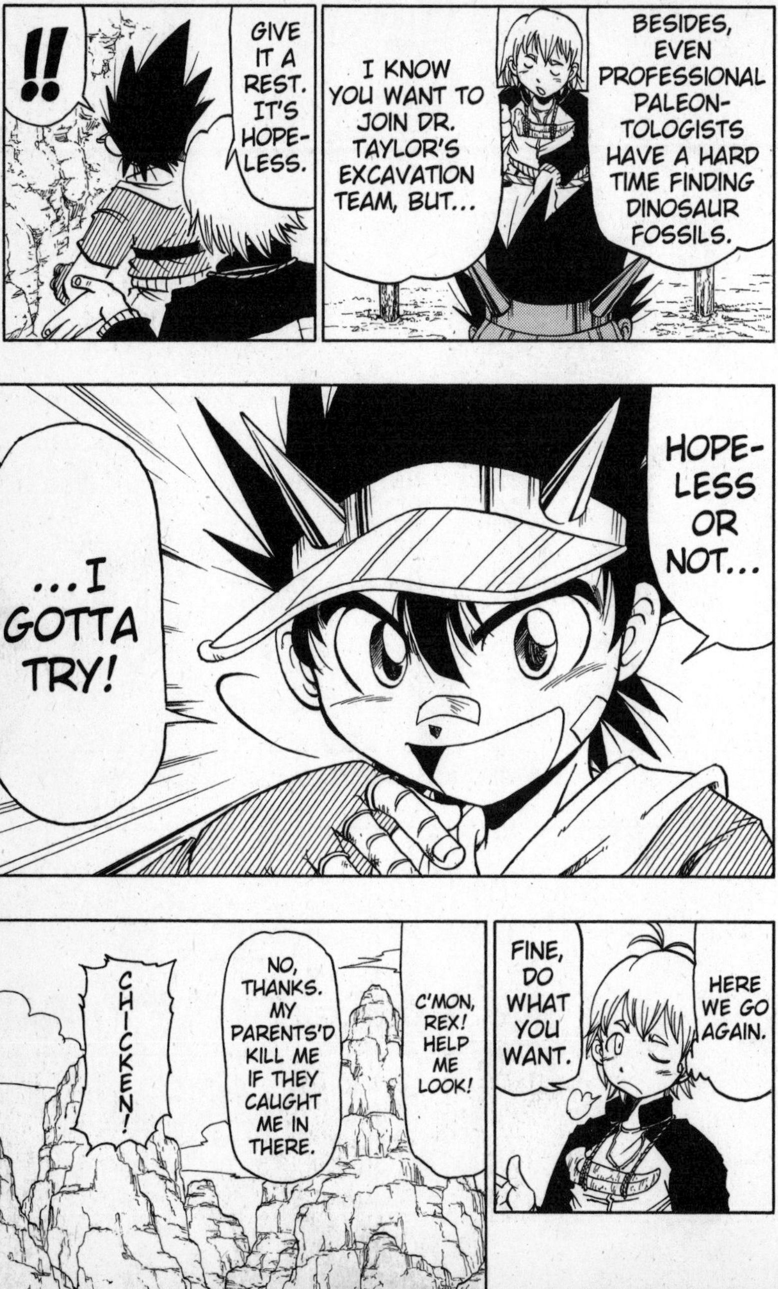

I KNOW YOU WANT TO JOIN DR. TAYLOR'S EXCAVATION TEAM, BUT...
BESIDES, EVEN PROFESSIONAL PALEON-TOLOGISTS HAVE A HARD TIME FINDING DINOSAUR FOSSILS.
GIVE IT A REST. IT'S HOPE-LESS.
!!
HOPE-LESS OR NOT...
...I GOTTA TRY!
HERE WE GO AGAIN.
FINE, DO WHAT YOU WANT.
C'MON, REX! HELP ME LOOK!
NO, THANKS. MY PARENTS'D KILL ME IF THEY CAUGHT ME IN THERE.
CHICKEN!

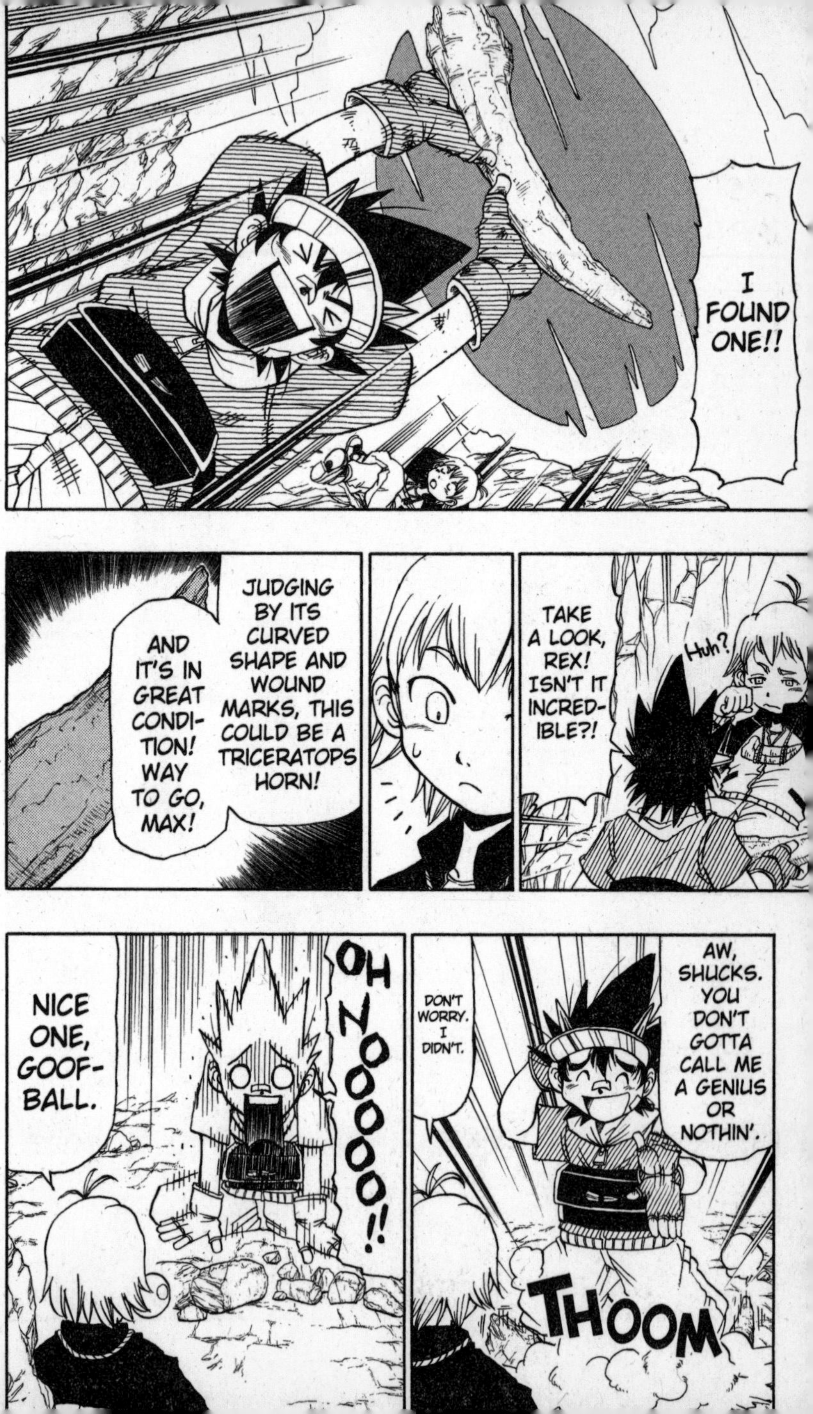
I FOUND ONE!!
TAKE A LOOK, REX! ISN'T IT INCREDIBLE?!
Huh?
JUDGING BY ITS CURVED SHAPE AND WOUND MARKS, THIS COULD BE A TRICERATOPS HORN!
AND IT'S IN GREAT CONDITION! WAY TO GO, MAX!
AW, SHUCKS. YOU DON'T GOTTA CALL ME A GENIUS OR NOTHIN'.
DON'T WORRY. I DIDN'T.
THOOM
OH NOOOOOO!!
NICE ONE, GOOF-BALL.

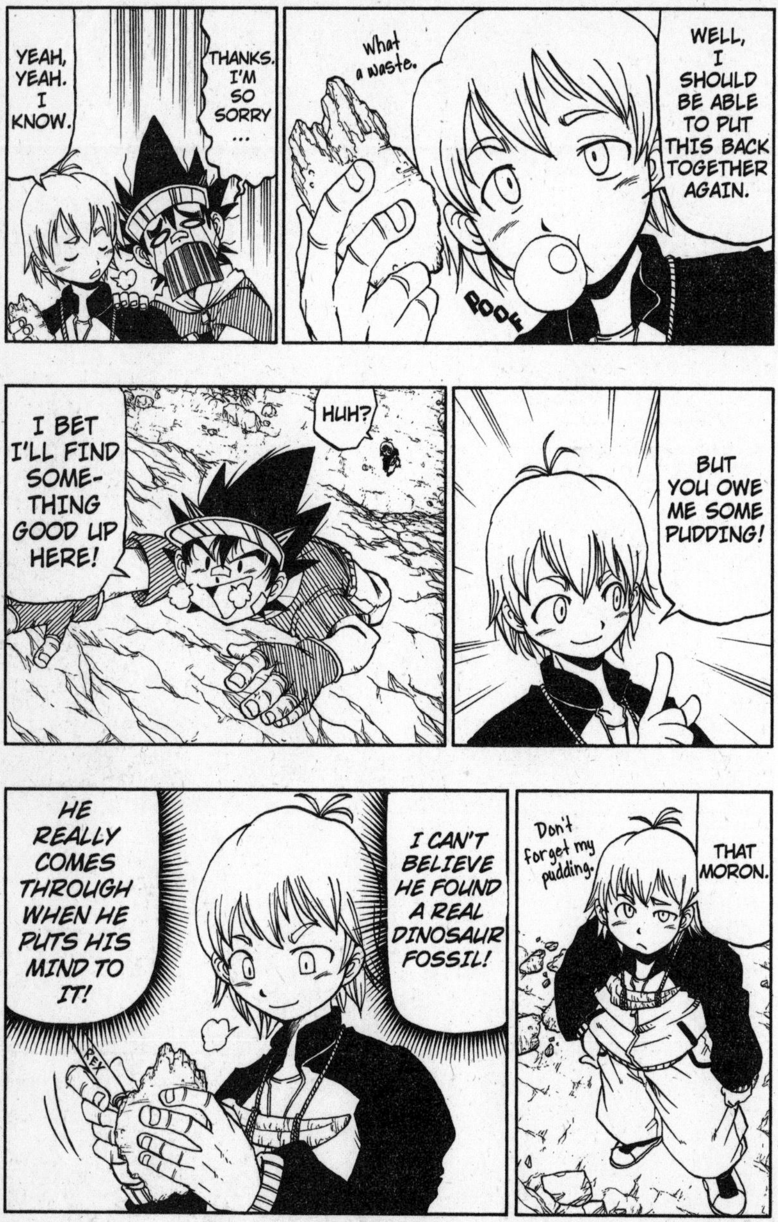
WELL, I SHOULD BE ABLE TO PUT THIS BACK TOGETHER AGAIN.
What a waste.
POOF
THANKS. I'M SO SORRY ...
YEAH, YEAH. I KNOW.
BUT YOU OWE ME SOME PUDDING!
HUH?
I BET I'LL FIND SOME-THING GOOD UP HERE!
THAT MORON.
Don't forget my pudding.
I CAN'T BELIEVE HE FOUND A REAL DINOSAUR FOSSIL!
HE REALLY COMES THROUGH WHEN HE PUTS HIS MIND TO IT!
REX

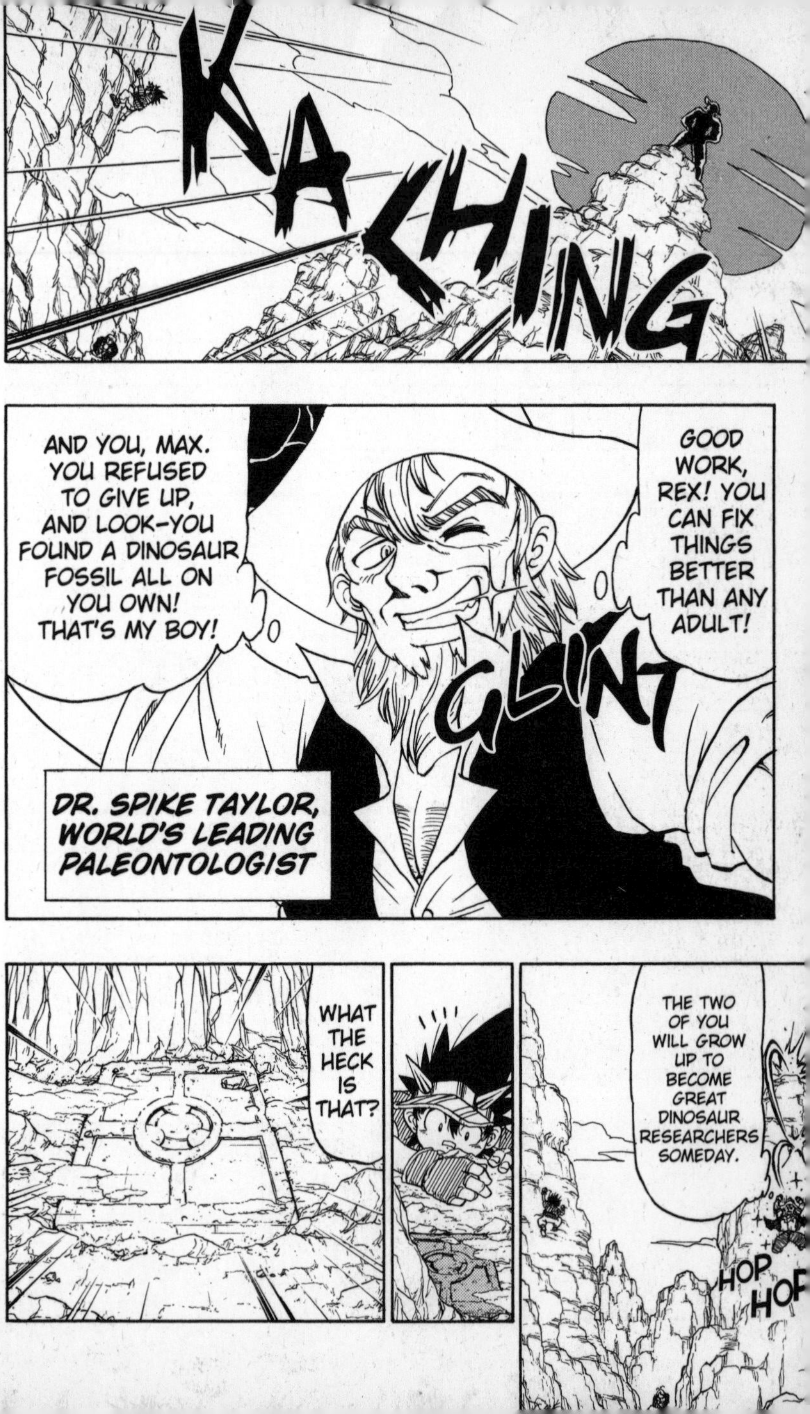
KA-CHING
GOOD WORK, REX! YOU CAN FIX THINGS BETTER THAN ANY ADULT!
AND YOU, MAX. YOU REFUSED TO GIVE UP, AND LOOK–YOU FOUND A DINOSAUR FOSSIL ALL ON YOU OWN! THAT'S MY BOY!
GLINT
DR. SPIKE TAYLOR, WORLD'S LEADING PALEONTOLOGIST
THE TWO OF YOU WILL GROW UP TO BECOME GREAT DINOSAUR RESEARCHERS SOMEDAY.
HOP
HOP
WHAT THE HECK IS THAT?

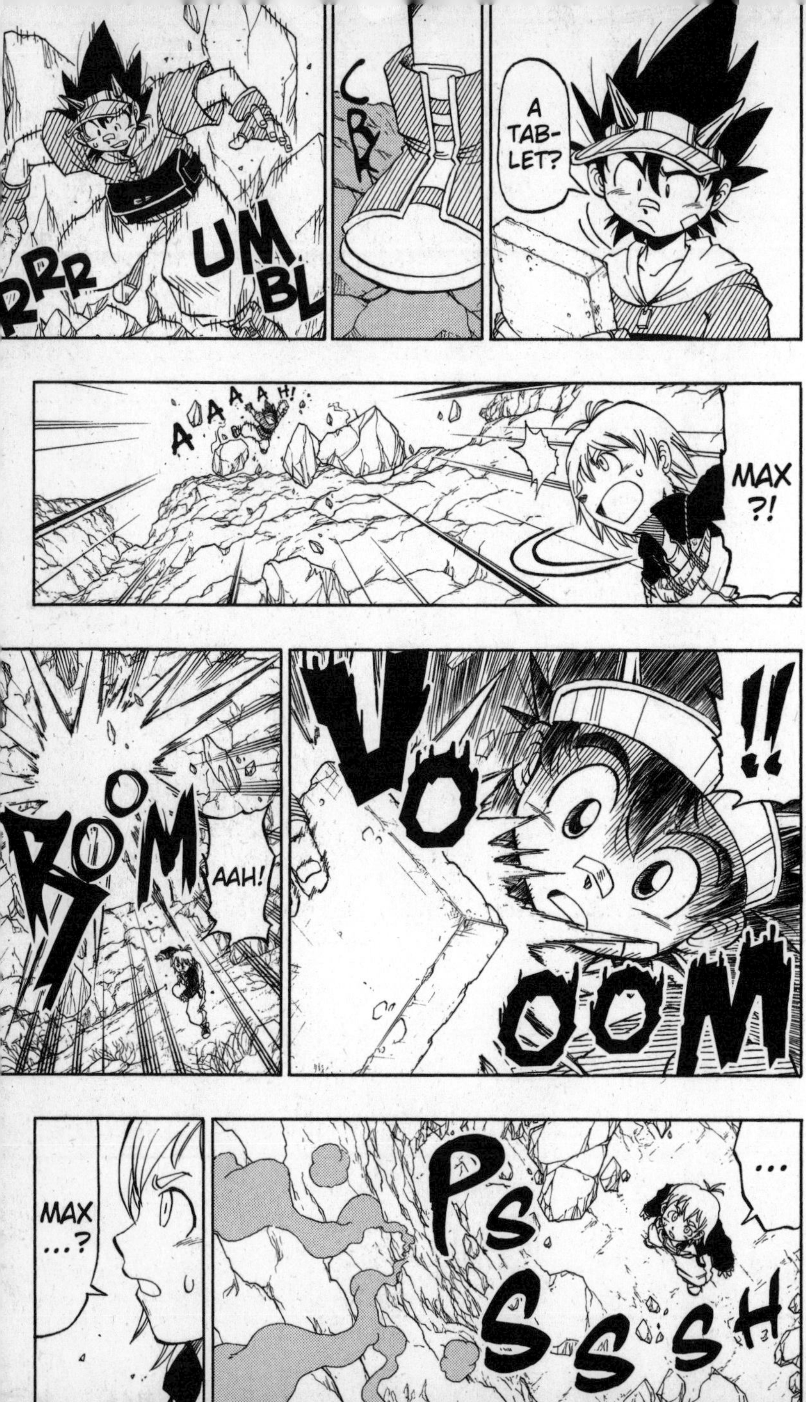
A TAB-LET?
RRR UM BL
MAX ?!
AAAAH!
VO !! OOM
ROOM
AAH!
...
PS SSSSH
MAX ...?

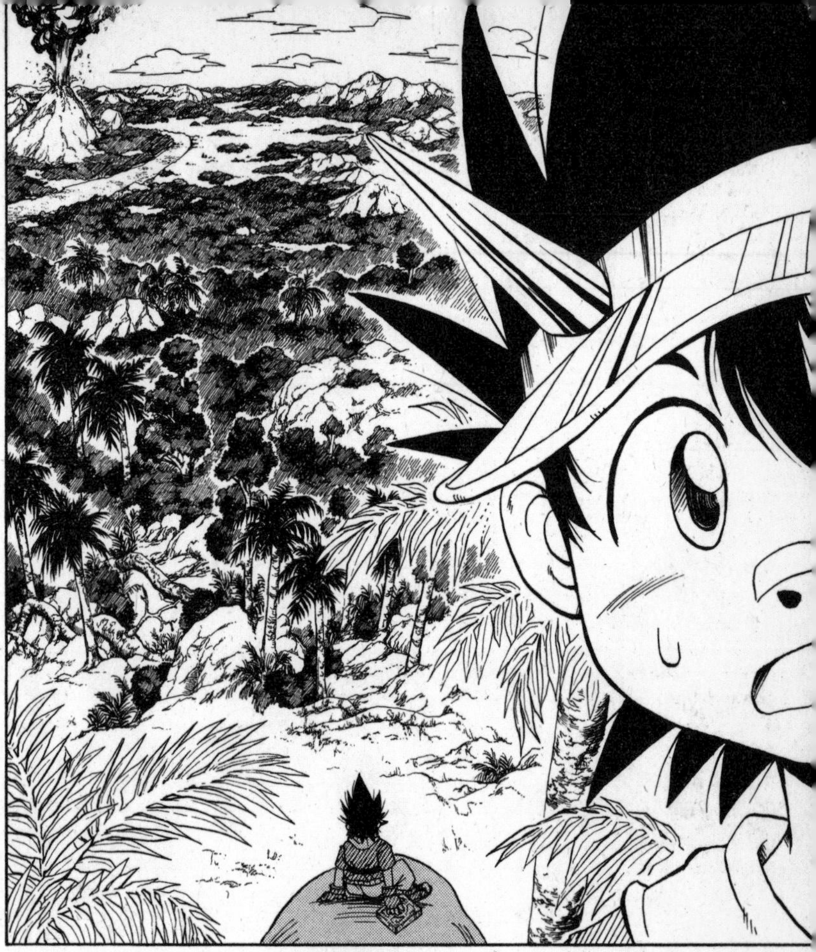

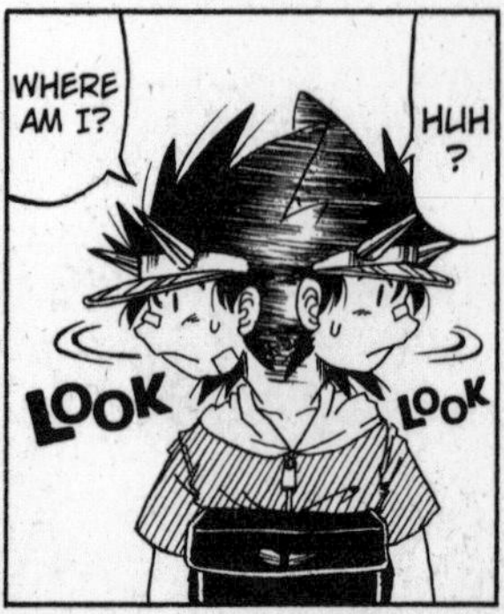
HUH ?
WHERE AM I?
LOOK
LOOK

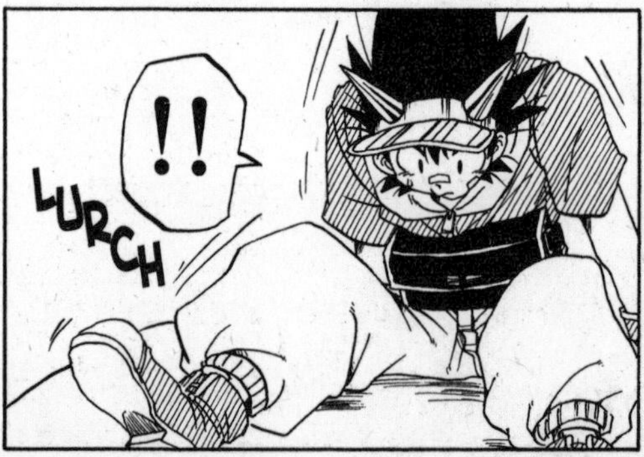
!!
LURCH

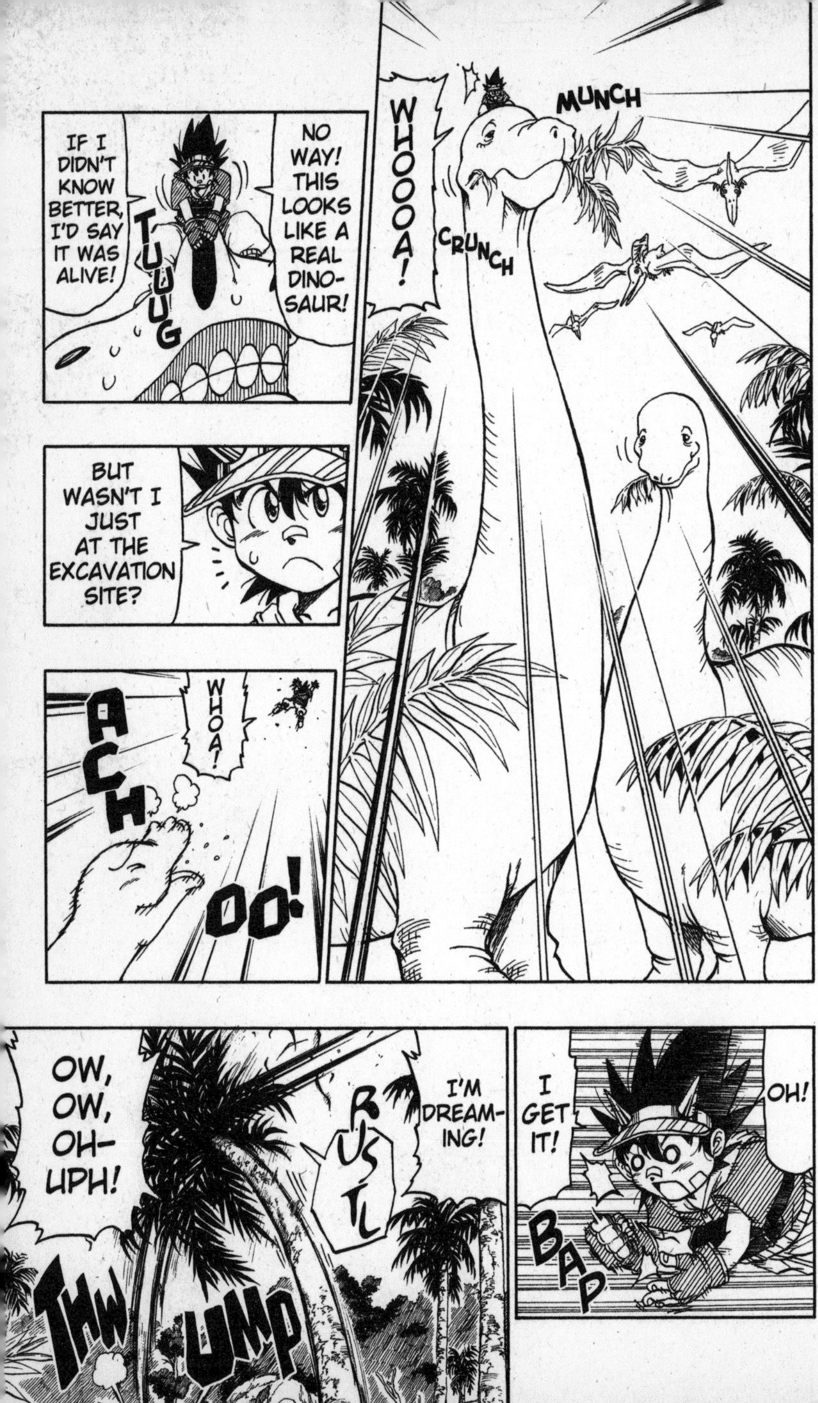
WHOOOOA!
MUNCH
CRUNCH
NO WAY! THIS LOOKS LIKE A REAL DINO-SAUR!
IF I DIDN'T KNOW BETTER, I'D SAY IT WAS ALIVE!
TUUUG
BUT WASN'T I JUST AT THE EXCAVATION SITE?
WHOA!
ACH
OO!
OH!
I GET IT!
BAP
I'M DREAM-ING!
RUSTL
OW, OW, OH-UPH!
THWUMP

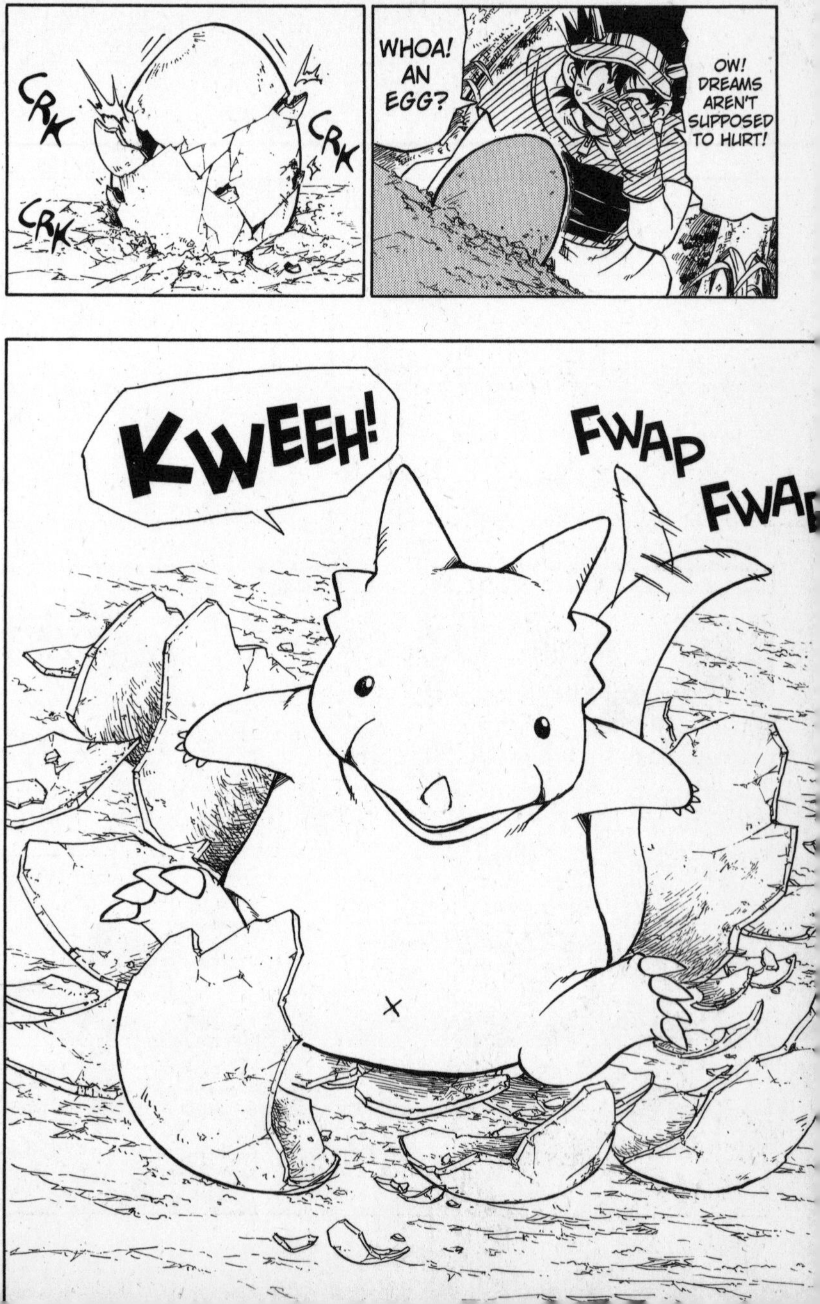
OW! DREAMS AREN'T SUPPOSED TO HURT!
WHOA! AN EGG?
CRK
CRK
CRK
FWAP
FWA
KWEEH!

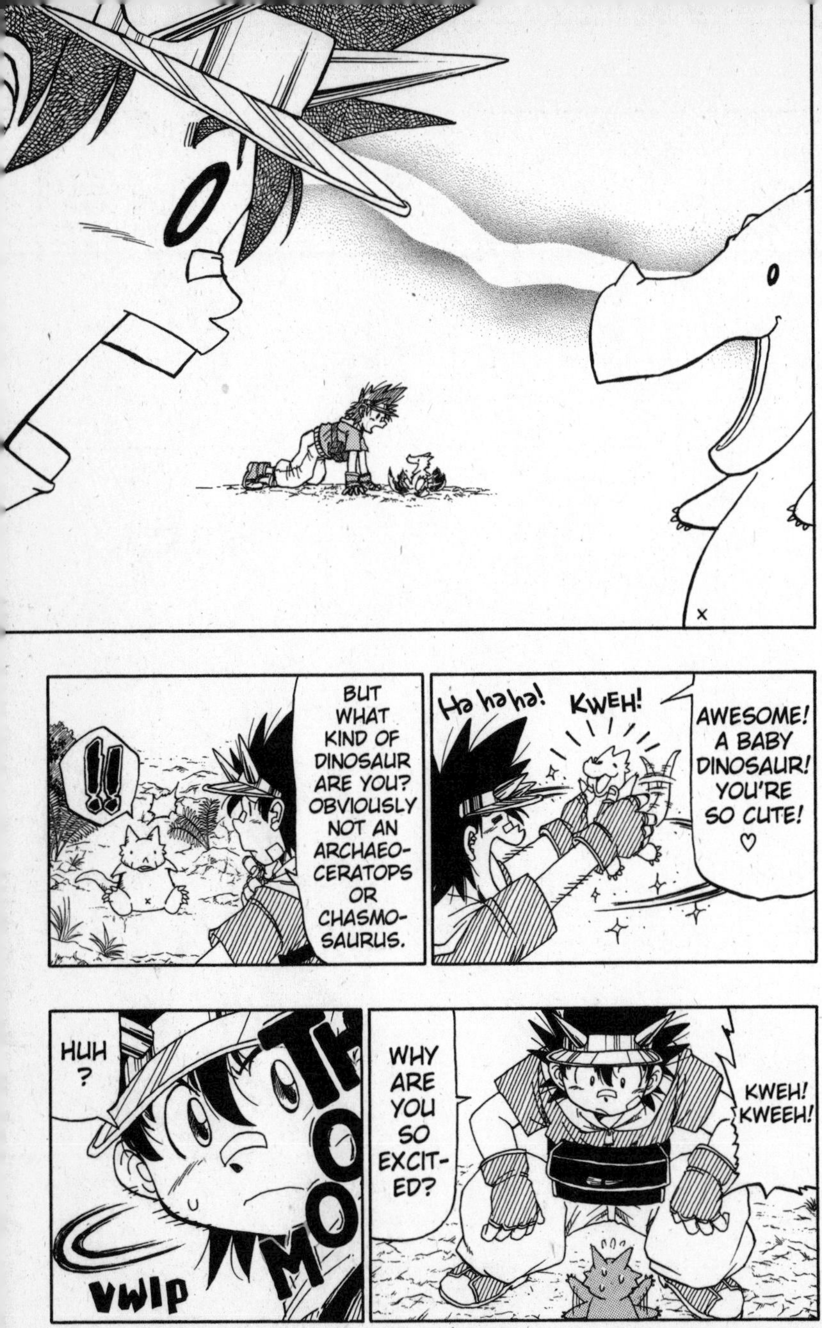
AWESOME! A BABY DINOSAUR! YOU'RE SO CUTE! ♡
KWEH!
Ha ha ha!
BUT WHAT KIND OF DINOSAUR ARE YOU? OBVIOUSLY NOT AN ARCHAEO-CERATOPS OR CHASMO-SAURUS.
!!
KWEH! KWEEH!
WHY ARE YOU SO EXCIT-ED?
THOOM
HUH?
VWIP

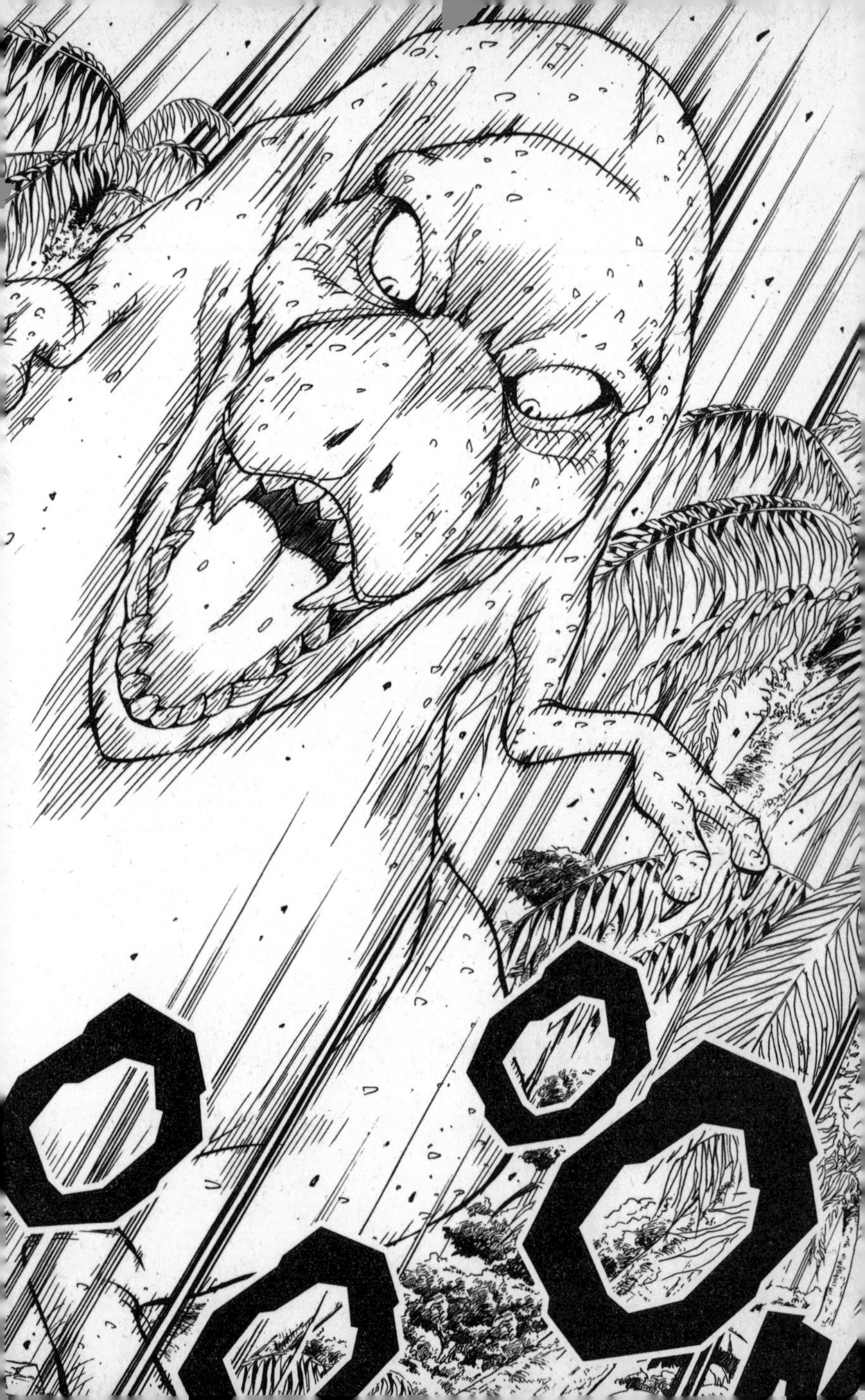

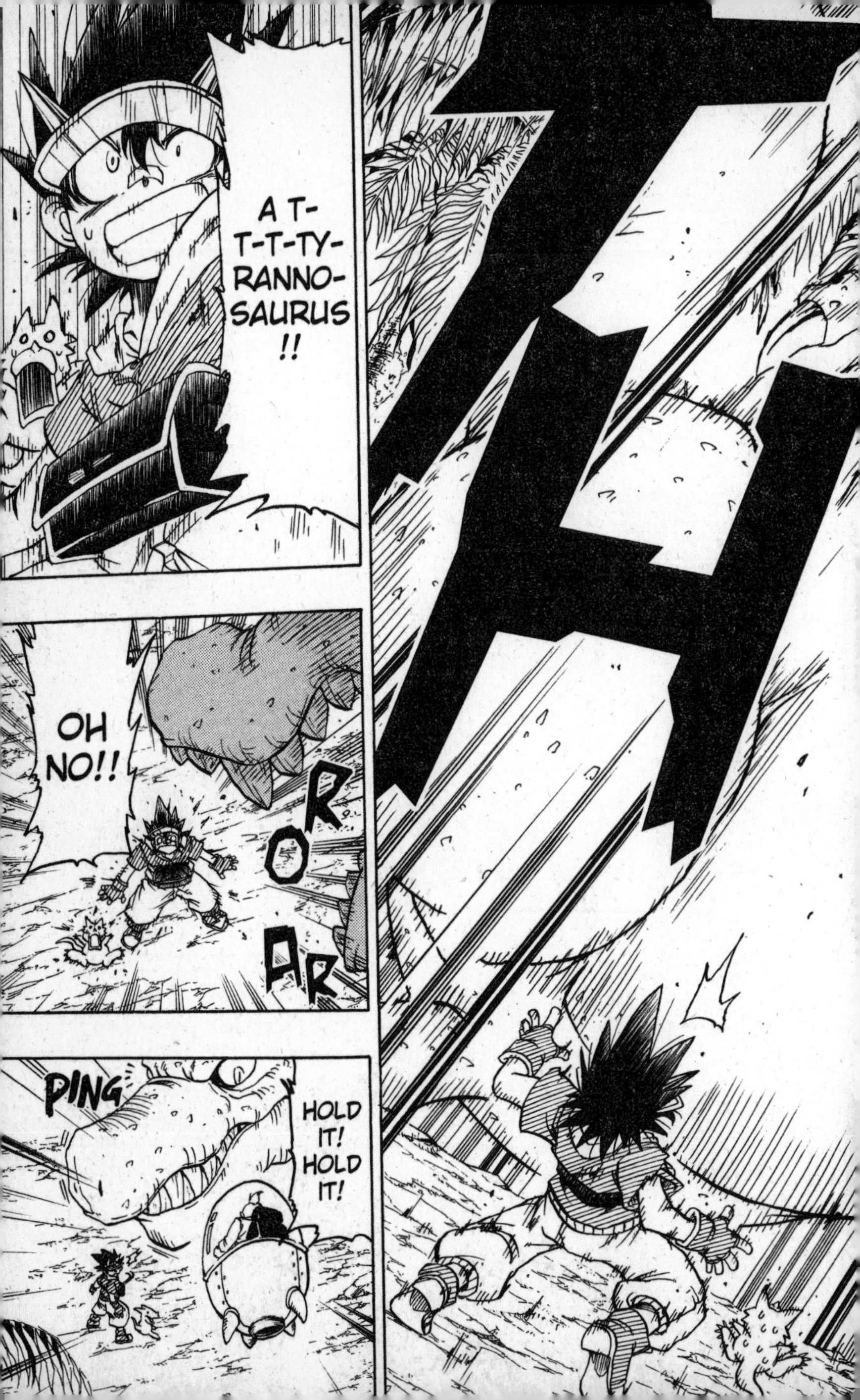
A T-T-T-TY-RANNO-SAURUS !!
OH NO!!
ROAR
HOLD IT! HOLD IT!
PING

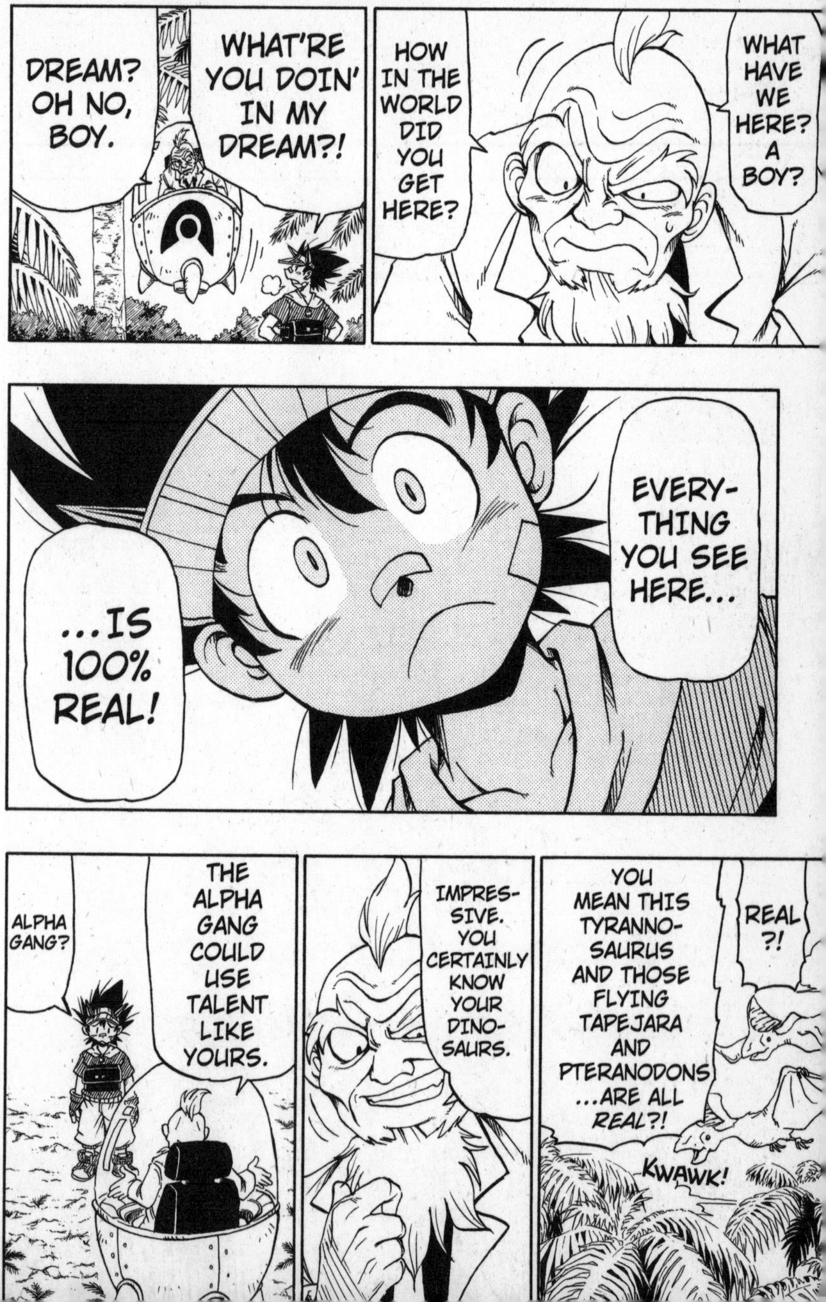
WHAT HAVE WE HERE? A BOY?
HOW IN THE WORLD DID YOU GET HERE?
WHAT'RE YOU DOIN' IN MY DREAM?!
DREAM? OH NO, BOY.
EVERY-THING YOU SEE HERE...
...IS 100% REAL!
REAL ?!
YOU MEAN THIS TYRANNO-SAURUS AND THOSE FLYING TAPEJARA AND PTERANODONS ...ARE ALL REAL?!
KWAWK!
IMPRES-SIVE. YOU CERTAINLY KNOW YOUR DINO-SAURS.
THE ALPHA GANG COULD USE TALENT LIKE YOURS.
ALPHA GANG?

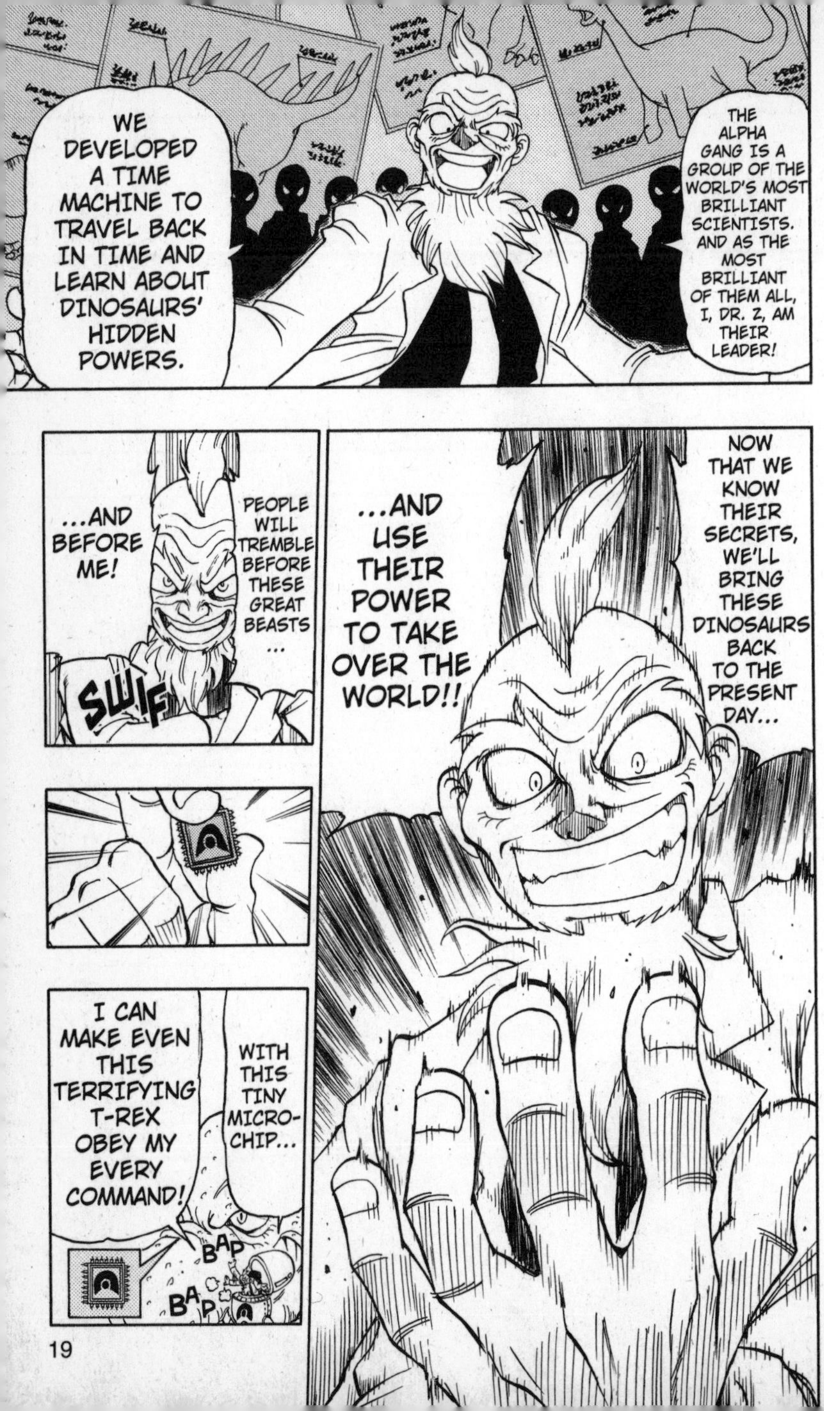
THE ALPHA GANG IS A GROUP OF THE WORLD'S MOST BRILLIANT SCIENTISTS. AND AS THE MOST BRILLIANT OF THEM ALL, I, DR. Z, AM THEIR LEADER!
WE DEVELOPED A TIME MACHINE TO TRAVEL BACK IN TIME AND LEARN ABOUT DINOSAURS' HIDDEN POWERS.
NOW THAT WE KNOW THEIR SECRETS, WE'LL BRING THESE DINOSAURS BACK TO THE PRESENT DAY...
...AND USE THEIR POWER TO TAKE OVER THE WORLD!!
PEOPLE WILL TREMBLE BEFORE THESE GREAT BEASTS...
...AND BEFORE ME!
SWIF
WITH THIS TINY MICRO-CHIP...
I CAN MAKE EVEN THIS TERRIFYING T-REX OBEY MY EVERY COMMAND!
BAP
BAP

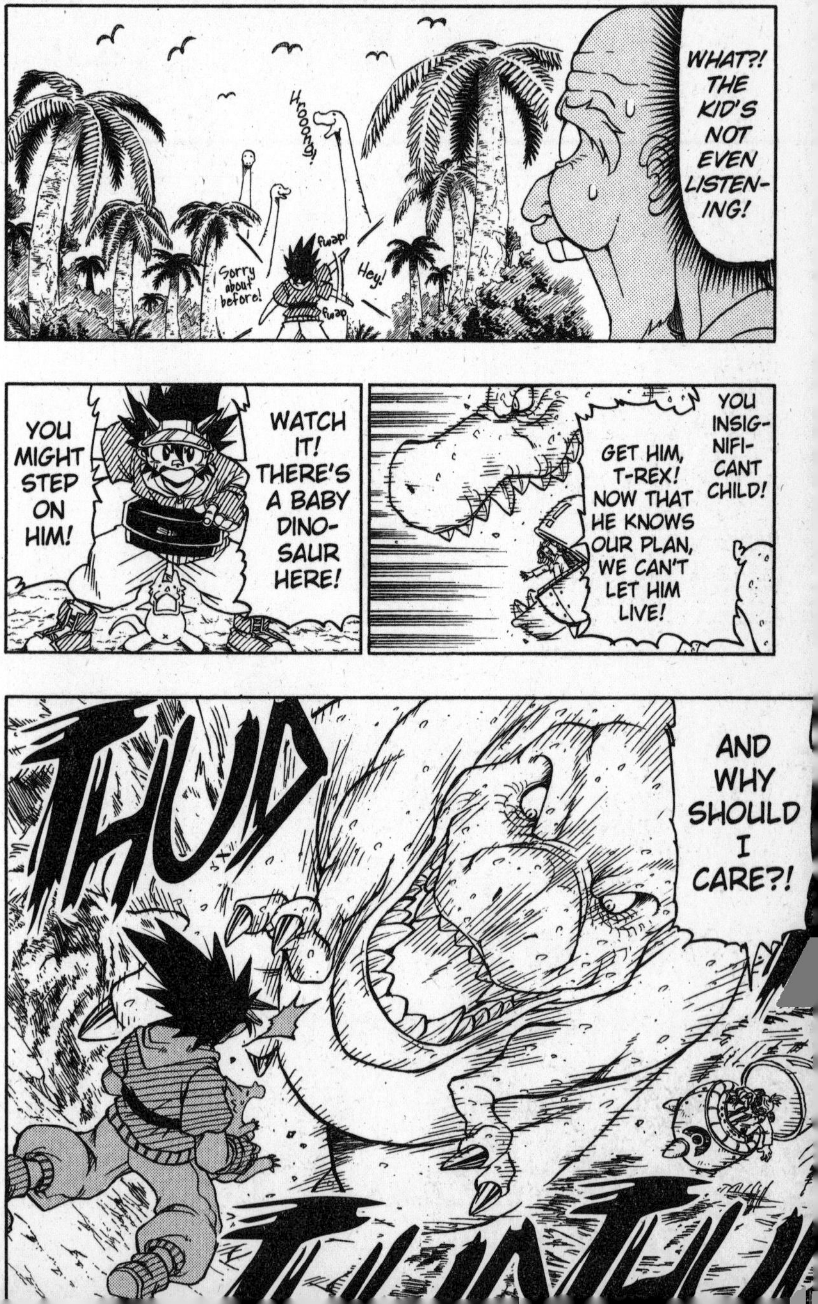
WHAT?! THE KID'S NOT EVEN LISTEN-ING!
Hrooong!
Hey!
fwap
Sorry about before!
fwap
YOU INSIG-NIFI-CANT CHILD!
GET HIM, T-REX! NOW THAT HE KNOWS OUR PLAN, WE CAN'T LET HIM LIVE!
WATCH IT! THERE'S A BABY DINO-SAUR HERE!
YOU MIGHT STEP ON HIM!
AND WHY SHOULD I CARE?!
THUD

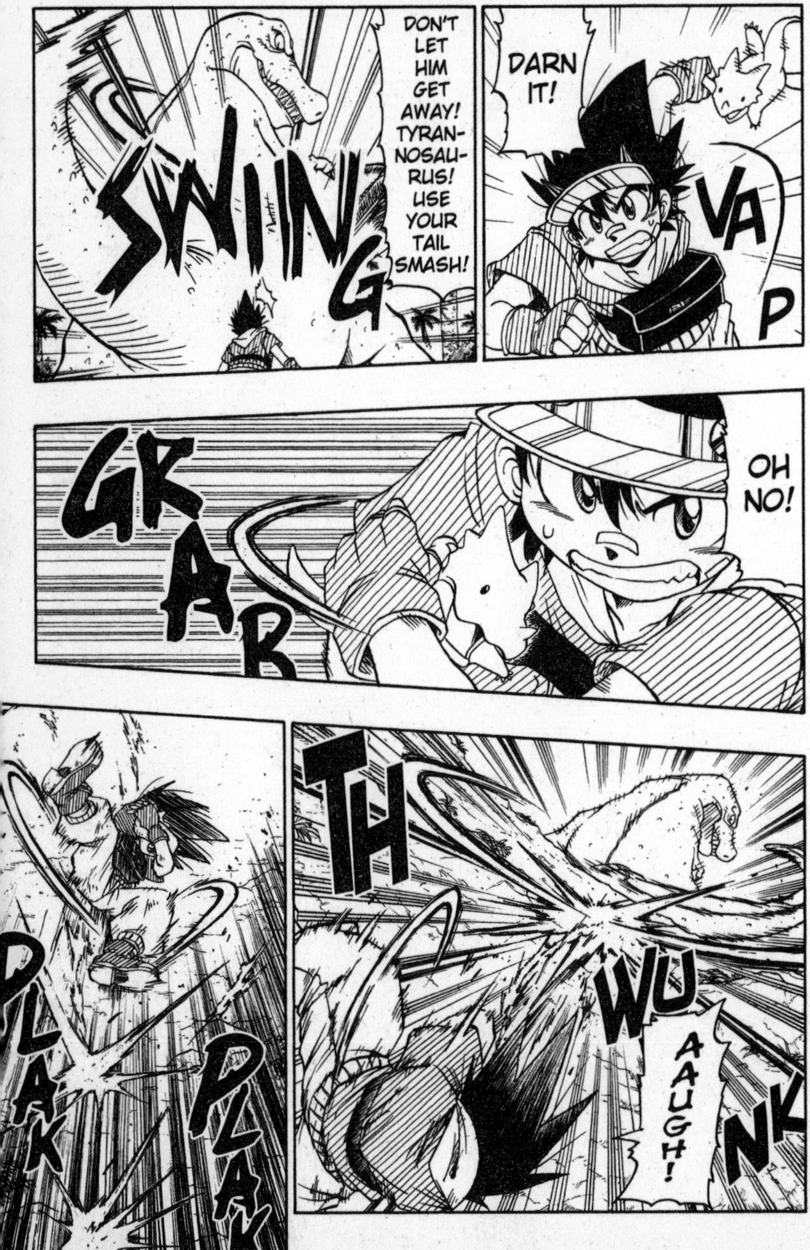
DARN IT!
VAP
DON'T LET HIM GET AWAY! TYRANNOSAURUS! USE YOUR TAIL SMASH!
SWING
OH NO!
GRAB
THWUNK
AAUGH!
PLAK
PLAK

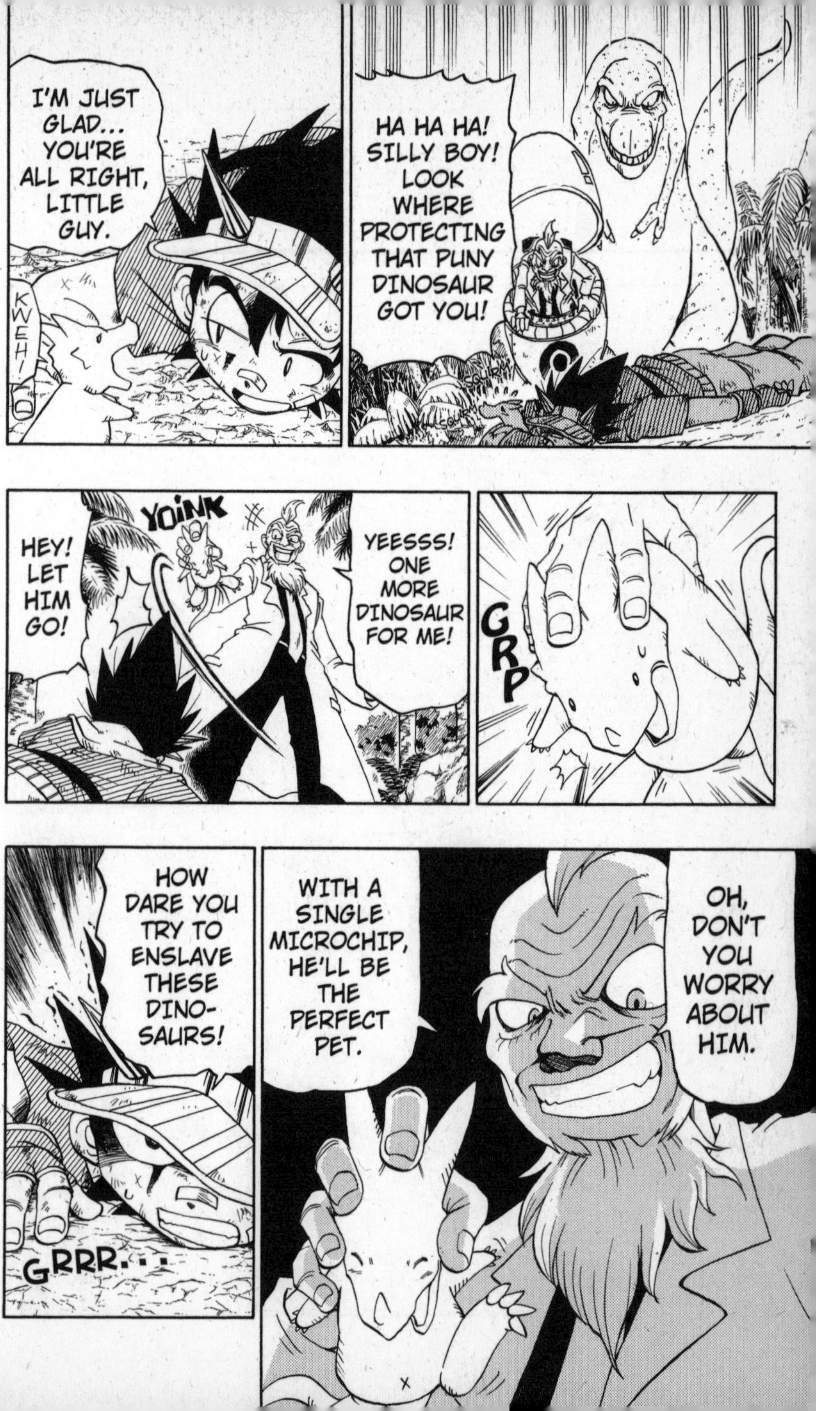
HA HA HA! SILLY BOY! LOOK WHERE PROTECTING THAT PUNY DINOSAUR GOT YOU!
SQUIRM
SQUIRM
I'M JUST GLAD... YOU'RE ALL RIGHT, LITTLE GUY.
KWEH!
GRP
YEESSS! ONE MORE DINOSAUR FOR ME!
YOINK
HEY! LET HIM GO!
OH, DON'T YOU WORRY ABOUT HIM.
WITH A SINGLE MICROCHIP, HE'LL BE THE PERFECT PET.
HOW DARE YOU TRY TO ENSLAVE THESE DINO-SAURS!
GRRR...

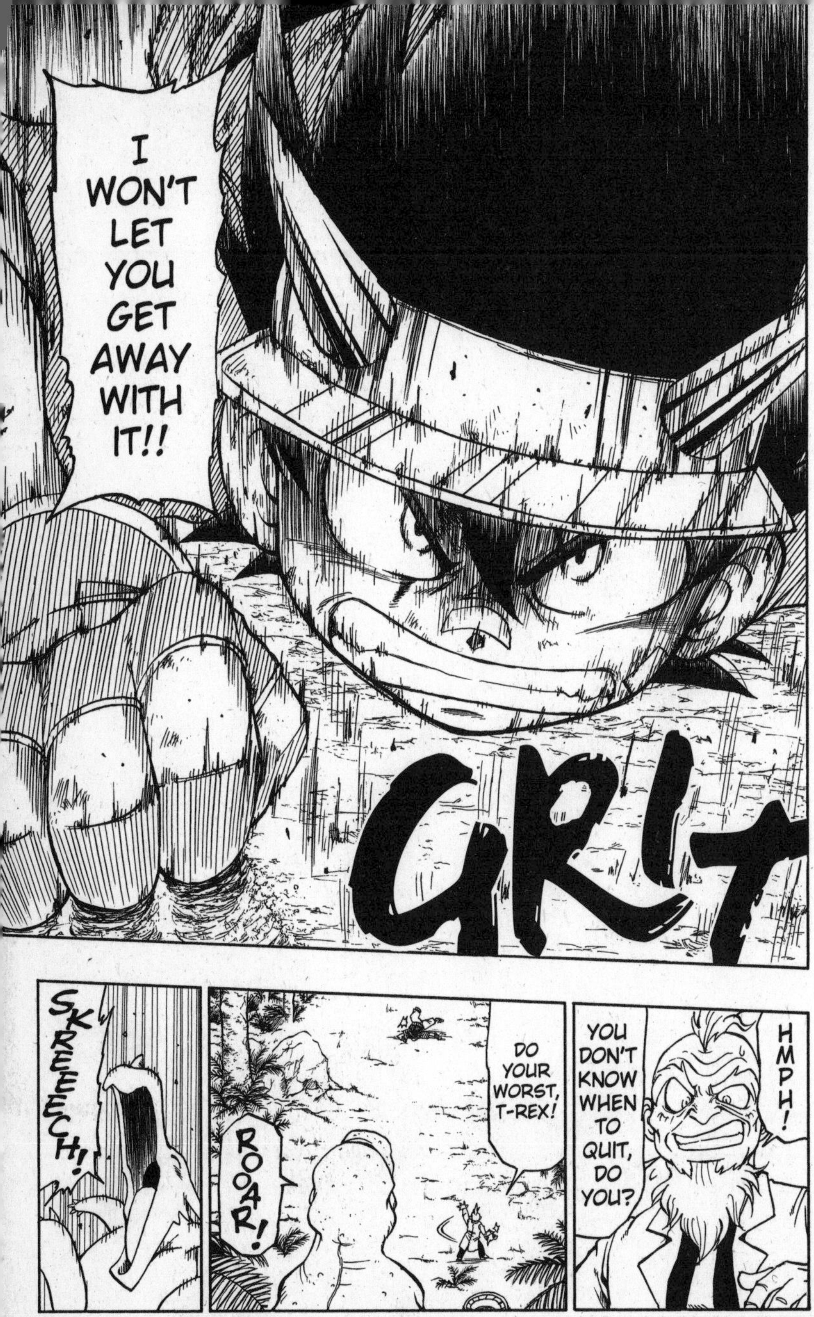
I WON'T LET YOU GET AWAY WITH IT!!
GRIT
HMPH!
YOU DON'T KNOW WHEN TO QUIT, DO YOU?
DO YOUR WORST, T-REX!
ROOAR!
SKREEECH!

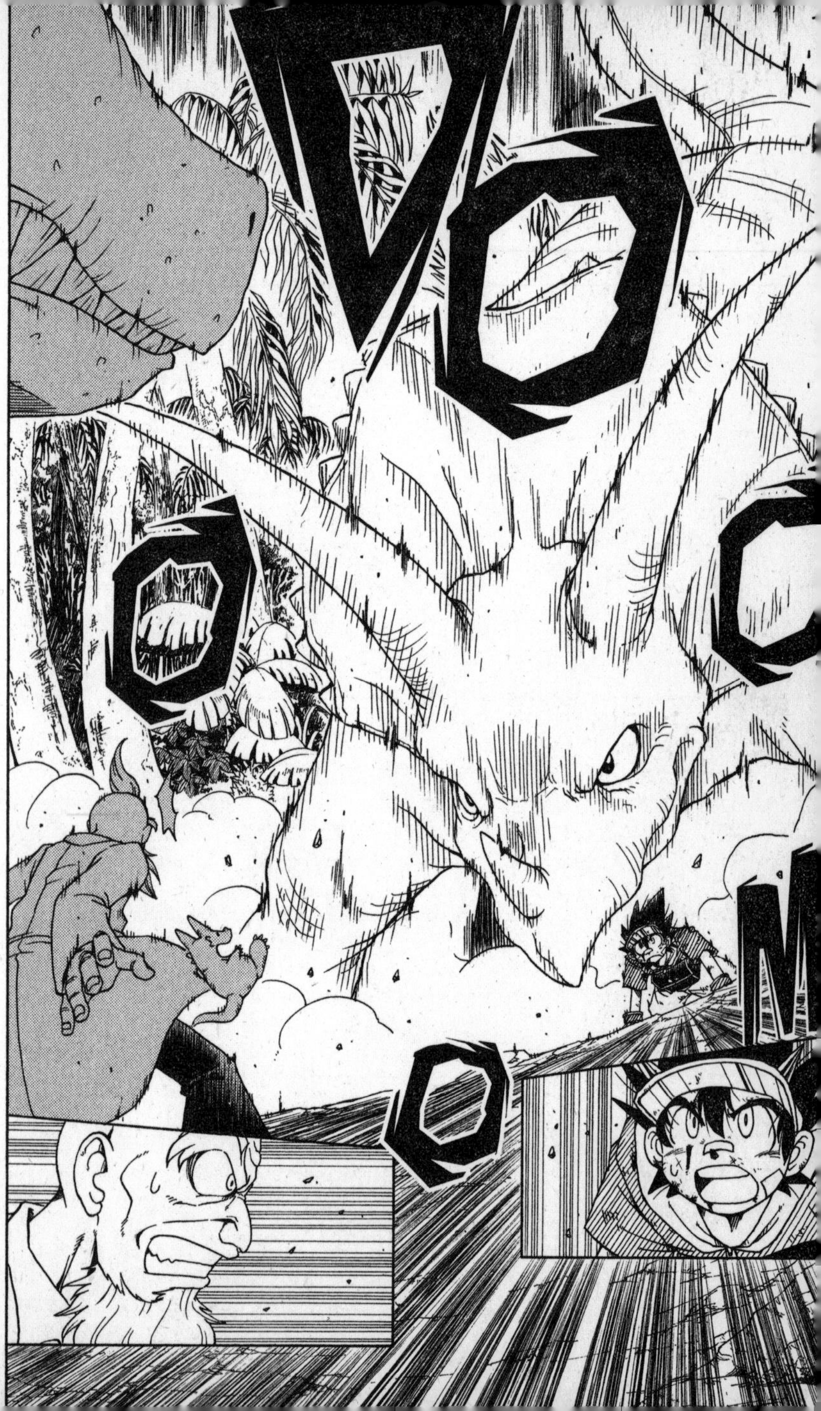
DOOOOM

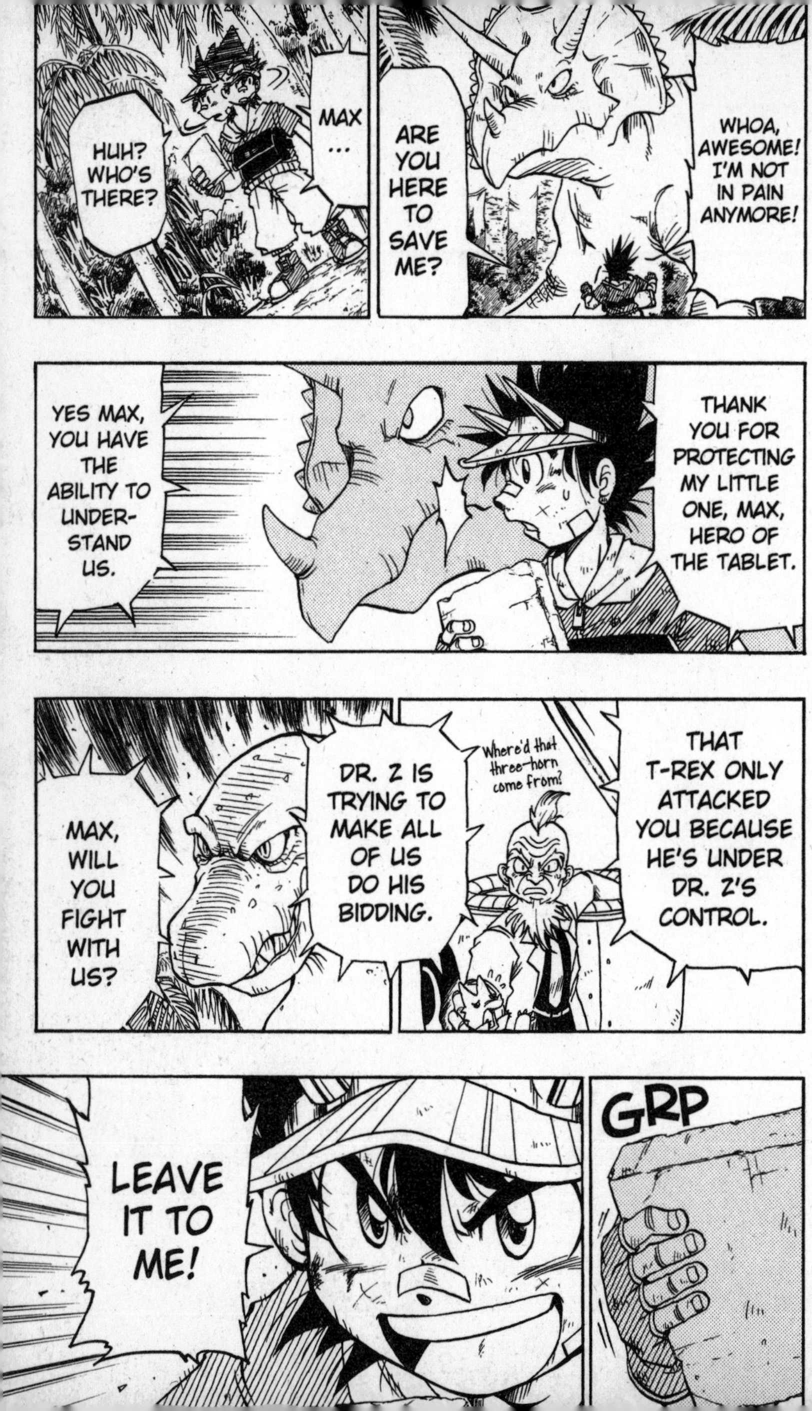
WHOA, AWESOME! I'M NOT IN PAIN ANYMORE!
ARE YOU HERE TO SAVE ME?
MAX ...
HUH? WHO'S THERE?
THANK YOU FOR PROTECTING MY LITTLE ONE, MAX, HERO OF THE TABLET.
YES MAX, YOU HAVE THE ABILITY TO UNDER-STAND US.
THAT T-REX ONLY ATTACKED YOU BECAUSE HE'S UNDER DR. Z'S CONTROL.
Where'd that three-horn come from?
DR. Z IS TRYING TO MAKE ALL OF US DO HIS BIDDING.
MAX, WILL YOU FIGHT WITH US?
GRP
LEAVE IT TO ME!

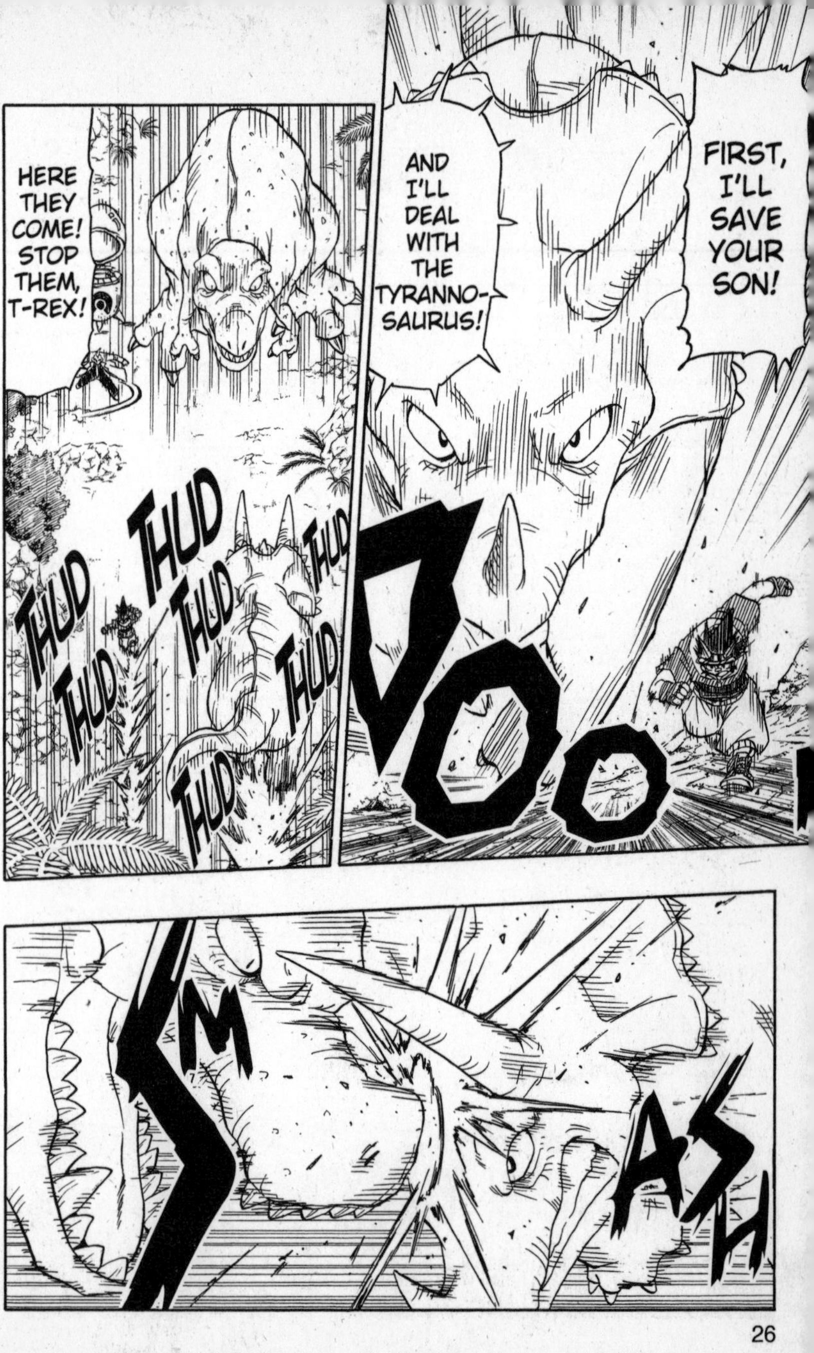
FIRST, I'LL SAVE YOUR SON!
AND I'LL DEAL WITH THE TYRANNOSAURUS!
DOOO
HERE THEY COME! STOP THEM, T-REX!
THUD THUD THUD THUD THUD THUD THUD

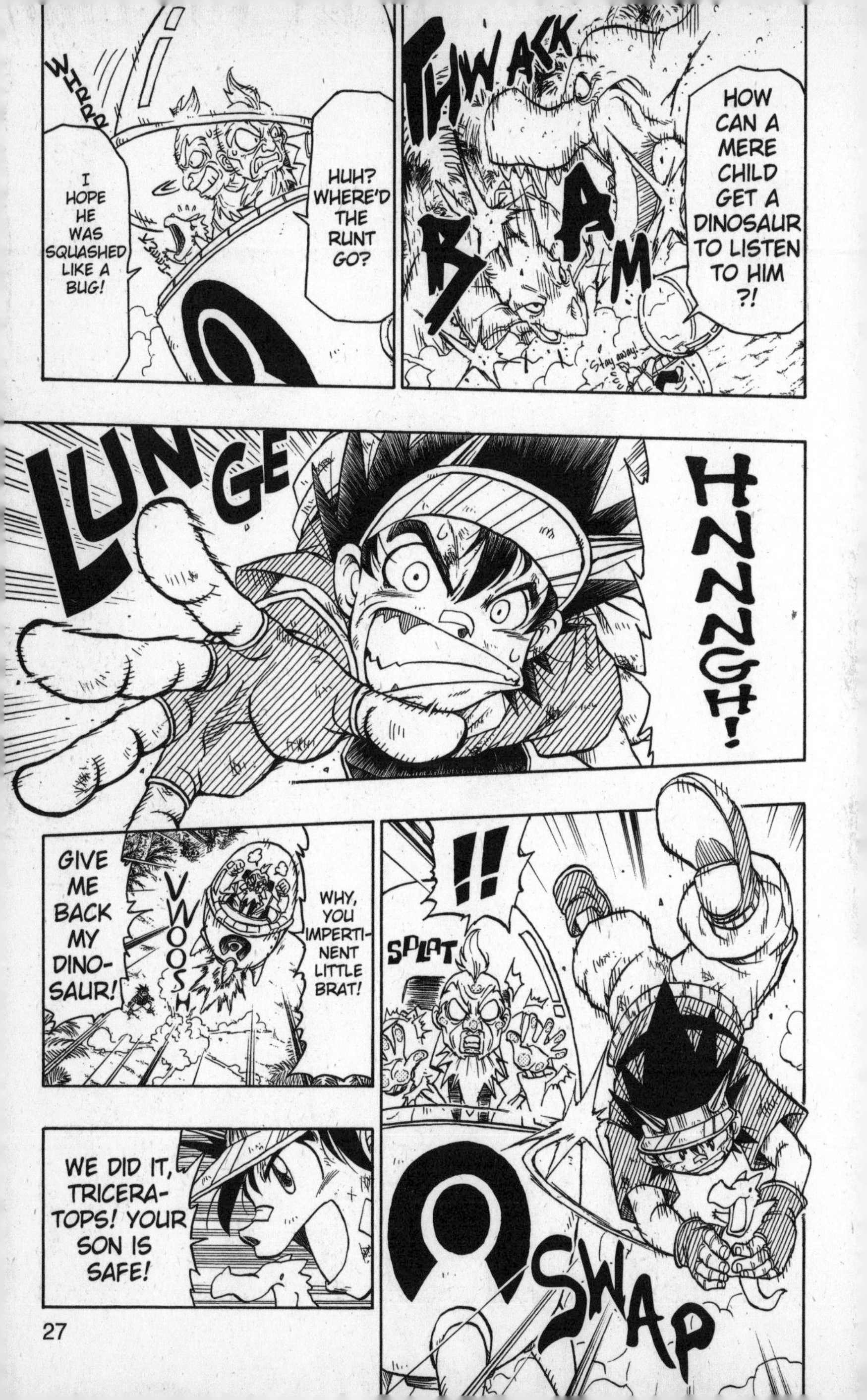
THWACK
HOW CAN A MERE CHILD GET A DINOSAUR TO LISTEN TO HIM ?!
BAM
Stay away!
WHRRR
HUH? WHERE'D THE RUNT GO?
I HOPE HE WAS SQUASHED LIKE A BUG!
HNNNGH!
LUNGE
!!
SPLAT
SWAP
WHY, YOU IMPERTI-NENT LITTLE BRAT!
VWOOSH
GIVE ME BACK MY DINO-SAUR!
WE DID IT, TRICERA-TOPS! YOUR SON IS SAFE!

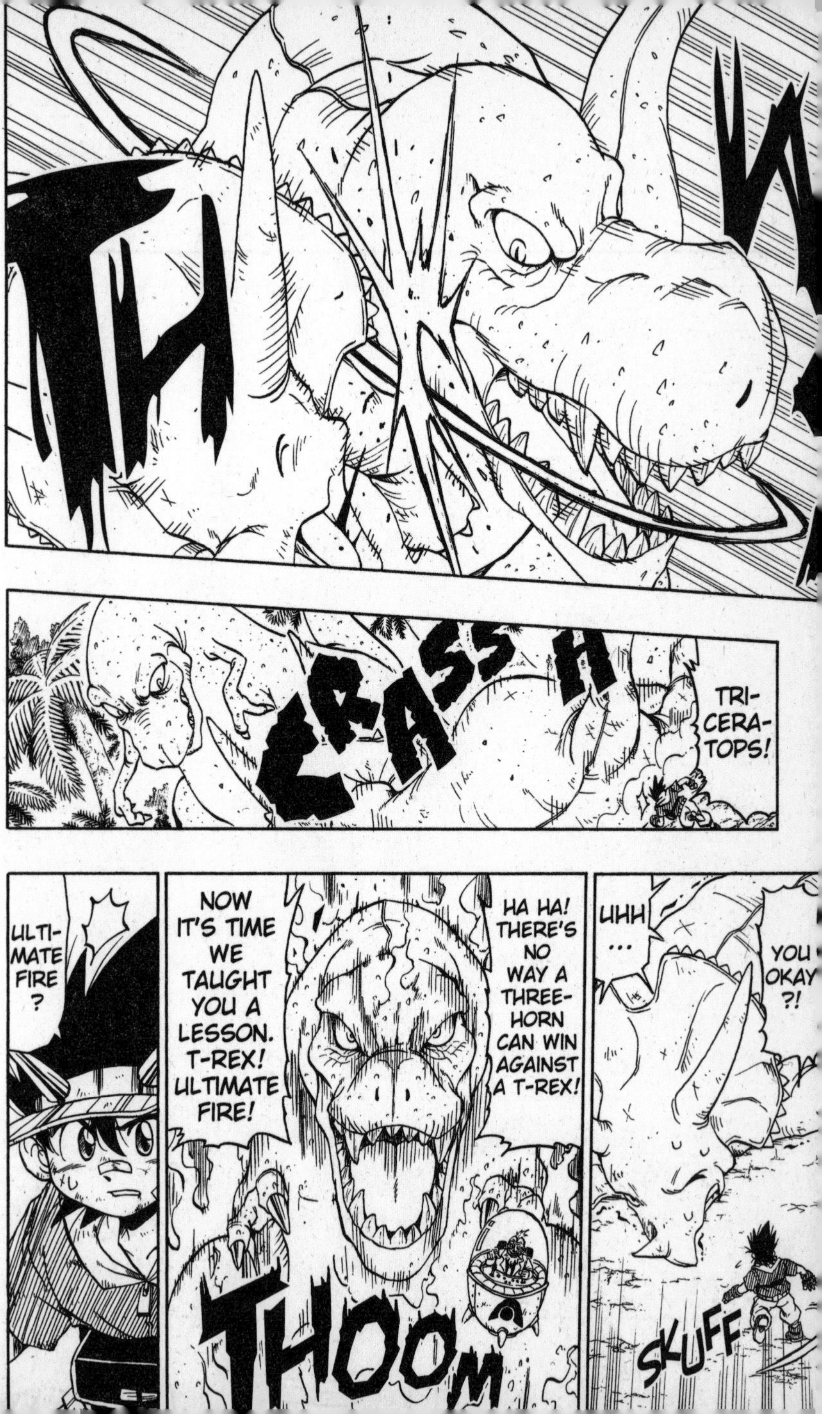
TRI-
CERA-
TOPS!
CRASSH
UHH
...
YOU
OKAY
?!
SKUFF
HA HA! THERE'S NO WAY A THREE-HORN CAN WIN AGAINST A T-REX!
NOW IT'S TIME WE TAUGHT YOU A LESSON. T-REX! ULTIMATE FIRE!
THOOM
ULTI-
MATE
FIRE
?

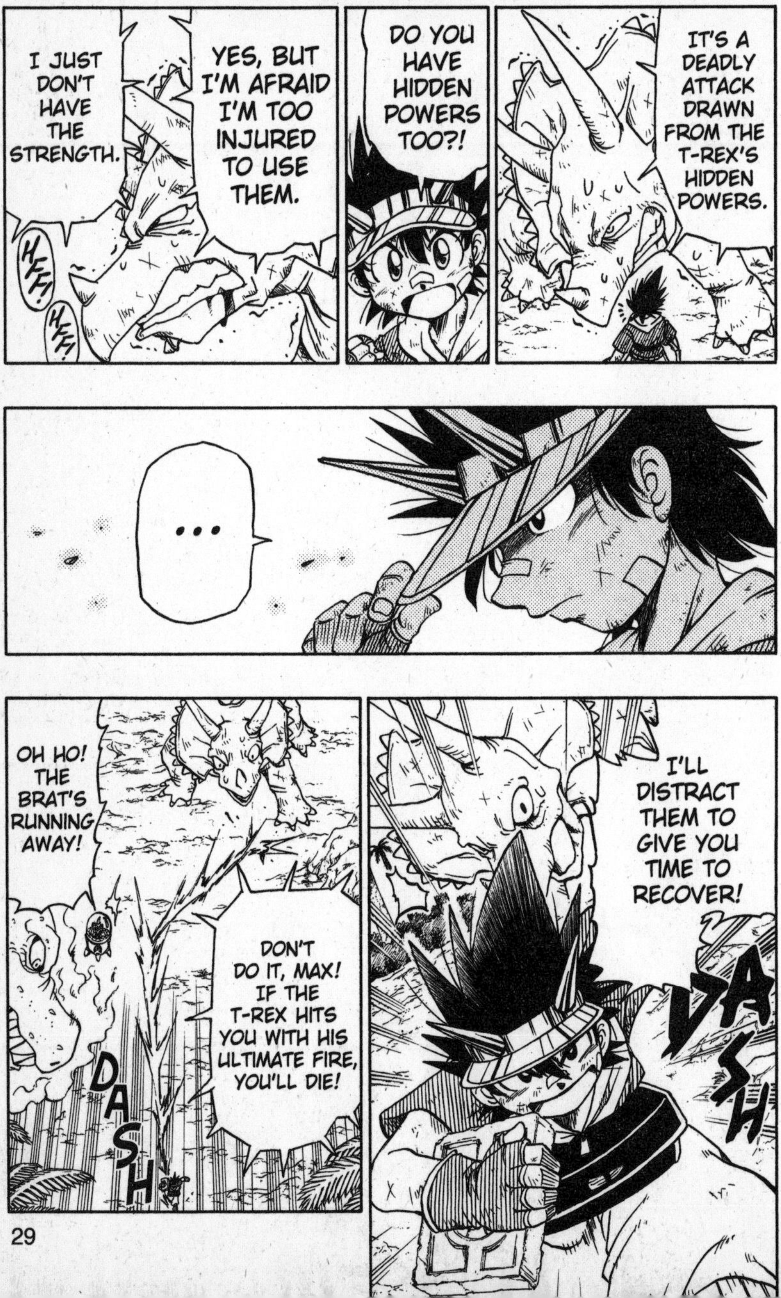
IT'S A DEADLY ATTACK DRAWN FROM THE T-REX'S HIDDEN POWERS.
DO YOU HAVE HIDDEN POWERS TOO?!
YES, BUT I'M AFRAID I'M TOO INJURED TO USE THEM.
I JUST DON'T HAVE THE STRENGTH.
HFF!
HFF!
...
I'LL DISTRACT THEM TO GIVE YOU TIME TO RECOVER!
DASH
OH HO! THE BRAT'S RUNNING AWAY!
DON'T DO IT, MAX! IF THE T-REX HITS YOU WITH HIS ULTIMATE FIRE, YOU'LL DIE!
DASH

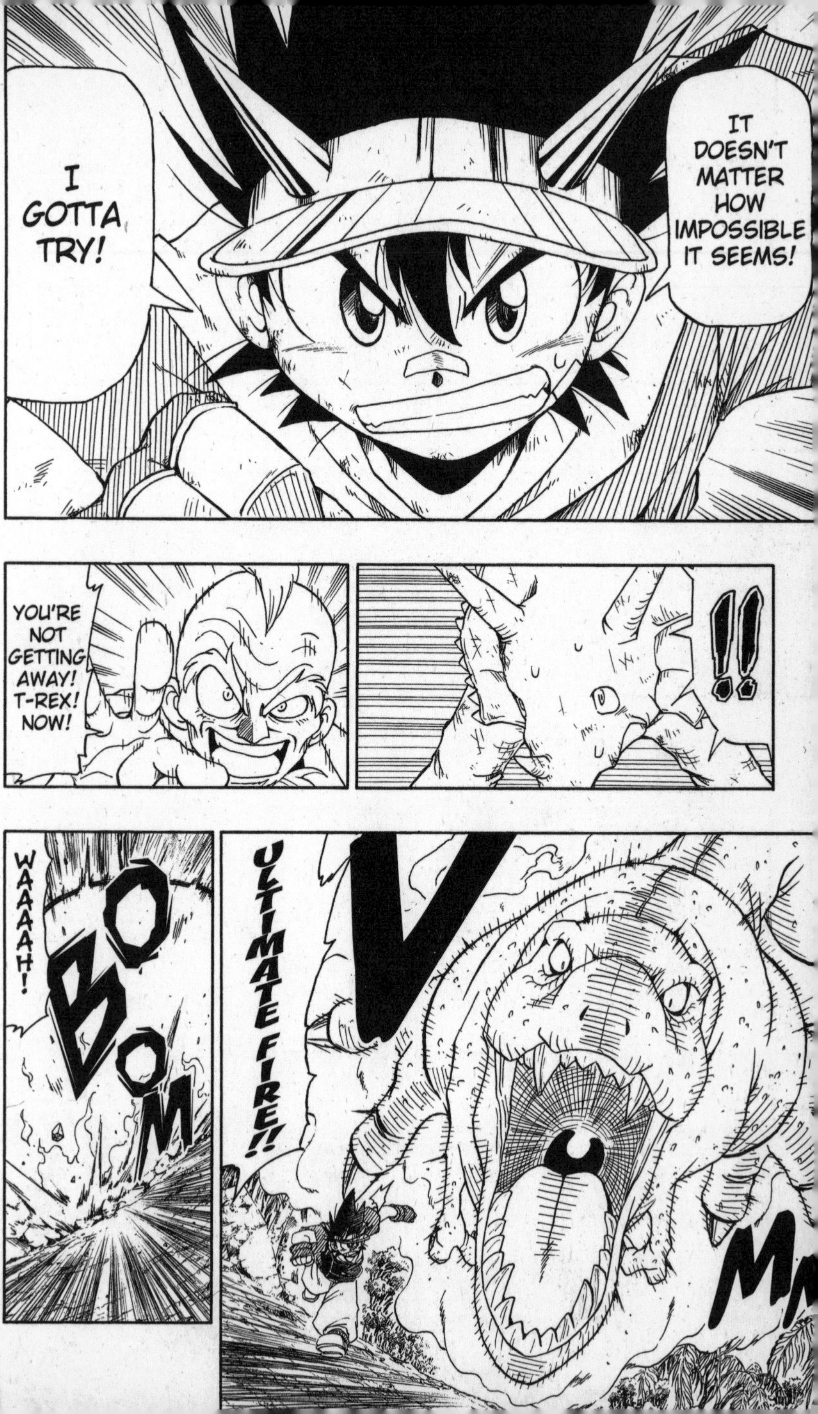
IT DOESN'T MATTER HOW IMPOSSIBLE IT SEEMS!
I GOTTA TRY!
!!
YOU'RE NOT GETTING AWAY! T-REX! NOW!
ULTIMATE FIRE!!
MM
WAAAAAH!
BOBOM

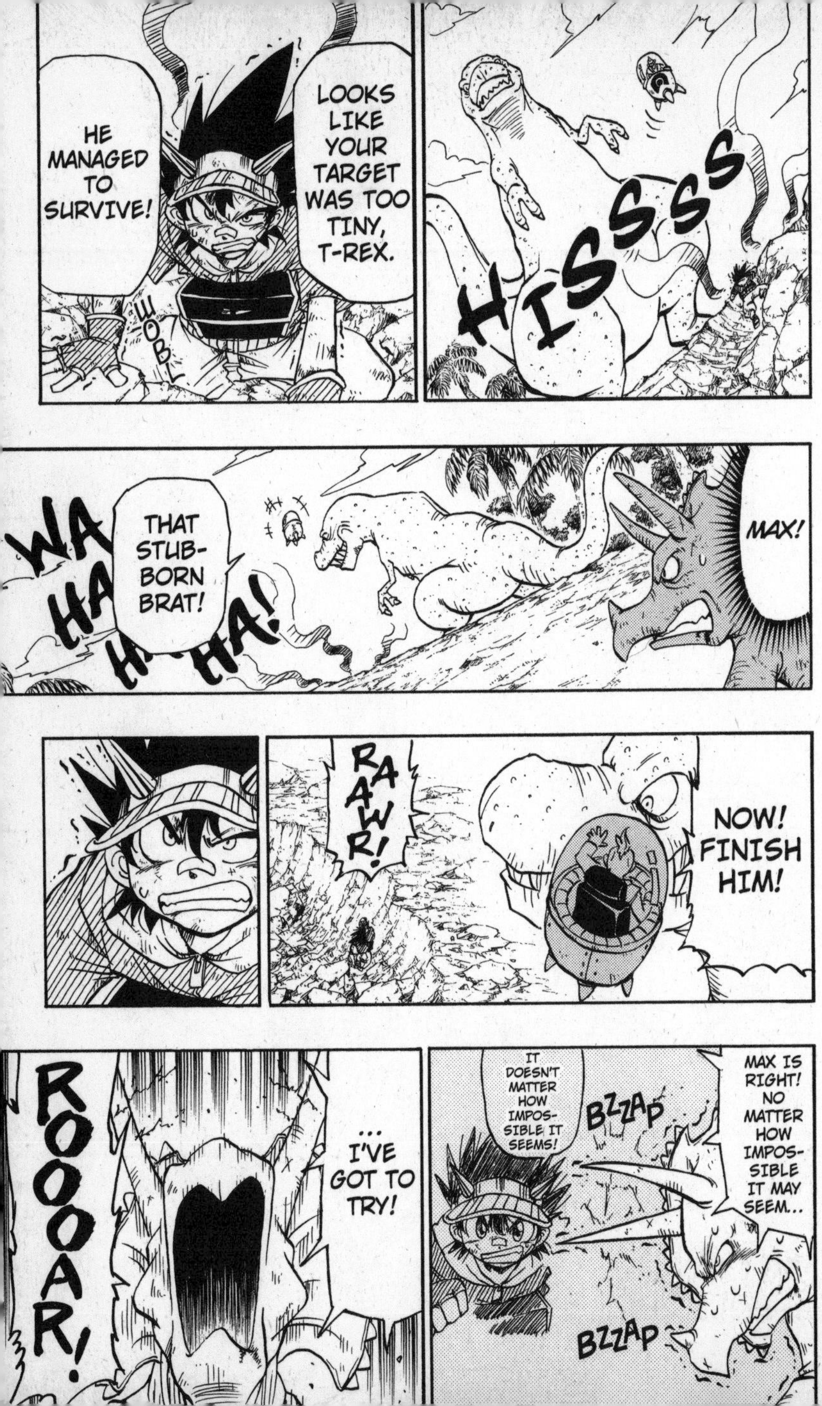
HISSSSS
LOOKS LIKE YOUR TARGET WAS TOO TINY, T-REX.
HE MANAGED TO SURVIVE!
MAX!
THAT STUB-BORN BRAT!
WA HA HA HA!
NOW! FINISH HIM!
RAWR!
MAX IS RIGHT! NO MATTER HOW IMPOS-SIBLE IT MAY SEEM...
IT DOESN'T MATTER HOW IMPOS-SIBLE IT SEEMS!
BZZAP
BZZAP
... I'VE GOT TO TRY!
ROOOAR!

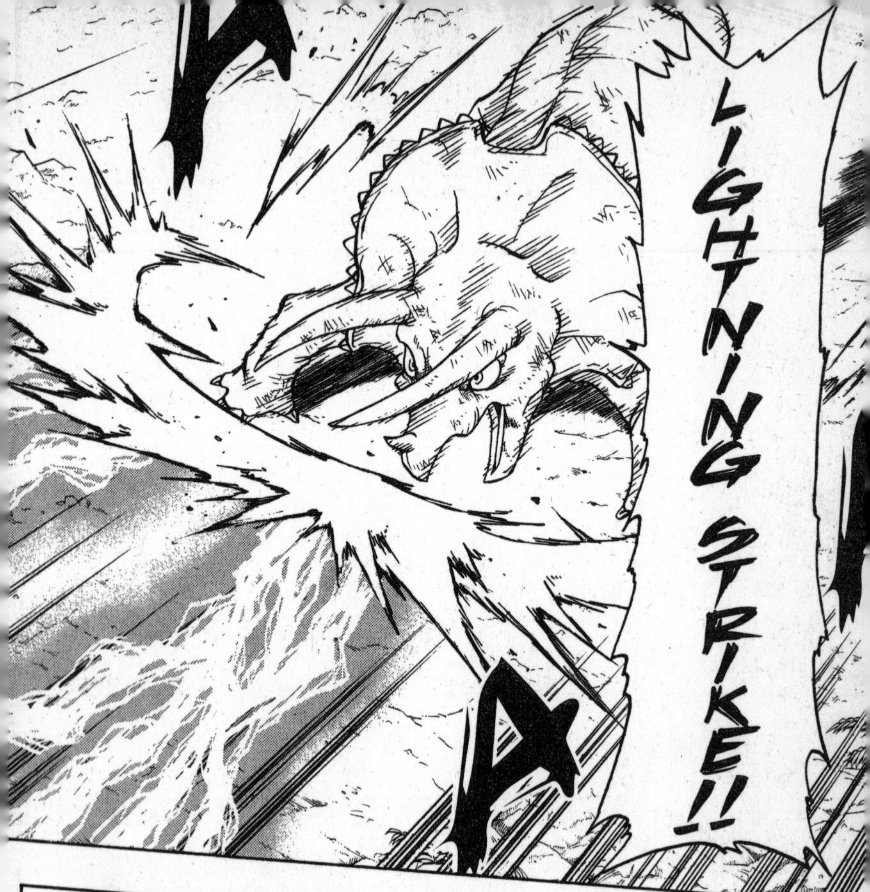
LIGHTNING STRIKE!!

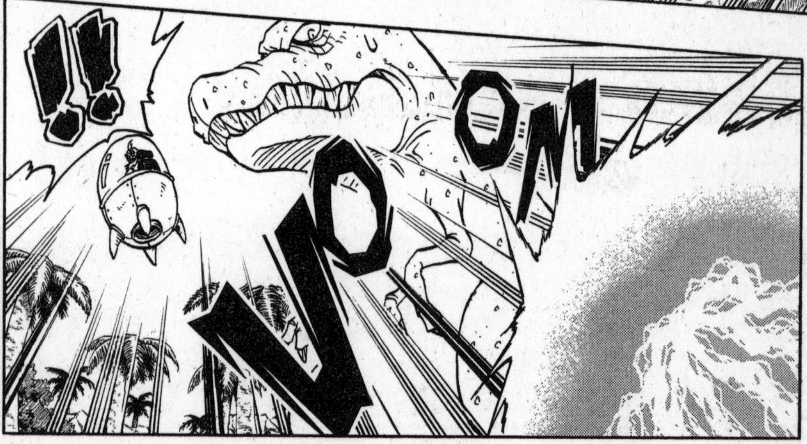
!!
VOOM

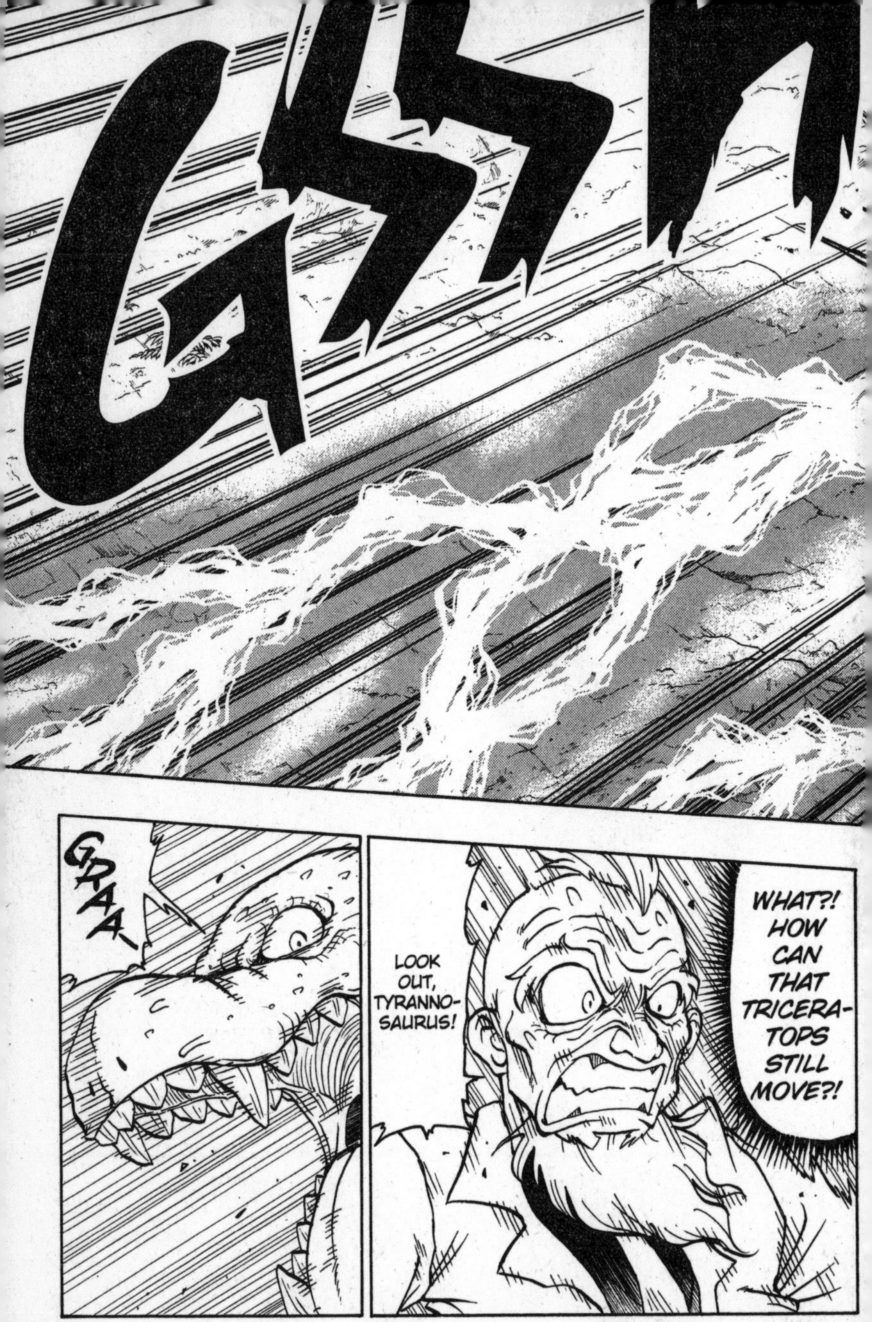
WHAT?! HOW CAN THAT TRICERA-TOPS STILL MOVE?!
LOOK OUT, TYRANNO-SAURUS!
GRAA-

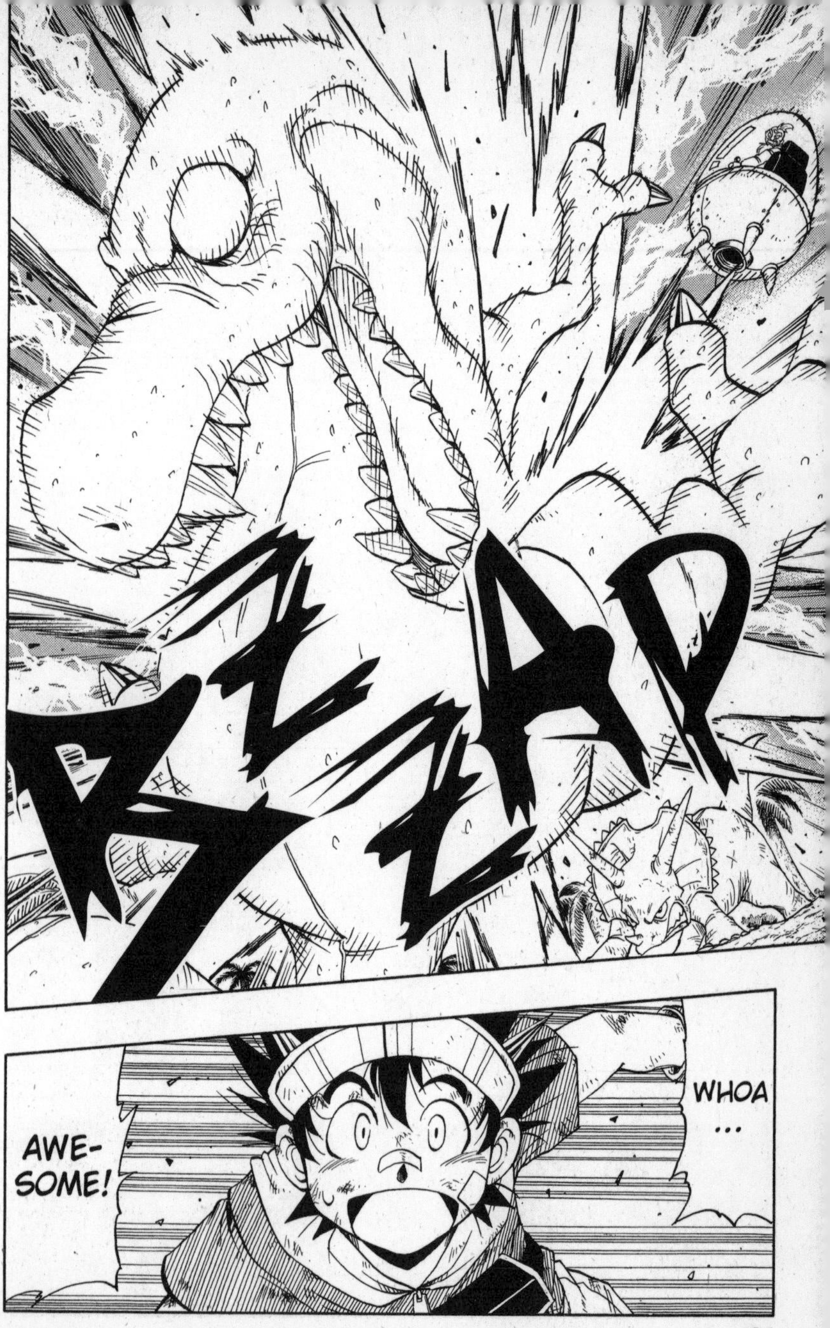
BZZAP
WHOA ...
AWE-SOME!

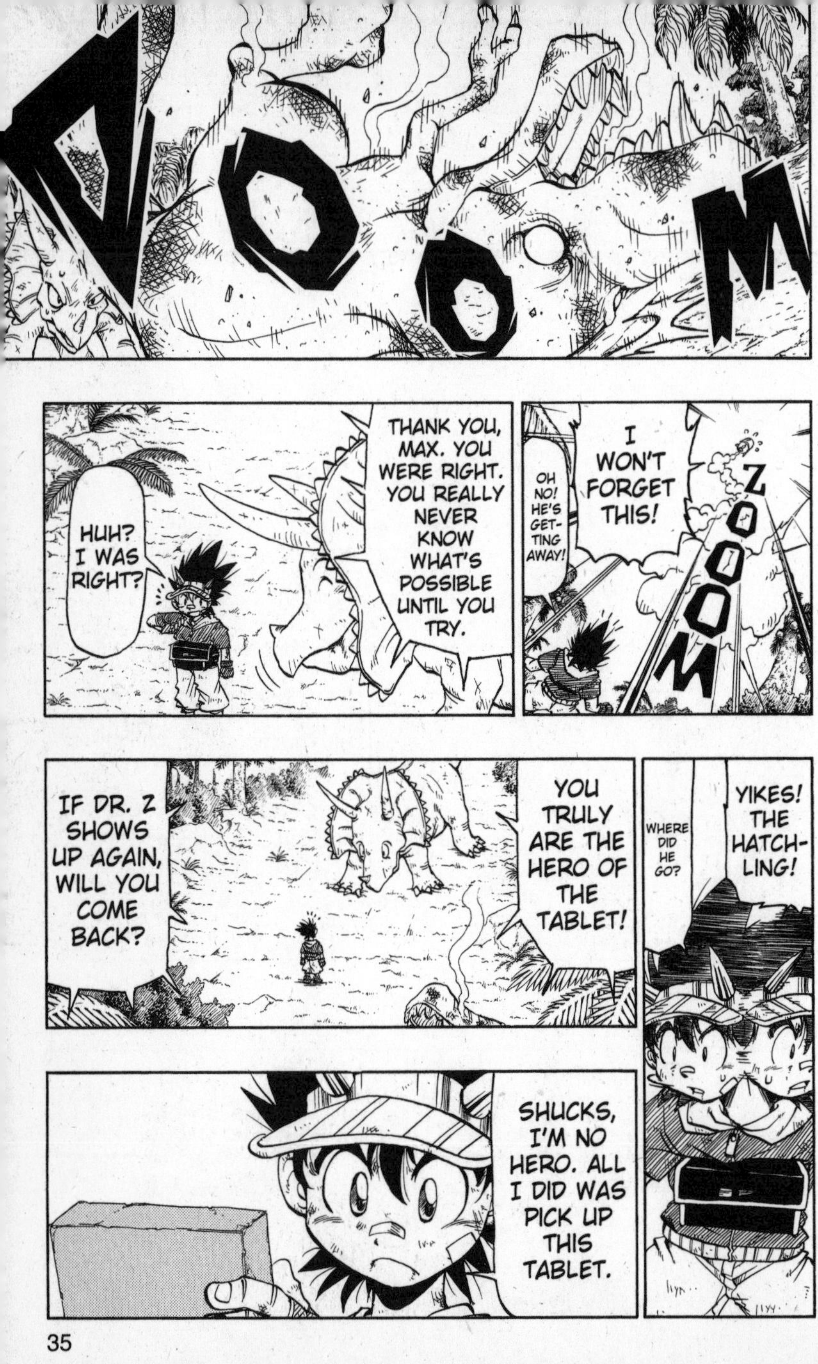
VOOOM
I WON'T FORGET THIS!
OH NO! HE'S GET-TING AWAY!
ZOOOM
THANK YOU, MAX. YOU WERE RIGHT. YOU REALLY NEVER KNOW WHAT'S POSSIBLE UNTIL YOU TRY.
HUH? I WAS RIGHT?
YIKES! THE HATCH-LING!
WHERE DID HE GO?
YOU TRULY ARE THE HERO OF THE TABLET!
IF DR. Z SHOWS UP AGAIN, WILL YOU COME BACK?
SHUCKS, I'M NO HERO. ALL I DID WAS PICK UP THIS TABLET.

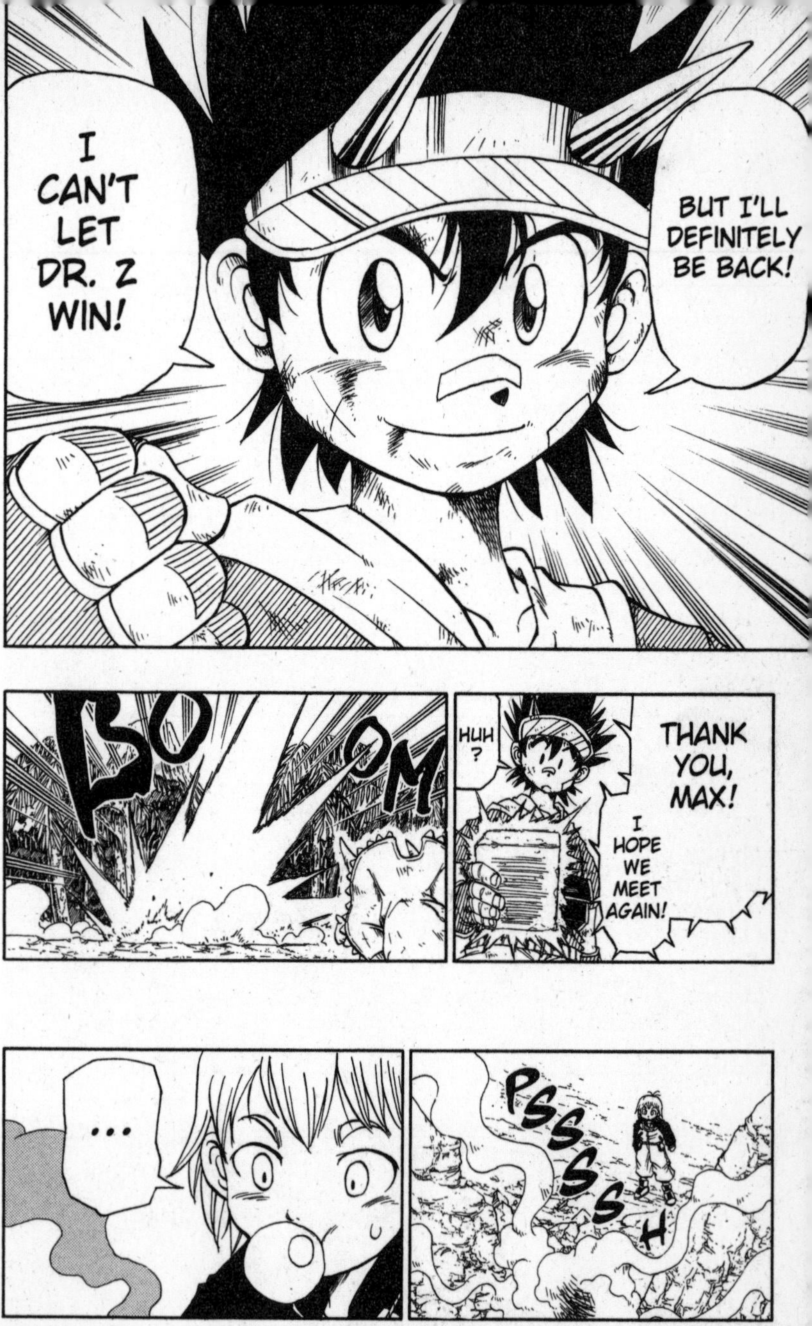
I CAN'T LET DR. Z WIN!
BUT I'LL DEFINITELY BE BACK!
THANK YOU, MAX!
I HOPE WE MEET AGAIN!
HUH?
BOOM
PSSSSSH
...

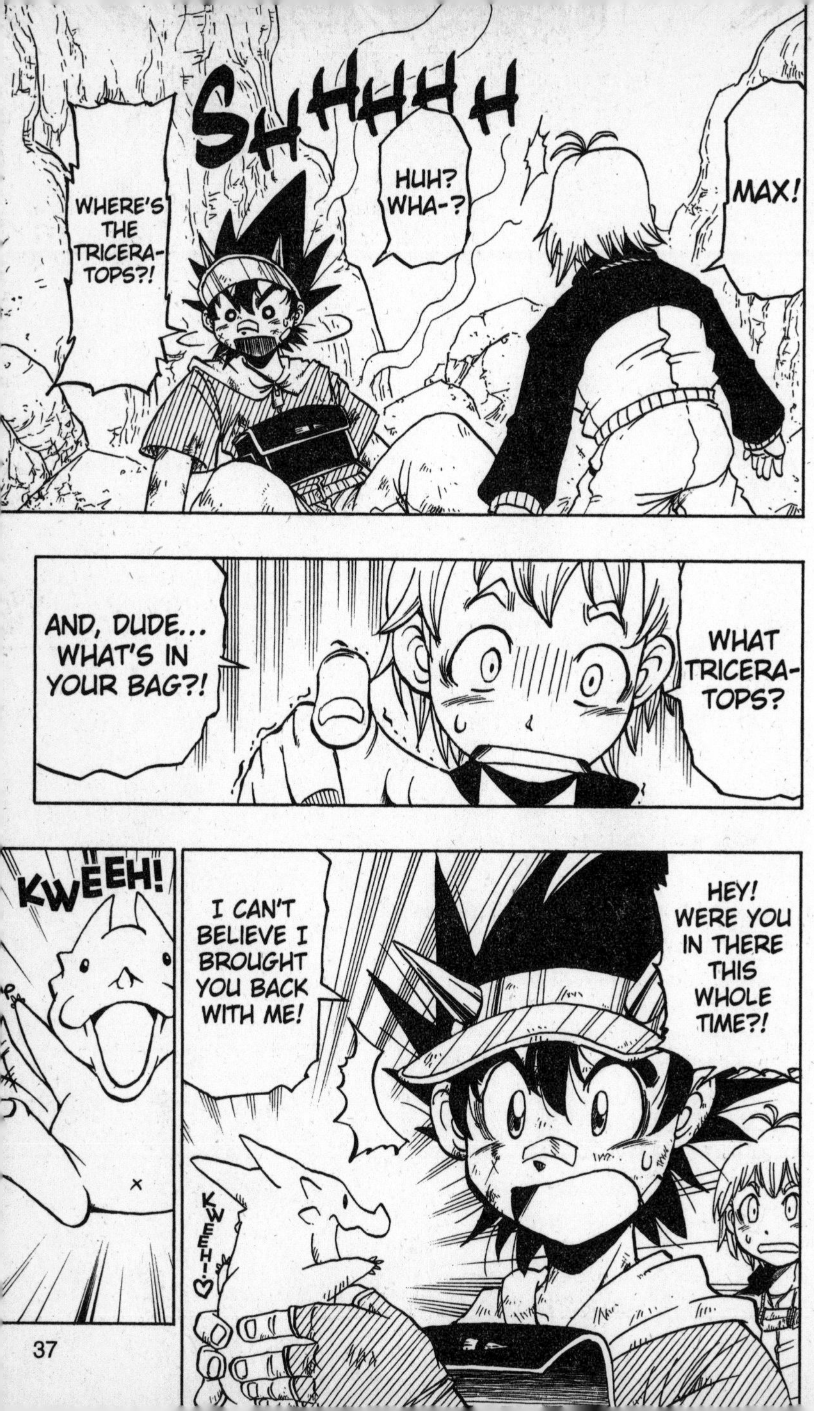
MAX!
SHHHHH
HUH? WHA-?
WHERE'S THE TRICERA-TOPS?!
WHAT TRICERA-TOPS?
AND, DUDE... WHAT'S IN YOUR BAG?!
HEY! WERE YOU IN THERE THIS WHOLE TIME?!
I CAN'T BELIEVE I BROUGHT YOU BACK WITH ME!
KWEEH!♡
KWEEH!

DIG IT!

Uncover facts about dinosaurs, their super moves and their trading card stats!

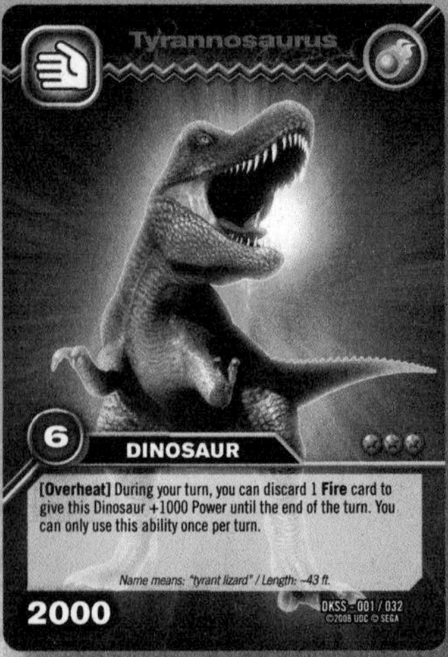
Tyrannosaurus
6
DINOSAUR
[Overheat] During your turn, you can discard 1 Fire card to give this Dinosaur +1000 Power until the end of the turn. You can only use this ability once per turn.
Name means: "tyrant lizard" / Length: ~43 ft.
2000
DKSS - 001 / 032
©2008 UDC © SEGA

TYRANNOSAURUS

Tyrannosaurus means "tyrant lizard"
Length: approx. 43 ft.
Lived in: Cretaceous Period
Discovered in: Canada and America
Just like its name suggests, the Tyrannosaurus is one of the most ferocious dinosaurs that ever lived.
Card Rarity: Silver Rare and Colossal Rare – Rarest of them all!
With its special **Overheat** ability it can increase its power to a stunning +3000, more than any other Dinosaur out there. The Tyrannosaurus is the Alpha Gang's greatest weapon!

LIGHTNING STRIKE

Card Rarity: Common
Lightning Strike lets any **Lightning** Dinosaur with a **Rock** icon blast out a powerful shock from its horn. Your opponent's Dinosaur will be blown away by the powerful +1000 power boost from this Super Move!

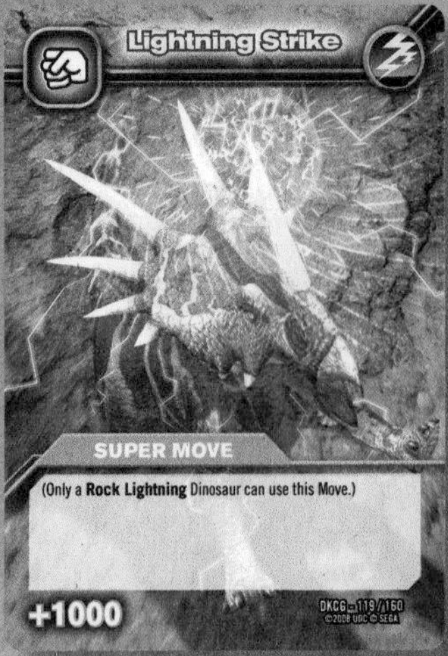
Lightning Strike
SUPER MOVE
(Only a Rock Lightning Dinosaur can use this Move.)
+1000
DKCG - 119 / 150
©2008 UDC © SEGA

CHAPTER 2
THE ALPHA GANG'S PLOT

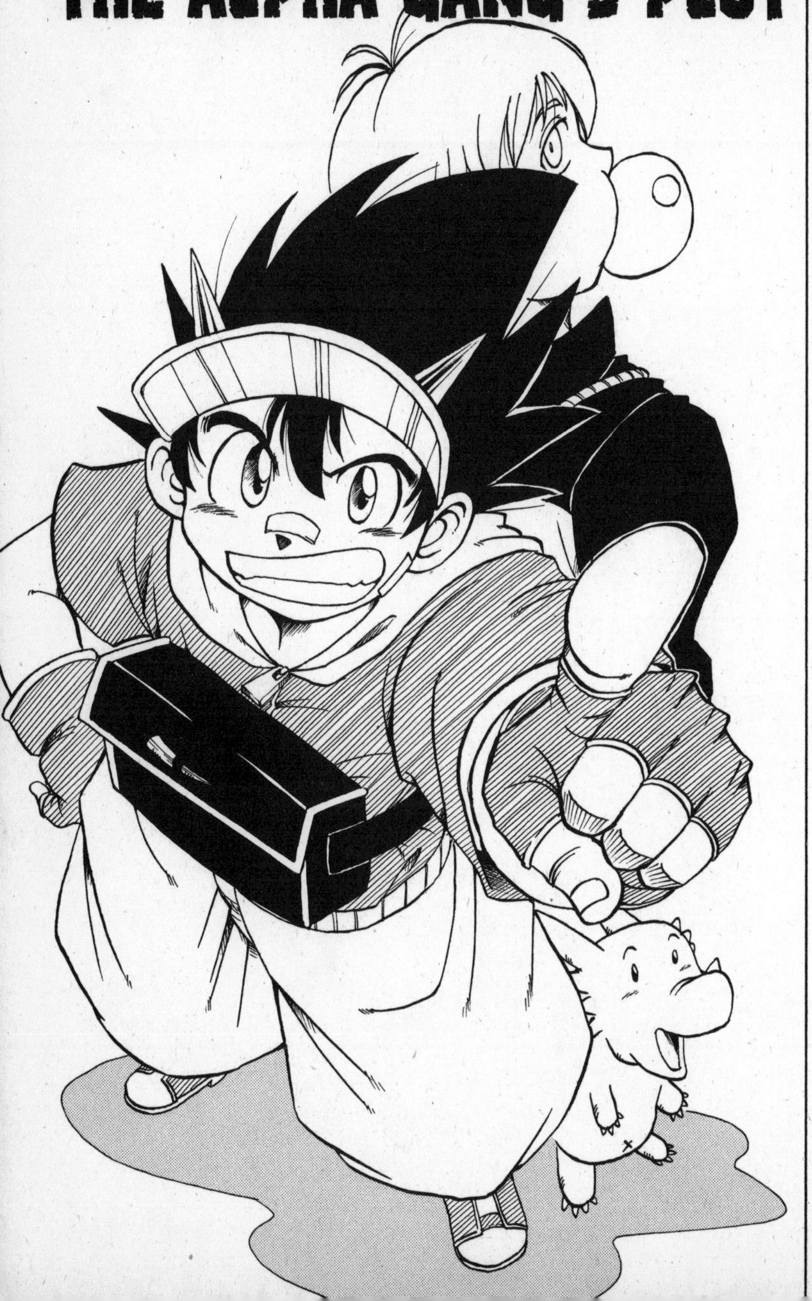

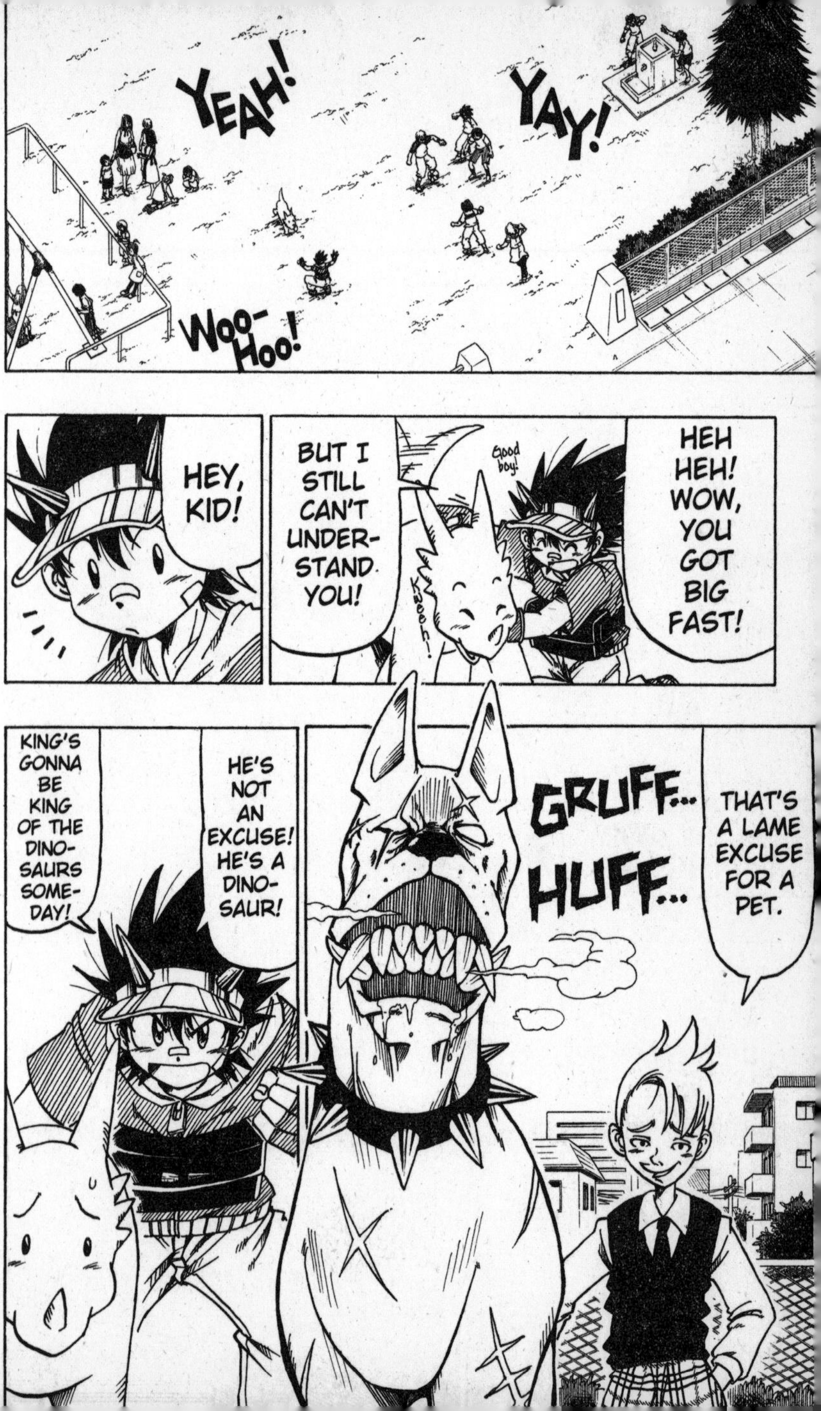
YAY!
YEAH!
WOO-HOO!
HEH HEH! WOW, YOU GOT BIG FAST!
Good boy!
Kween!
BUT I STILL CAN'T UNDERSTAND YOU!
HEY, KID!
THAT'S A LAME EXCUSE FOR A PET.
GRUFF...
HUFF...
HE'S NOT AN EXCUSE! HE'S A DINOSAUR!
KING'S GONNA BE KING OF THE DINOSAURS SOMEDAY!

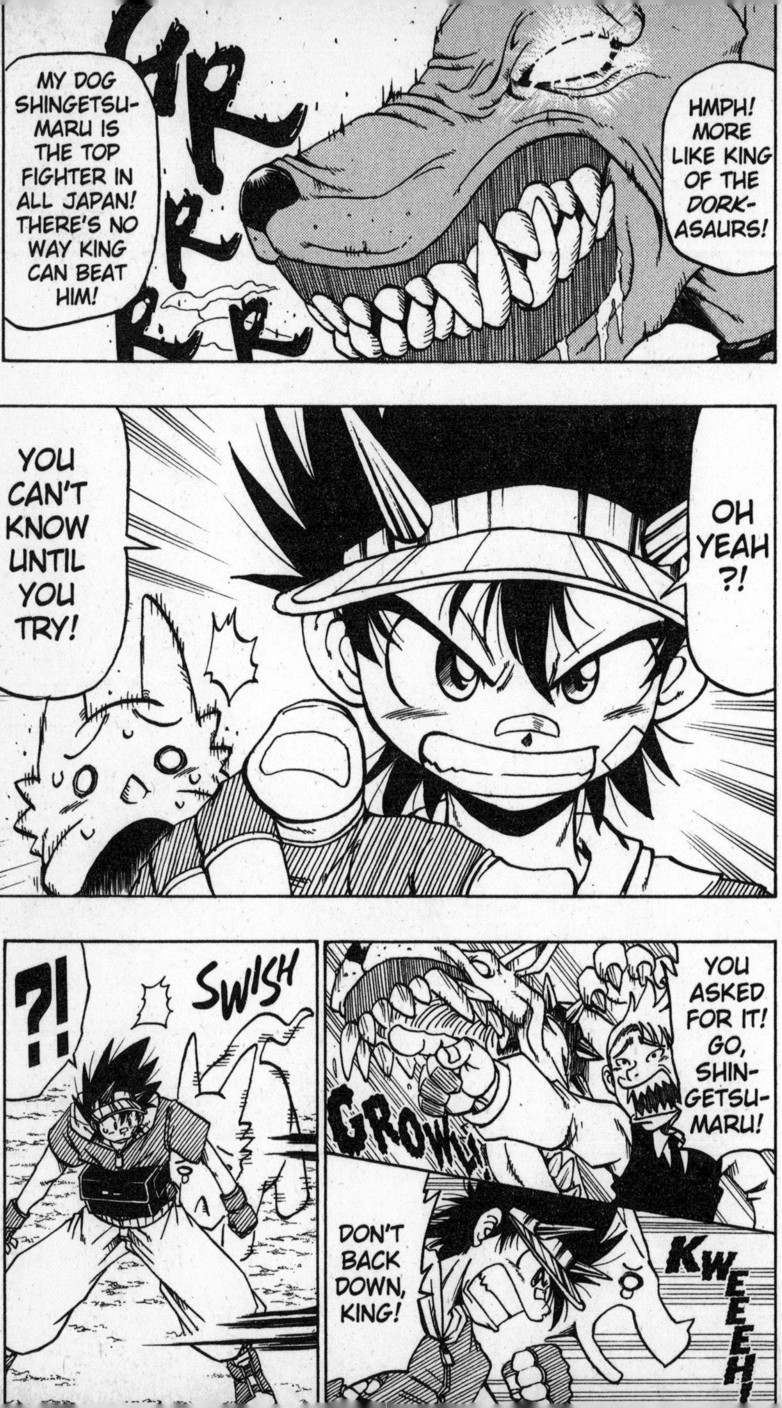
HMPH! MORE LIKE KING OF THE DORK-ASAURS!
MY DOG SHINGETSU-MARU IS THE TOP FIGHTER IN ALL JAPAN! THERE'S NO WAY KING CAN BEAT HIM!
OH YEAH?!
YOU CAN'T KNOW UNTIL YOU TRY!
YOU ASKED FOR IT! GO, SHIN-GETSU-MARU!
GROWL
KWEEEH!
DON'T BACK DOWN, KING!
?!
SWISH

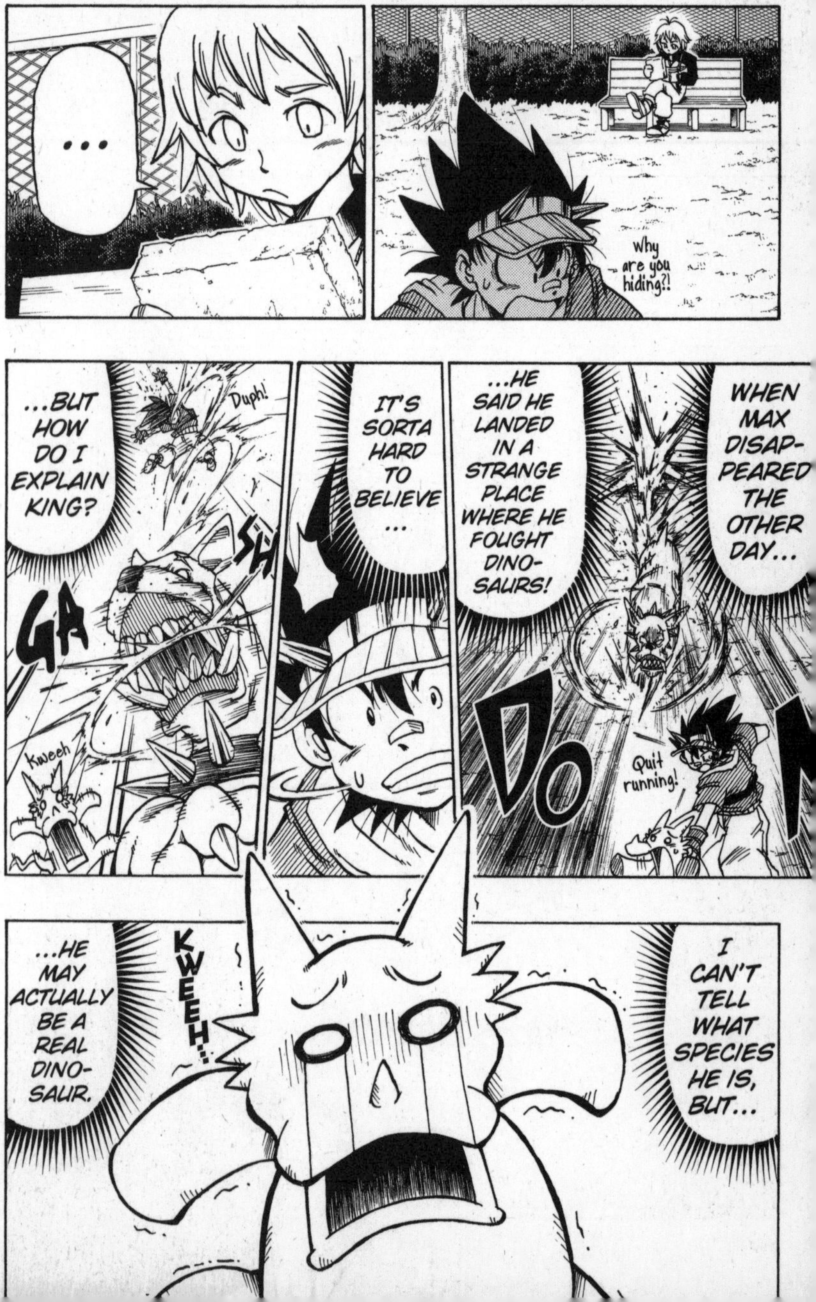
Why are you hiding?!
...
WHEN MAX DISAPPEARED THE OTHER DAY...
...HE SAID HE LANDED IN A STRANGE PLACE WHERE HE FOUGHT DINOSAURS!
DO
Quit running!
IT'S SORTA HARD TO BELIEVE...
...BUT HOW DO I EXPLAIN KING?
Duph!
SH
GA
Kweeh
I CAN'T TELL WHAT SPECIES HE IS, BUT...
KWEEH!!
...HE MAY ACTUALLY BE A REAL DINOSAUR.

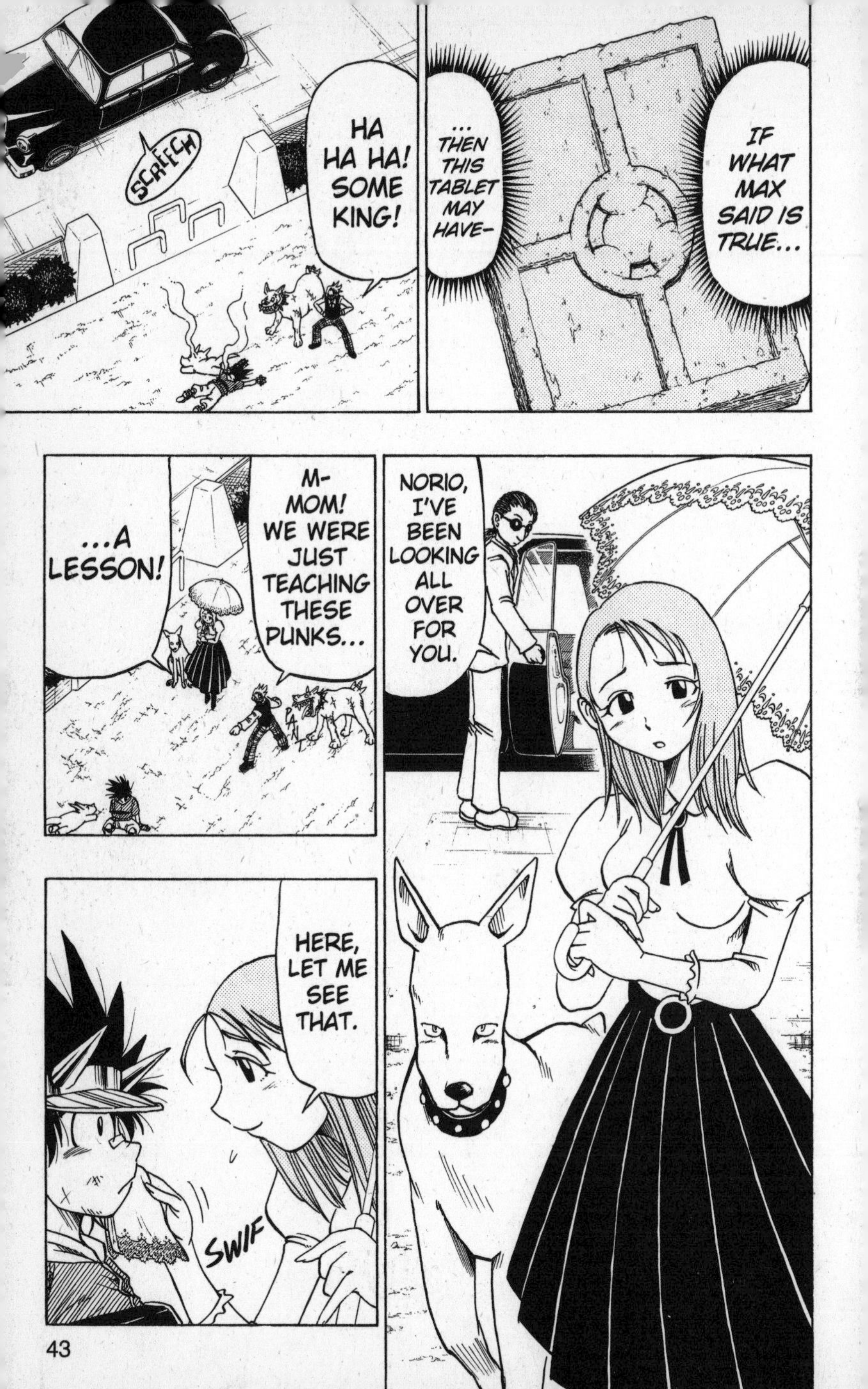
IF WHAT MAX SAID IS TRUE...
...THEN THIS TABLET MAY HAVE-
HA HA HA! SOME KING!
SCREECH
NORIO, I'VE BEEN LOOKING ALL OVER FOR YOU.
M-MOM! WE WERE JUST TEACHING THESE PUNKS...
...A LESSON!
PANT
HERE, LET ME SEE THAT.
SWIF

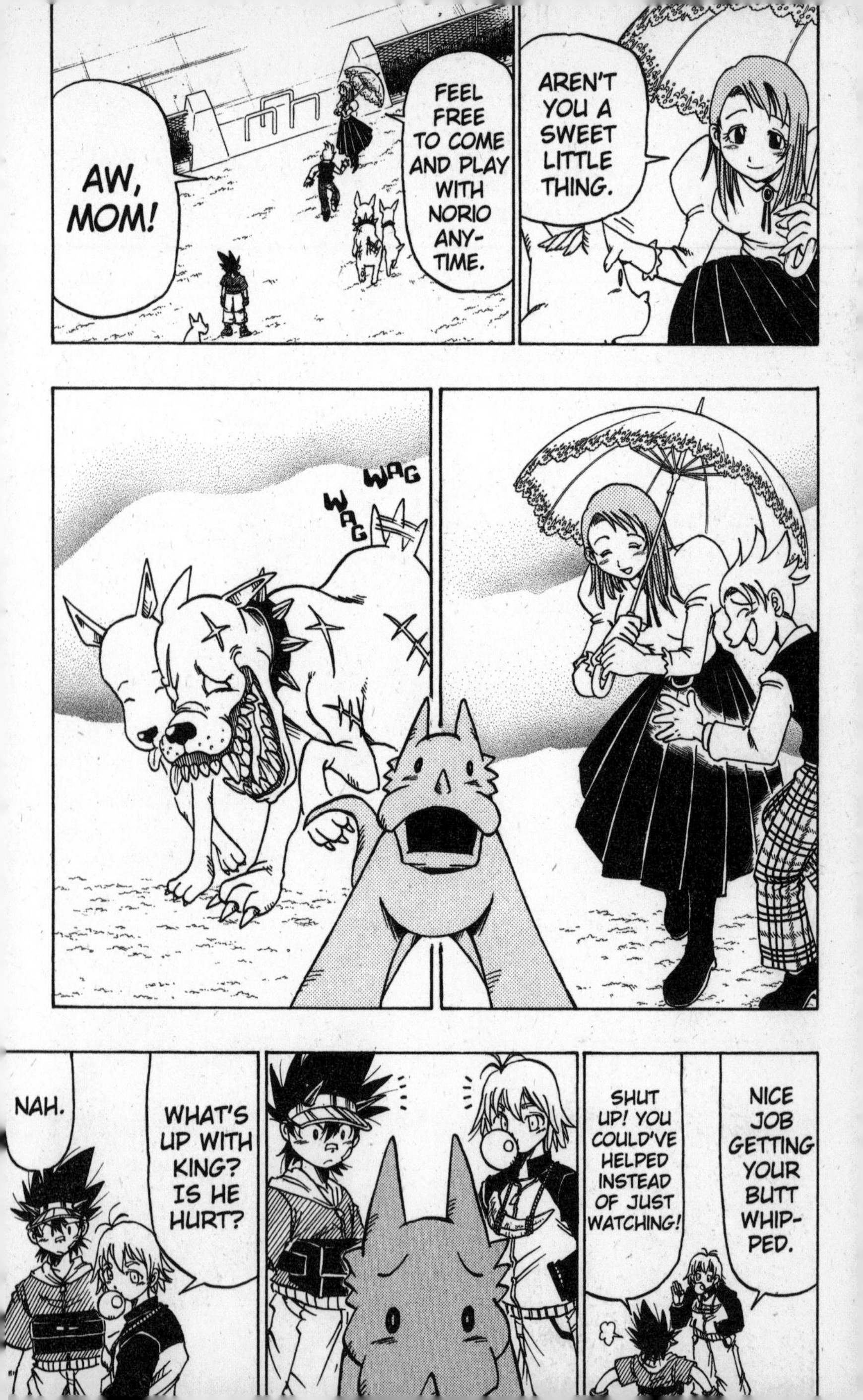
AREN'T YOU A SWEET LITTLE THING.
FEEL FREE TO COME AND PLAY WITH NORIO ANY-TIME.
AW, MOM!
WAG
WAG
NICE JOB GETTING YOUR BUTT WHIP-PED.
SHUT UP! YOU COULD'VE HELPED INSTEAD OF JUST WATCHING!
WHAT'S UP WITH KING? IS HE HURT?
NAH.

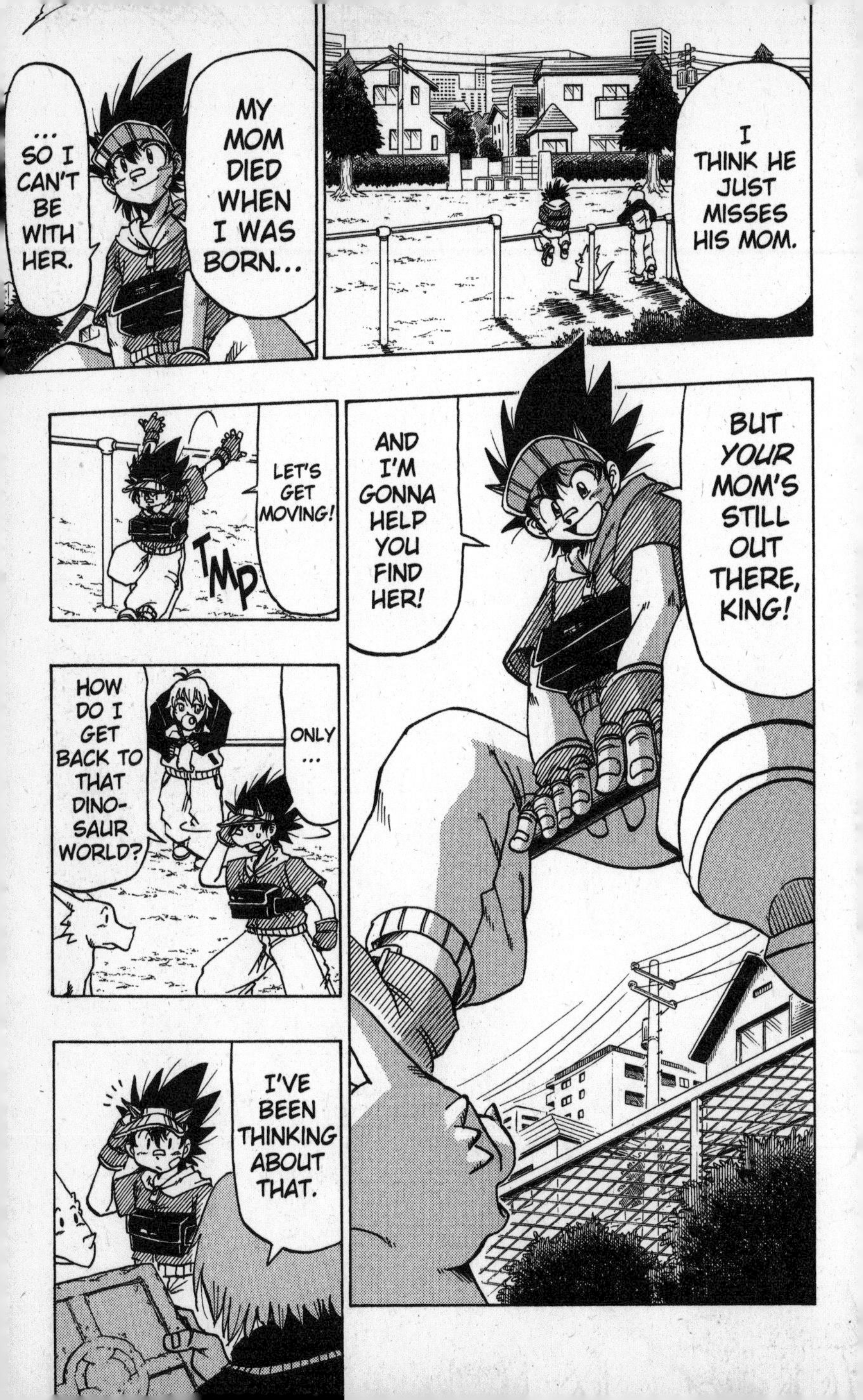
I THINK HE JUST MISSES HIS MOM.
MY MOM DIED WHEN I WAS BORN...
... SO I CAN'T BE WITH HER.
BUT YOUR MOM'S STILL OUT THERE, KING!
AND I'M GONNA HELP YOU FIND HER!
LET'S GET MOVING!
TMP
ONLY ...
HOW DO I GET BACK TO THAT DINO-SAUR WORLD?
I'VE BEEN THINKING ABOUT THAT.

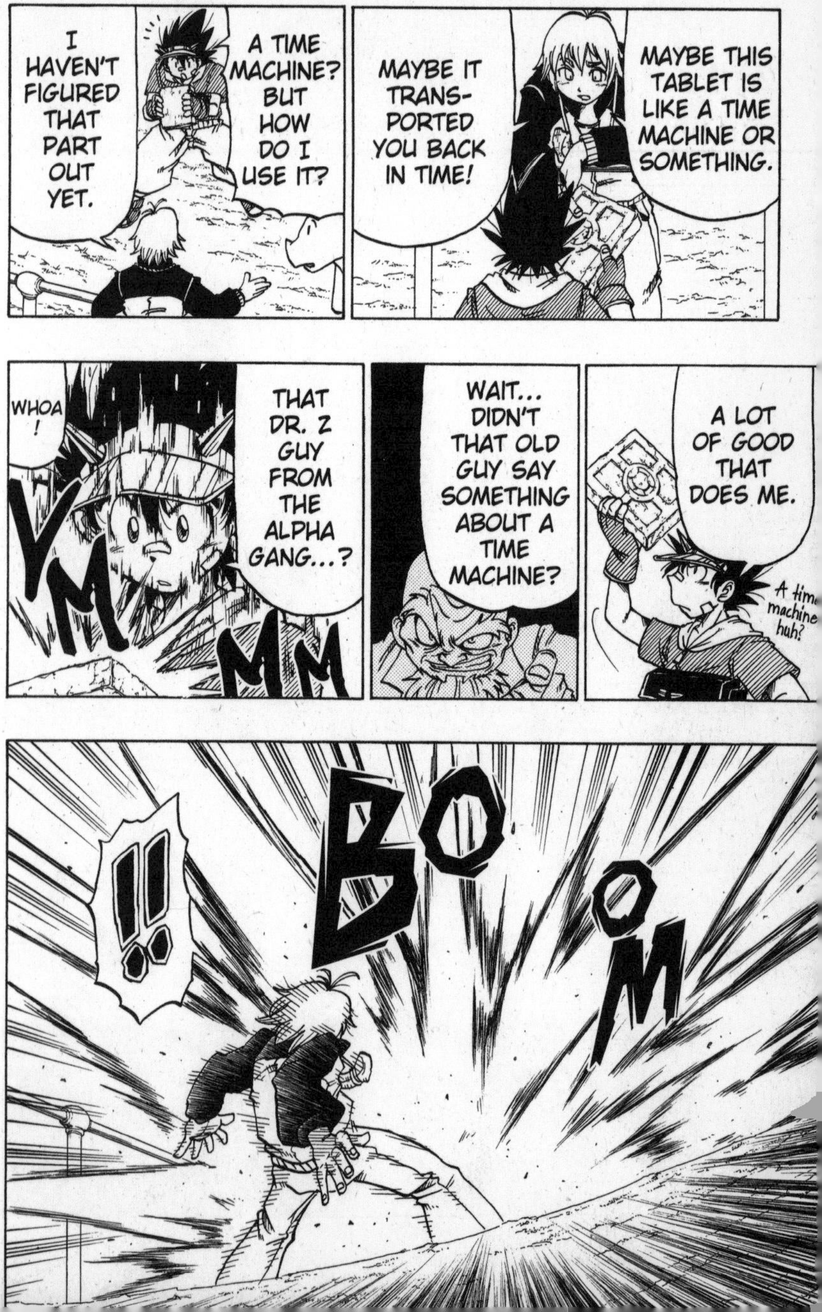
MAYBE THIS TABLET IS LIKE A TIME MACHINE OR SOMETHING.
MAYBE IT TRANS-PORTED YOU BACK IN TIME!
A TIME MACHINE? BUT HOW DO I USE IT?
I HAVEN'T FIGURED THAT PART OUT YET.
A LOT OF GOOD THAT DOES ME.
A tim machine huh?
WAIT... DIDN'T THAT OLD GUY SAY SOMETHING ABOUT A TIME MACHINE?
THAT DR. Z GUY FROM THE ALPHA GANG...?
WHOA!
YMMM
!!
BOOM

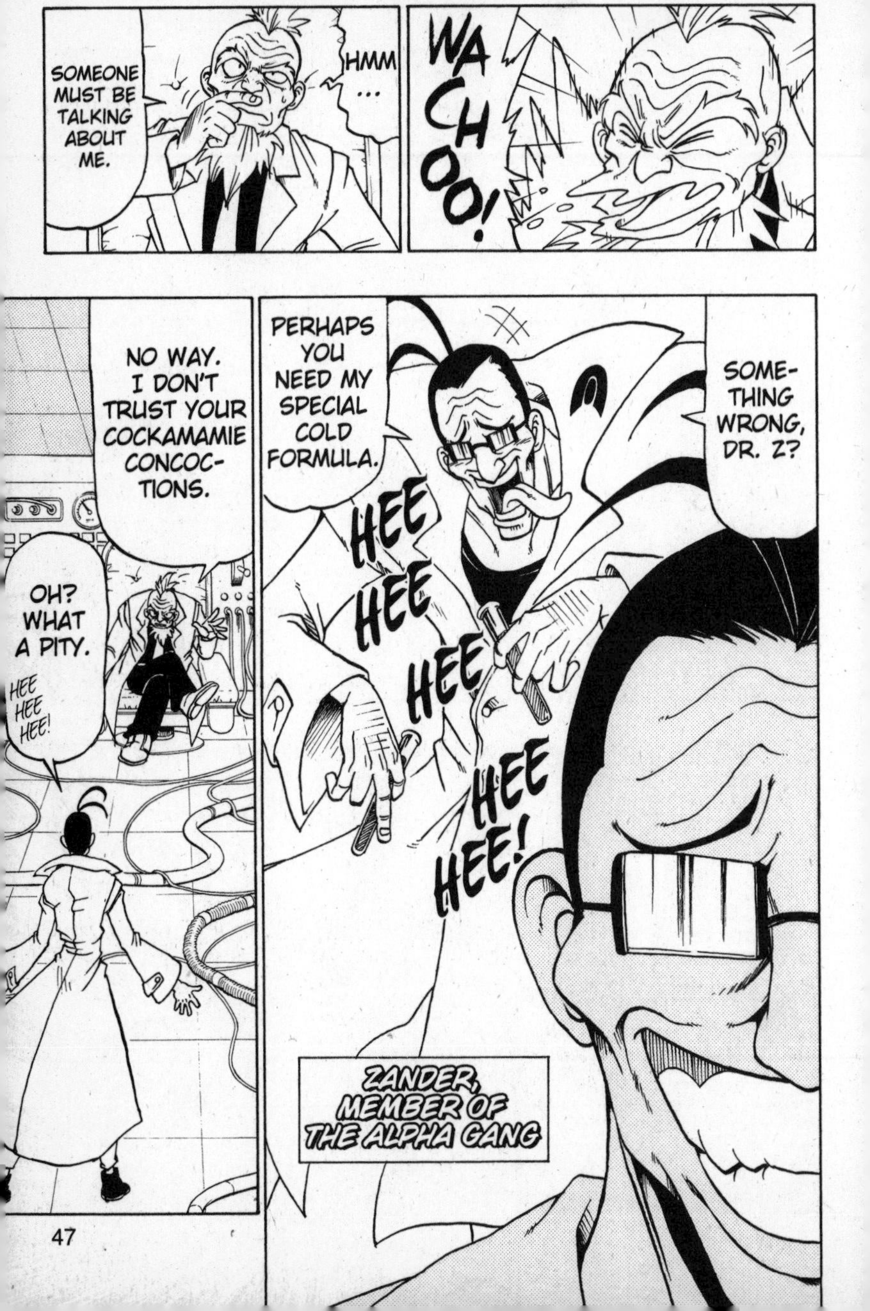
WACHOO!
HMM ...
SOMEONE MUST BE TALKING ABOUT ME.
SOME-THING WRONG, DR. Z?
PERHAPS YOU NEED MY SPECIAL COLD FORMULA.
HEE HEE HEE HEE HEE!
ZANDER, MEMBER OF THE ALPHA GANG
NO WAY. I DON'T TRUST YOUR COCKAMAMIE CONCOC-TIONS.
OH? WHAT A PITY.
HEE HEE HEE!

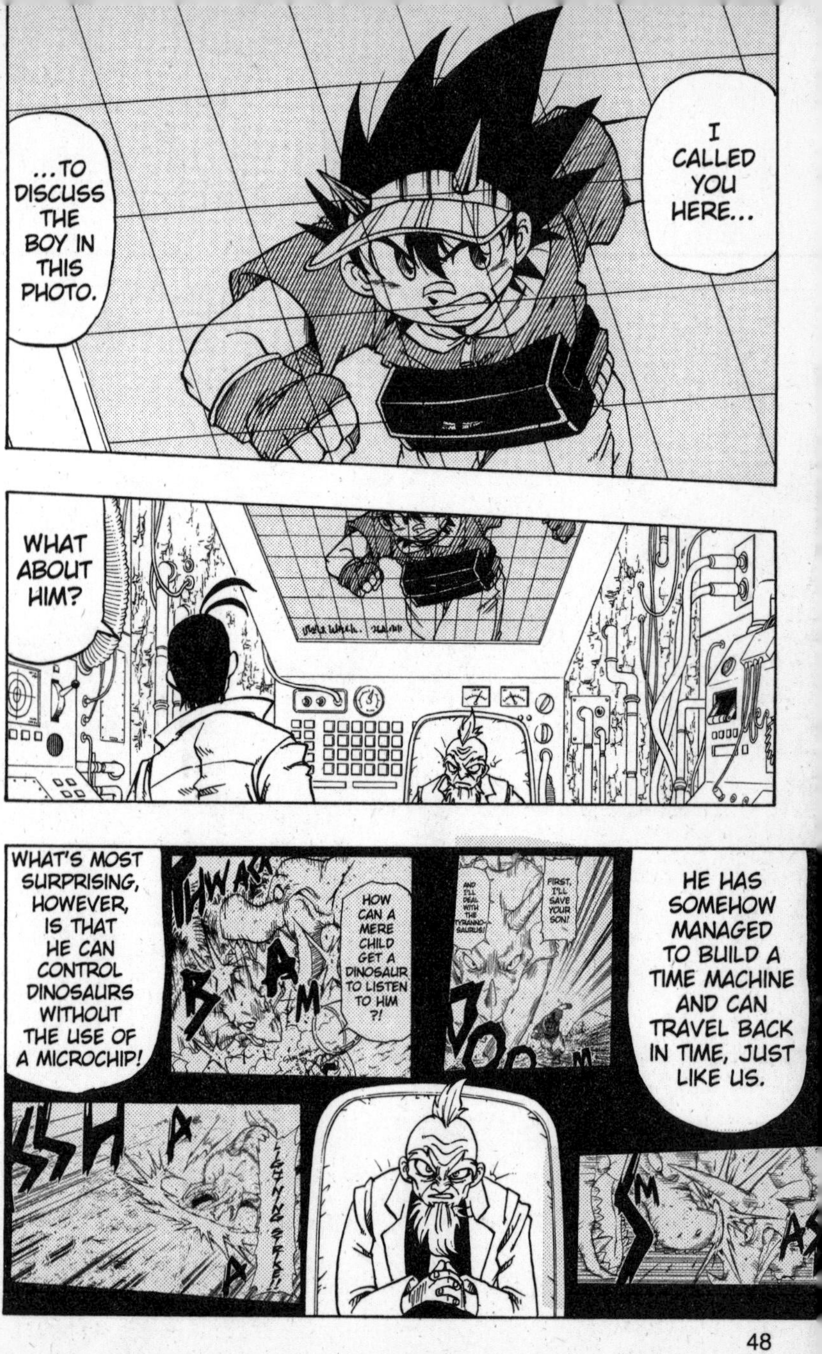
I CALLED YOU HERE...
...TO DISCUSS THE BOY IN THIS PHOTO.
WHAT ABOUT HIM?
HE HAS SOMEHOW MANAGED TO BUILD A TIME MACHINE AND CAN TRAVEL BACK IN TIME, JUST LIKE US.
FIRST, I'LL SAVE YOUR SON!
AND I'LL DEAL WITH THE TYRANNOSAURUS!
HOW CAN A MERE CHILD GET A DINOSAUR TO LISTEN TO HIM?!
BAM
WHAT'S MOST SURPRISING, HOWEVER, IS THAT HE CAN CONTROL DINOSAURS WITHOUT THE USE OF A MICROCHIP!
LIGHTNING STRIKE!

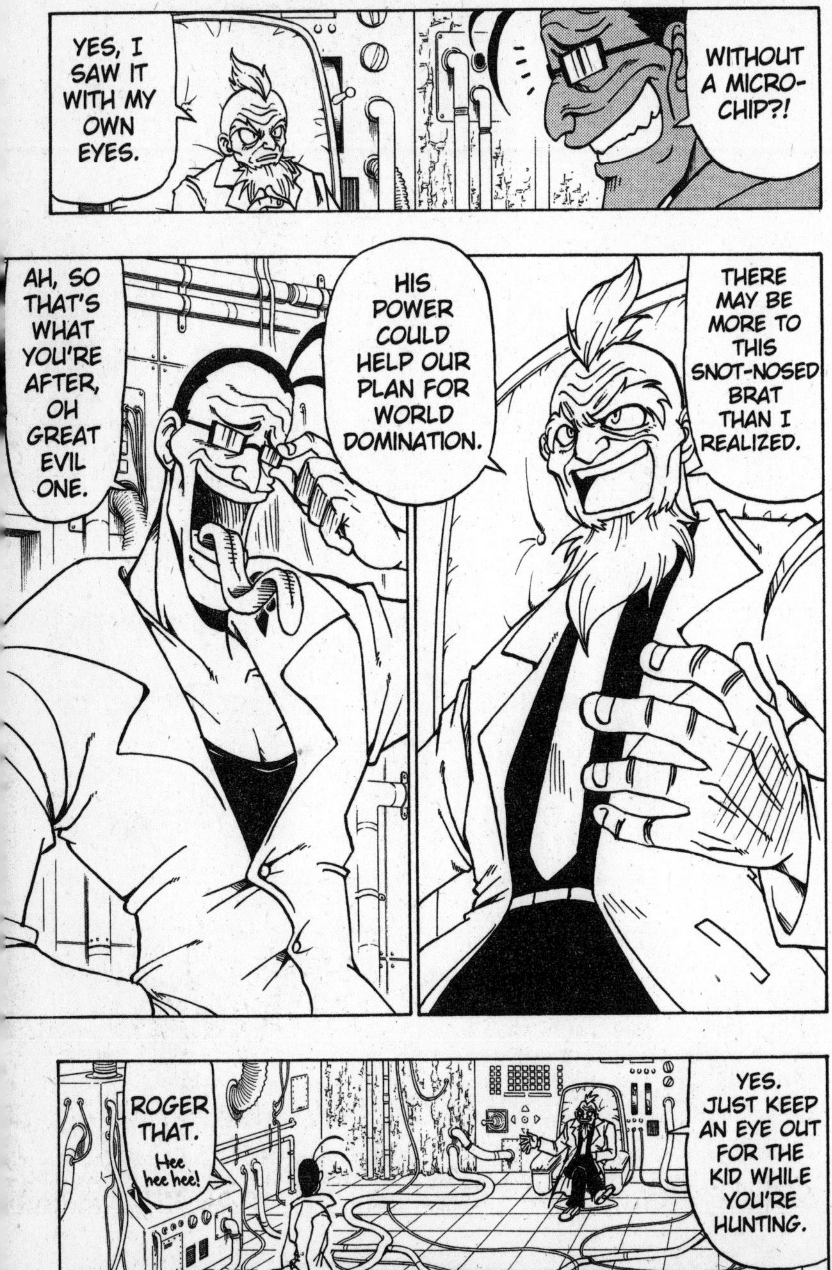
WITHOUT A MICRO-CHIP?!
YES, I SAW IT WITH MY OWN EYES.
THERE MAY BE MORE TO THIS SNOT-NOSED BRAT THAN I REALIZED.
HIS POWER COULD HELP OUR PLAN FOR WORLD DOMINATION.
AH, SO THAT'S WHAT YOU'RE AFTER, OH GREAT EVIL ONE.
YES. JUST KEEP AN EYE OUT FOR THE KID WHILE YOU'RE HUNTING.
ROGER THAT.
Hee hee hee!

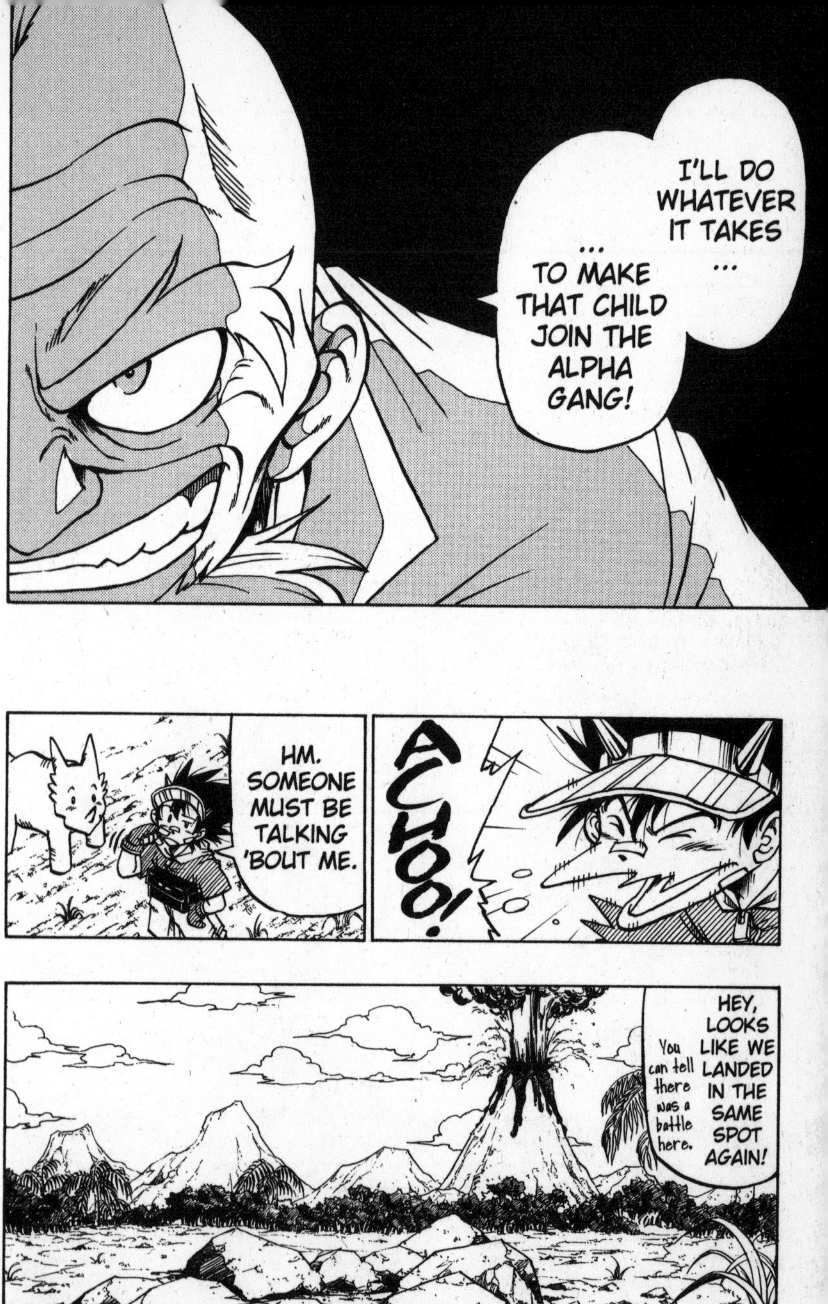
I'LL DO WHATEVER IT TAKES ...
... TO MAKE THAT CHILD JOIN THE ALPHA GANG!
ACHOO!
HM. SOMEONE MUST BE TALKING 'BOUT ME.
HEY, LOOKS LIKE WE LANDED IN THE SAME SPOT AGAIN!
You can tell there was a battle here.

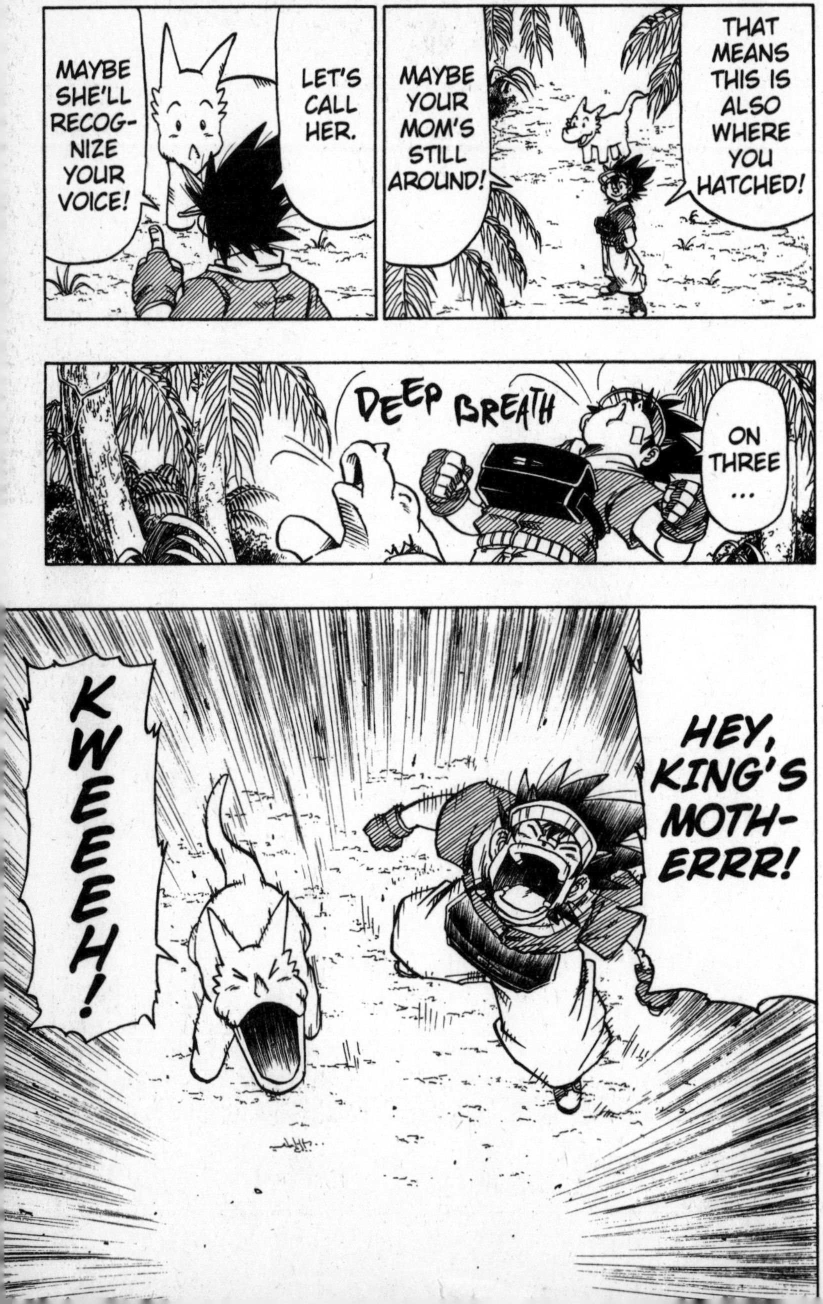
THAT MEANS THIS IS ALSO WHERE YOU HATCHED!
MAYBE YOUR MOM'S STILL AROUND!
LET'S CALL HER.
MAYBE SHE'LL RECOG-NIZE YOUR VOICE!
ON THREE ...
DEEP BREATH
HEY, KING'S MOTH-ERRR!
KWEEEEH!

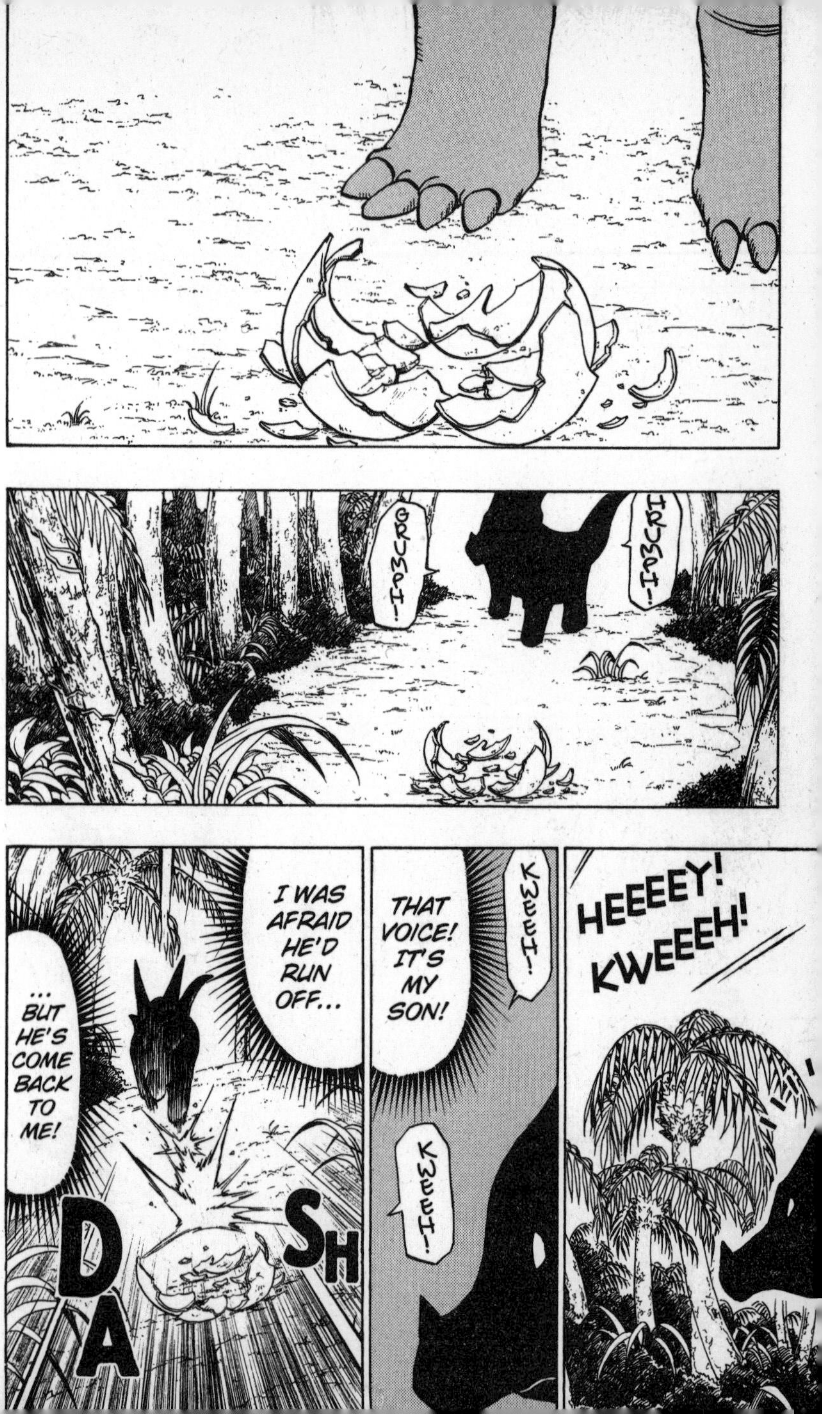
HRUMPH!
GRUMPH!
HEEEEY! KWEEEH!
KWEEH!
THAT VOICE! IT'S MY SON!
I WAS AFRAID HE'D RUN OFF...
KWEEH!
...BUT HE'S COME BACK TO ME!
DASH

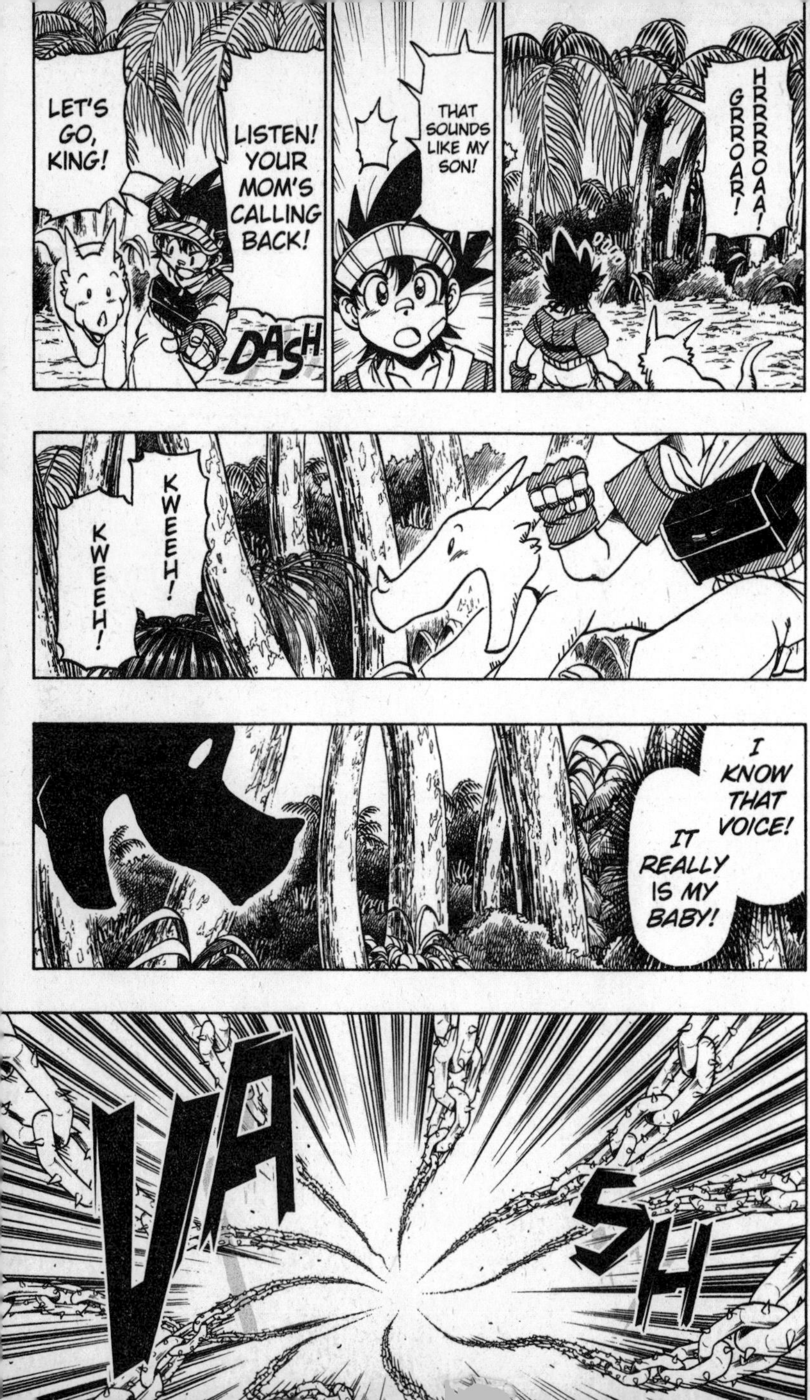
HRRROAA!
GRRROAR!
THAT SOUNDS LIKE MY SON!
LISTEN! YOUR MOM'S CALLING BACK!
LET'S GO, KING!
DASH
KWEEH!
KWEEH!
I KNOW THAT VOICE!
IT REALLY IS MY BABY!
VA
SH

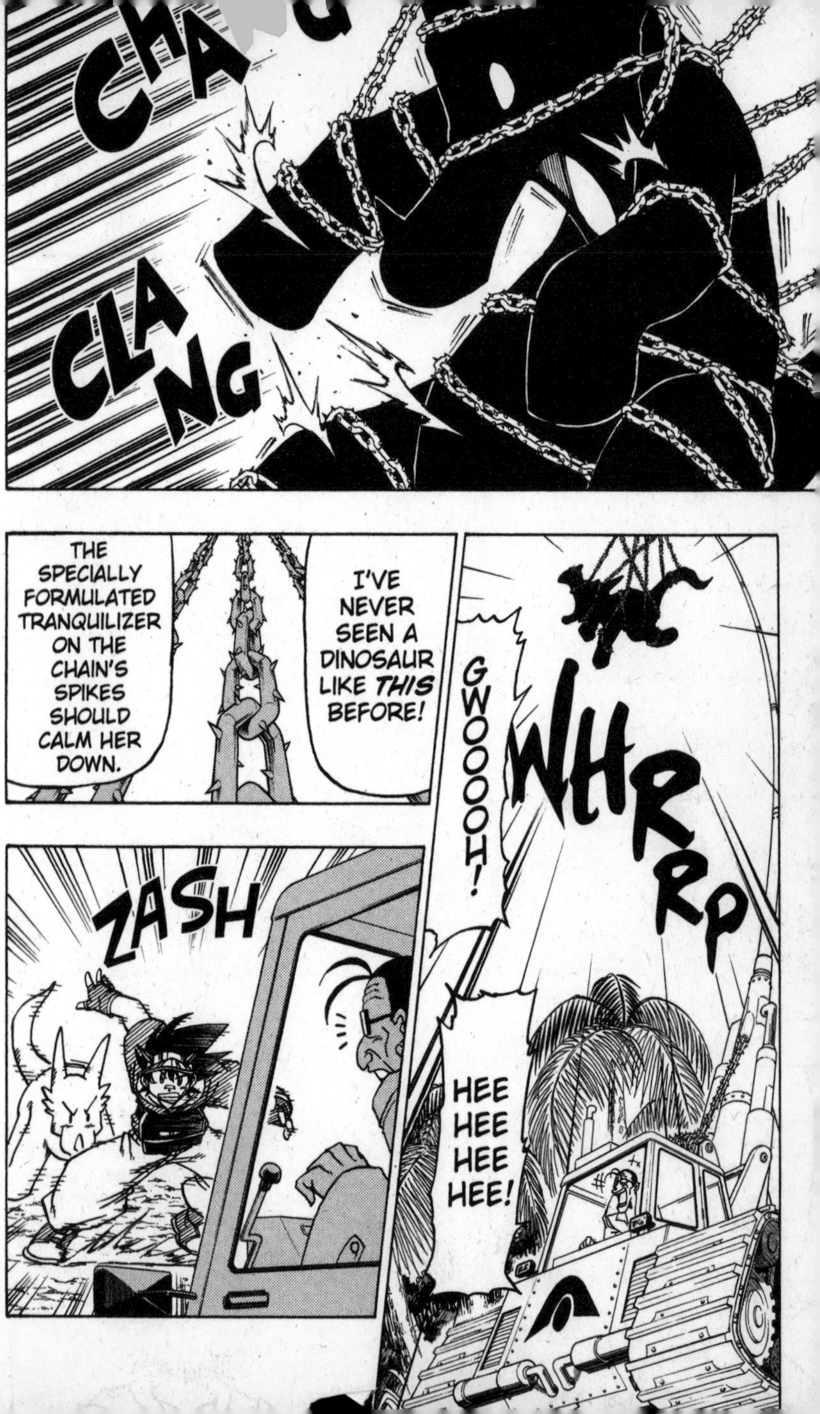
CHANG
CLANG
GWOOOOOH!
WHRRP
HEE HEE HEE HEE!
I'VE NEVER SEEN A DINOSAUR LIKE *THIS* BEFORE!
THE SPECIALLY FORMULATED TRANQUILIZER ON THE CHAIN'S SPIKES SHOULD CALM HER DOWN.
ZASH

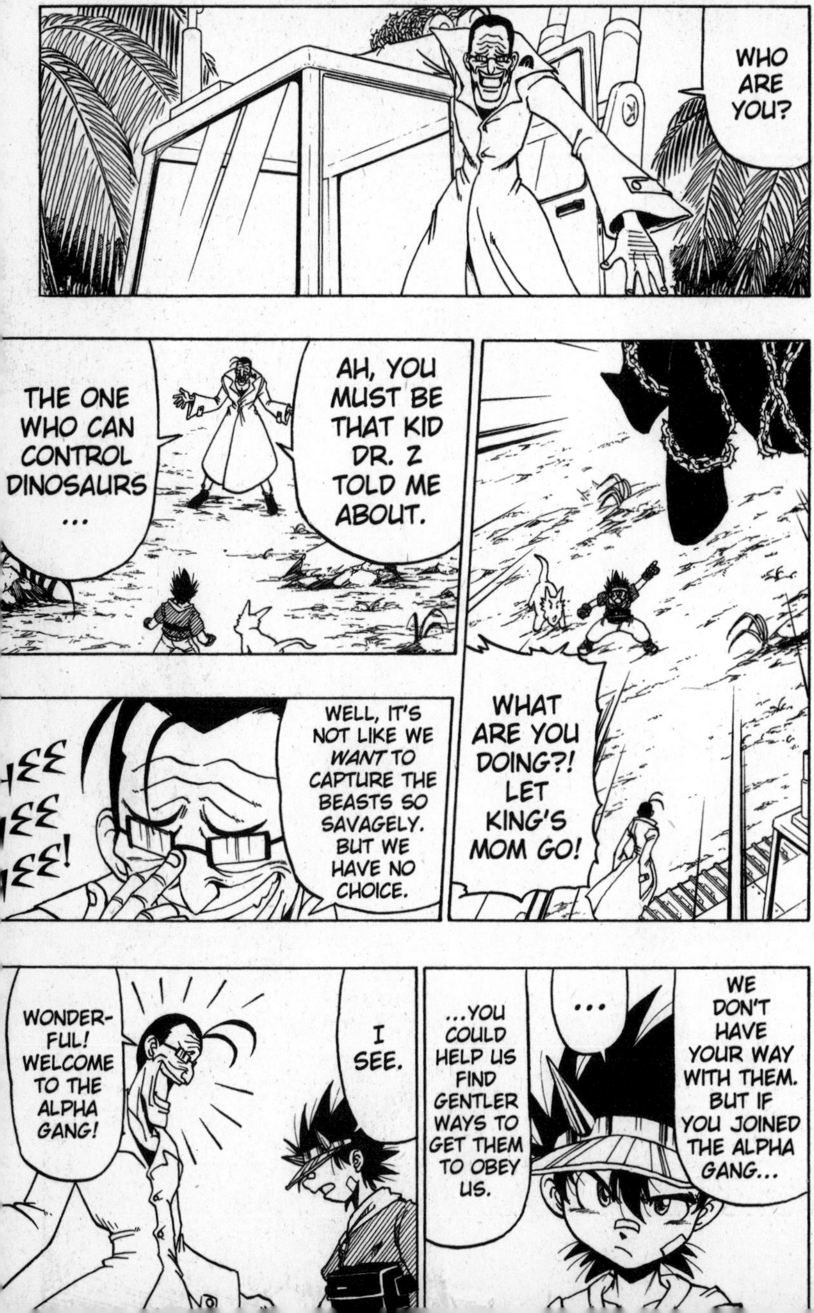
WHO ARE YOU?
AH, YOU MUST BE THAT KID DR. Z TOLD ME ABOUT.
THE ONE WHO CAN CONTROL DINOSAURS ...
WHAT ARE YOU DOING?! LET KING'S MOM GO!
WELL, IT'S NOT LIKE WE WANT TO CAPTURE THE BEASTS SO SAVAGELY. BUT WE HAVE NO CHOICE.
WE DON'T HAVE YOUR WAY WITH THEM. BUT IF YOU JOINED THE ALPHA GANG...
...
...YOU COULD HELP US FIND GENTLER WAYS TO GET THEM TO OBEY US.
I SEE.
WONDERFUL! WELCOME TO THE ALPHA GANG!

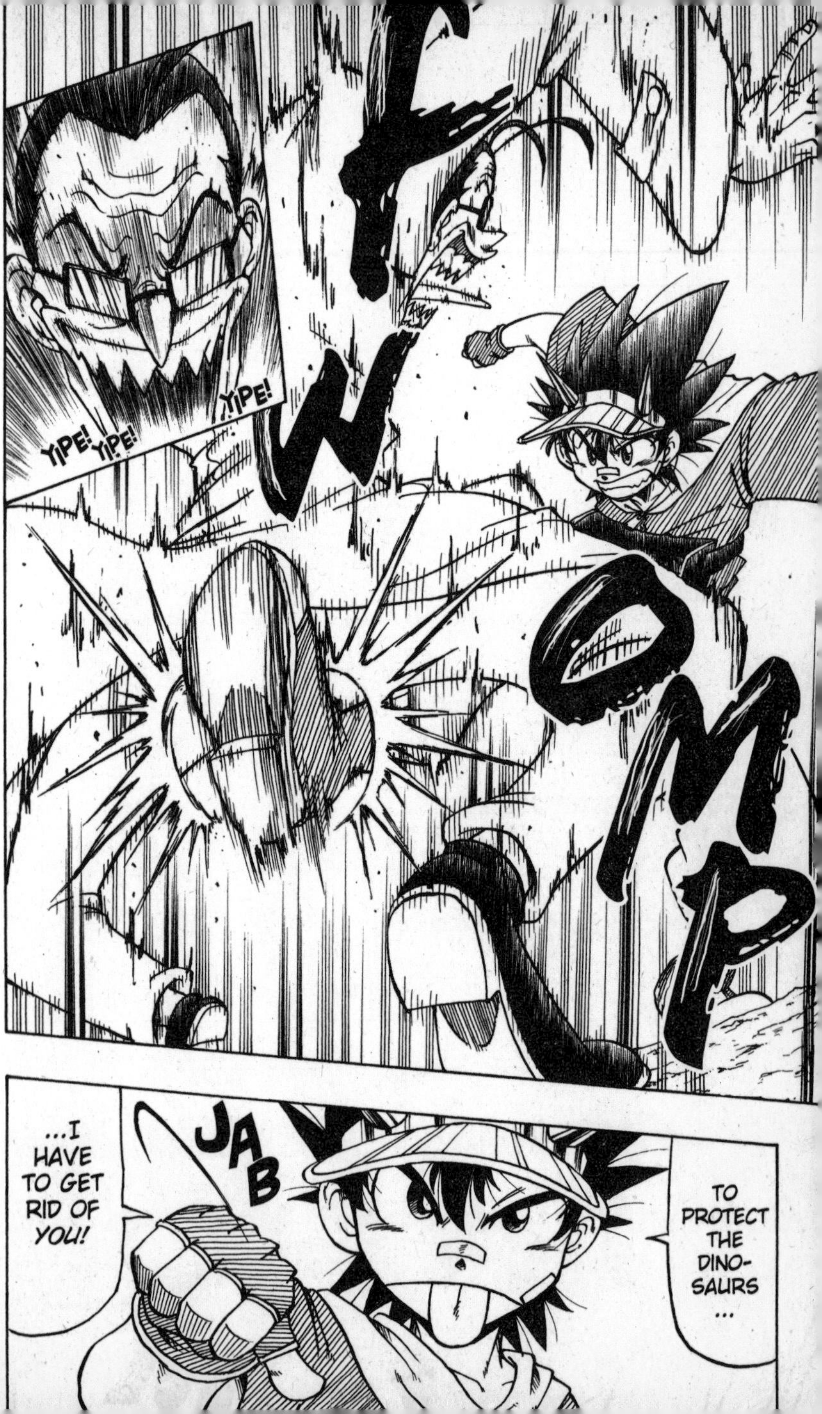

YIPE!
YIPE!
YIPE!
TO PROTECT THE DINOSAURS ...
JAB
...I HAVE TO GET RID OF YOU!

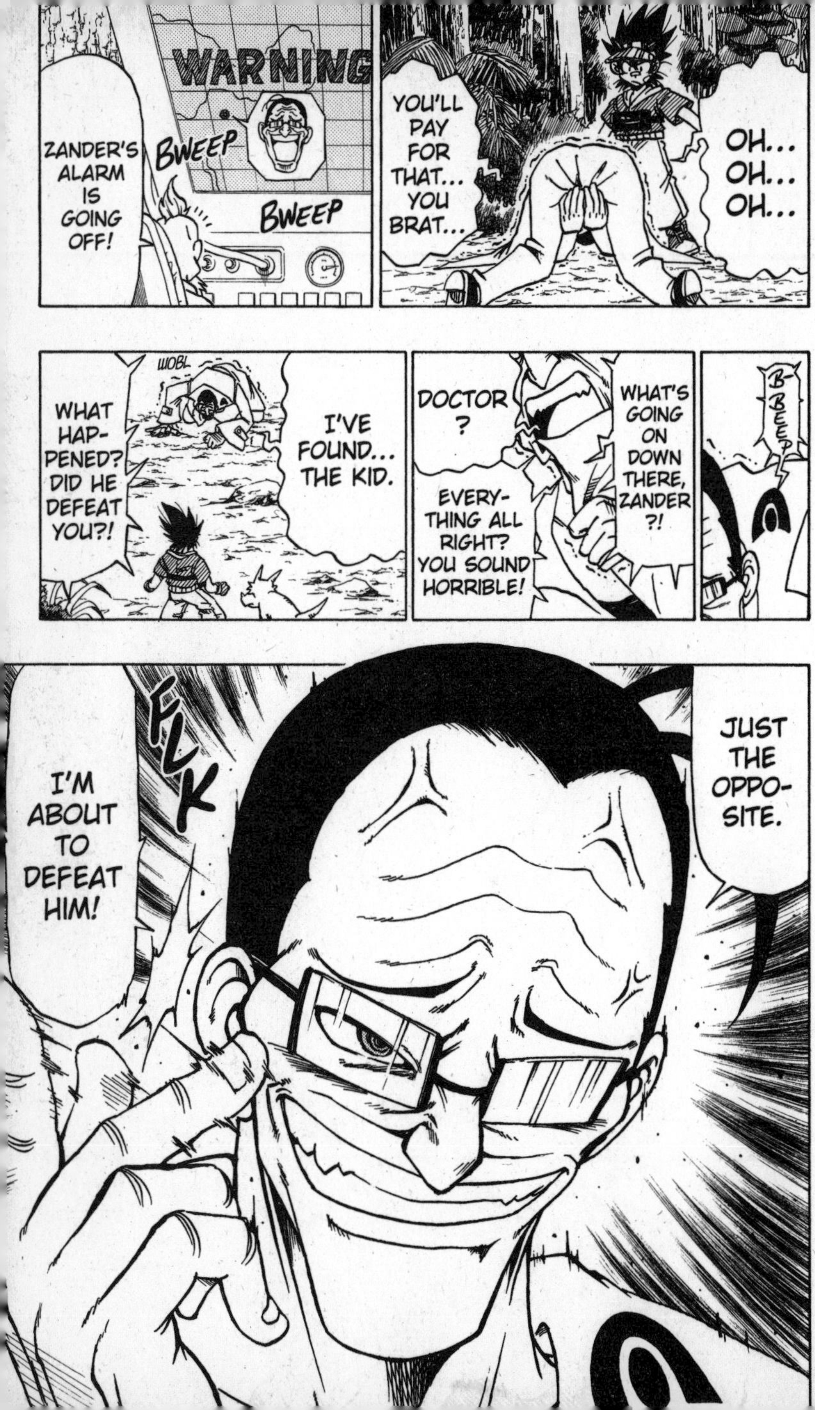
OH... OH... OH...
YOU'LL PAY FOR THAT... YOU BRAT...
WARNING
BWEEP
ZANDER'S ALARM IS GOING OFF!
BWEEP
B-BEEEP
WHAT'S GOING ON DOWN THERE, ZANDER?!
DOCTOR?
EVERY-THING ALL RIGHT? YOU SOUND HORRIBLE!
WOBL
I'VE FOUND... THE KID.
WHAT HAP-PENED? DID HE DEFEAT YOU?!
JUST THE OPPO-SITE.
FLK
I'M ABOUT TO DEFEAT HIM!

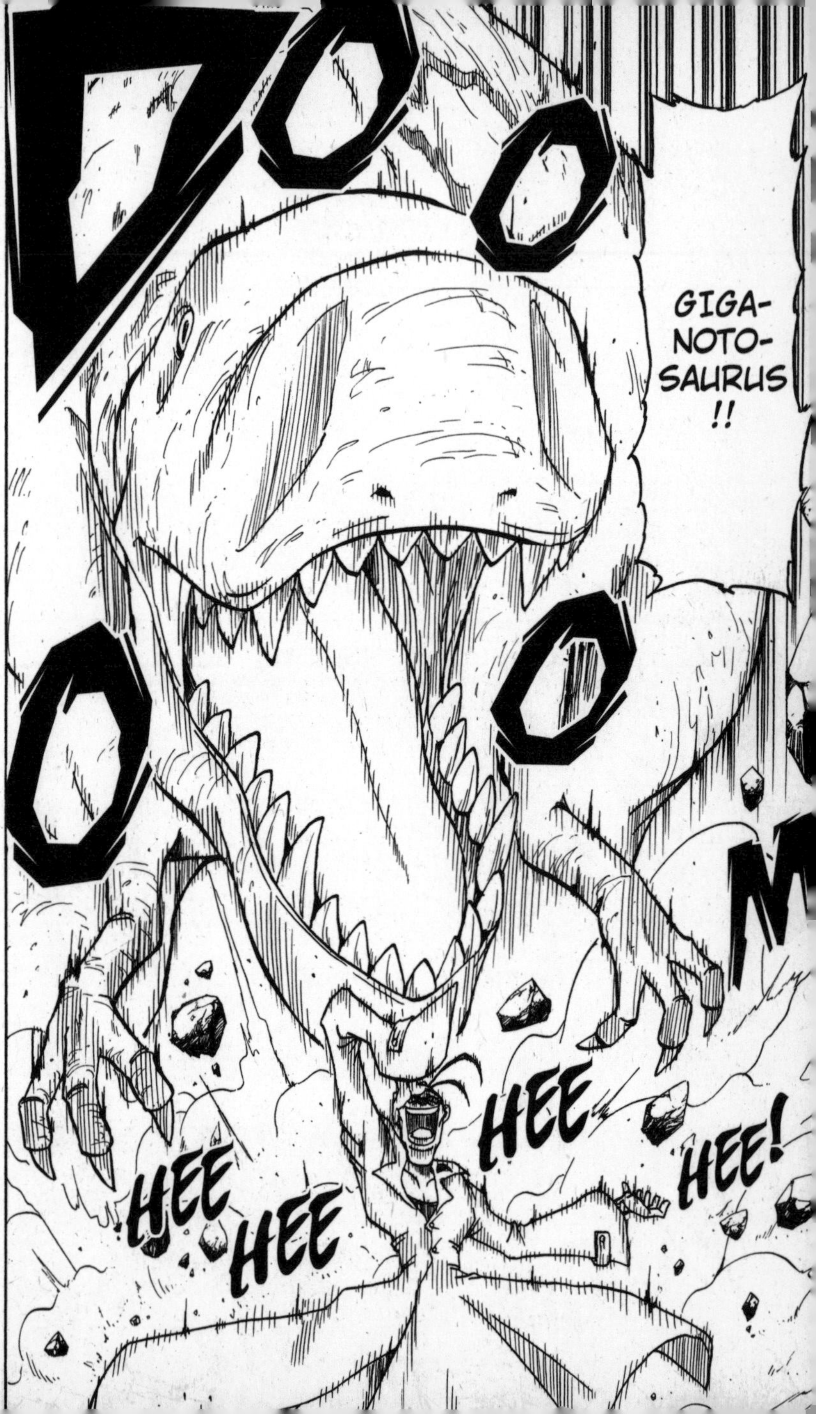
GIGA-NOTO-SAURUS!!
DOOOOM
HEE HEE HEE HEE!

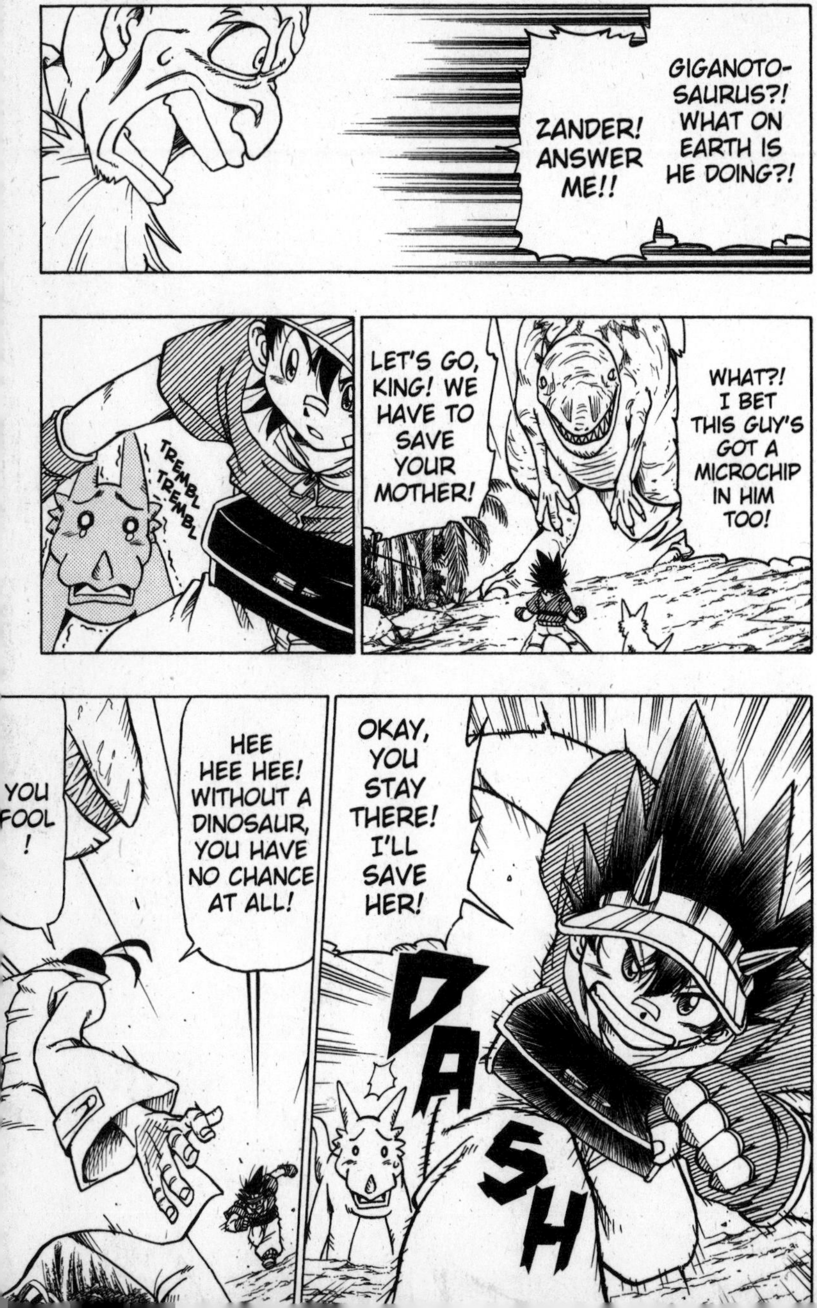
GIGANOTO-SAURUS?! WHAT ON EARTH IS HE DOING?!
ZANDER! ANSWER ME!!
WHAT?! I BET THIS GUY'S GOT A MICROCHIP IN HIM TOO!
LET'S GO, KING! WE HAVE TO SAVE YOUR MOTHER!
TREMBL TREMBL
OKAY, YOU STAY THERE! I'LL SAVE HER!
DASH
HEE HEE HEE! WITHOUT A DINOSAUR, YOU HAVE NO CHANCE AT ALL!
YOU FOOL!

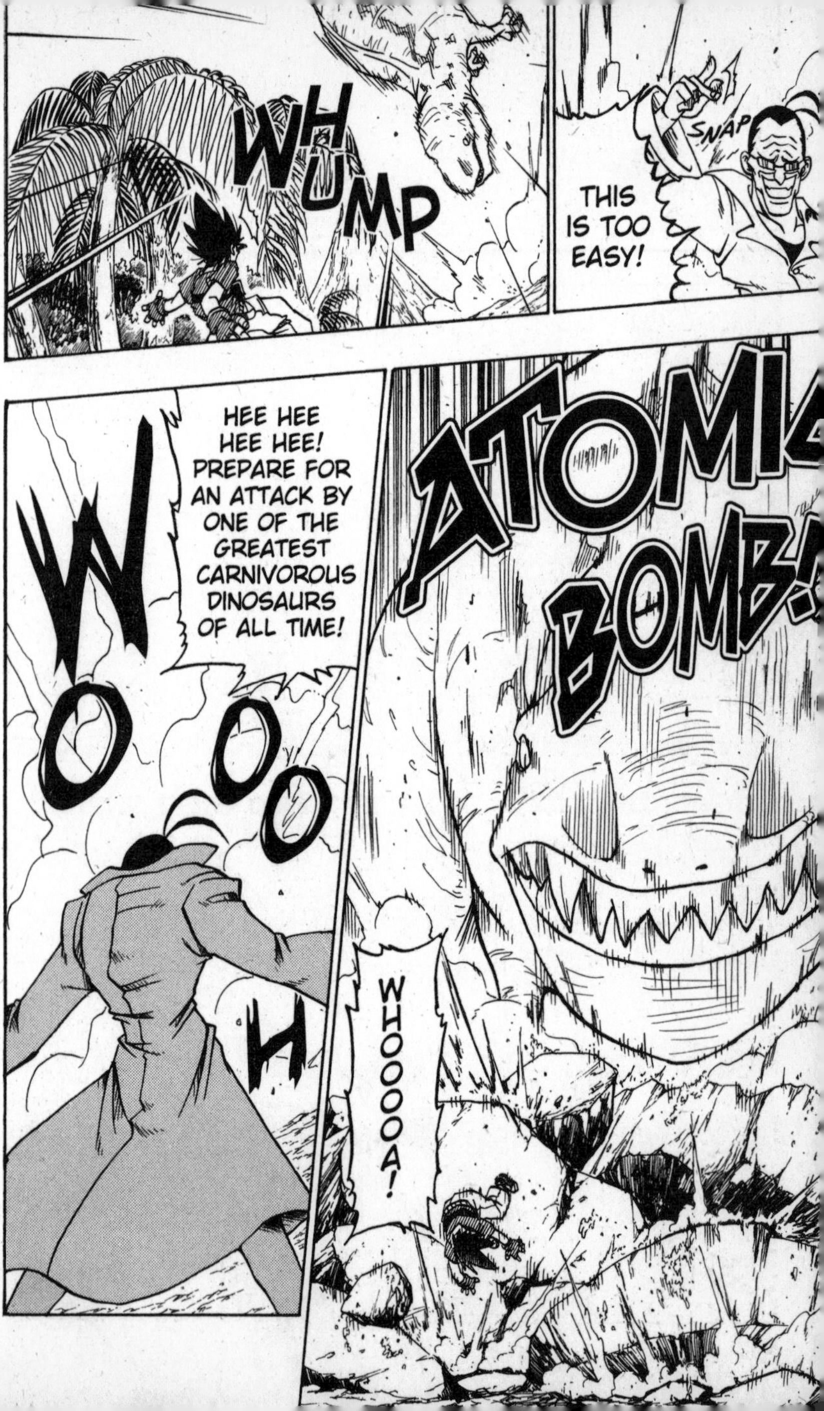
SNAP
THIS IS TOO EASY!
WHUMP
ATOMIC BOMB!
WHOOOOA!
HEE HEE HEE HEE! PREPARE FOR AN ATTACK BY ONE OF THE GREATEST CARNIVOROUS DINOSAURS OF ALL TIME!
WOOOH

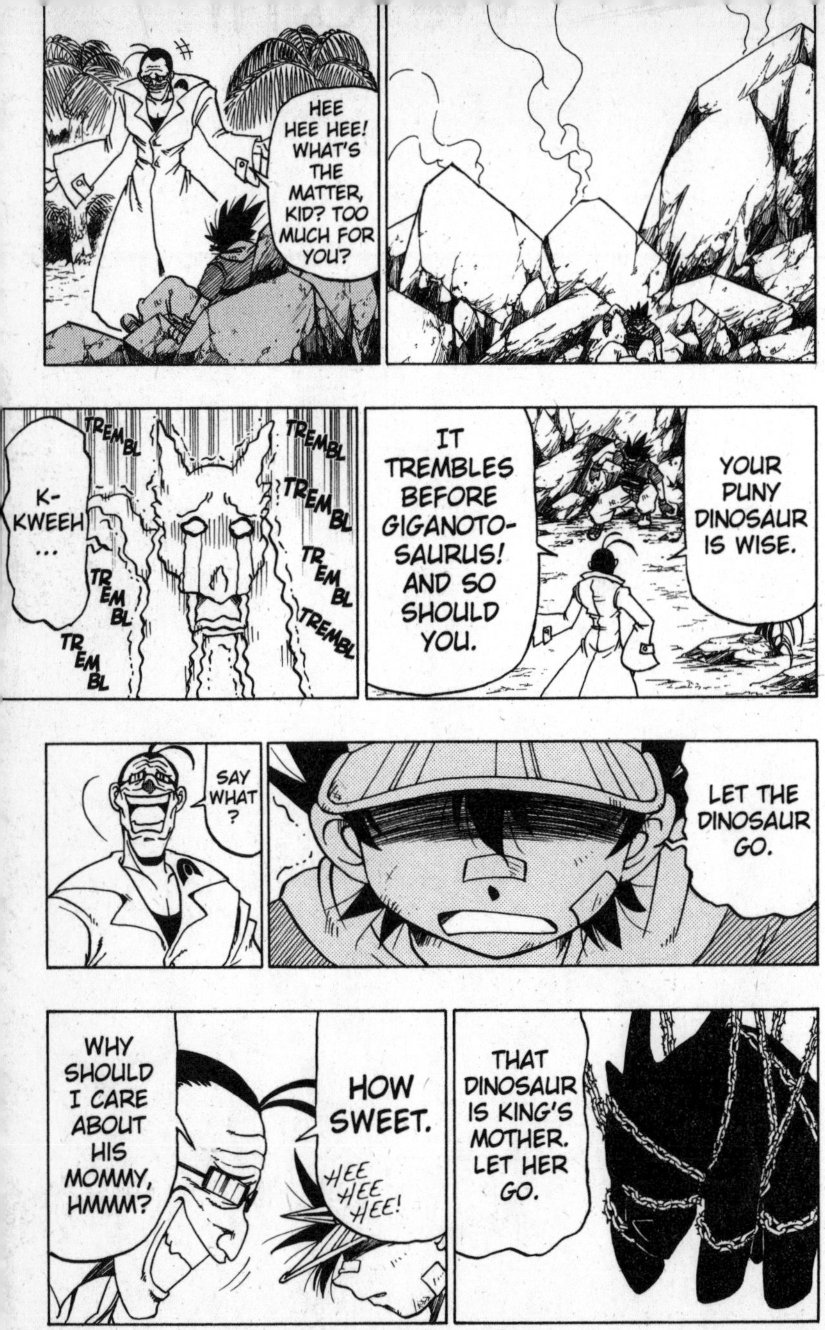
HEE HEE HEE! WHAT'S THE MATTER, KID? TOO MUCH FOR YOU?
YOUR PUNY DINOSAUR IS WISE.
IT TREMBLES BEFORE GIGANOTO-SAURUS! AND SO SHOULD YOU.
TREMBL
TREMBL
TREMBL
TREMBL
TREMBL
TREMBL
TREMBL
K-KWEEH...
LET THE DINOSAUR GO.
SAY WHAT?
THAT DINOSAUR IS KING'S MOTHER. LET HER GO.
HOW SWEET.
HEE HEE HEE!
WHY SHOULD I CARE ABOUT HIS MOMMY, HMMM?

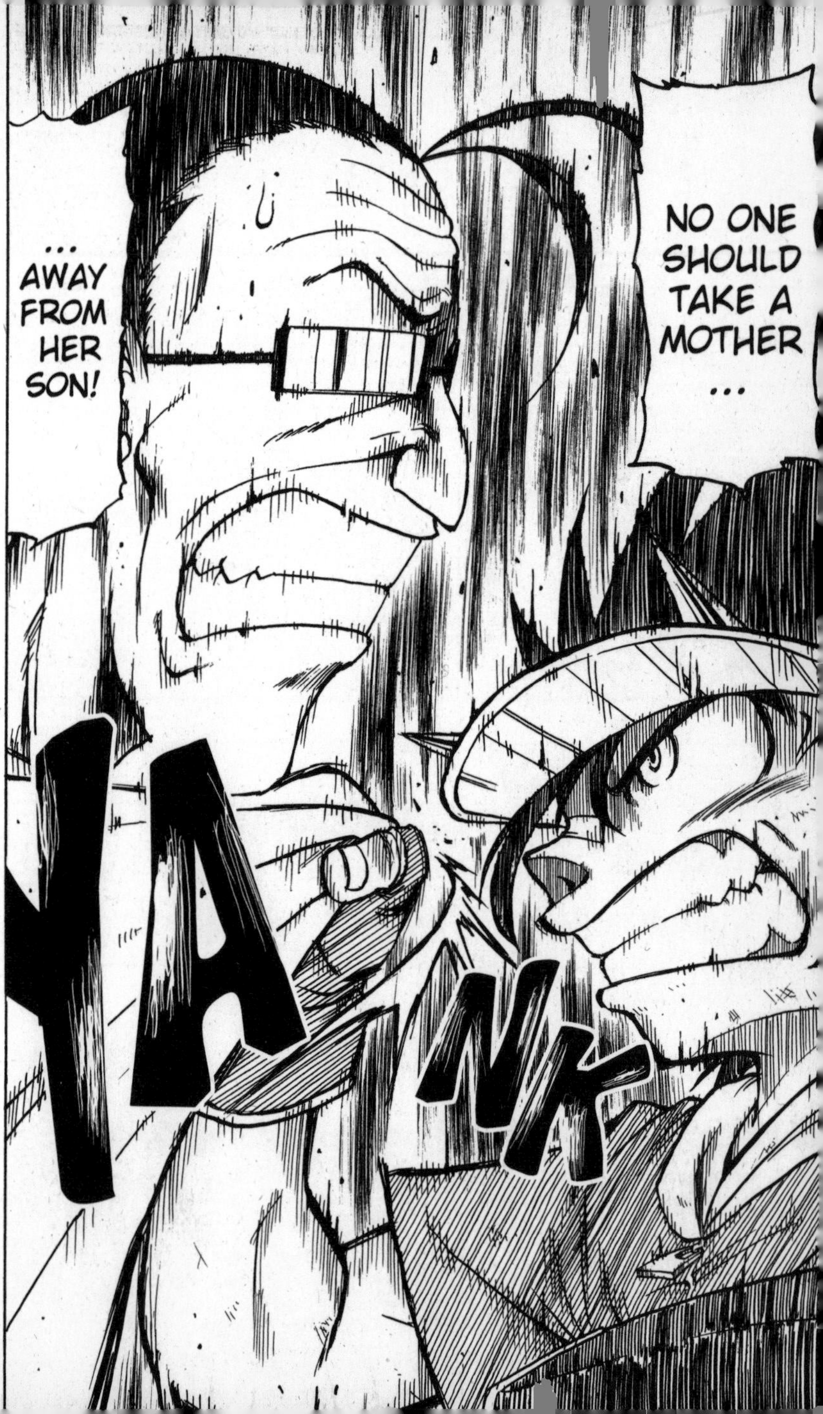
NO ONE SHOULD TAKE A MOTHER ...
... AWAY FROM HER SON!
YANK

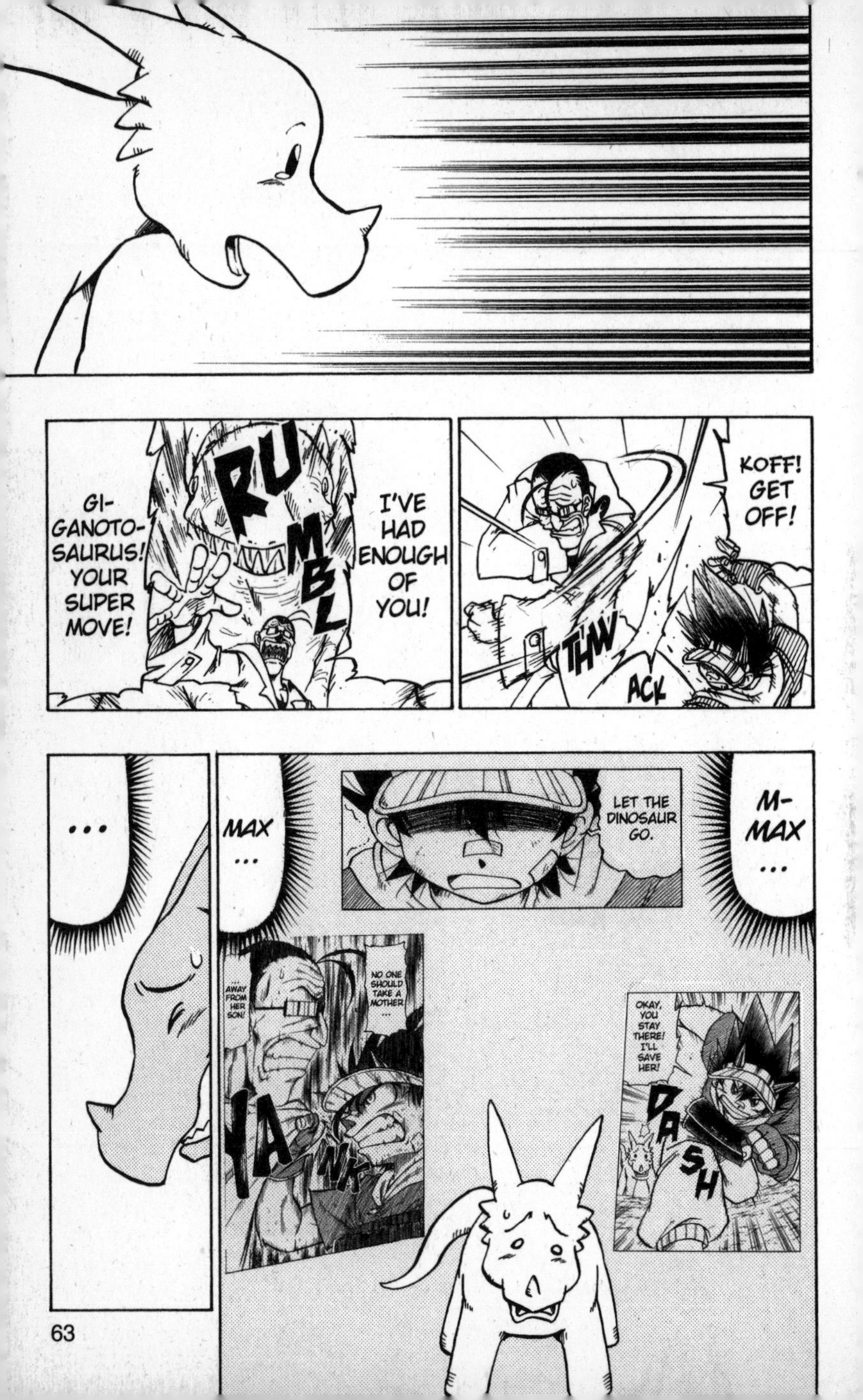
KOFF! GET OFF!
THW
ACK
I'VE HAD ENOUGH OF YOU!
RUMBL
GI-GANOTO-SAURUS! YOUR SUPER MOVE!
M-MAX ...
LET THE DINOSAUR GO.
MAX ...
...
OKAY, YOU STAY THERE! I'LL SAVE HER!
DASH
NO ONE SHOULD TAKE A MOTHER ...
... AWAY FROM HER SON!
YANK

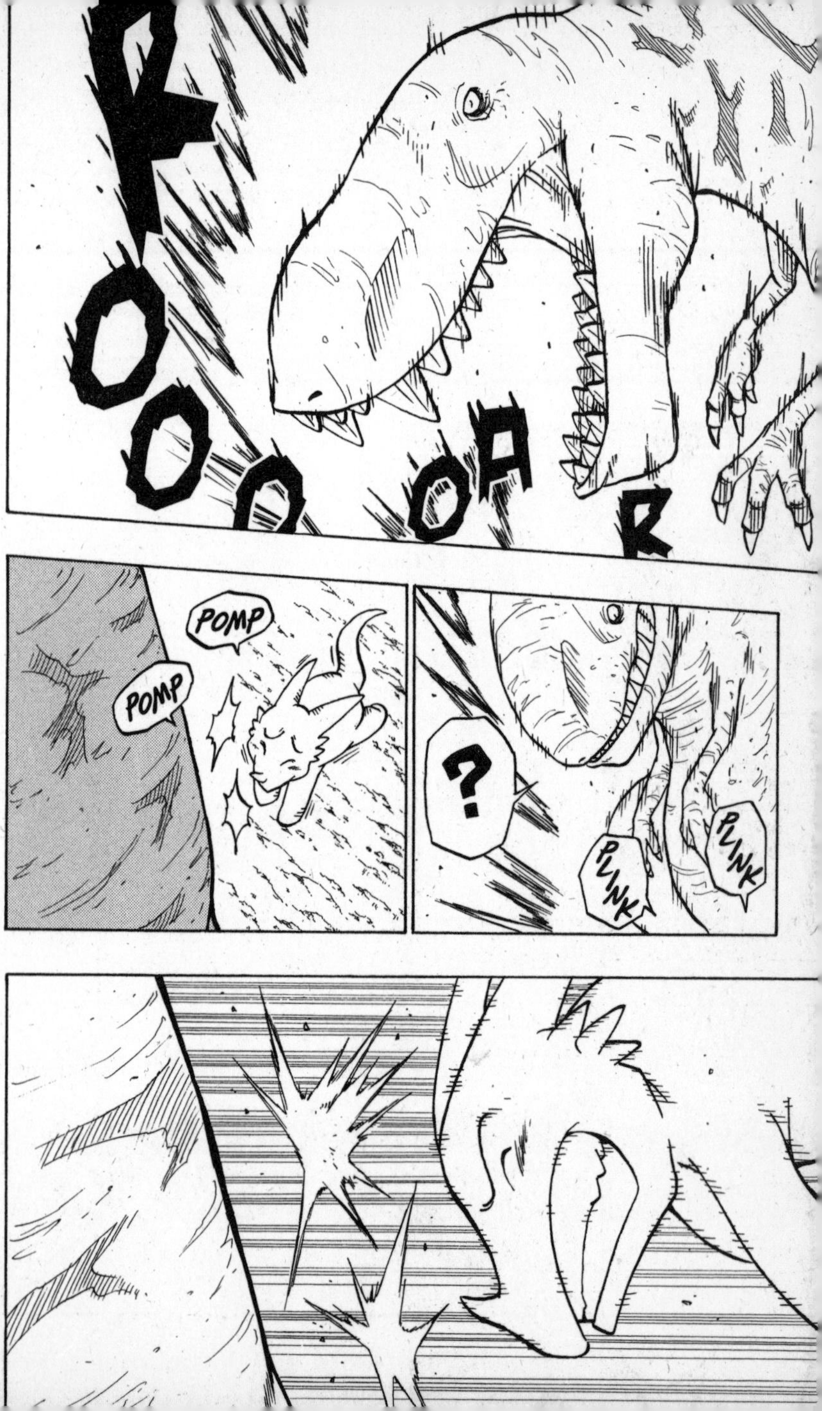
ROOOOOOAR
?
PLINK
PLINK
POMP
POMP

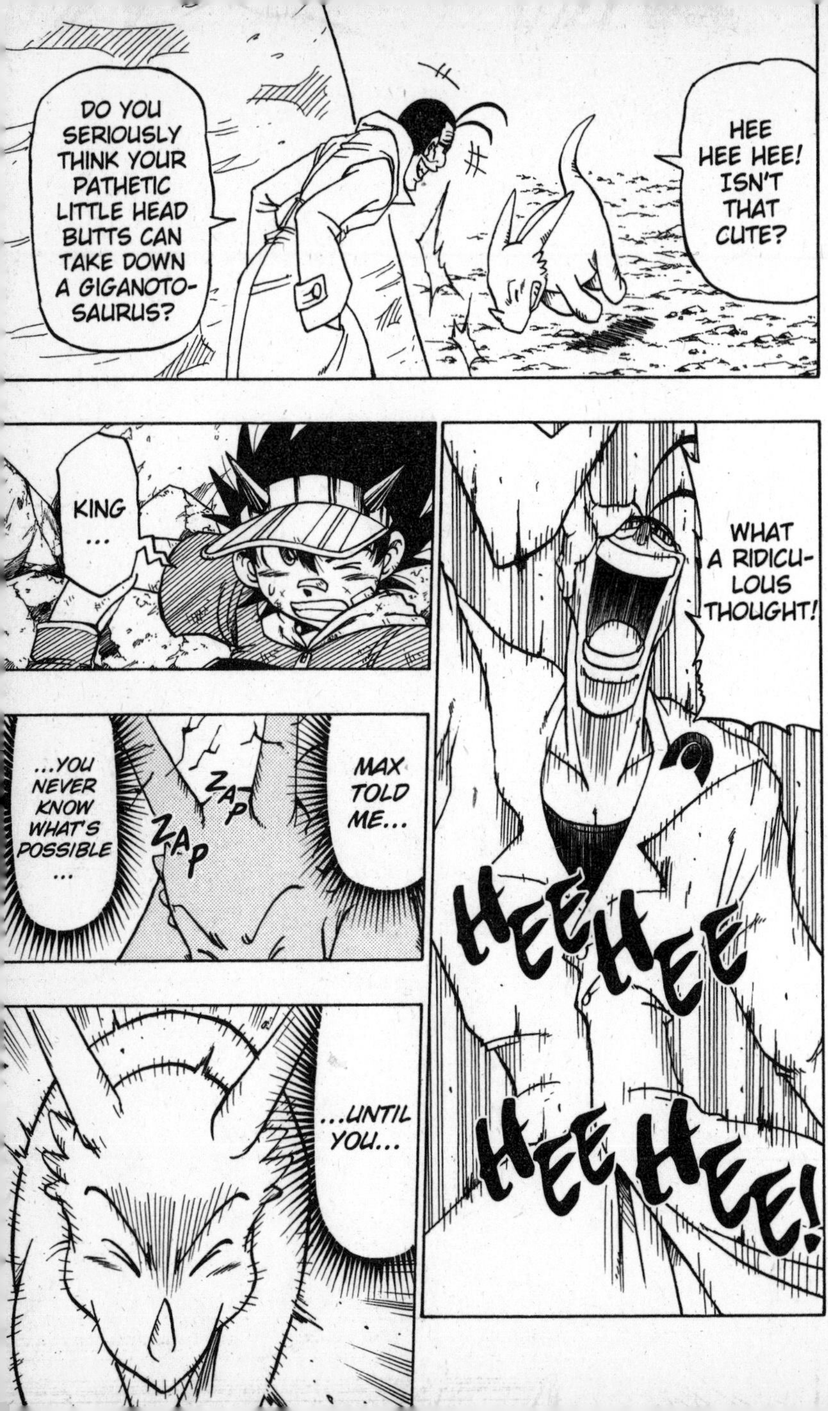
HEE HEE HEE! ISN'T THAT CUTE?
DO YOU SERIOUSLY THINK YOUR PATHETIC LITTLE HEAD BUTTS CAN TAKE DOWN A GIGANOTO-SAURUS?
WHAT A RIDICU-LOUS THOUGHT!
HEE HEE
HEE HEE!
KING ...
MAX TOLD ME...
ZAP
ZAP
...YOU NEVER KNOW WHAT'S POSSIBLE ...
...UNTIL YOU...

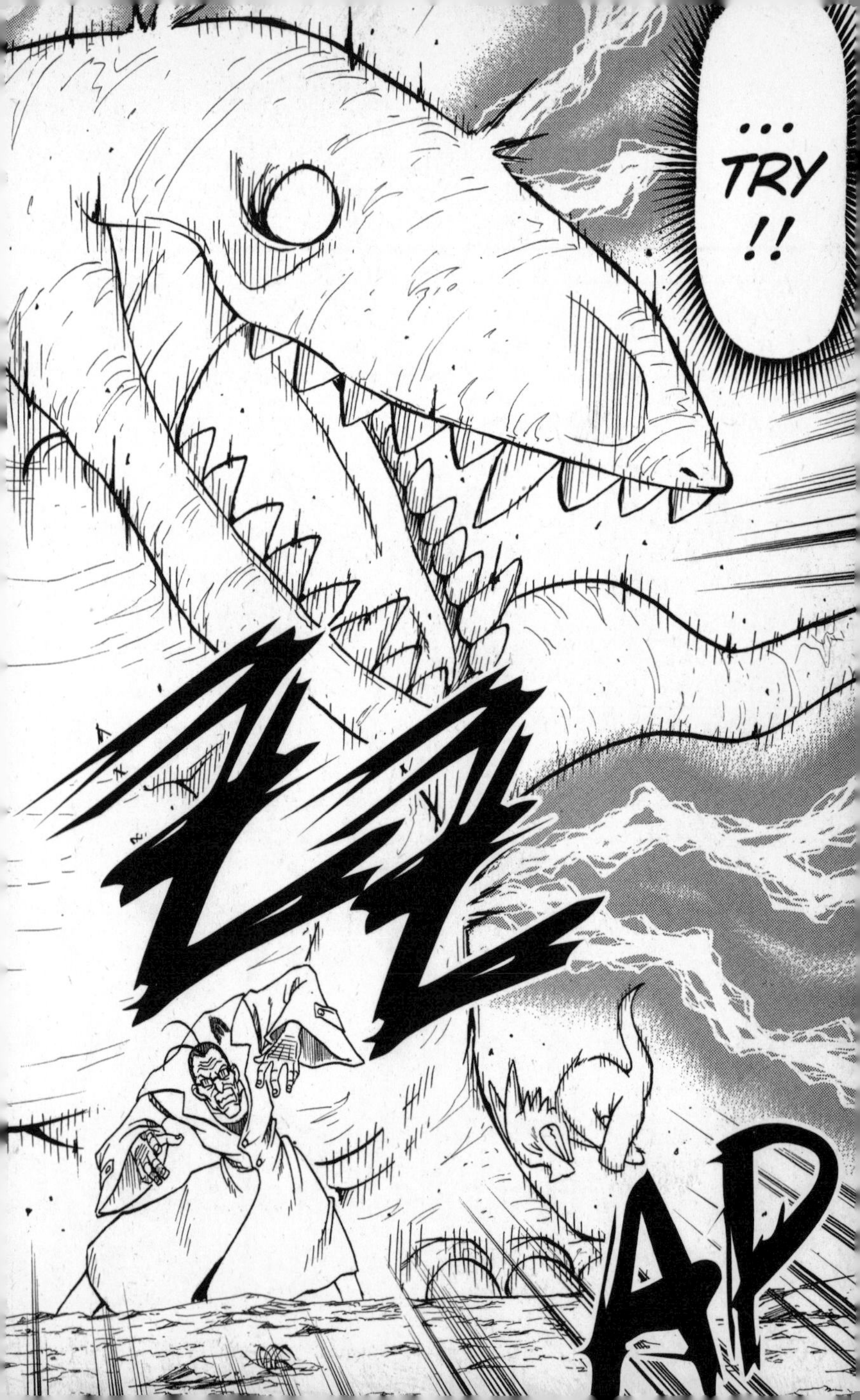
...TRY!!
ZZAP

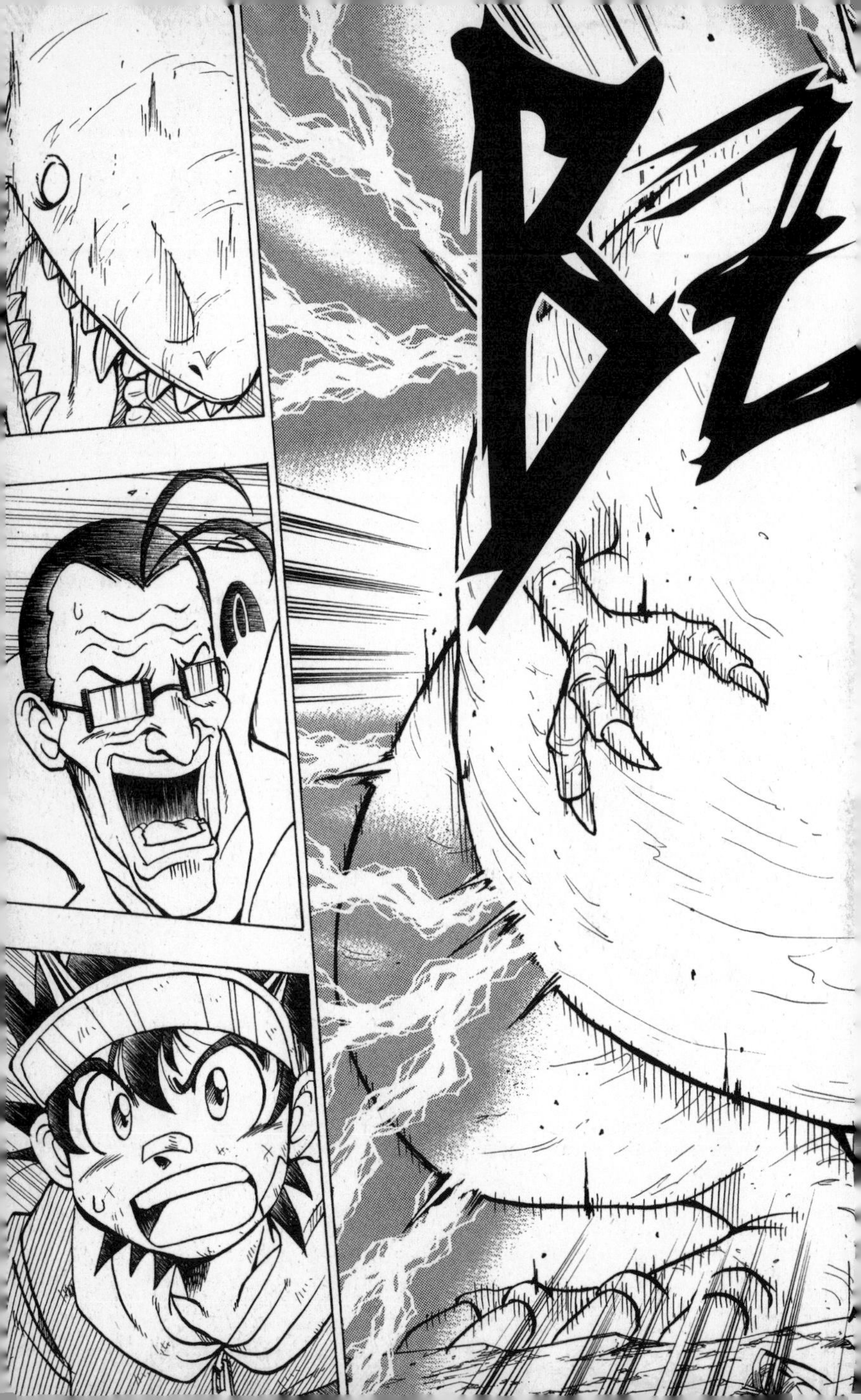

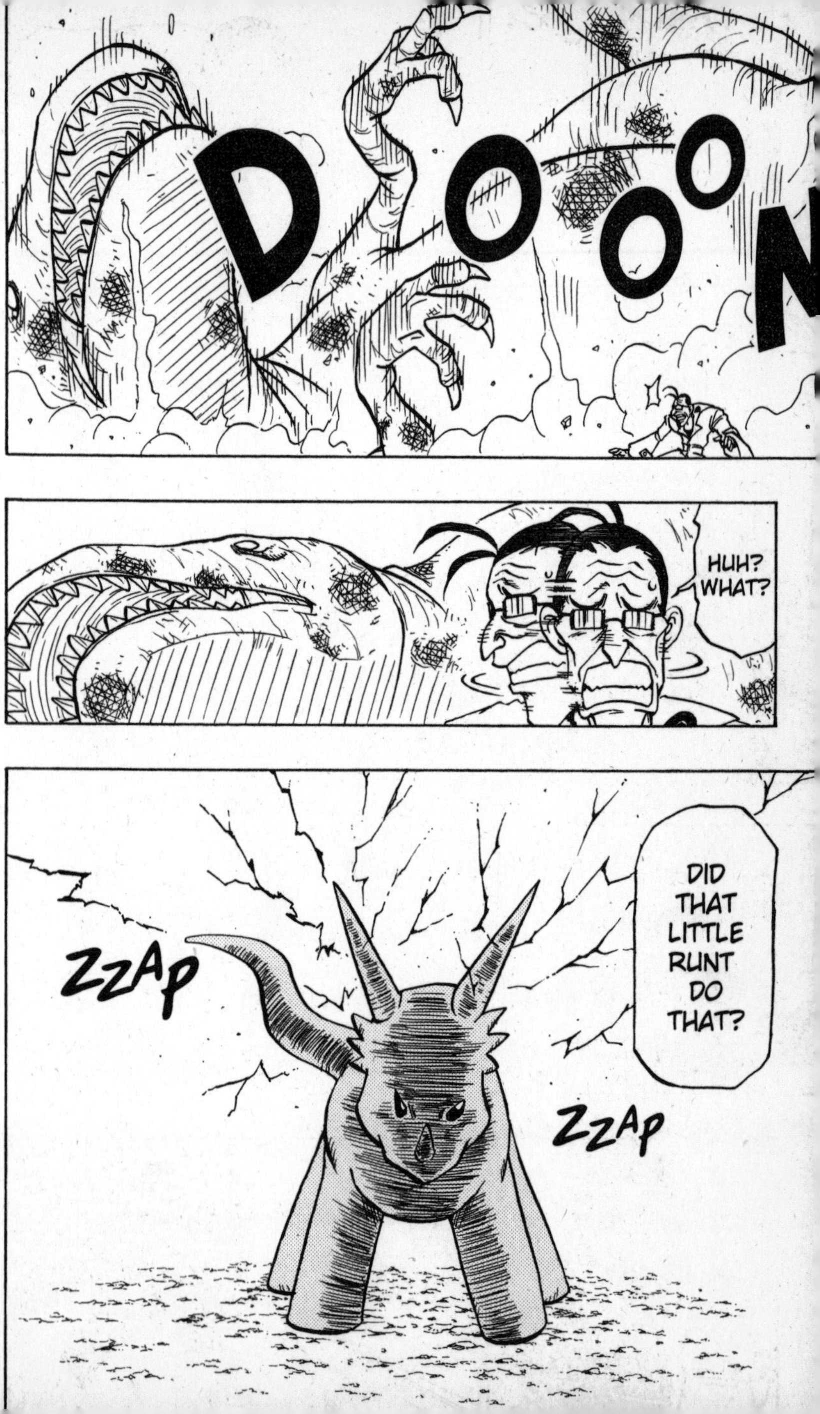
DOOON
HUH? WHAT?
DID THAT LITTLE RUNT DO THAT?
ZZAP
ZZAP

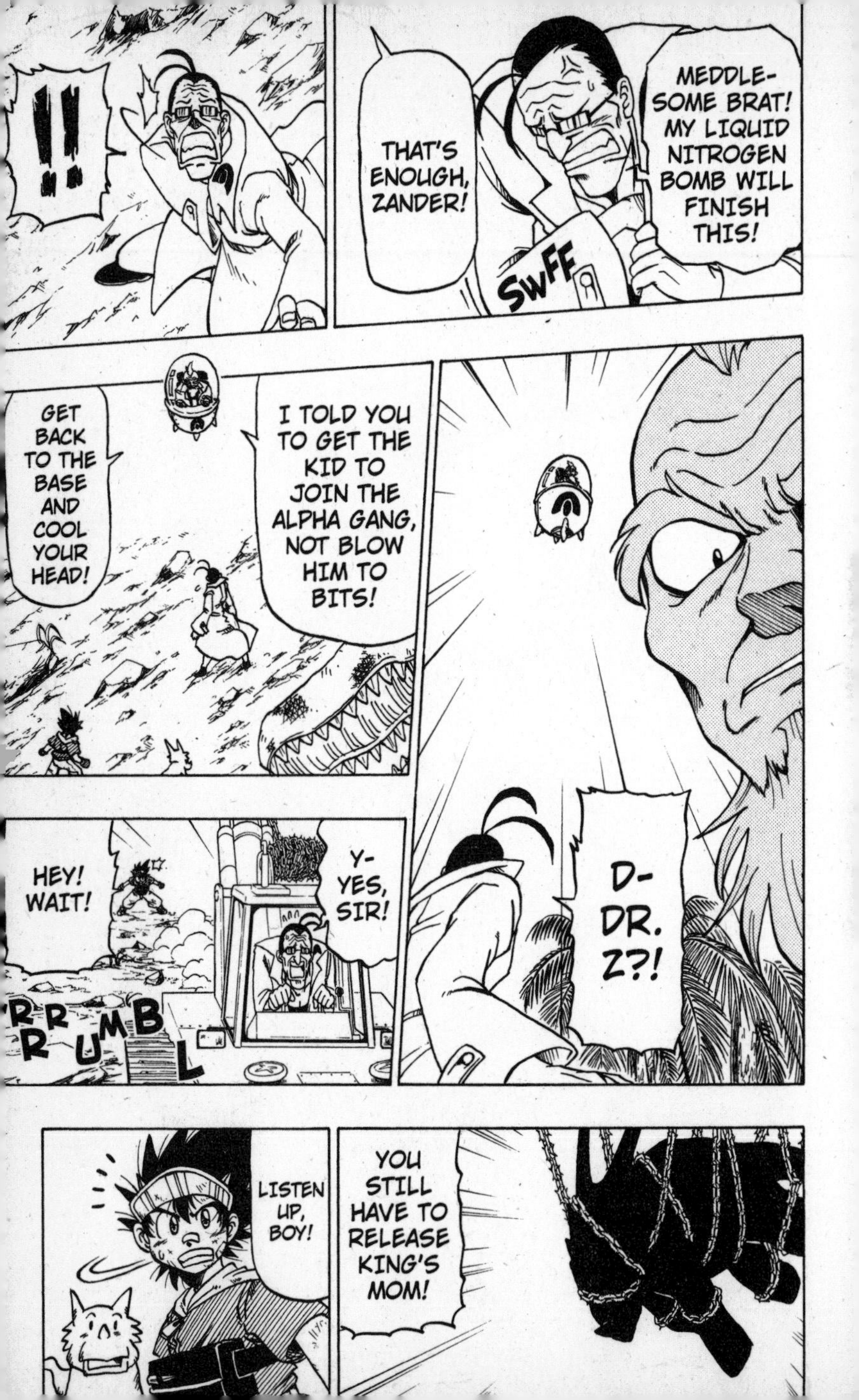
MEDDLE-SOME BRAT! MY LIQUID NITROGEN BOMB WILL FINISH THIS!
SWFF
THAT'S ENOUGH, ZANDER!
!!
D-DR. Z?!
I TOLD YOU TO GET THE KID TO JOIN THE ALPHA GANG, NOT BLOW HIM TO BITS!
GET BACK TO THE BASE AND COOL YOUR HEAD!
Y-YES, SIR!
HEY! WAIT!
RRRUMBL
YOU STILL HAVE TO RELEASE KING'S MOM!
LISTEN UP, BOY!

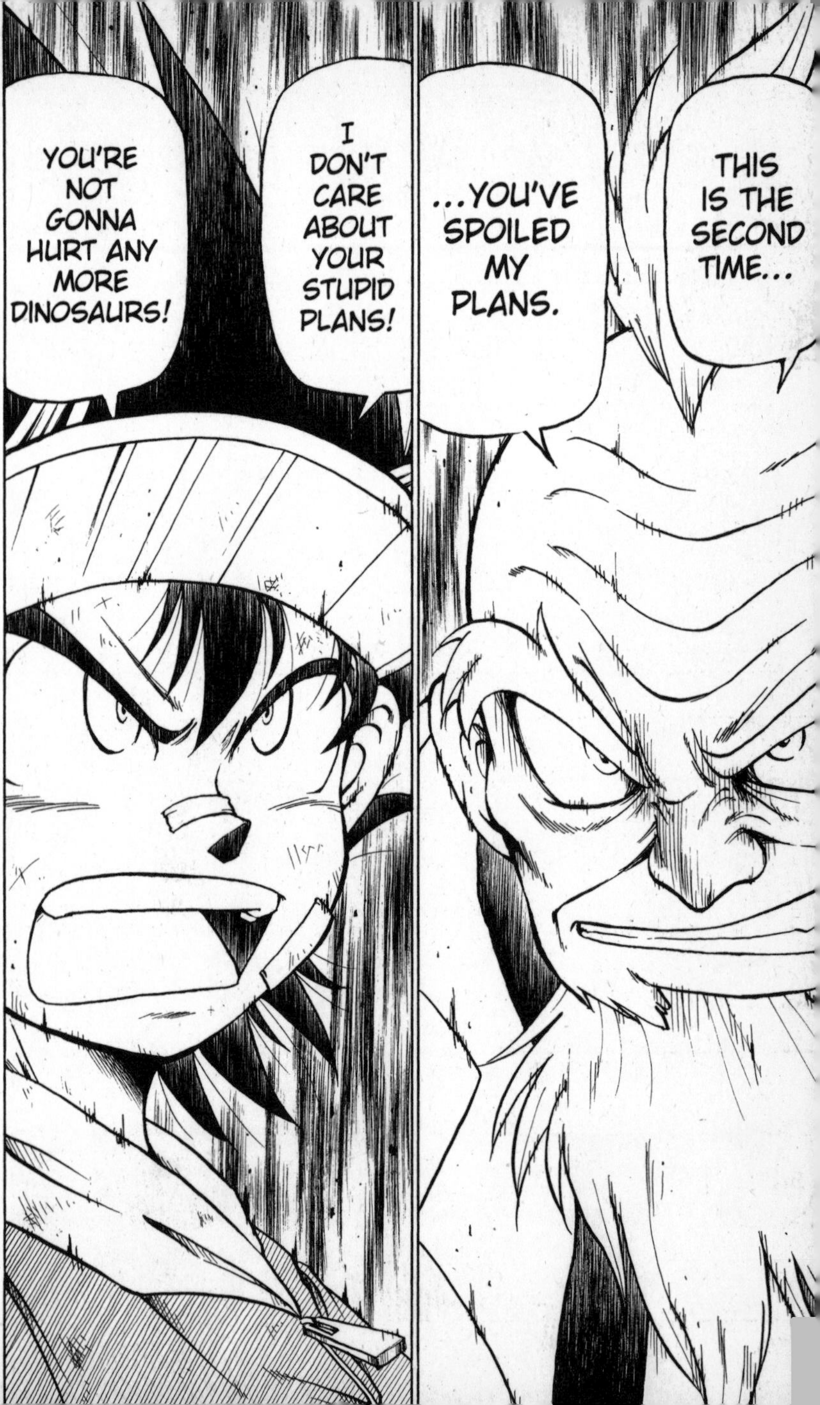
THIS IS THE SECOND TIME...
...YOU'VE SPOILED MY PLANS.
I DON'T CARE ABOUT YOUR STUPID PLANS!
YOU'RE NOT GONNA HURT ANY MORE DINOSAURS!

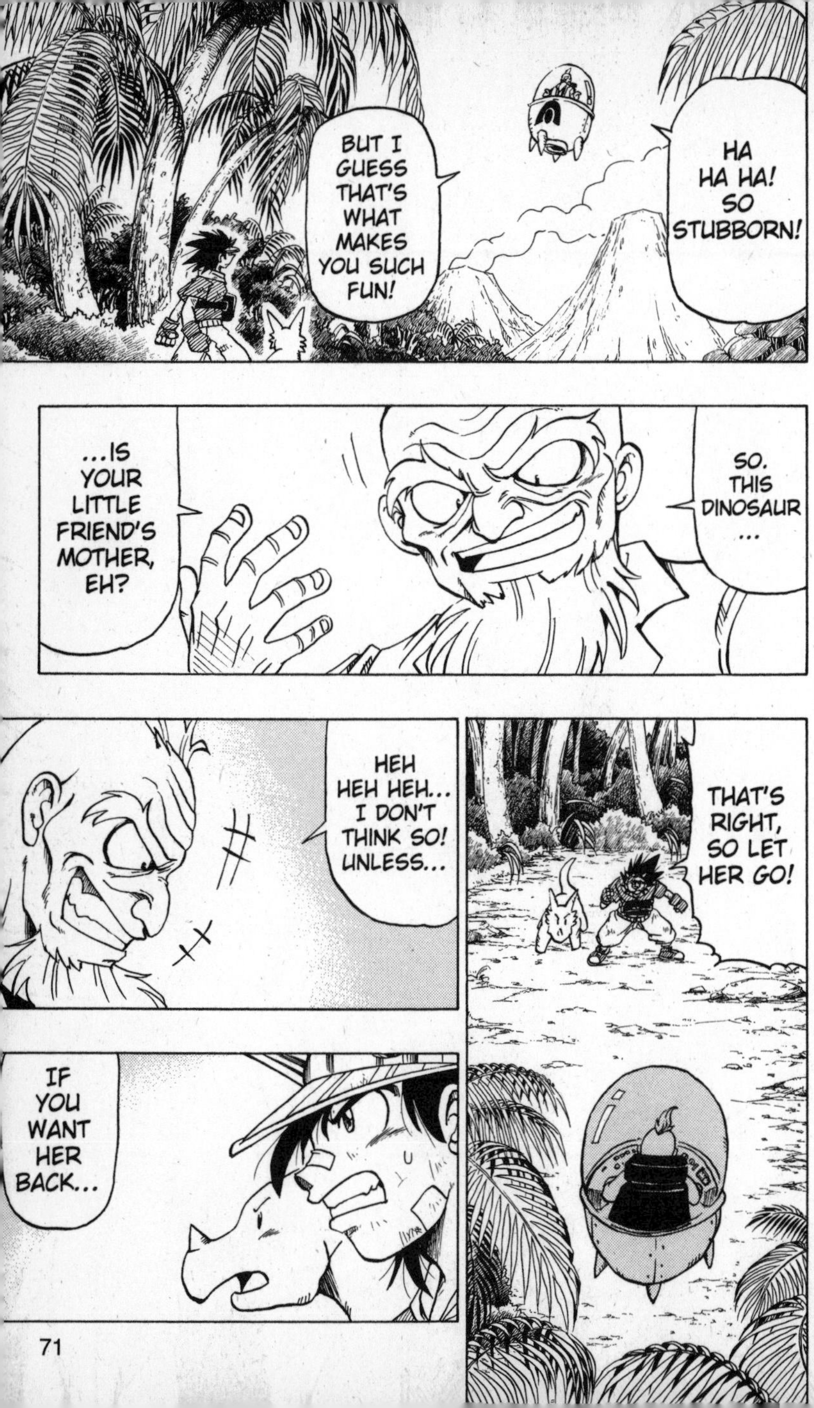
HA HA HA! SO STUBBORN!
BUT I GUESS THAT'S WHAT MAKES YOU SUCH FUN!
SO. THIS DINOSAUR ...
...IS YOUR LITTLE FRIEND'S MOTHER, EH?
THAT'S RIGHT, SO LET HER GO!
HEH HEH HEH... I DON'T THINK SO! UNLESS...
IF YOU WANT HER BACK...

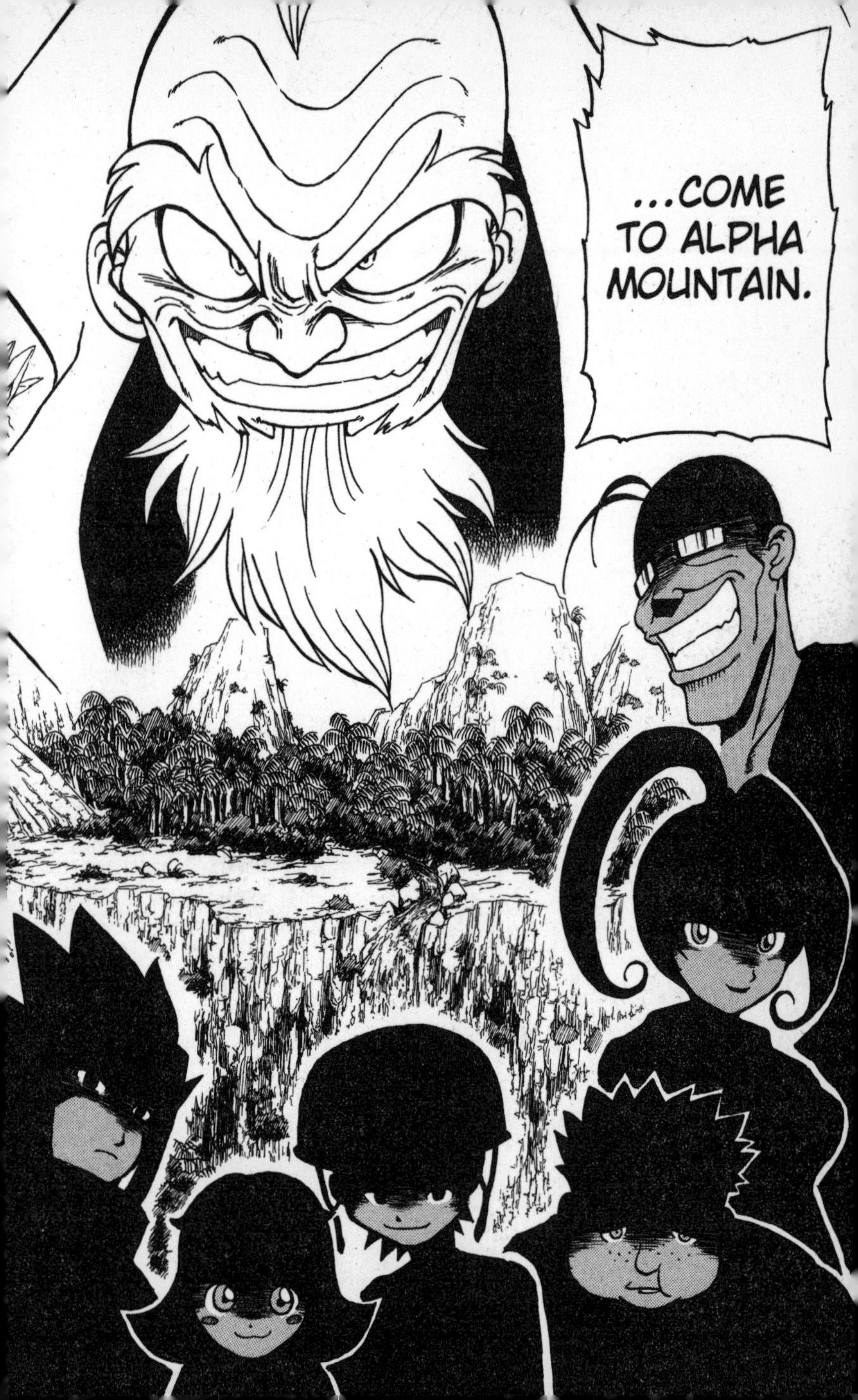
...COME TO ALPHA MOUNTAIN.

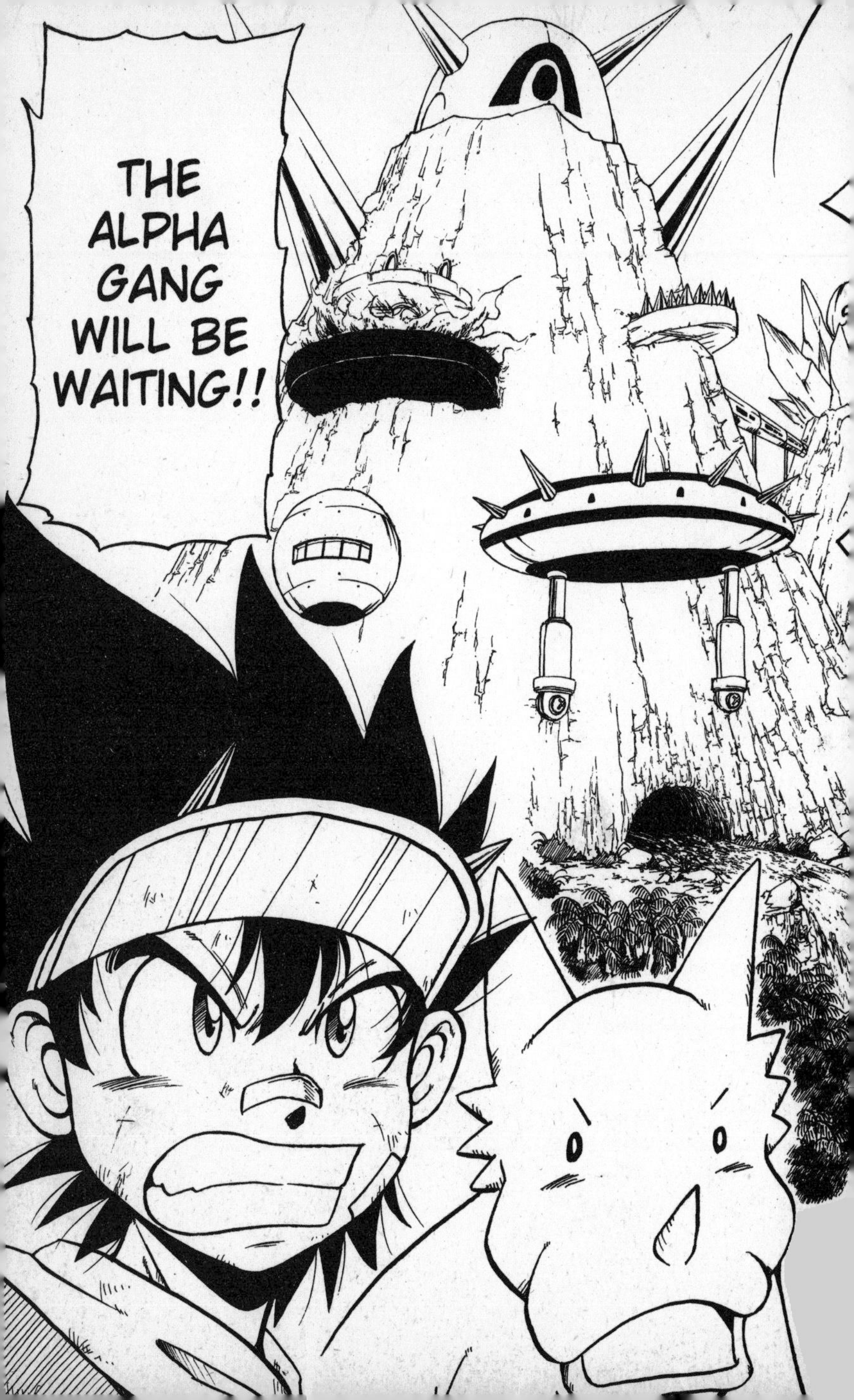
THE ALPHA GANG WILL BE WAITING!!

DIG IT!

Uncover facts about dinosaurs, their super moves and their trading card stats!

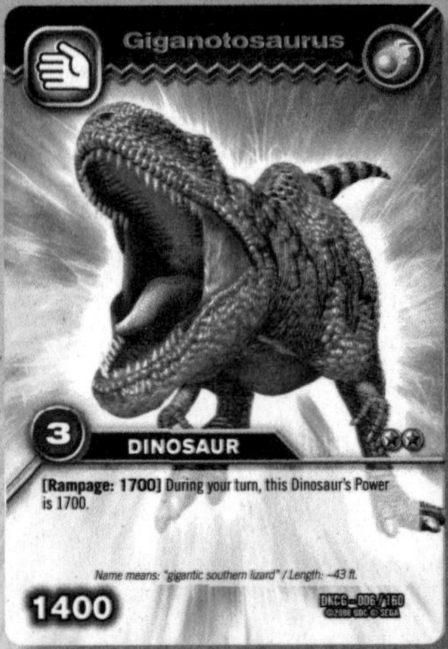

Giganotosaurus
3
DINOSAUR
[Rampage: 1700] During your turn, this Dinosaur's Power is 1700.
Name means: "gigantic southern lizard" / Length: ~43 ft.
1400
DKCG - 006 / 160
©2008 UDC © SEGA

GIGANOTOSAURUS

Giganotosaurus means "gigantic southern lizard"
Length: approx. 43 ft.
Lived in: Cretaceous Period
Discovered in: Argentina
Although it was a little bigger than the Tyrannosaurus, the Giganotosaurus had a smaller brain. But that doesn't mean it isn't a fierce fighter!
Card Rarity: Common
Giganotosaurus's **Rampage** ability makes it best on offense. Make sure you hold on to a powerful Move to defend against it!

ATOMIC BOMB

Card Rarity: Common
A deadly drop that spells doom for your opponents! Atomic Bomb is a regular Move, which means that any Dinosaur can use it. But if a level-three Dinosaur drops an Atomic Bomb, it gets powered up with +800 power instead of the usual +500. The extra power allows your level-three Dino to take out more powerful Dinosaurs.

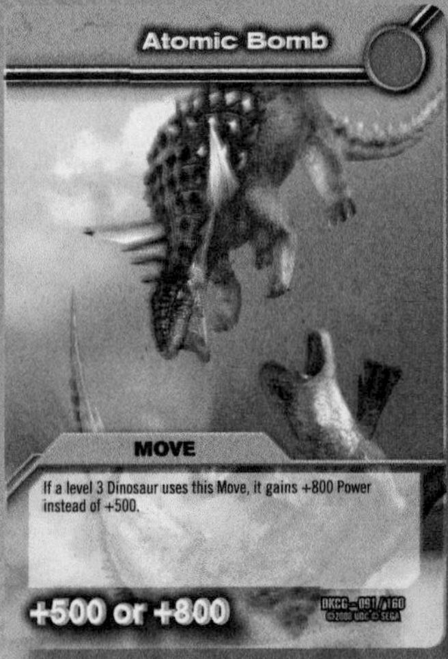

Atomic Bomb
MOVE
If a level 3 Dinosaur uses this Move, it gains +800 Power instead of +500.
+500 or +800
DKCG - 091 / 160
©2008 UDC © SEGA

CHAPTER 3
THE ULTIMATE DUO

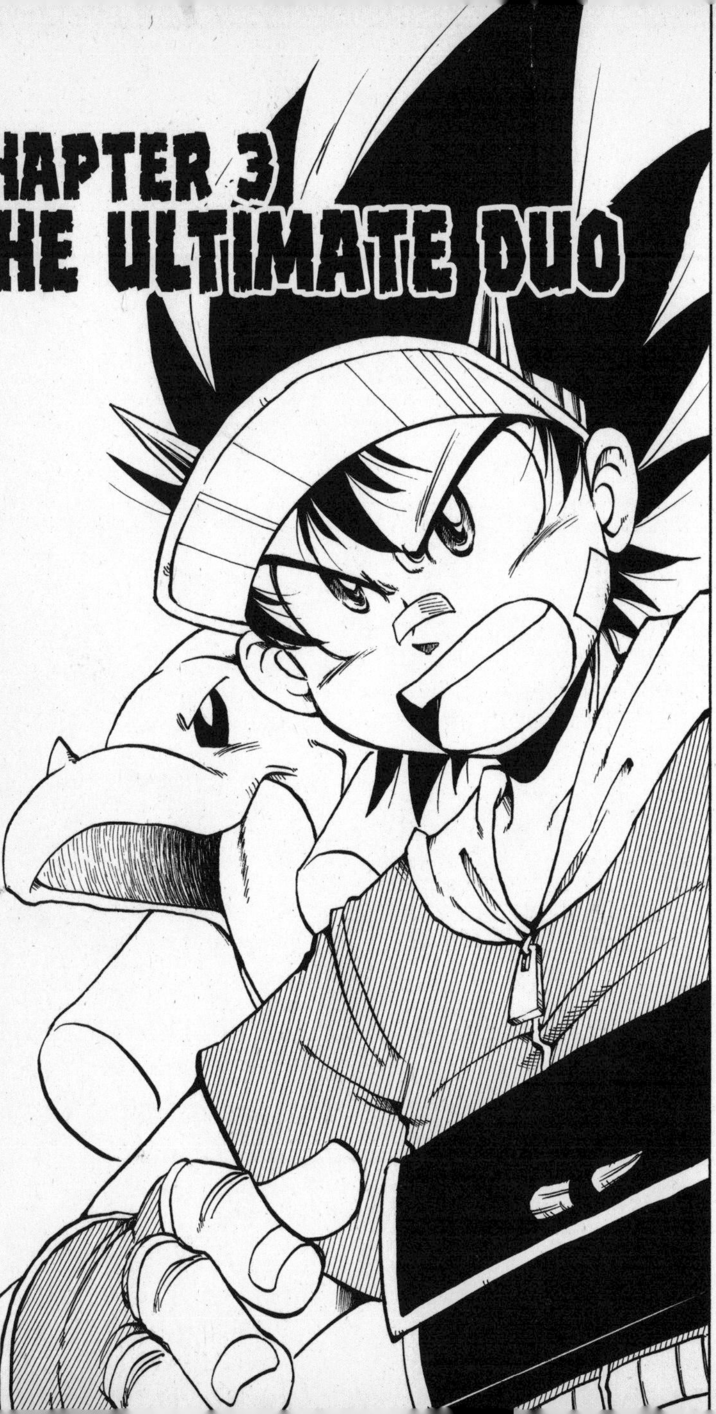

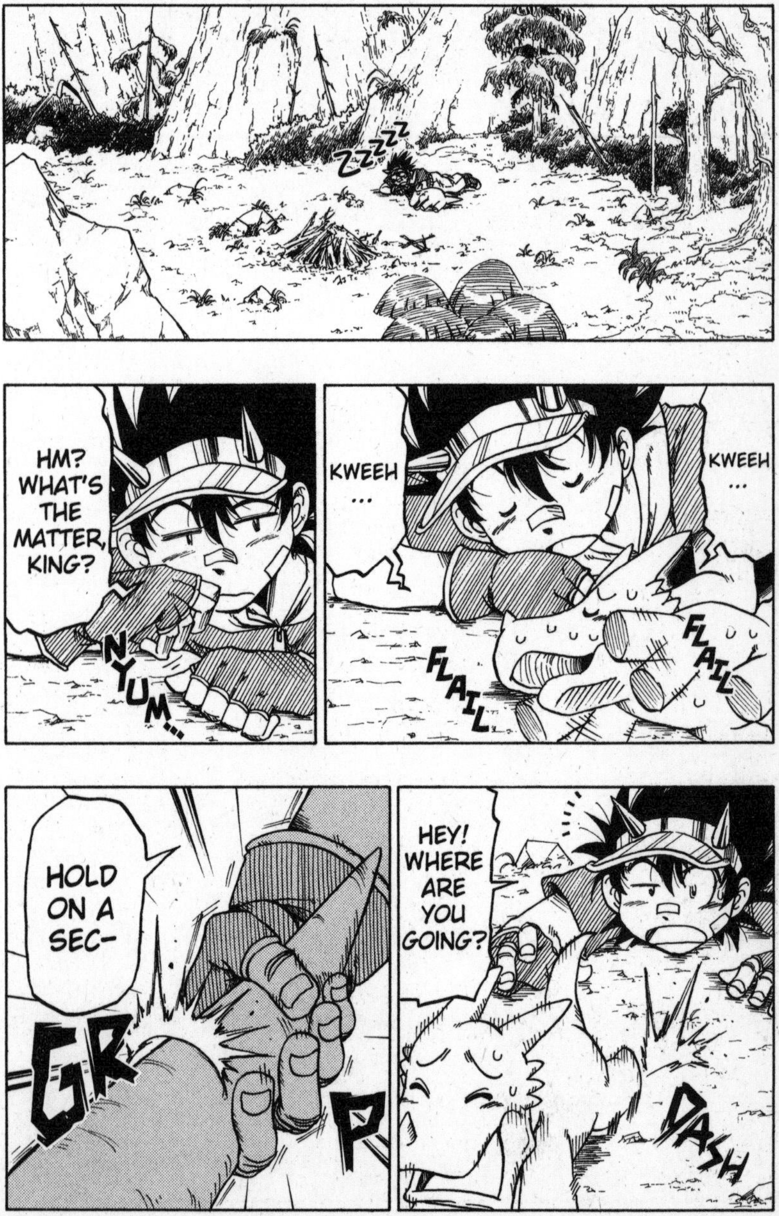
ZZZZZ
KWEEH ...
KWEEH ...
FLAIL
FLAIL
HM? WHAT'S THE MATTER, KING?
NYUM...
HEY! WHERE ARE YOU GOING?
DASH
HOLD ON A SEC-
GRP

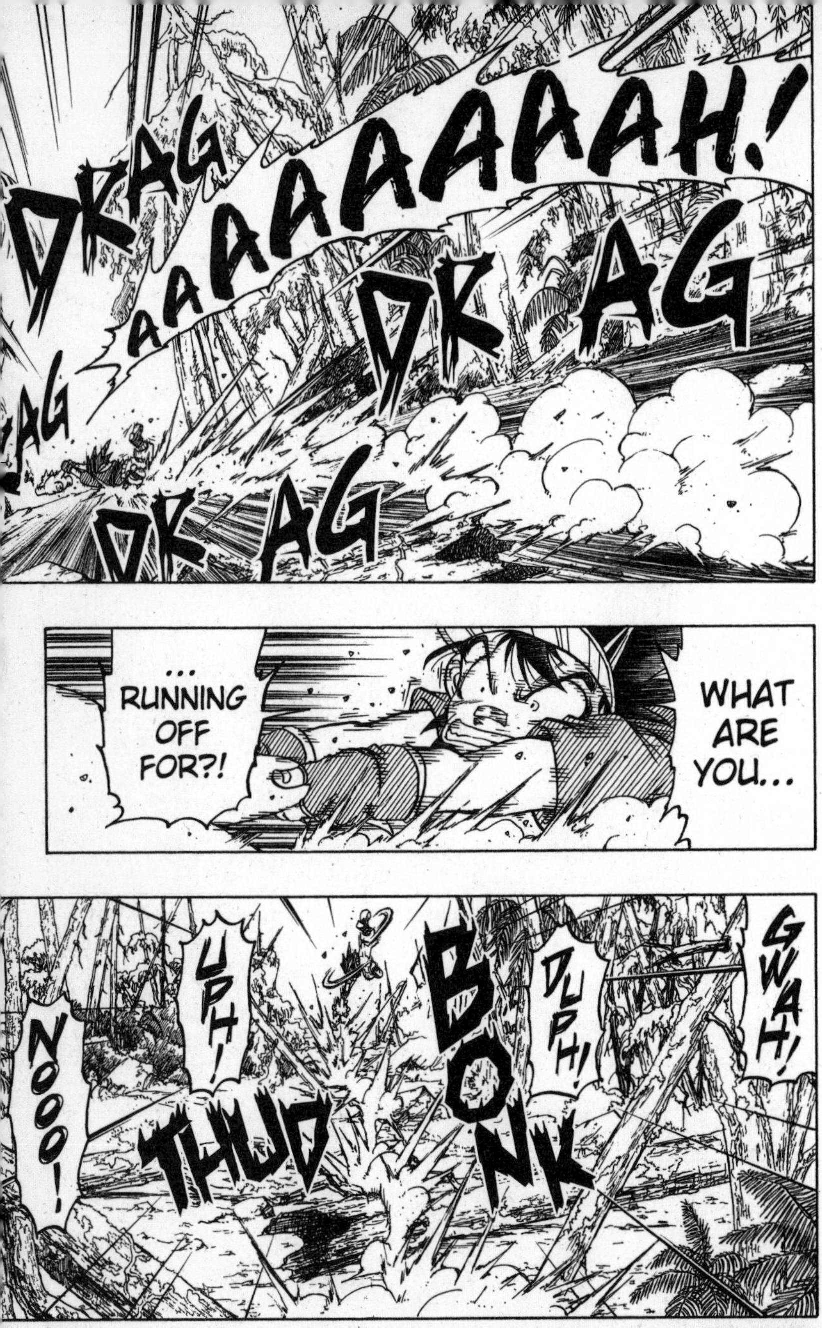
AAAAAAAH!
DRAG
DRAG
DRAG
AG
WHAT ARE YOU...
...RUNNING OFF FOR?!
GWAH!
DUPH!
BONK
UPH!
THUD
NOOOO!

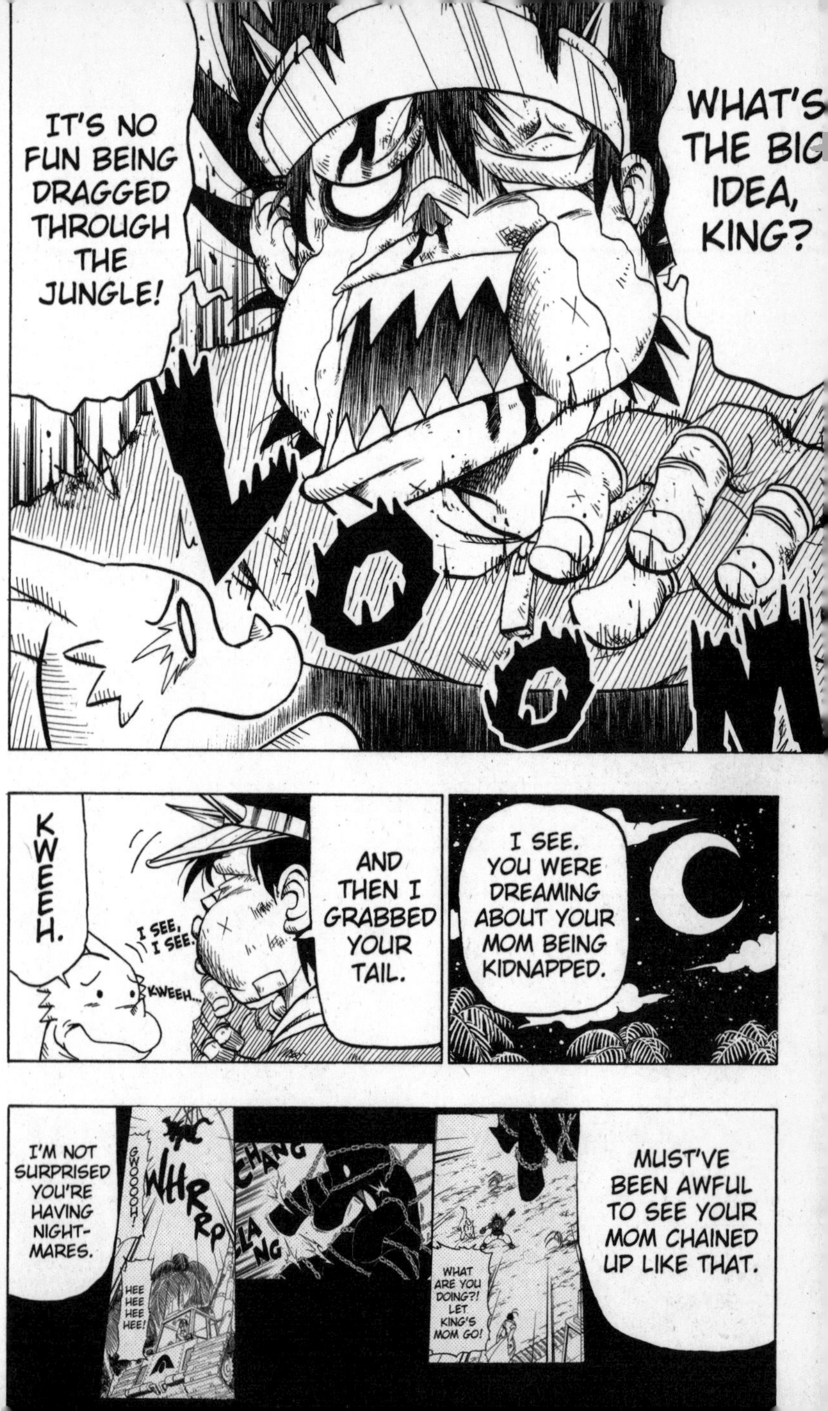
WHAT'S THE BIG IDEA, KING?
IT'S NO FUN BEING DRAGGED THROUGH THE JUNGLE!
VOOM
I SEE. YOU WERE DREAMING ABOUT YOUR MOM BEING KIDNAPPED.
AND THEN I GRABBED YOUR TAIL.
I SEE, I SEE.
KWEEH...
KWEEH.
MUST'VE BEEN AWFUL TO SEE YOUR MOM CHAINED UP LIKE THAT.
WHAT ARE YOU DOING?! LET KING'S MOM GO!
CHANG
CLANG
GWOOOOOH!
WHRRp
HEE HEE HEE HEE!
I'M NOT SURPRISED YOU'RE HAVING NIGHT-MARES.

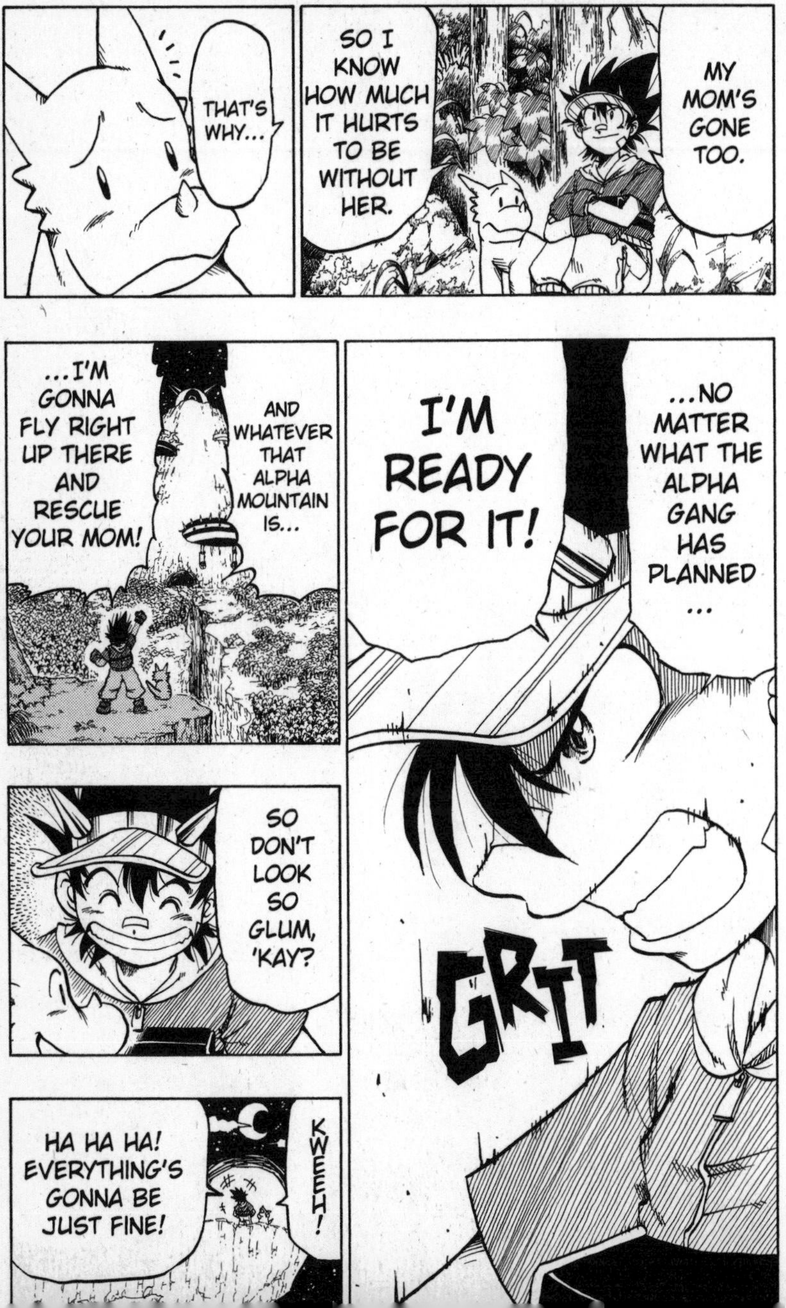
MY MOM'S GONE TOO.
SO I KNOW HOW MUCH IT HURTS TO BE WITHOUT HER.
THAT'S WHY...
...NO MATTER WHAT THE ALPHA GANG HAS PLANNED...
I'M READY FOR IT!
GRIT
AND WHATEVER THAT ALPHA MOUNTAIN IS...
...I'M GONNA FLY RIGHT UP THERE AND RESCUE YOUR MOM!
SO DON'T LOOK SO GLUM, 'KAY?
KWEEH!
HA HA HA! EVERYTHING'S GONNA BE JUST FINE!

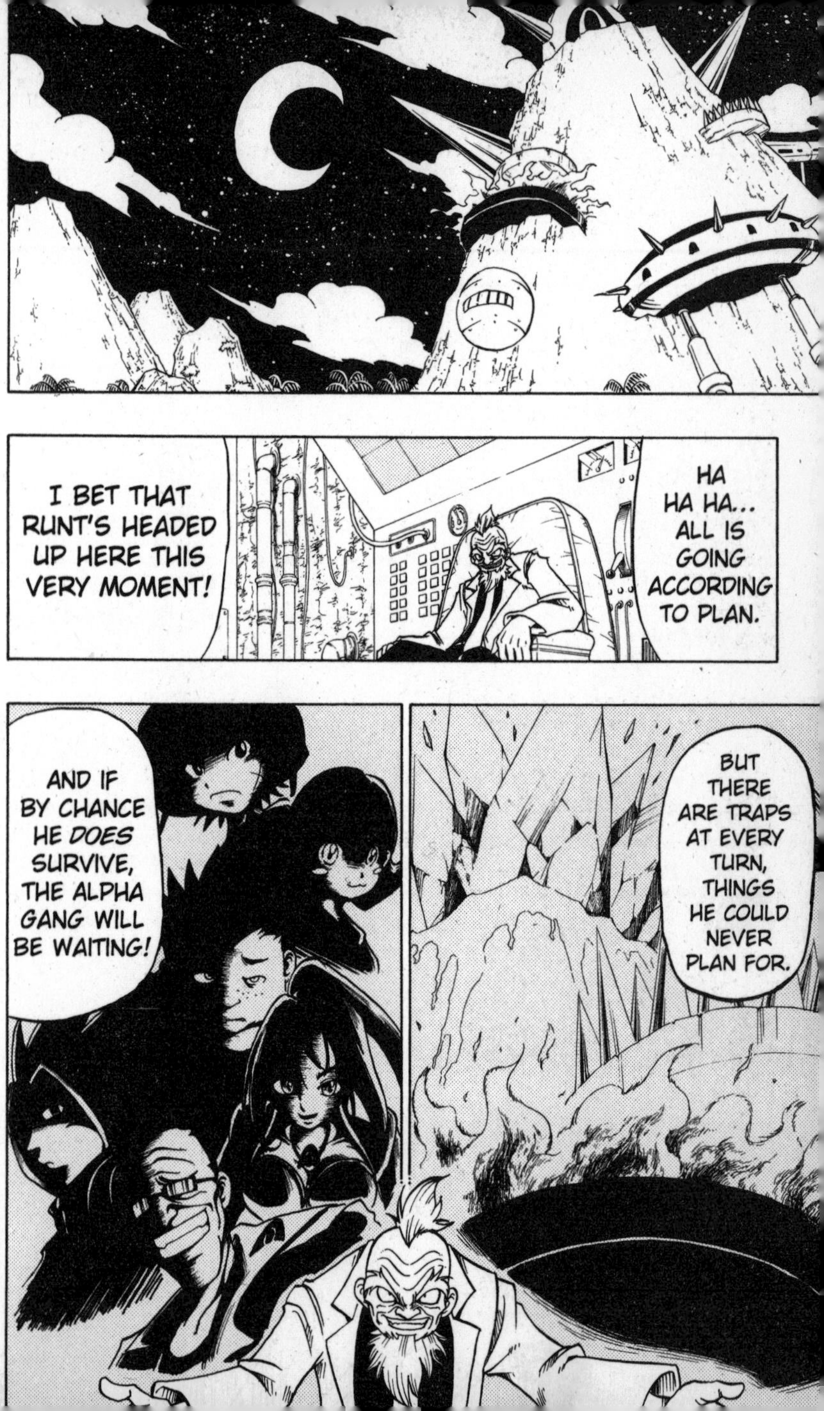
HA HA HA... ALL IS GOING ACCORDING TO PLAN.
I BET THAT RUNT'S HEADED UP HERE THIS VERY MOMENT!
BUT THERE ARE TRAPS AT EVERY TURN, THINGS HE COULD NEVER PLAN FOR.
AND IF BY CHANCE HE *DOES* SURVIVE, THE ALPHA GANG WILL BE WAITING!

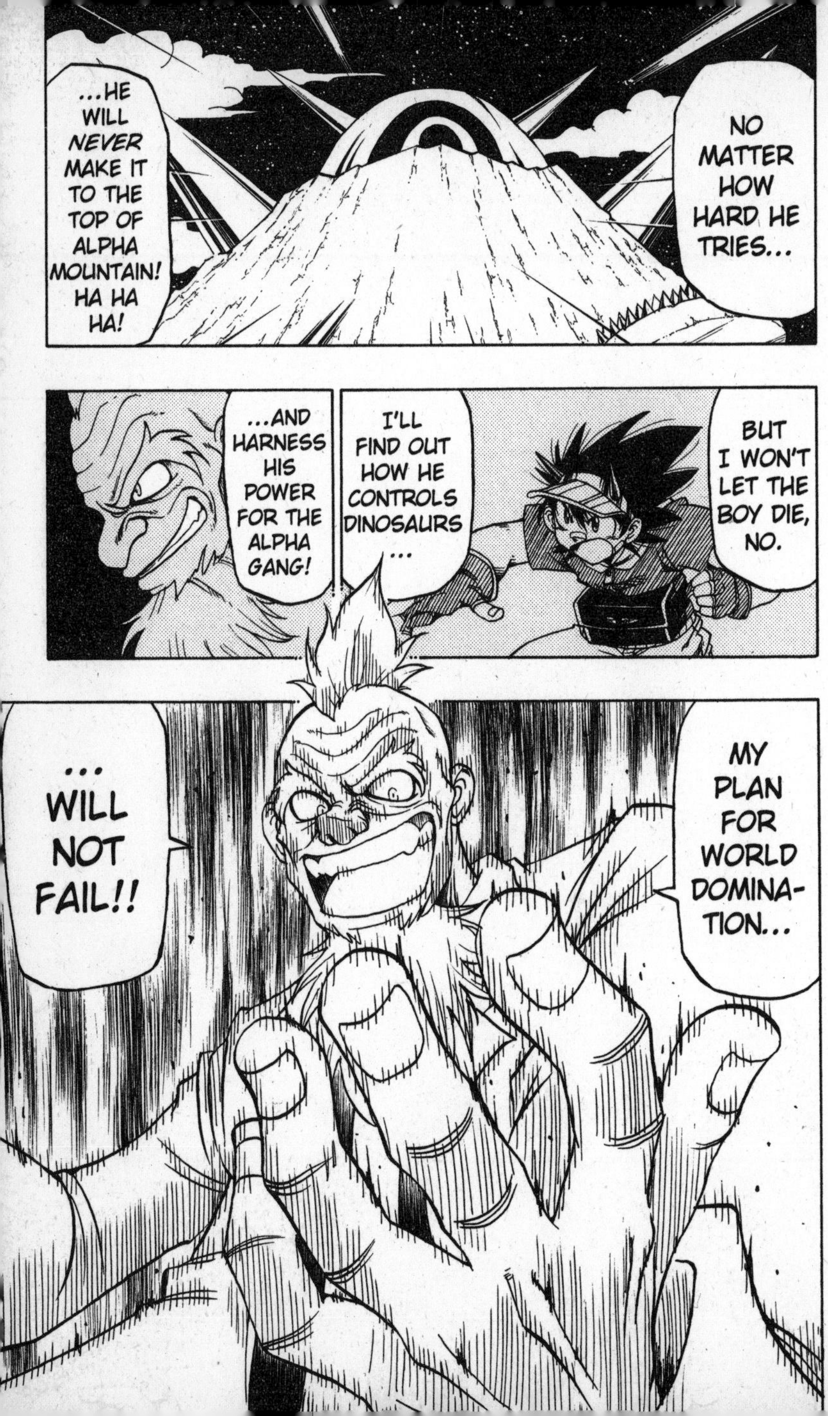
NO MATTER HOW HARD HE TRIES...
...HE WILL *NEVER* MAKE IT TO THE TOP OF ALPHA MOUNTAIN! HA HA HA!
BUT I WON'T LET THE BOY DIE, NO.
I'LL FIND OUT HOW HE CONTROLS DINOSAURS...
...AND HARNESS HIS POWER FOR THE ALPHA GANG!
MY PLAN FOR WORLD DOMINA-TION...
...WILL NOT FAIL!!

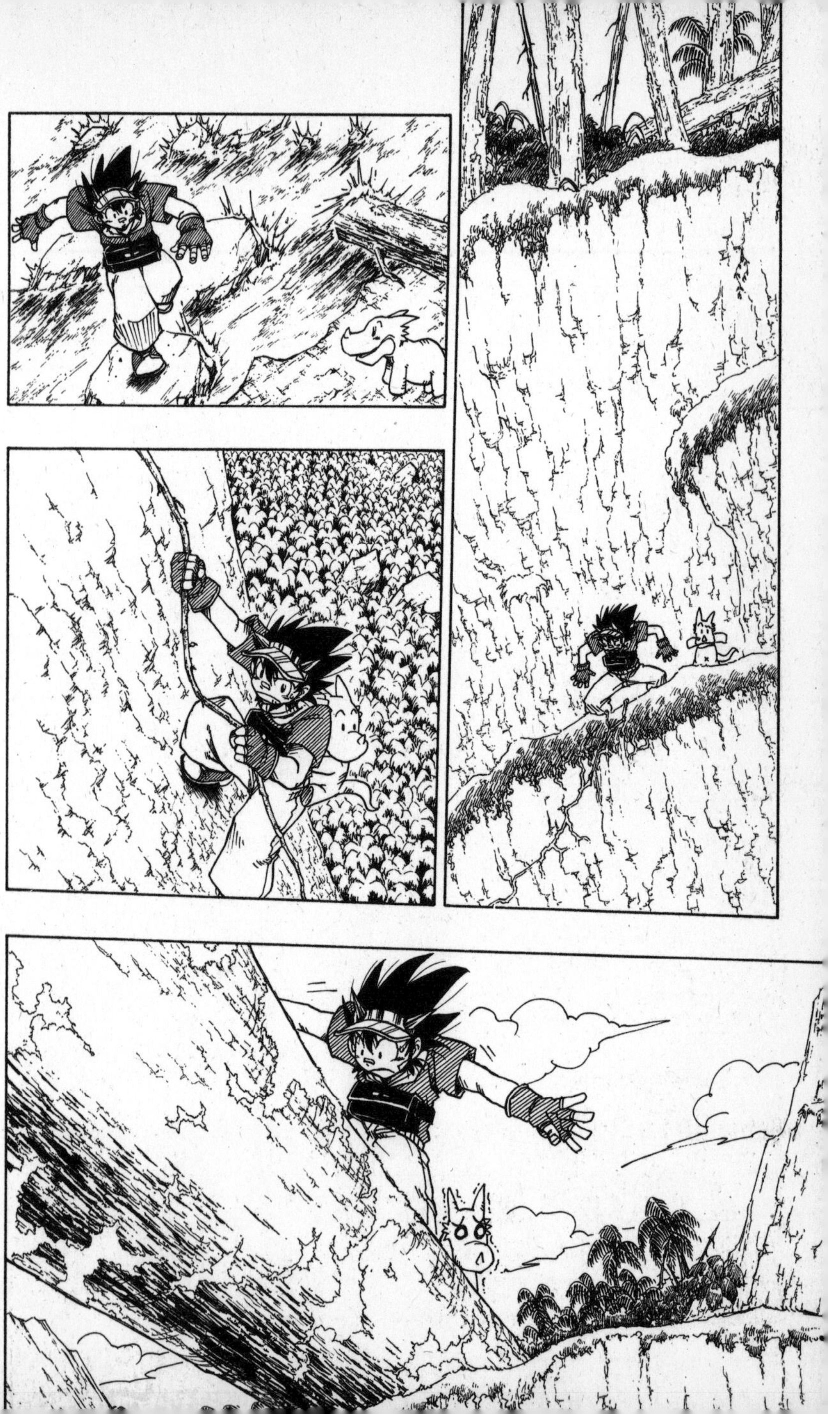

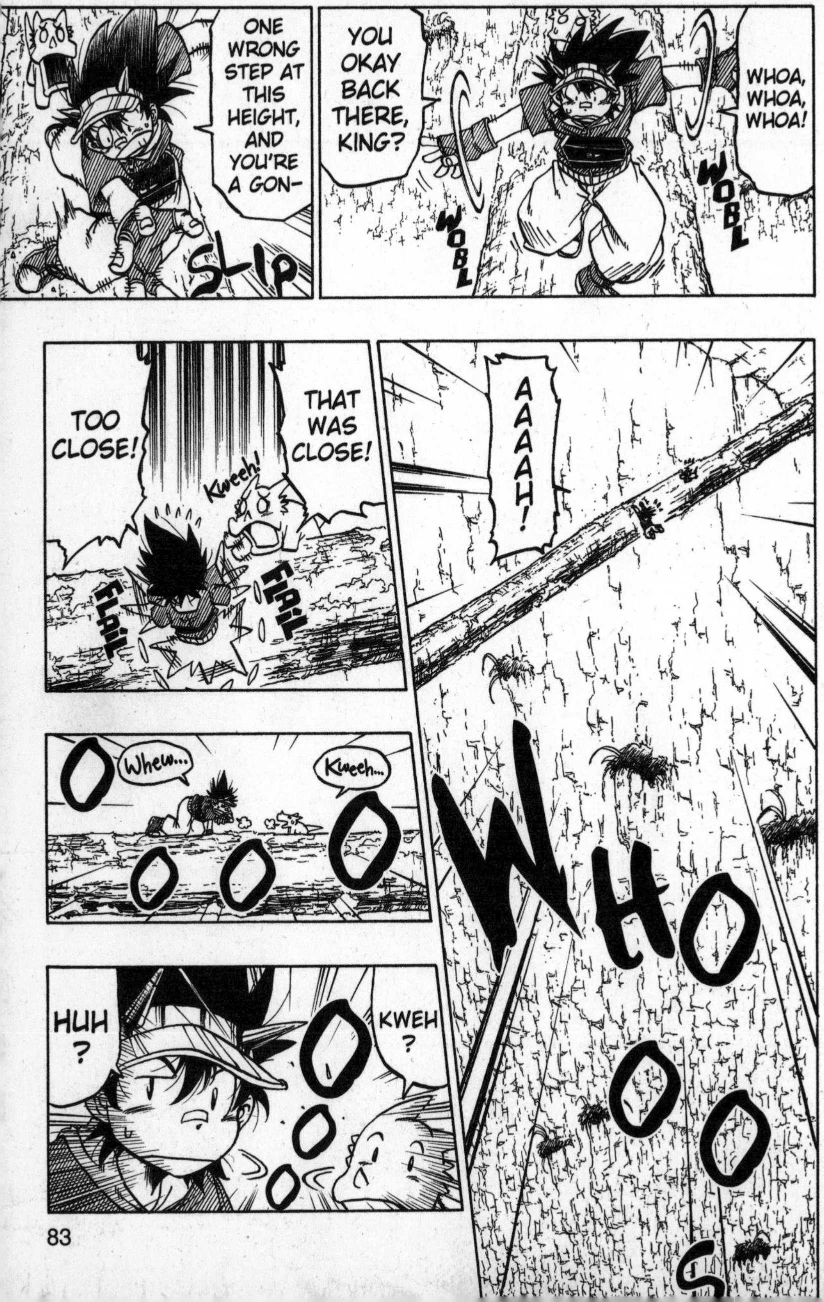
WHOA, WHOA, WHOA!
WOBL
WOBL
YOU OKAY BACK THERE, KING?
ONE WRONG STEP AT THIS HEIGHT, AND YOU'RE A GON-
SLIP
AAAAAH!
WHOOOOOS
THAT WAS CLOSE!
TOO CLOSE!
Kweeh!
FLAIL
FLAIL
Kweeh...
Whew...
OOOO
KWEH?
HUH?
OOOO

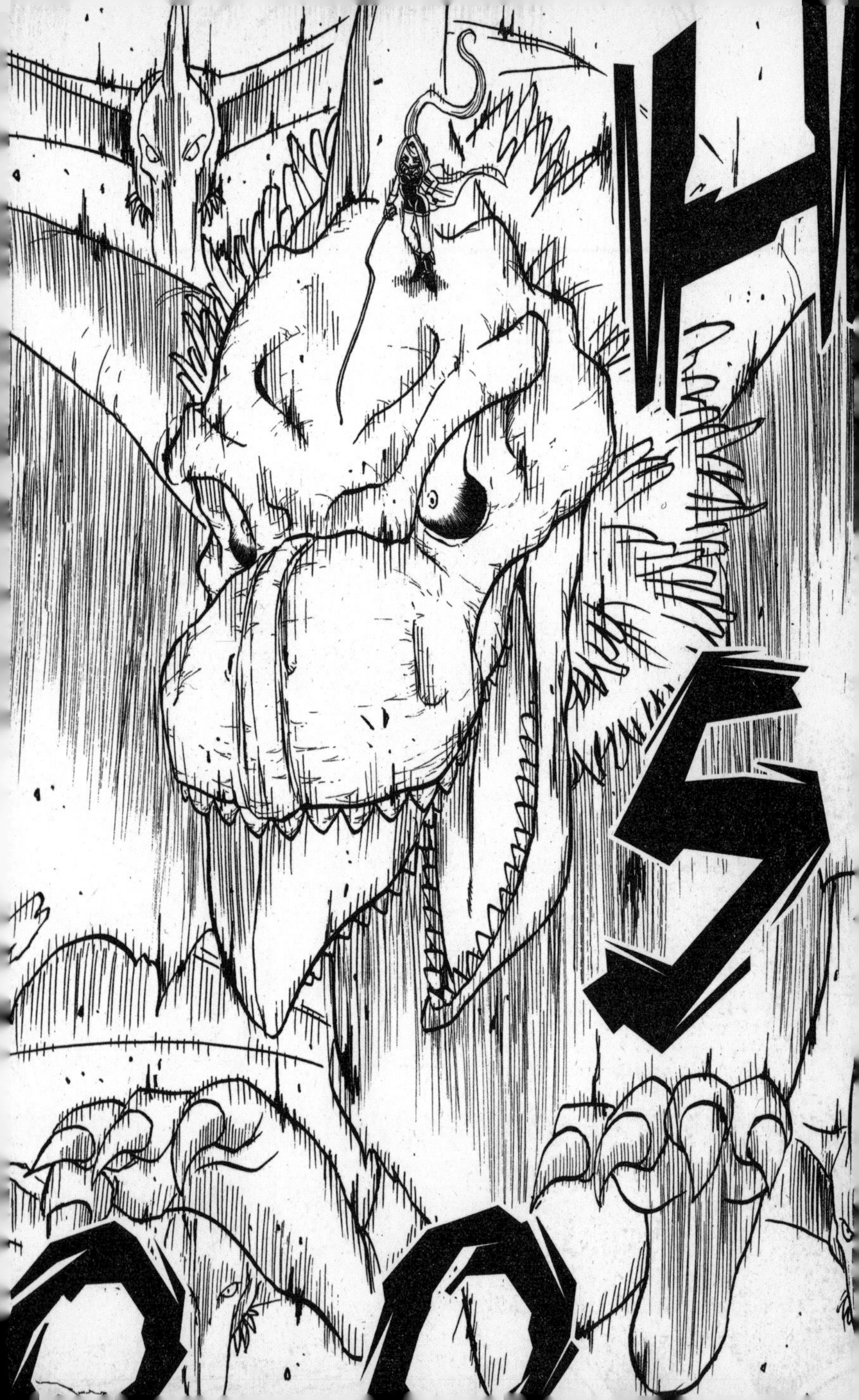

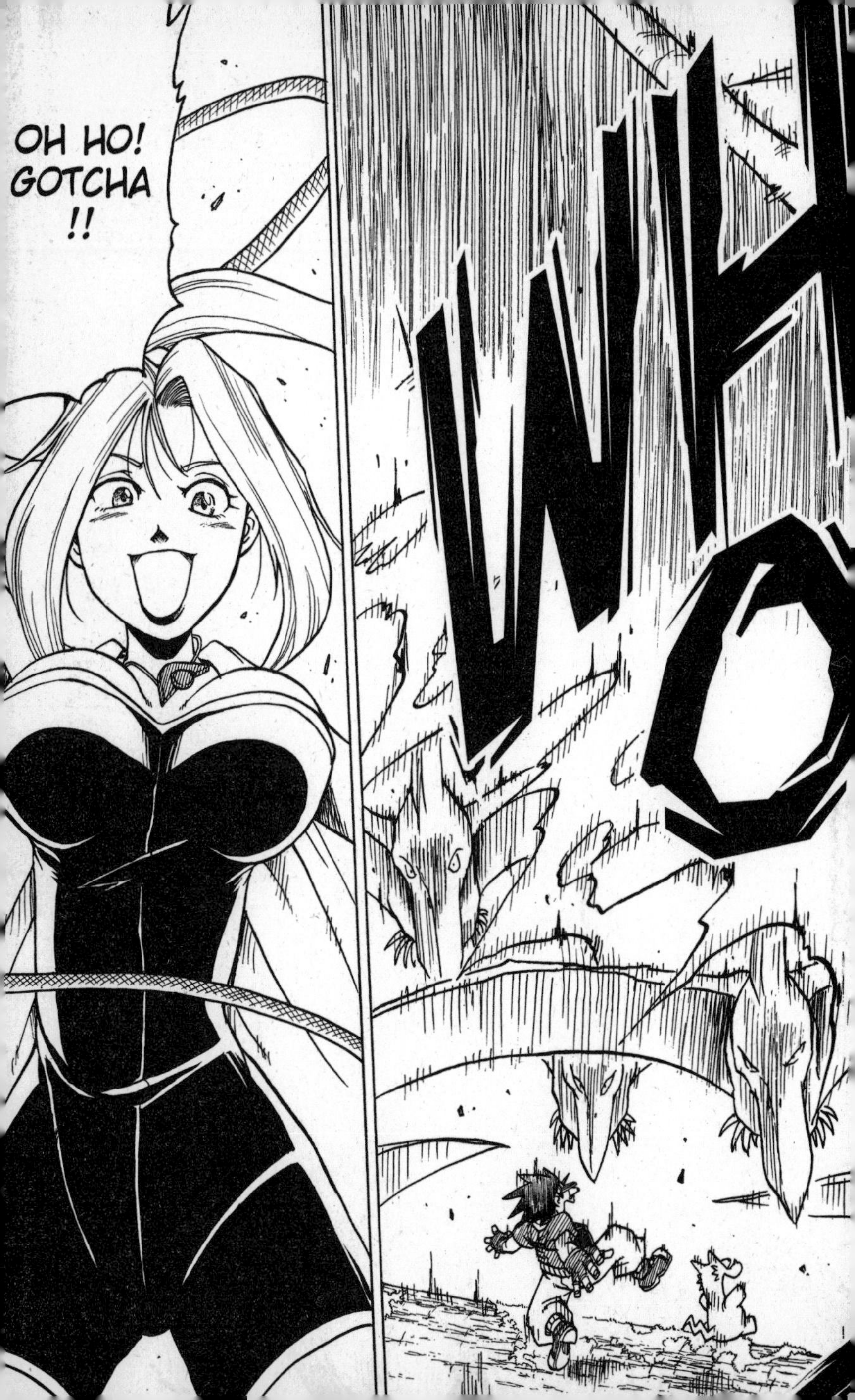
OH HO! GOTCHA !!

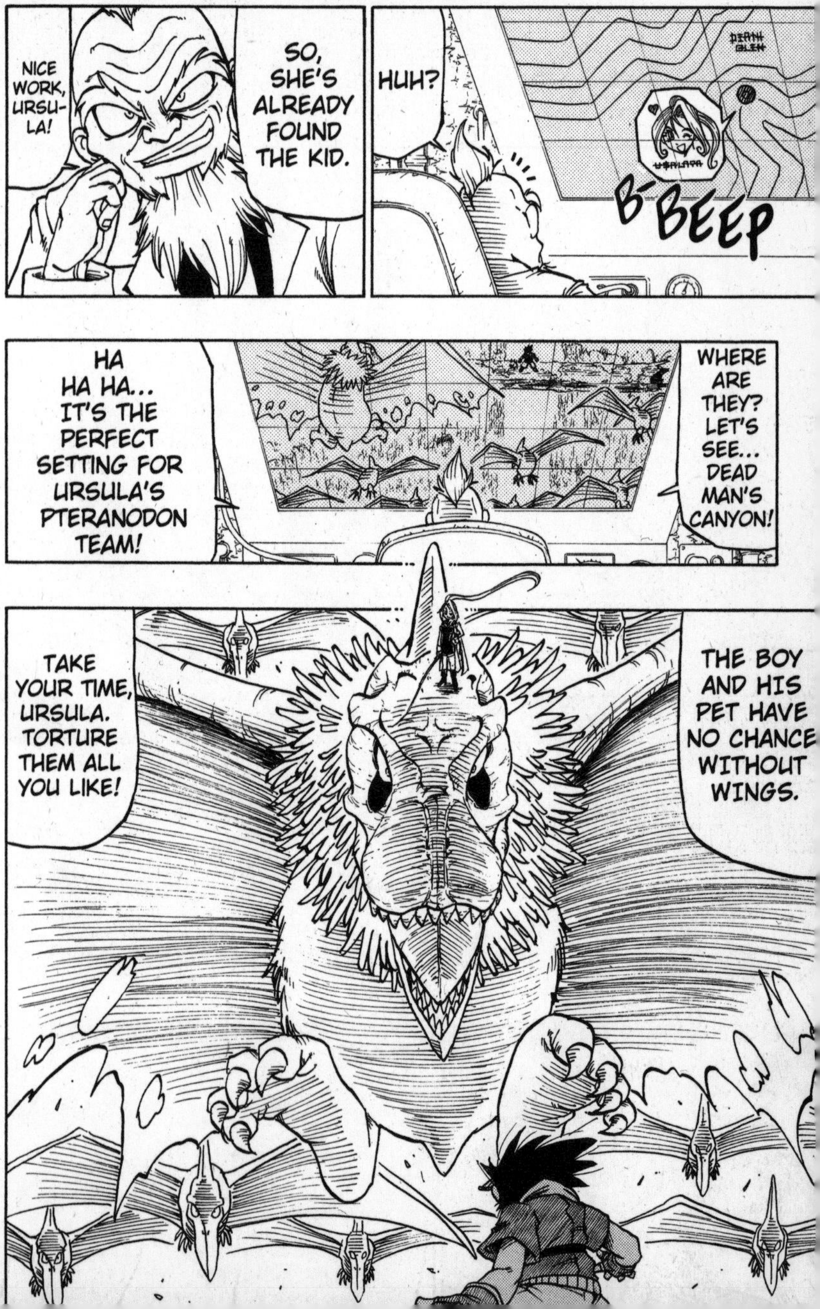
HUH?
B-BEEP
SO, SHE'S ALREADY FOUND THE KID.
NICE WORK, URSU-LA!
WHERE ARE THEY? LET'S SEE... DEAD MAN'S CANYON!
HA HA HA... IT'S THE PERFECT SETTING FOR URSULA'S PTERANODON TEAM!
THE BOY AND HIS PET HAVE NO CHANCE WITHOUT WINGS.
TAKE YOUR TIME, URSULA. TORTURE THEM ALL YOU LIKE!

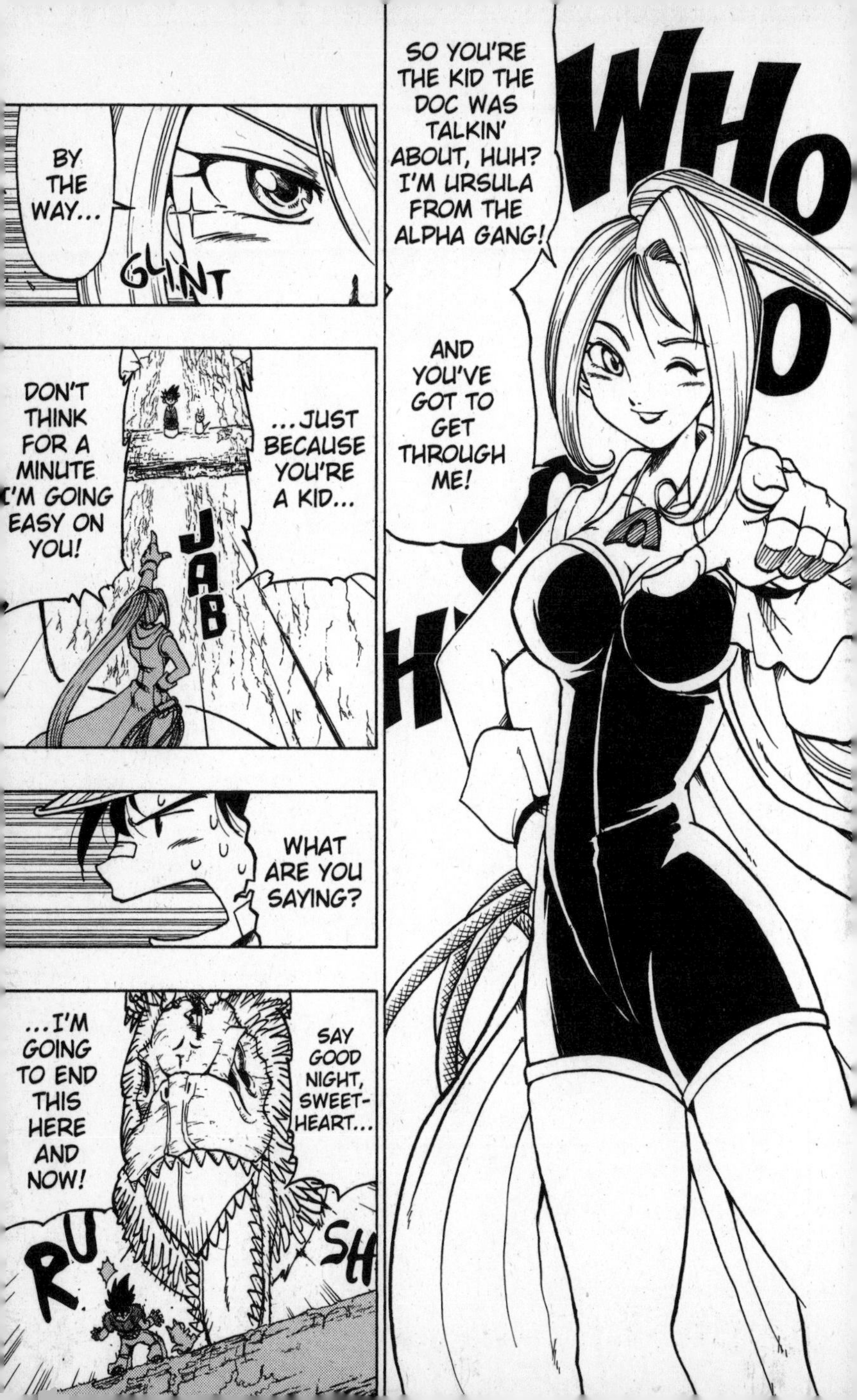
WHO
SO YOU'RE THE KID THE DOC WAS TALKIN' ABOUT, HUH? I'M URSULA FROM THE ALPHA GANG!
AND YOU'VE GOT TO GET THROUGH ME!
BY THE WAY...
GLINT
...JUST BECAUSE YOU'RE A KID...
DON'T THINK FOR A MINUTE I'M GOING EASY ON YOU!
JAB
WHAT ARE YOU SAYING?
SAY GOOD NIGHT, SWEET-HEART...
...I'M GOING TO END THIS HERE AND NOW!
SH
RU

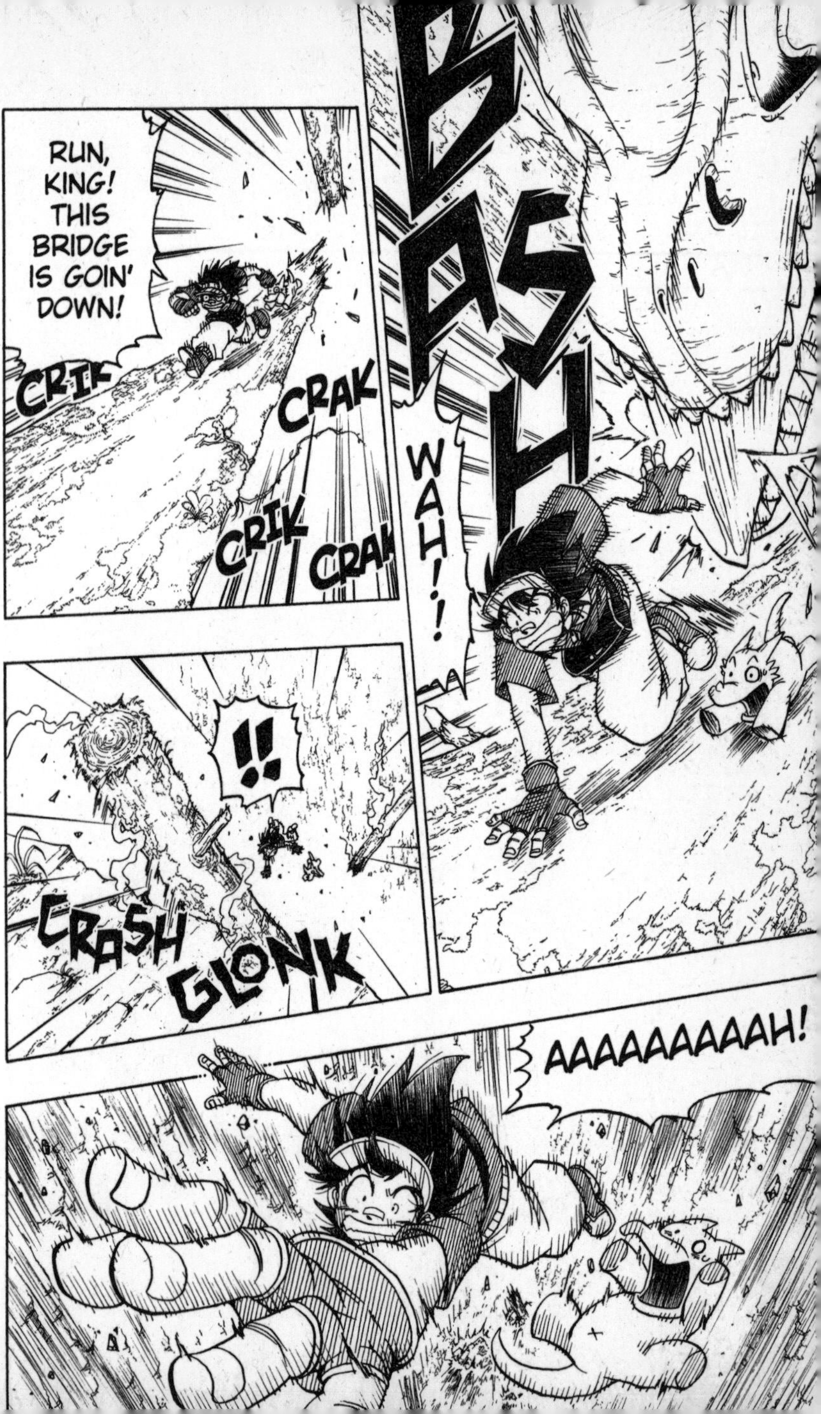
BASH
WAH!!
RUN, KING! THIS BRIDGE IS GOIN' DOWN!
CRIK
CRAK
CRIK
CRAK
!!
CRASH
GLONK
AAAAAAAAAH!

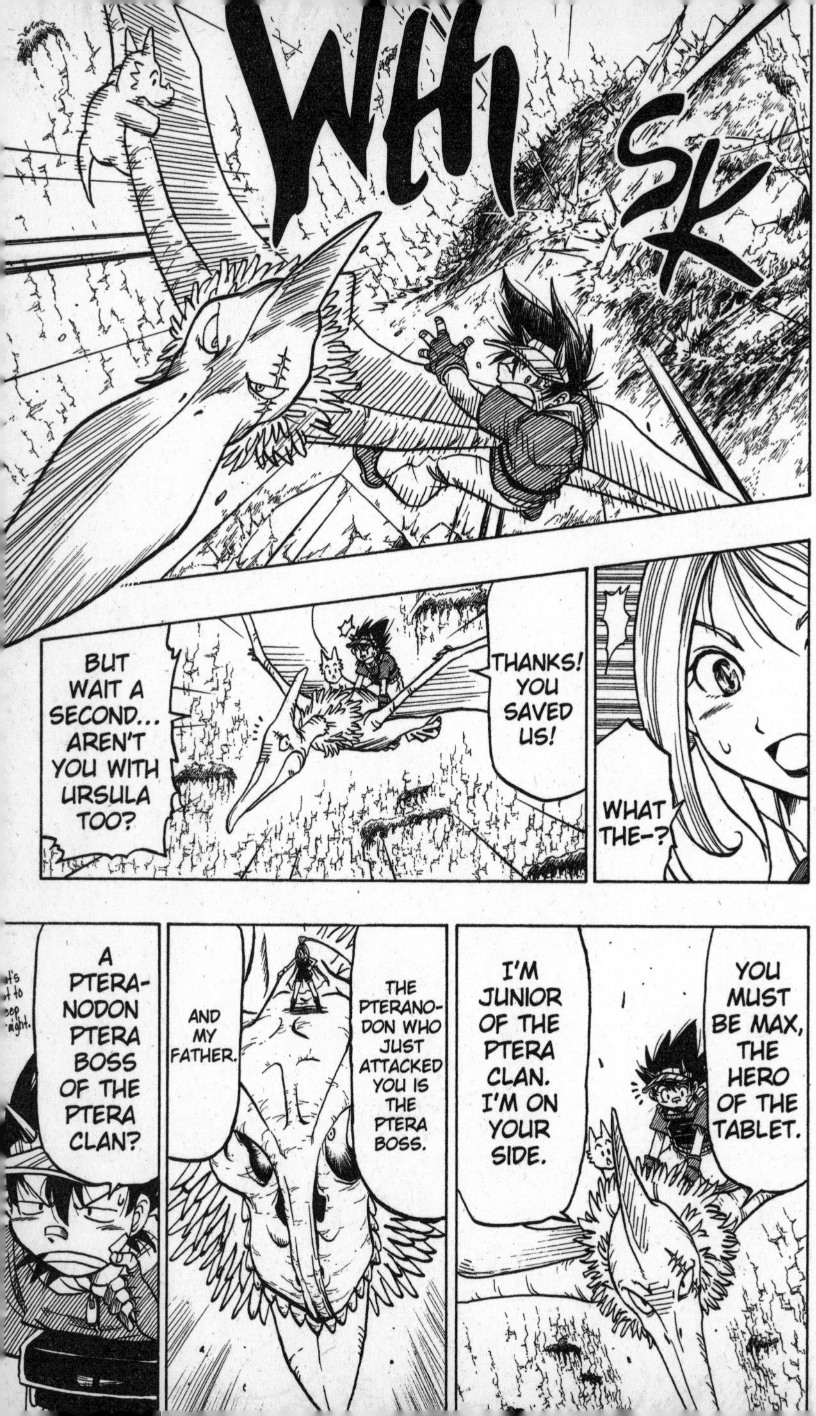
WHISK
WHAT THE-?
THANKS! YOU SAVED US!
BUT WAIT A SECOND... AREN'T YOU WITH URSULA TOO?
YOU MUST BE MAX, THE HERO OF THE TABLET.
I'M JUNIOR OF THE PTERA CLAN. I'M ON YOUR SIDE.
THE PTERANODON WHO JUST ATTACKED YOU IS THE PTERA BOSS.
AND MY FATHER.
A PTERANODON PTERA BOSS OF THE PTERA CLAN?

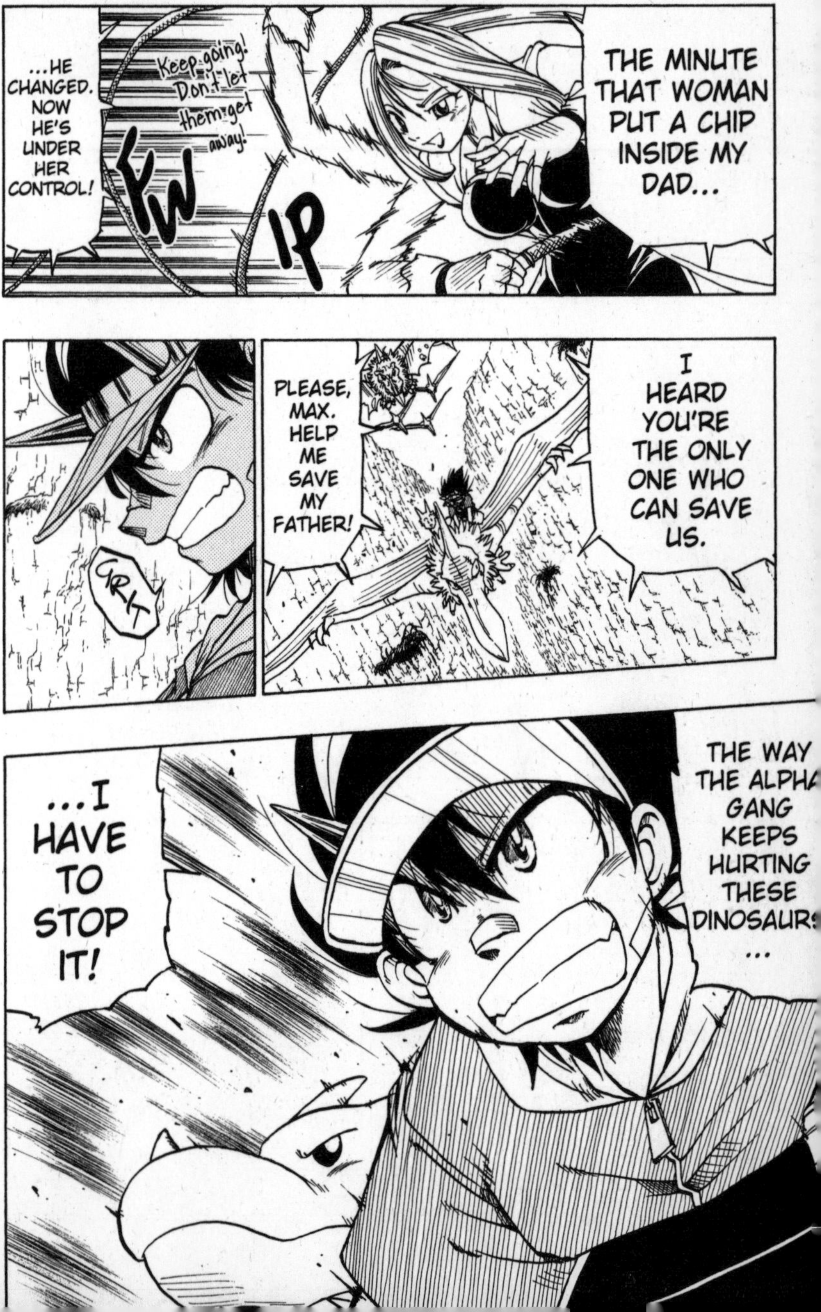
THE MINUTE THAT WOMAN PUT A CHIP INSIDE MY DAD...
Keep going! Don't let them get away!
...HE CHANGED. NOW HE'S UNDER HER CONTROL!
I HEARD YOU'RE THE ONLY ONE WHO CAN SAVE US.
PLEASE, MAX. HELP ME SAVE MY FATHER!
GRIT
THE WAY THE ALPH GANG KEEPS HURTING THESE DINOSAUR ...
...I HAVE TO STOP IT!

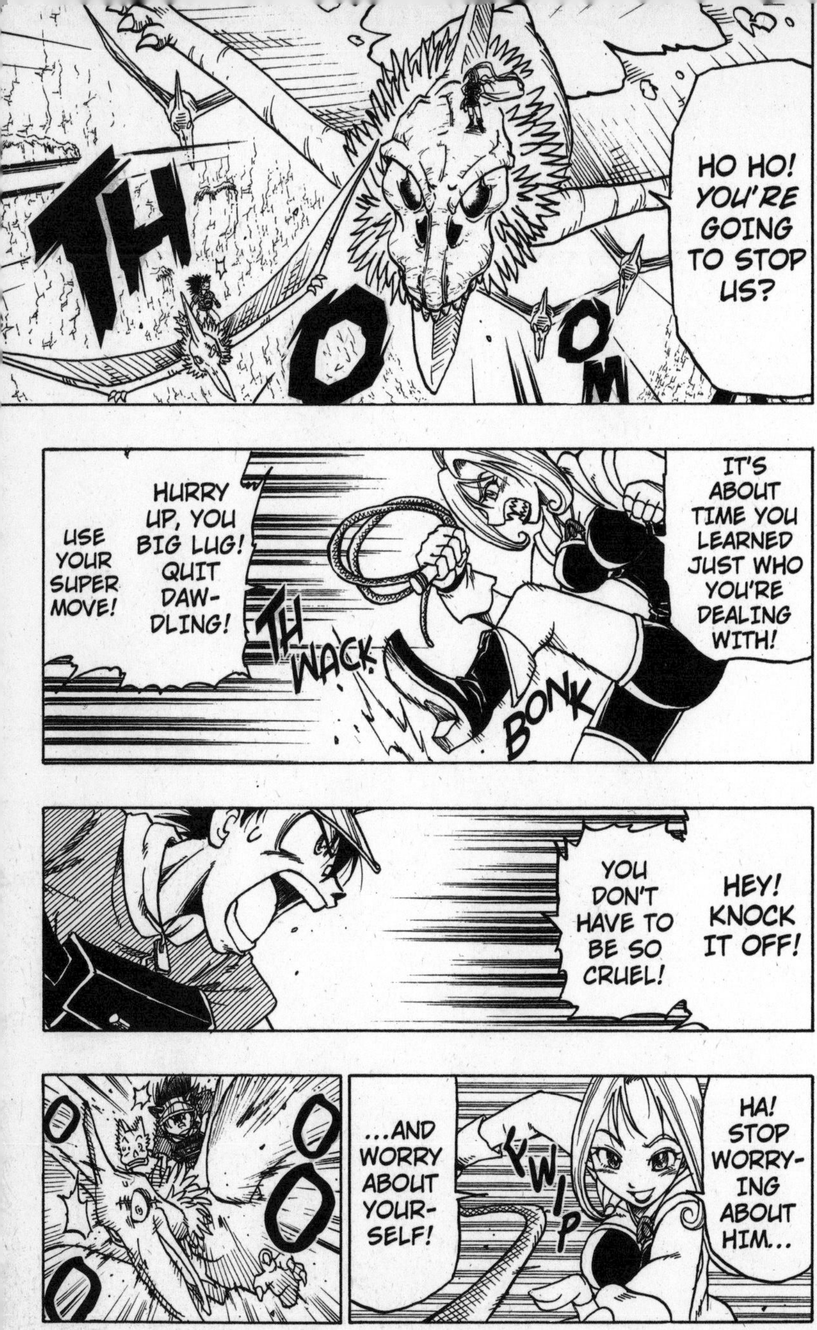
HO HO! YOU'RE GOING TO STOP US?
THOOM
IT'S ABOUT TIME YOU LEARNED JUST WHO YOU'RE DEALING WITH!
HURRY UP, YOU BIG LUG! QUIT DAWDLING!
USE YOUR SUPER MOVE!
THWACK
BONK
HEY! KNOCK IT OFF!
YOU DON'T HAVE TO BE SO CRUEL!
HA! STOP WORRYING ABOUT HIM...
...AND WORRY ABOUT YOURSELF!
FWIP

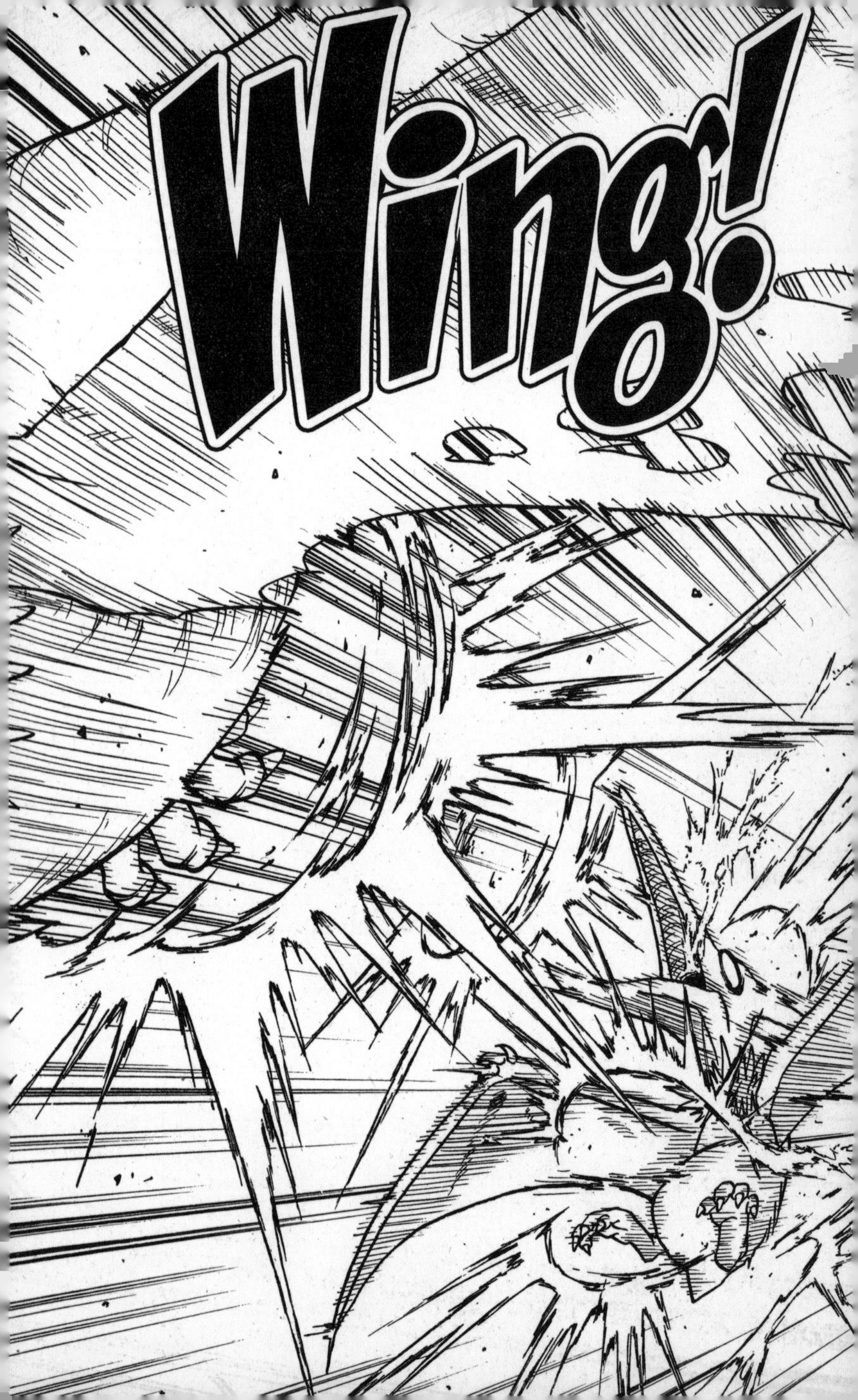
Wing!

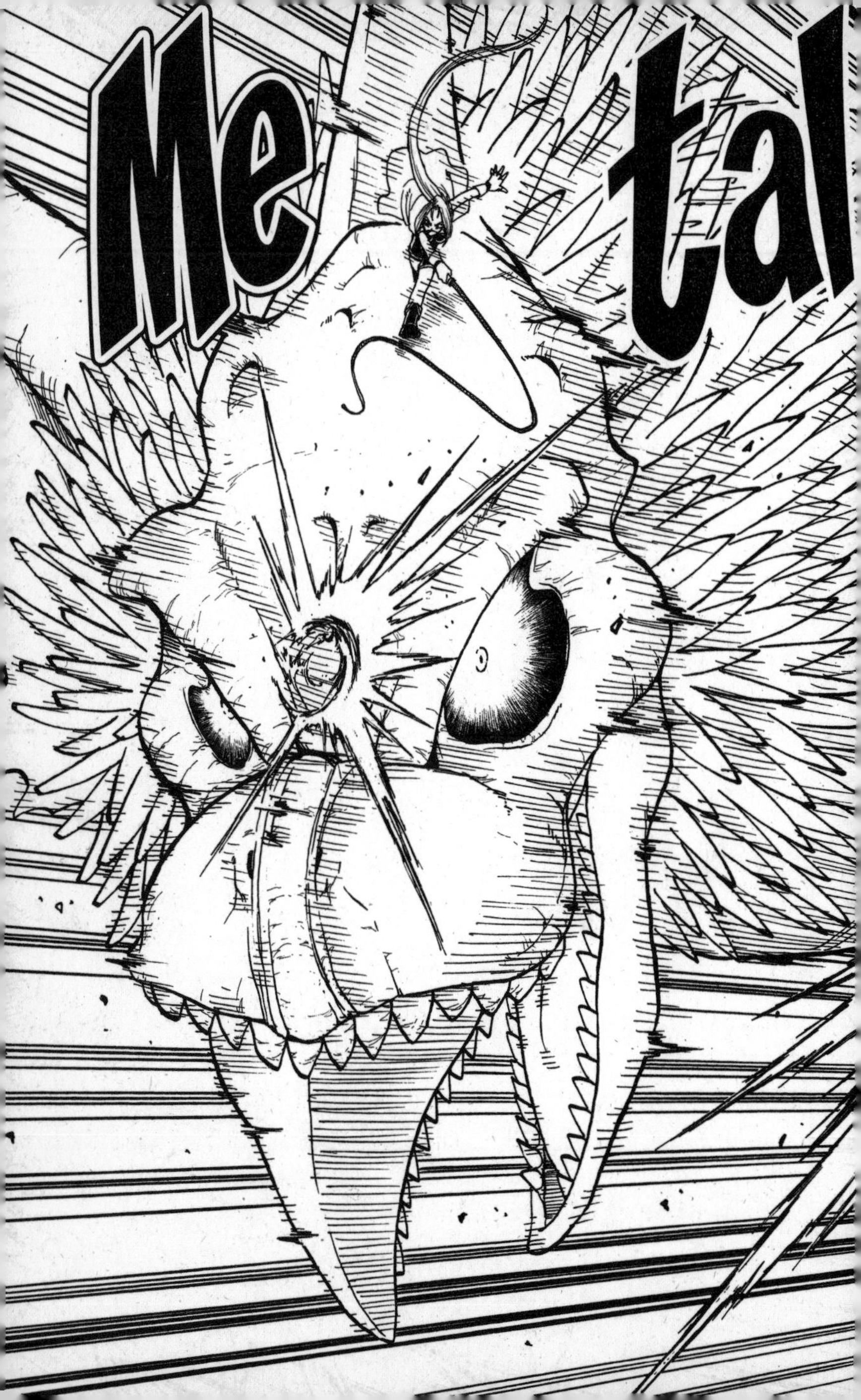
Me
tal

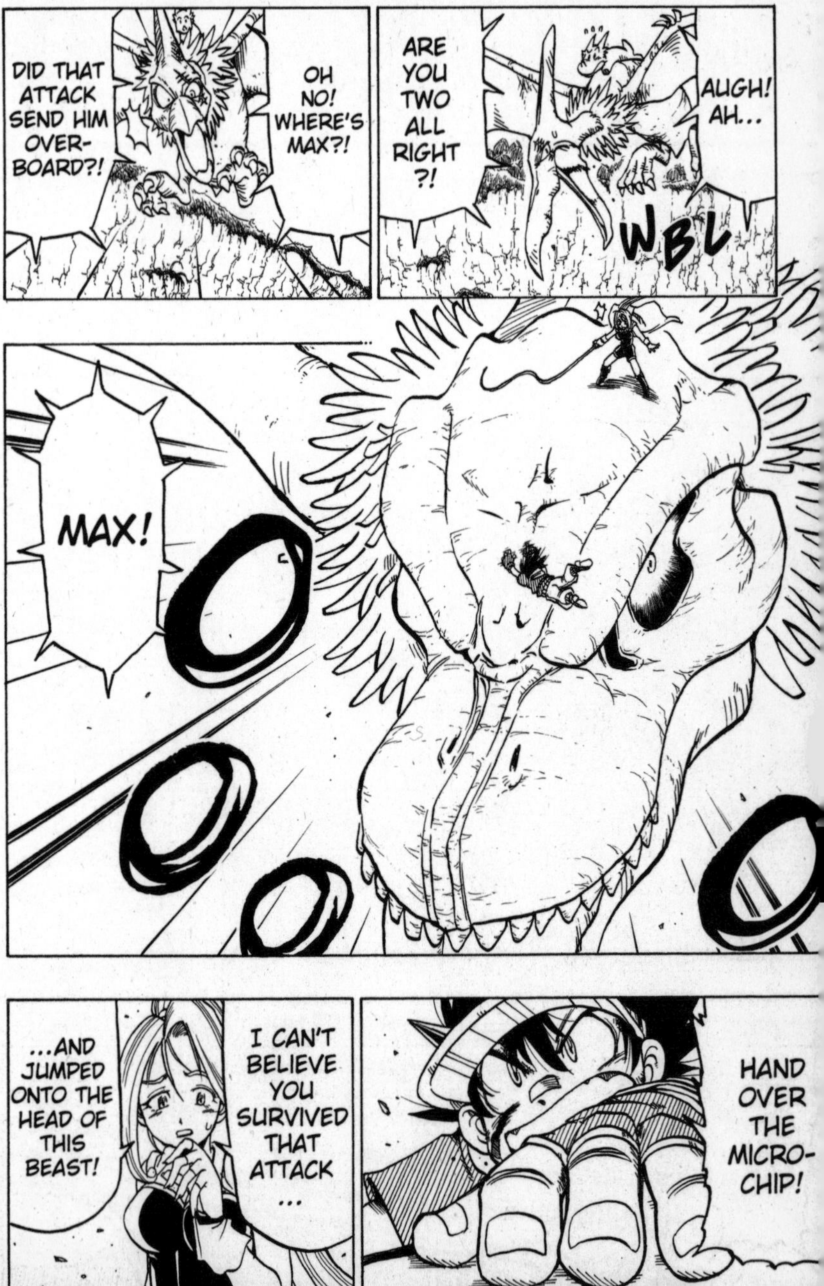
AUGH! AH...
ARE YOU TWO ALL RIGHT?!
WBL
OH NO! WHERE'S MAX?!
DID THAT ATTACK SEND HIM OVER-BOARD?!
MAX!
HAND OVER THE MICRO-CHIP!
I CAN'T BELIEVE YOU SURVIVED THAT ATTACK...
...AND JUMPED ONTO THE HEAD OF THIS BEAST!

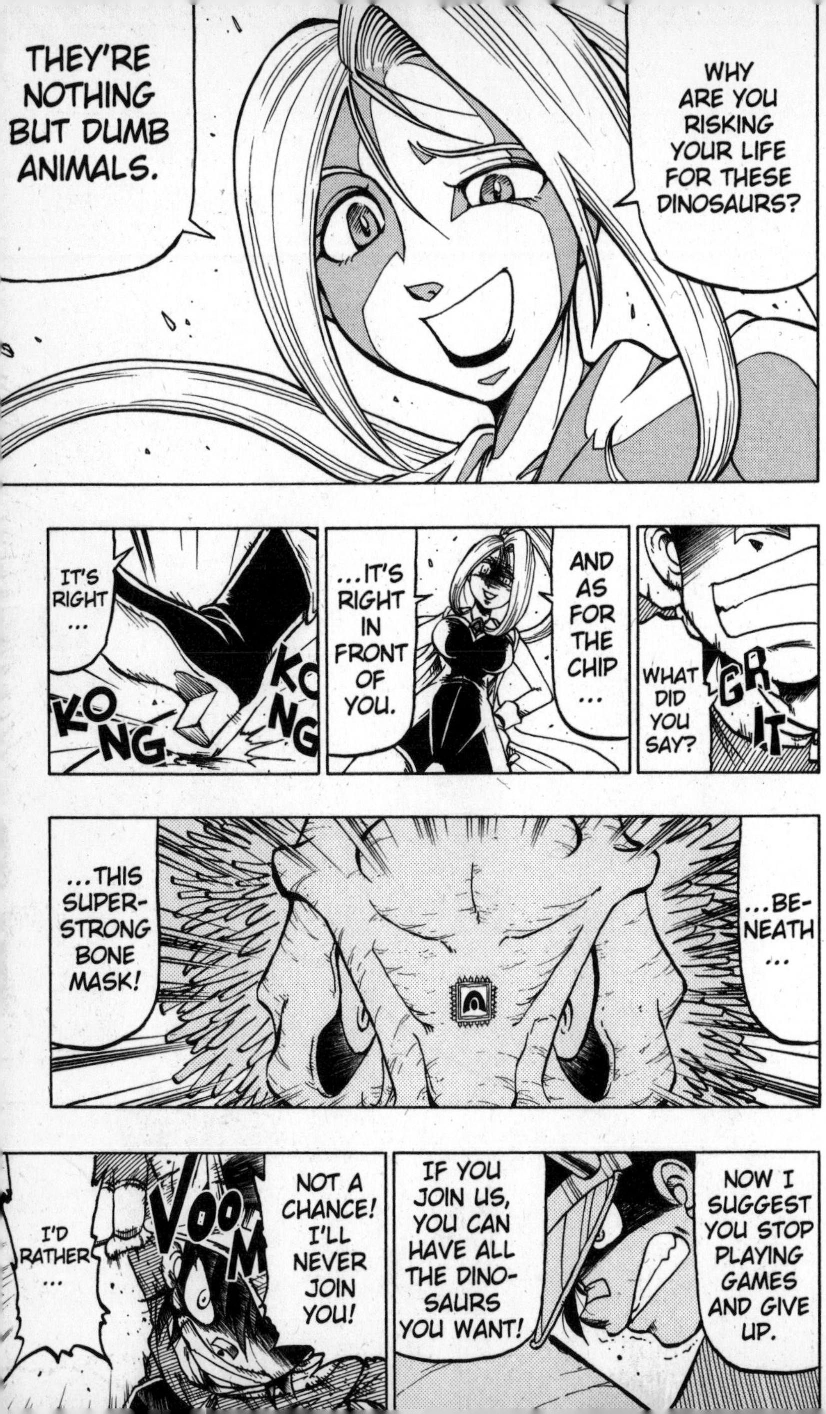
WHY ARE YOU RISKING YOUR LIFE FOR THESE DINOSAURS?
THEY'RE NOTHING BUT DUMB ANIMALS.
WHAT DID YOU SAY?
GRIT
AND AS FOR THE CHIP...
...IT'S RIGHT IN FRONT OF YOU.
IT'S RIGHT...
KONG
KONG
...BENEATH...
...THIS SUPER-STRONG BONE MASK!
NOW I SUGGEST YOU STOP PLAYING GAMES AND GIVE UP.
IF YOU JOIN US, YOU CAN HAVE ALL THE DINOSAURS YOU WANT!
NOT A CHANCE! I'LL NEVER JOIN YOU!
VOOM
I'D RATHER...

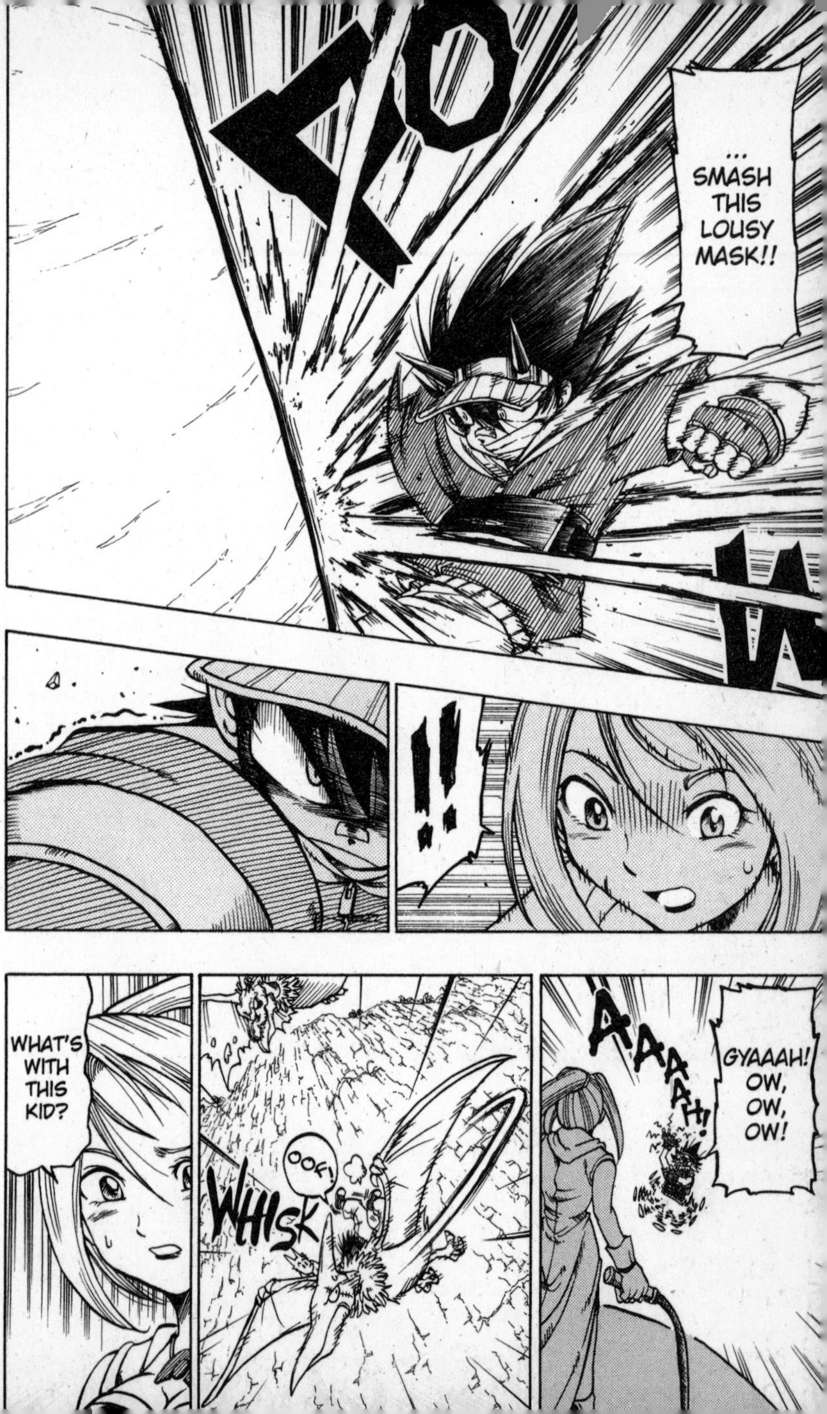
... SMASH THIS LOUSY MASK!!
!!
GYAAAH! OW, OW, OW!
AAAAAH!
OOF!
WHISK
WHAT'S WITH THIS KID?

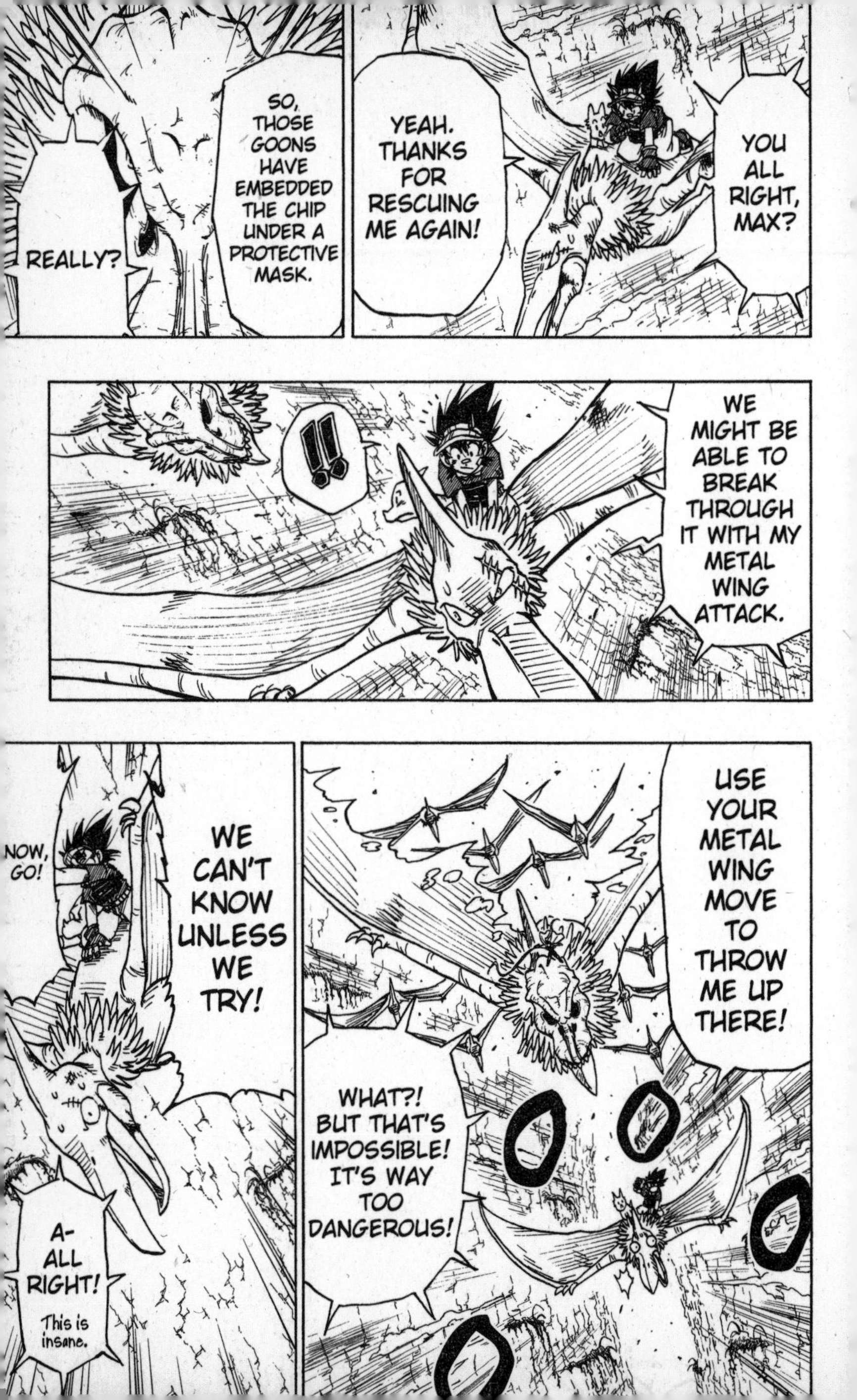
YOU ALL RIGHT, MAX?
YEAH. THANKS FOR RESCUING ME AGAIN!
SO, THOSE GOONS HAVE EMBEDDED THE CHIP UNDER A PROTECTIVE MASK.
REALLY?
WE MIGHT BE ABLE TO BREAK THROUGH IT WITH MY METAL WING ATTACK.
!!
USE YOUR METAL WING MOVE TO THROW ME UP THERE!
WHAT?! BUT THAT'S IMPOSSIBLE! IT'S WAY TOO DANGEROUS!
WE CAN'T KNOW UNLESS WE TRY!
NOW, GO!
A- ALL RIGHT!
This is insane.

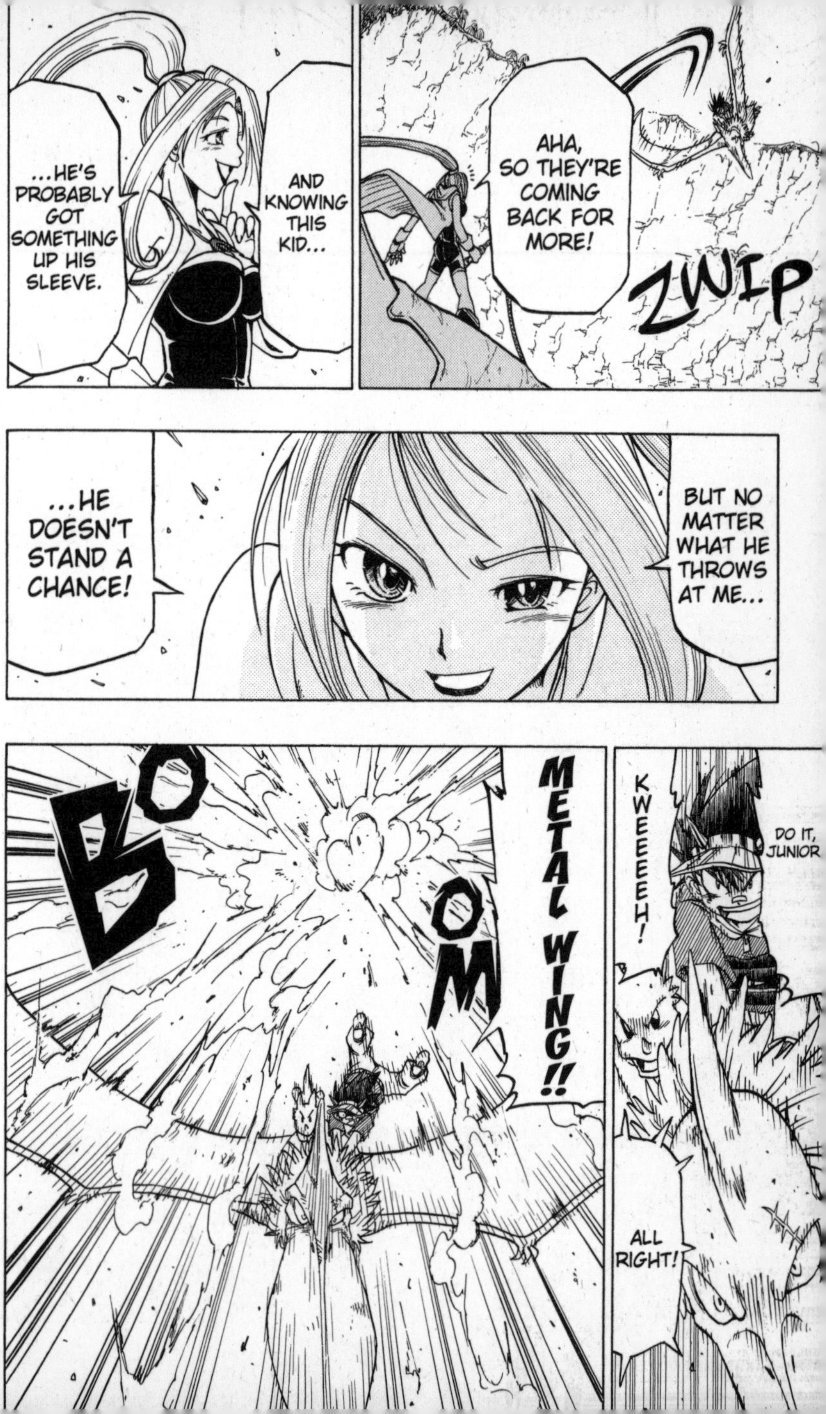
AHA, SO THEY'RE COMING BACK FOR MORE!
ZWIP
AND KNOWING THIS KID...
...HE'S PROBABLY GOT SOMETHING UP HIS SLEEVE.
BUT NO MATTER WHAT HE THROWS AT ME...
...HE DOESN'T STAND A CHANCE!
KWEEEEEH!
DO IT, JUNIOR
ALL RIGHT!
BOOM
METAL WING!!

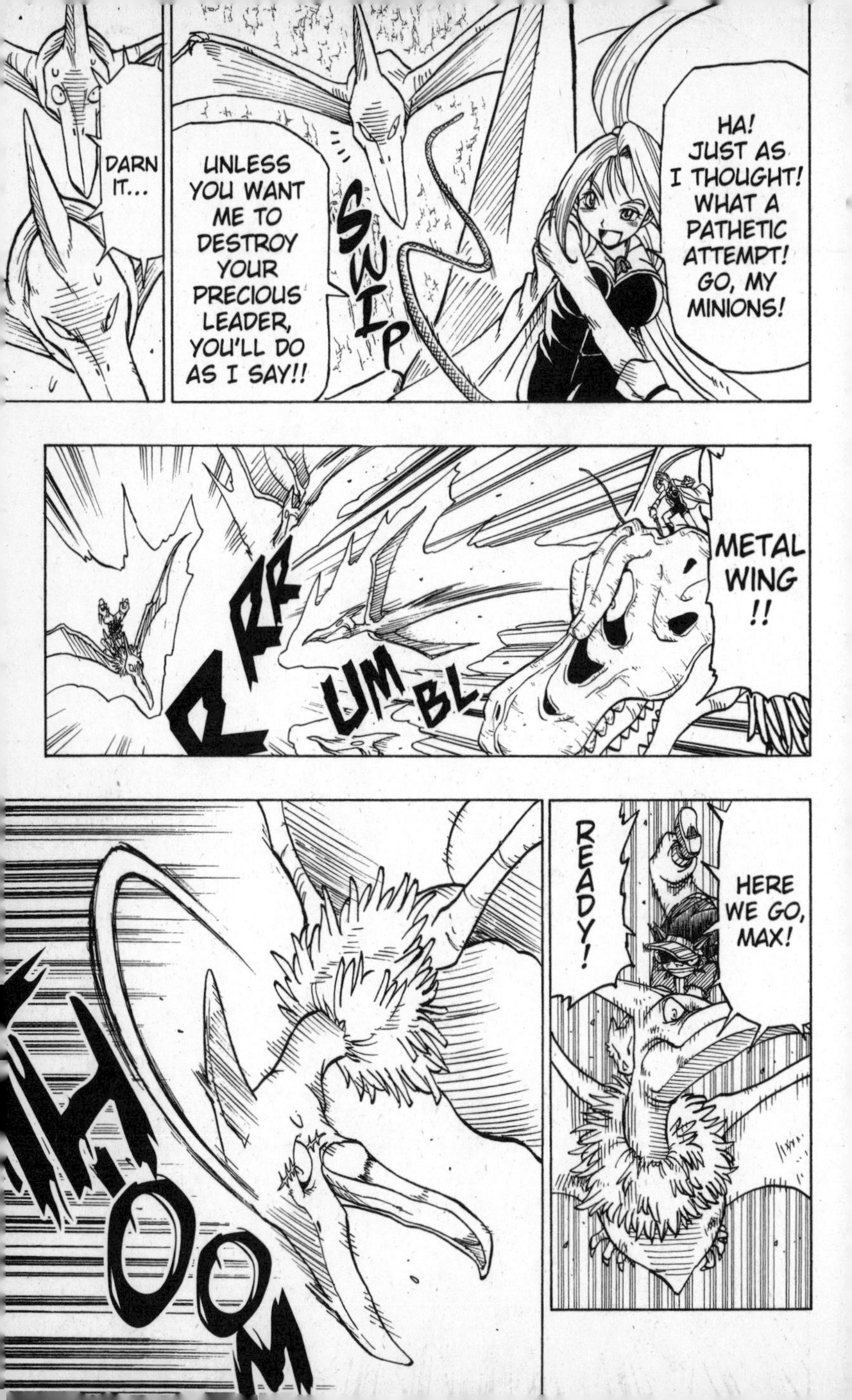
HA! JUST AS I THOUGHT! WHAT A PATHETIC ATTEMPT! GO, MY MINIONS!
SWIIP
UNLESS YOU WANT ME TO DESTROY YOUR PRECIOUS LEADER, YOU'LL DO AS I SAY!!
DARN IT...
METAL WING!!
RRRUMBL
HERE WE GO, MAX!
READY!
WHOOOM

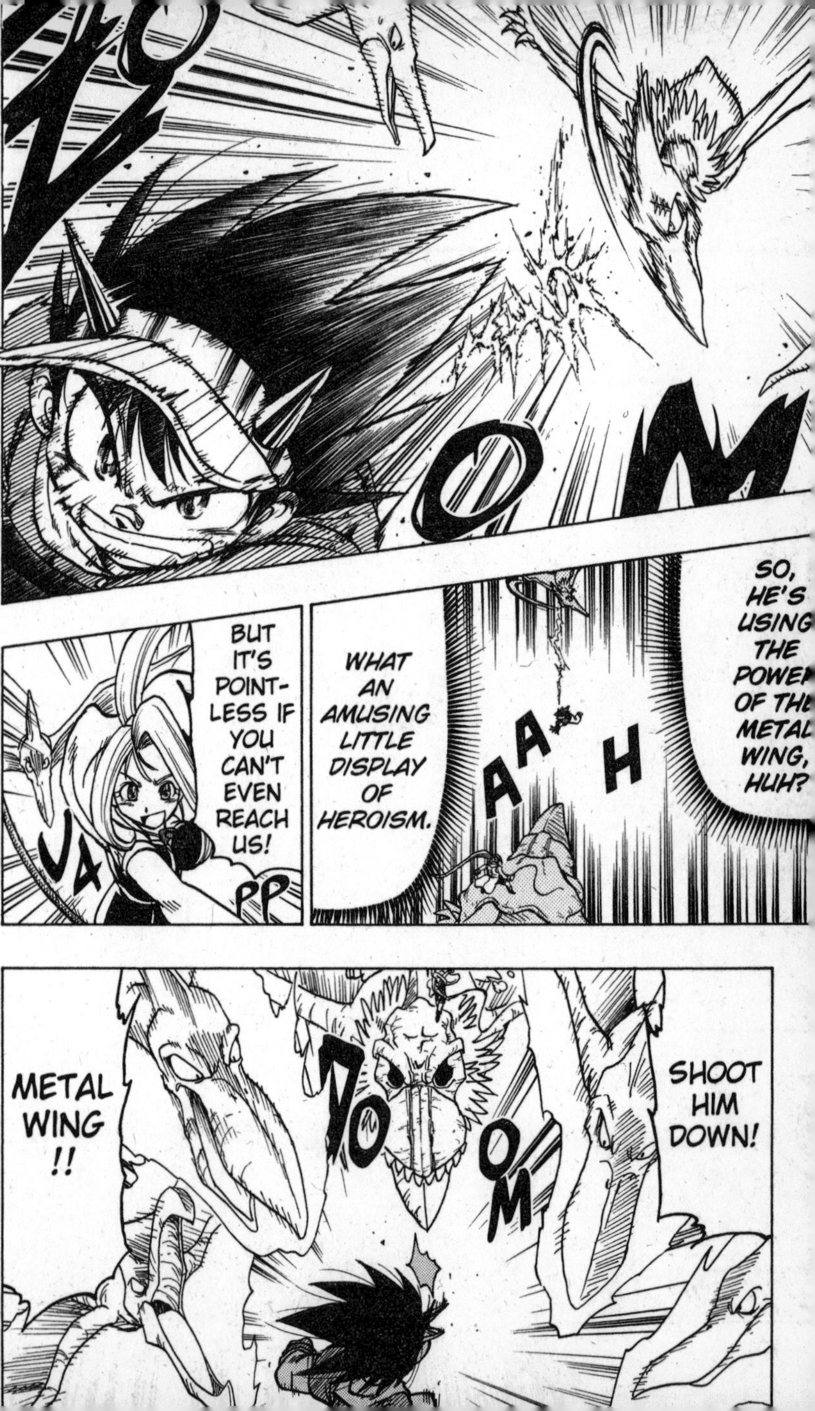
SO, HE'S USING THE POWER OF THE METAL WING, HUH?
AAH
WHAT AN AMUSING LITTLE DISPLAY OF HEROISM.
BUT IT'S POINT-LESS IF YOU CAN'T EVEN REACH US!
SHOOT HIM DOWN!
METAL WING!!

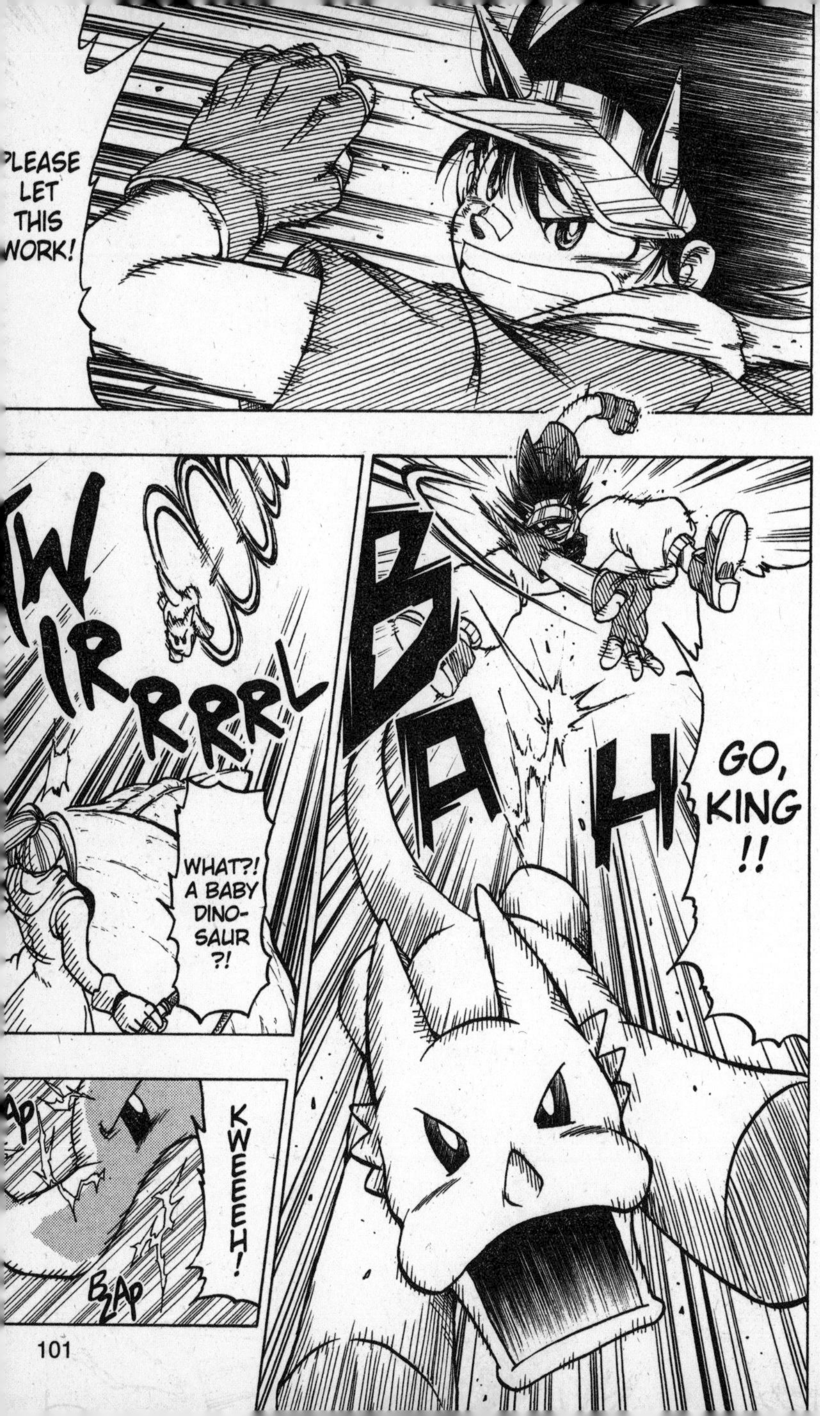
PLEASE LET THIS WORK!
BAH
GO, KING!!
TWIRRRRL
WHAT?! A BABY DINOSAUR?!
ZAP
KWEEEEH!
BZAP

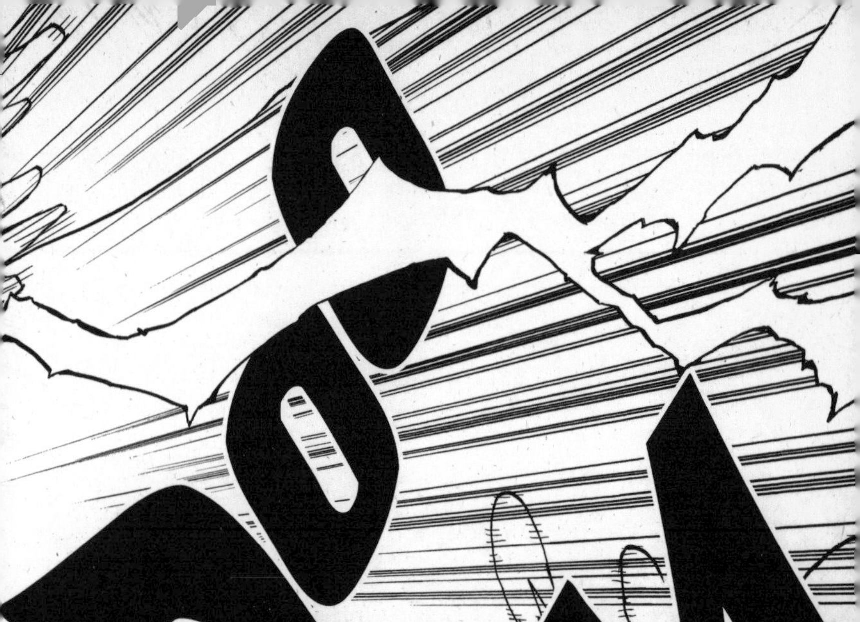
BOOM
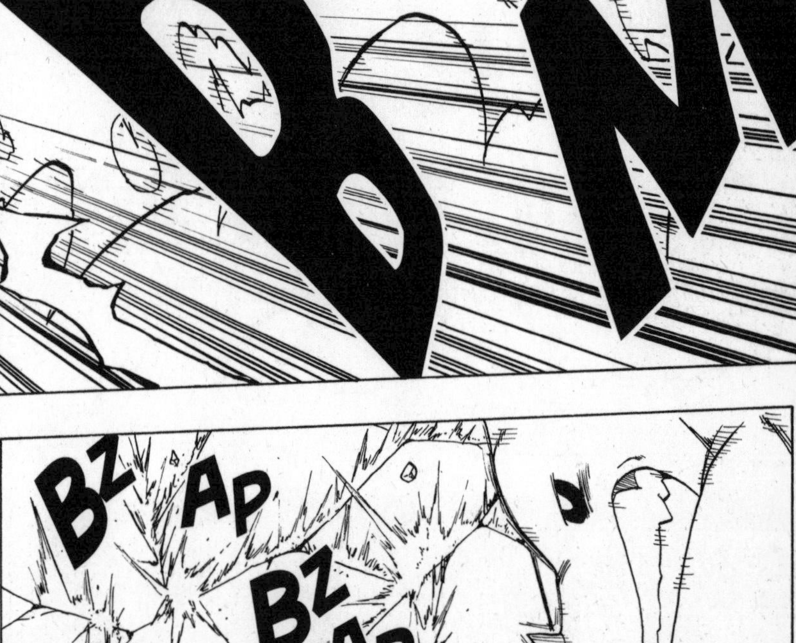
BZAP
BZAP

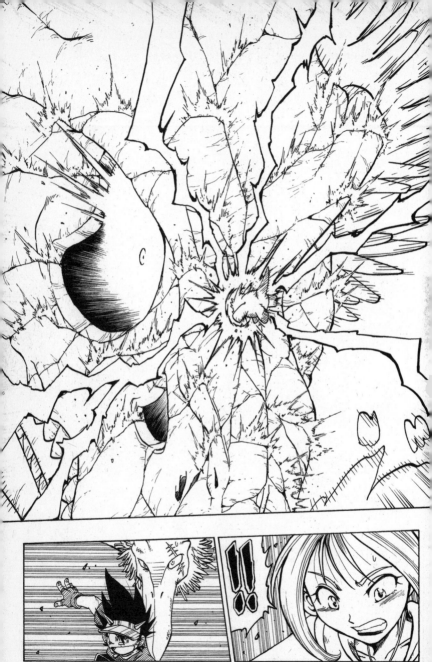

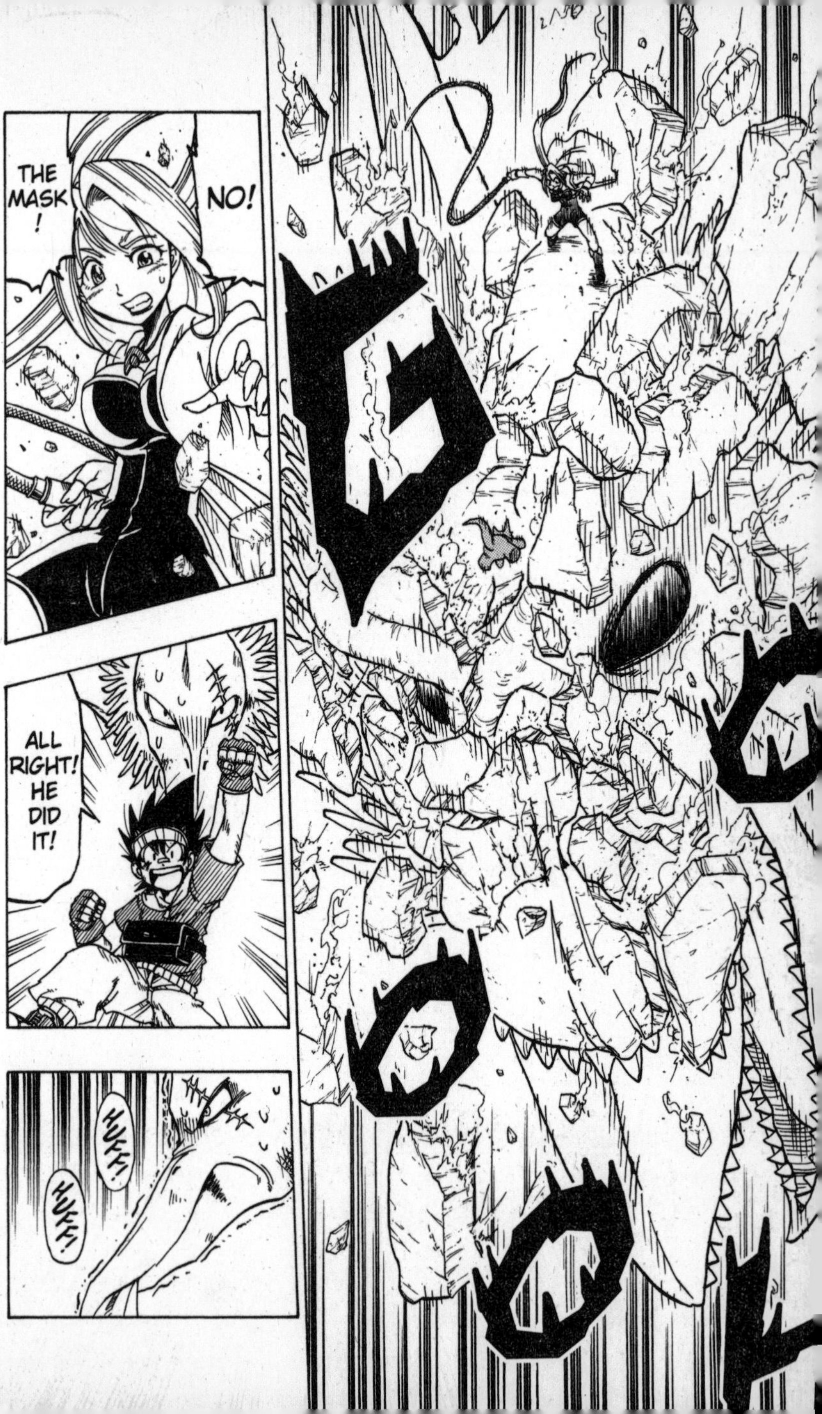
THE MASK!
NO!
ALL RIGHT! HE DID IT!
HUFF!
HUFF!

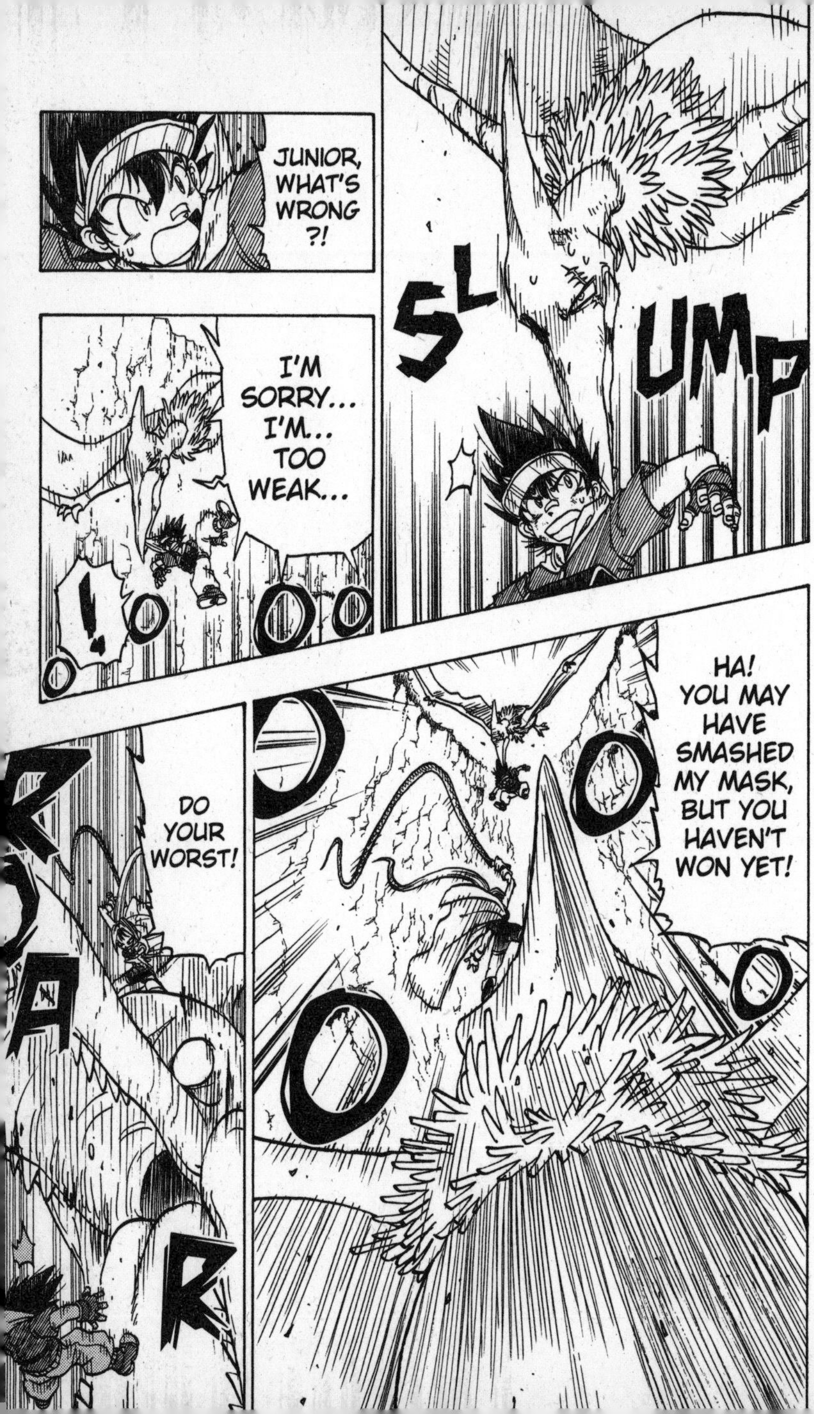
SLUMP
JUNIOR, WHAT'S WRONG?!
I'M SORRY... I'M... TOO WEAK...
HA! YOU MAY HAVE SMASHED MY MASK, BUT YOU HAVEN'T WON YET!
DO YOUR WORST!

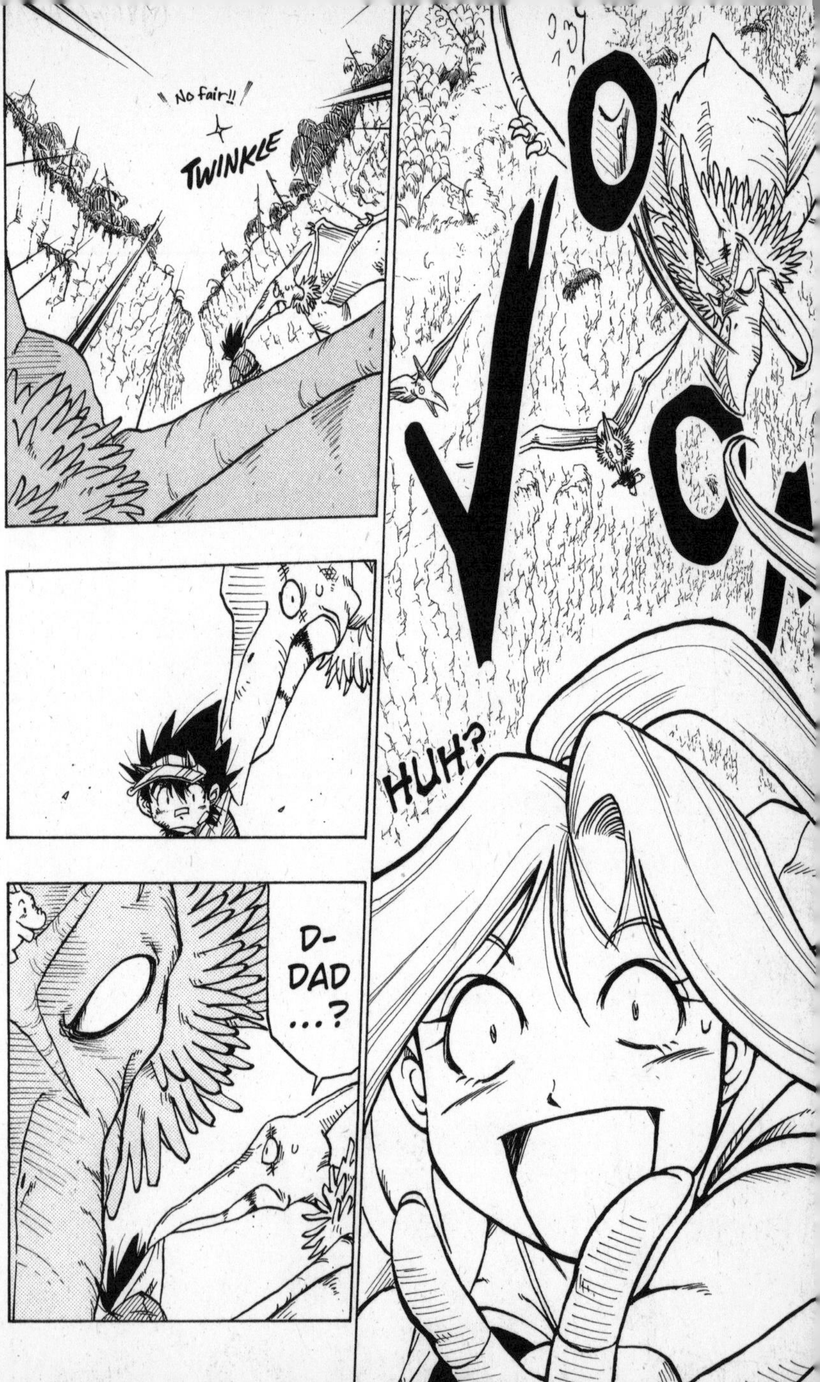
HUH?
No fair!!
TWINKLE
D-DAD ...?

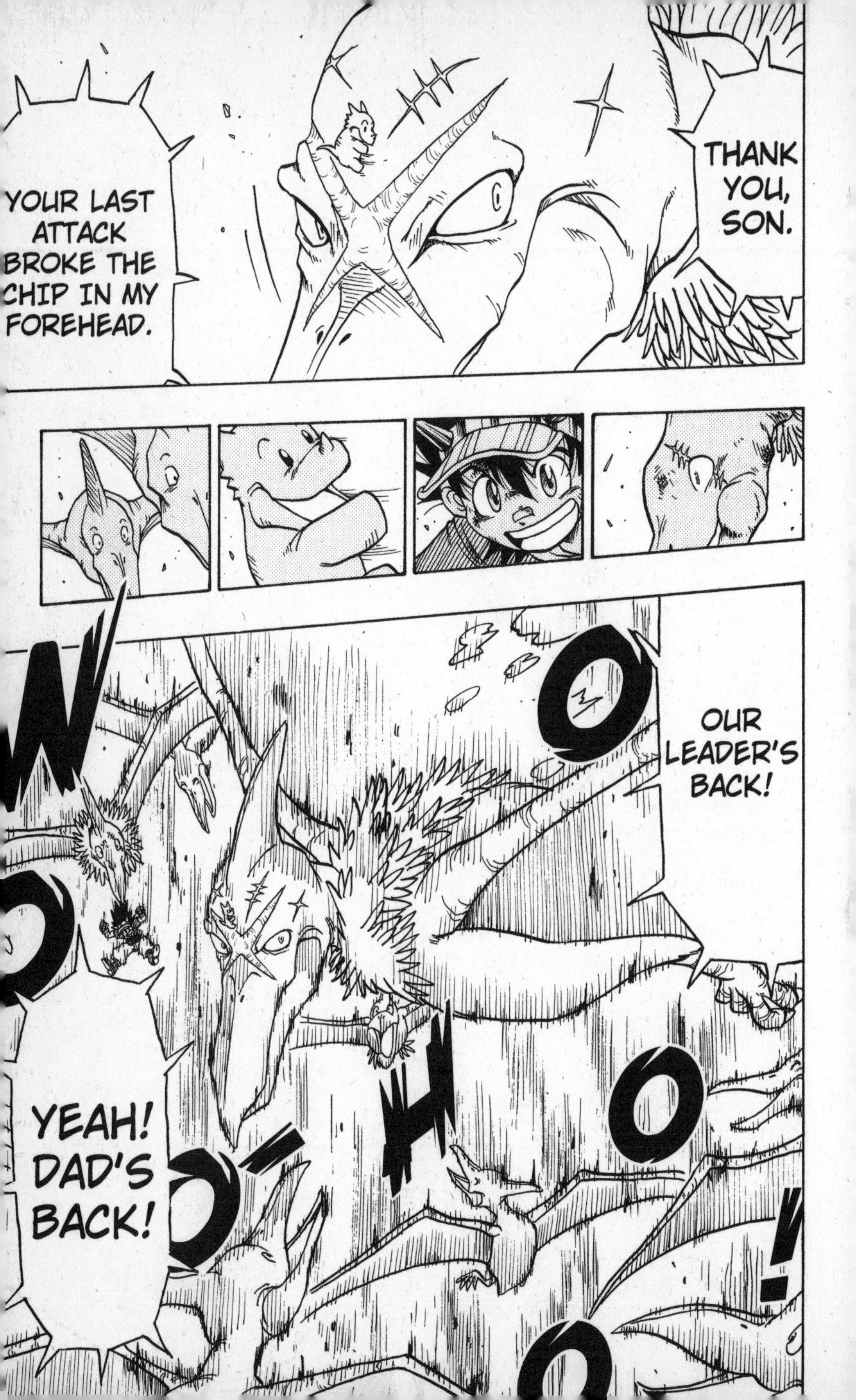
THANK YOU, SON.
YOUR LAST ATTACK BROKE THE CHIP IN MY FOREHEAD.
OUR LEADER'S BACK!
WHOOOO!
YEAH! DAD'S BACK!

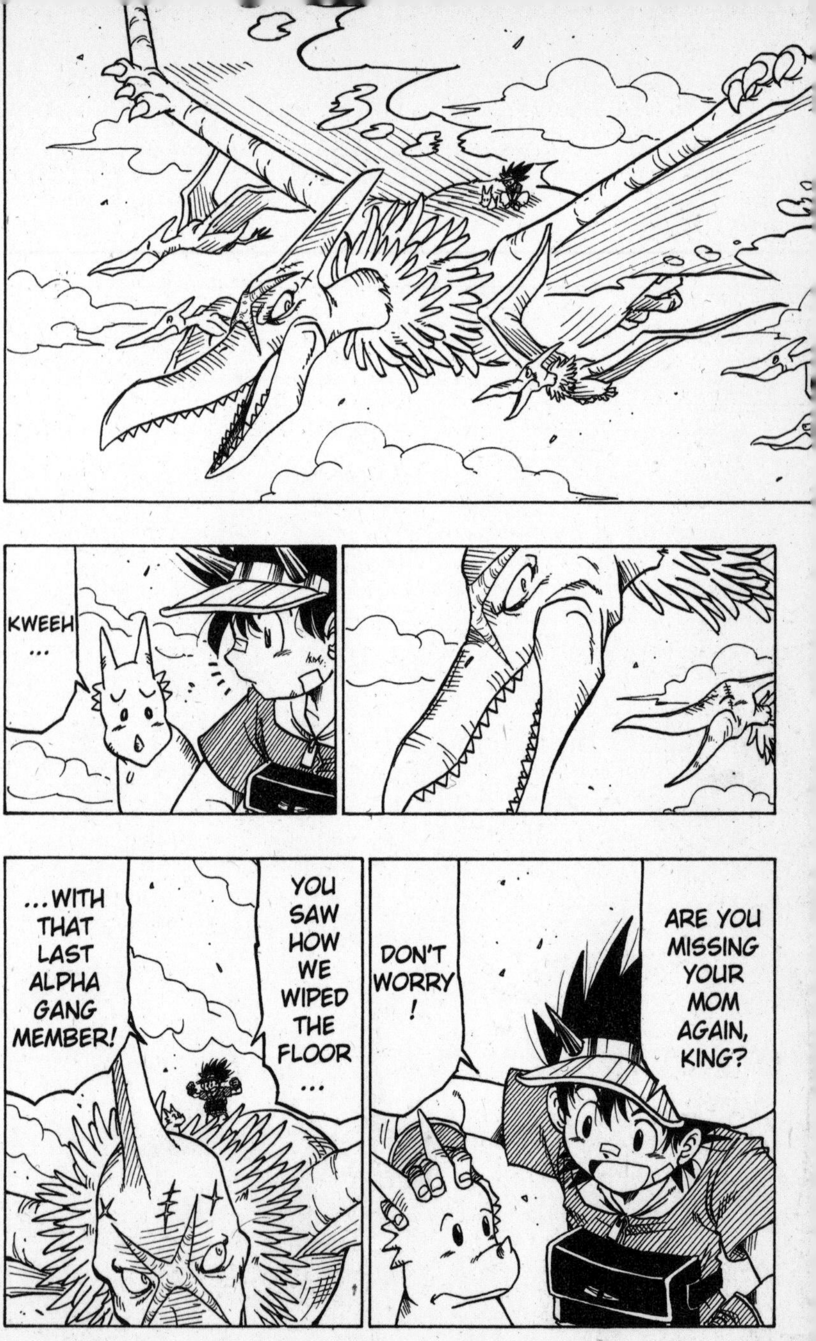
KWEEH ...
ARE YOU MISSING YOUR MOM AGAIN, KING?
DON'T WORRY!
YOU SAW HOW WE WIPED THE FLOOR ...
...WITH THAT LAST ALPHA GANG MEMBER!

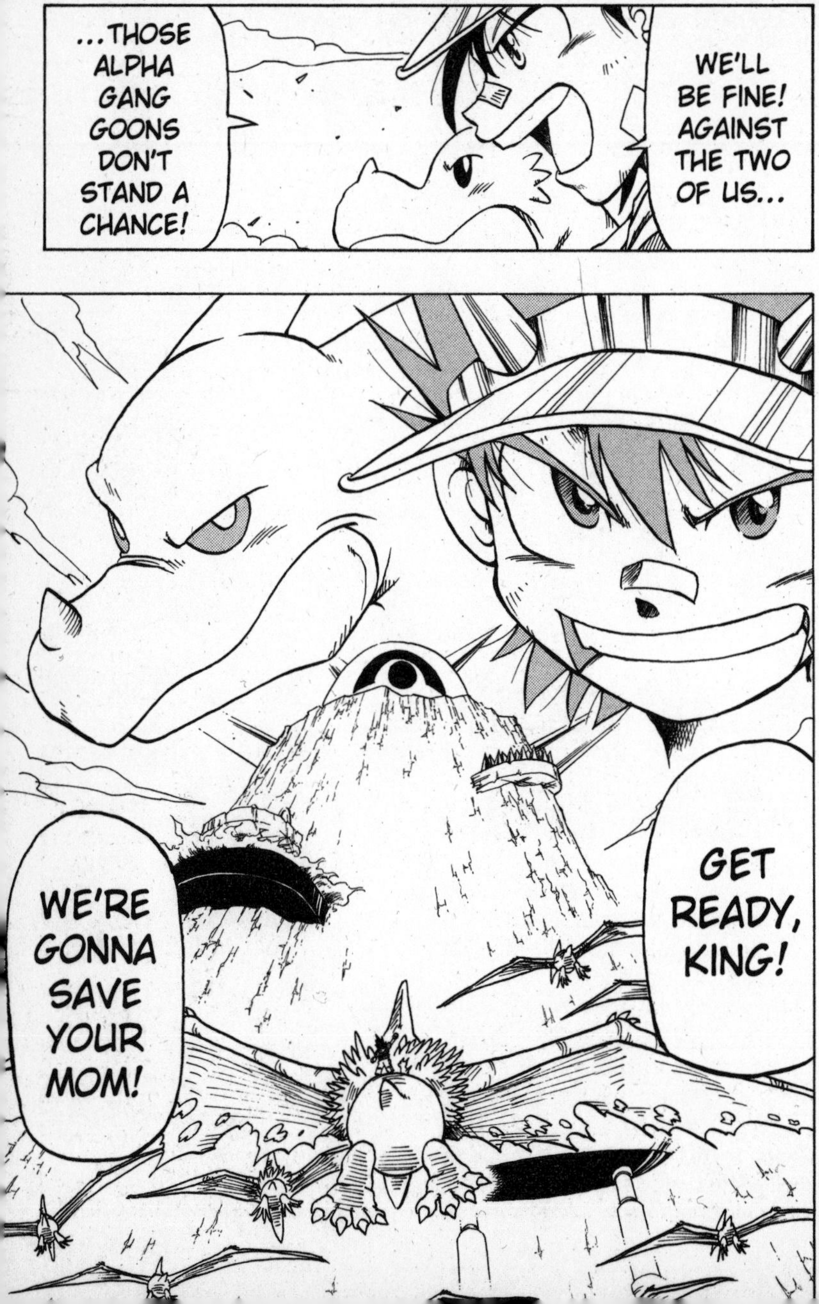
WE'LL BE FINE! AGAINST THE TWO OF US...
...THOSE ALPHA GANG GOONS DON'T STAND A CHANCE!
GET READY, KING!
WE'RE GONNA SAVE YOUR MOM!

DIG IT!

Uncover facts about dinosaurs, their super moves and their trading card stats!

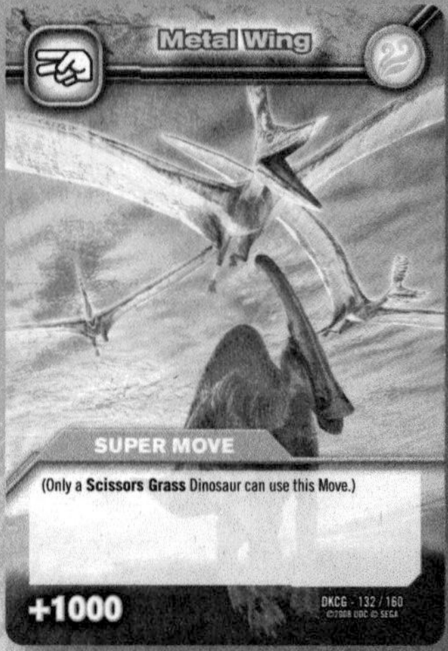

Metal Wing
SUPER MOVE
(Only a Scissors Grass Dinosaur can use this Move.)
+1000
DKCG - 132 / 160
©2008 UDC © SEGA

METAL WING

Card Rarity: Common

With Metal Wing, your **Grass** Dinosaurs can call on some help from above. A whole flock of Pterodactyls arrive, giving your Dinosaur a bonus of +1000 power! This mighty Super Move can only be used by a **Grass** Dinosaur with the **Scissors** icon.

STEGOSAURUS

Stegosaurus isn't mentioned in this chapter, but it does make an appearance later in the book. See if you can spot it!

Stegosaurus means "plated lizard"

Length: approx. 30 ft.

Lived in: Jurassic Period

Discovered in: America

The Stegosaurus is one of the most famous of all dinosaurs. Its spiked tail gave it a powerful defense.

Card Rarity: Gold Rare and Colossal Rare

With Stegosaurus's special **Quake** ability, your opponent can't afford to ignore it!

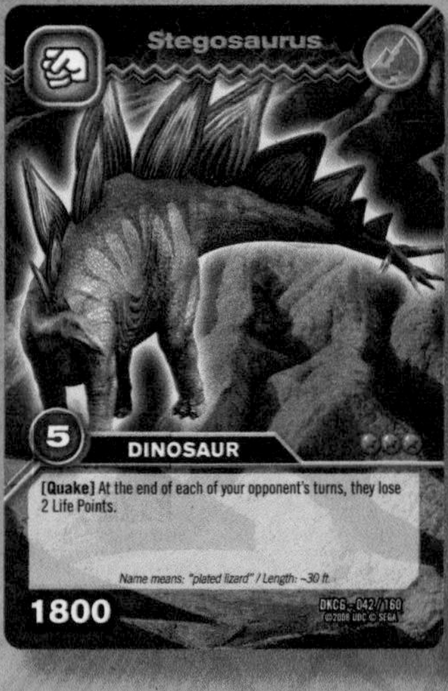

Stegosaurus
5
DINOSAUR
[Quake] At the end of each of your opponent's turns, they lose 2 Life Points.
Name means: "plated lizard" / Length: ~30 ft
1800
DKCG - 042 / 160
©2008 UDC © SEGA

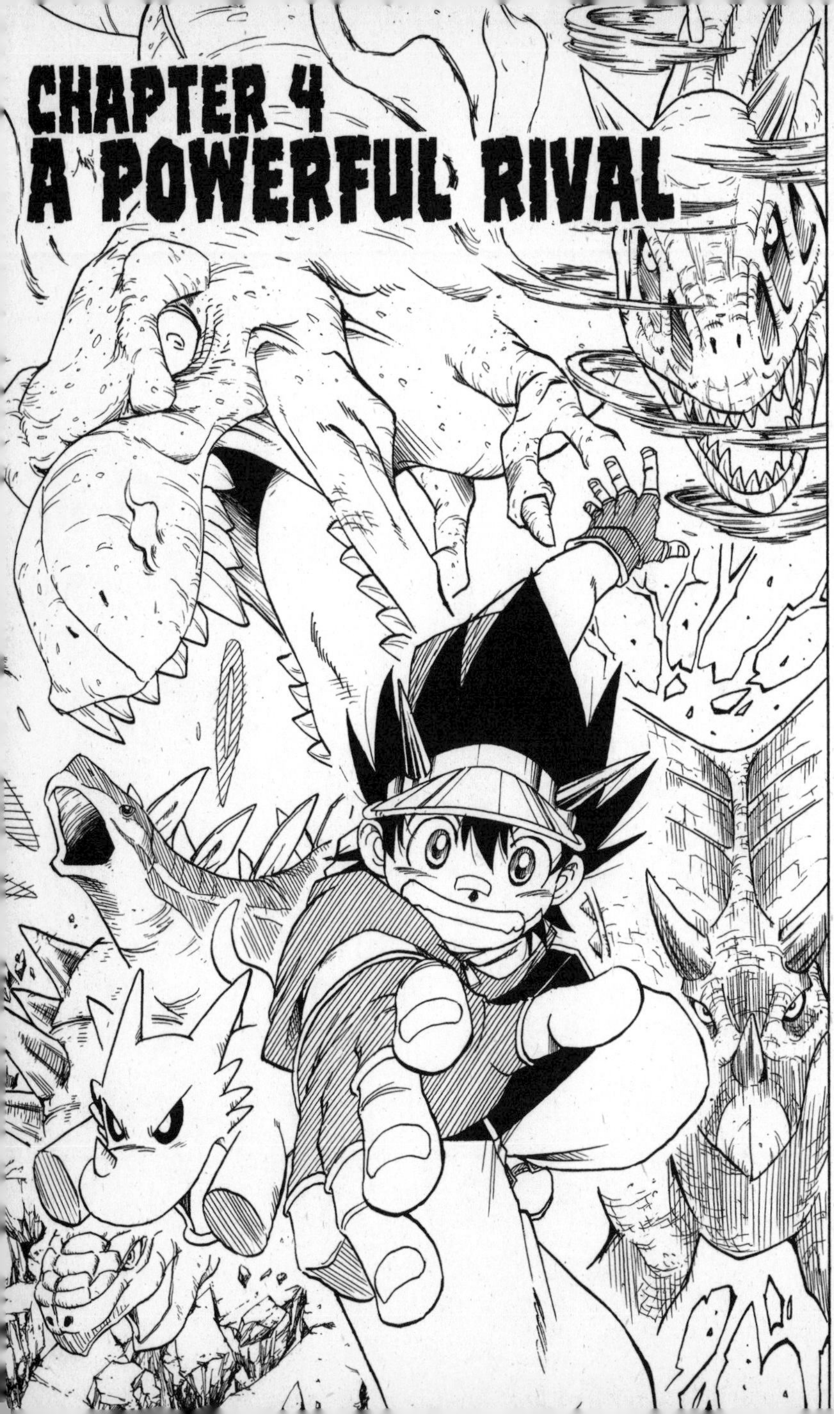
CHAPTER 4
A POWERFUL RIVAL

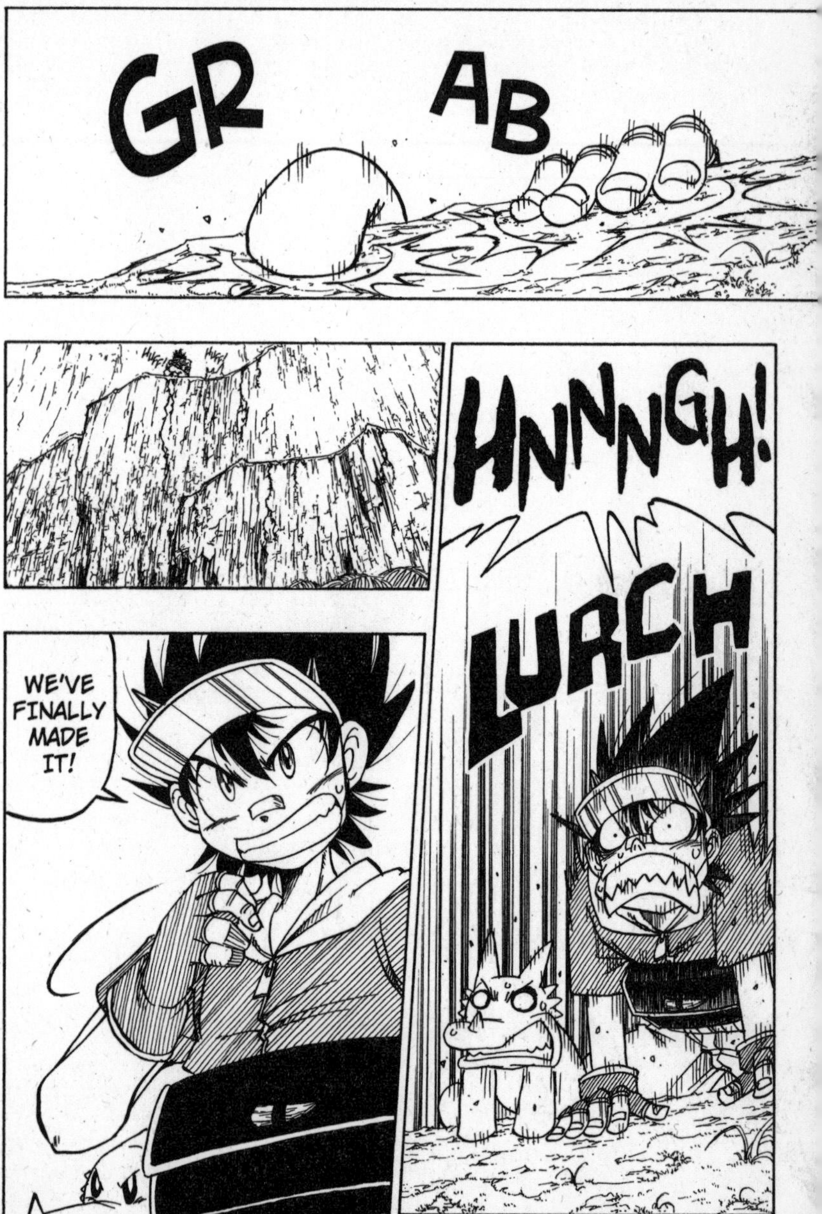
GRAB
HNNNGH!
LURCH
WE'VE FINALLY MADE IT!

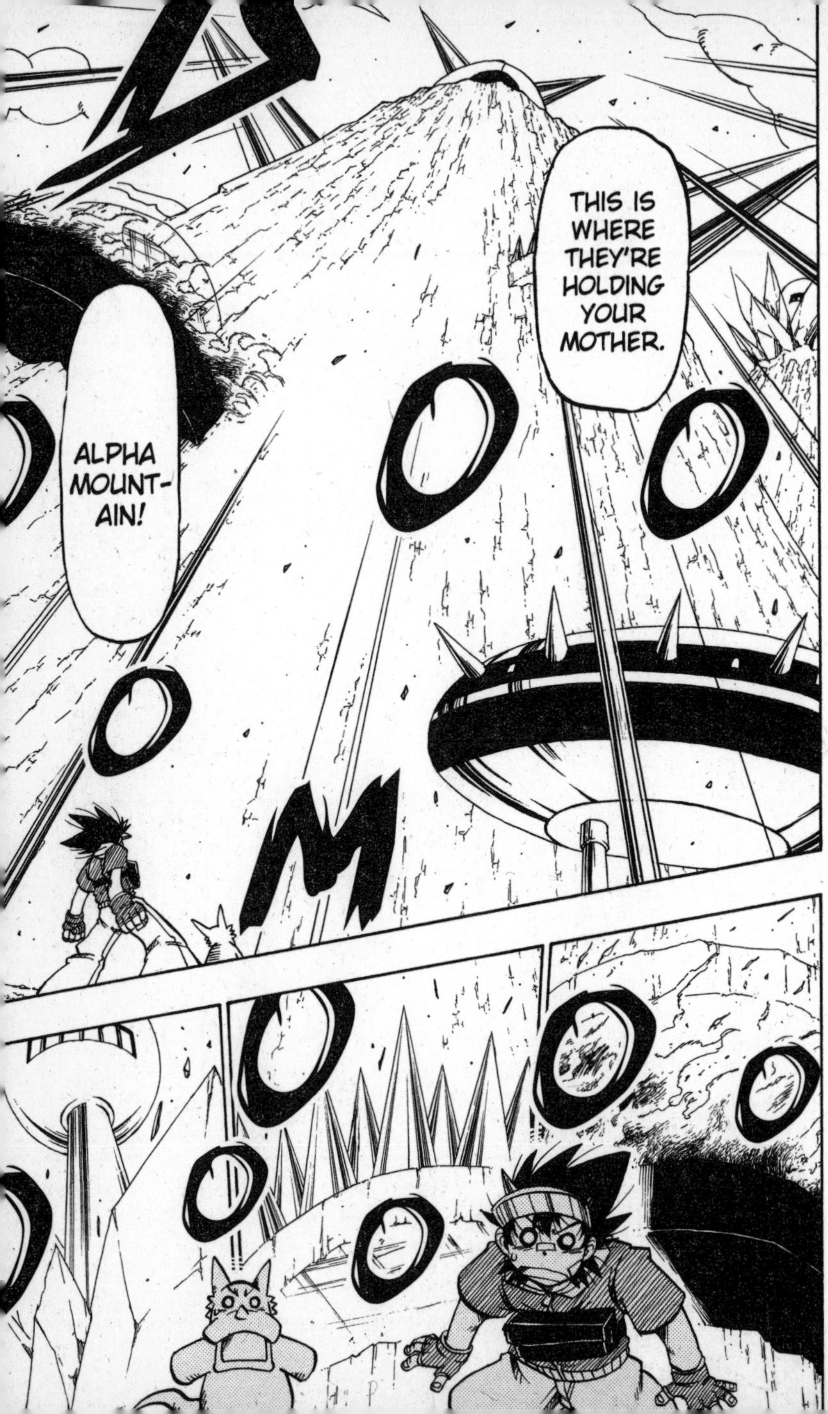
THIS IS WHERE THEY'RE HOLDING YOUR MOTHER.
ALPHA MOUNT-AIN!

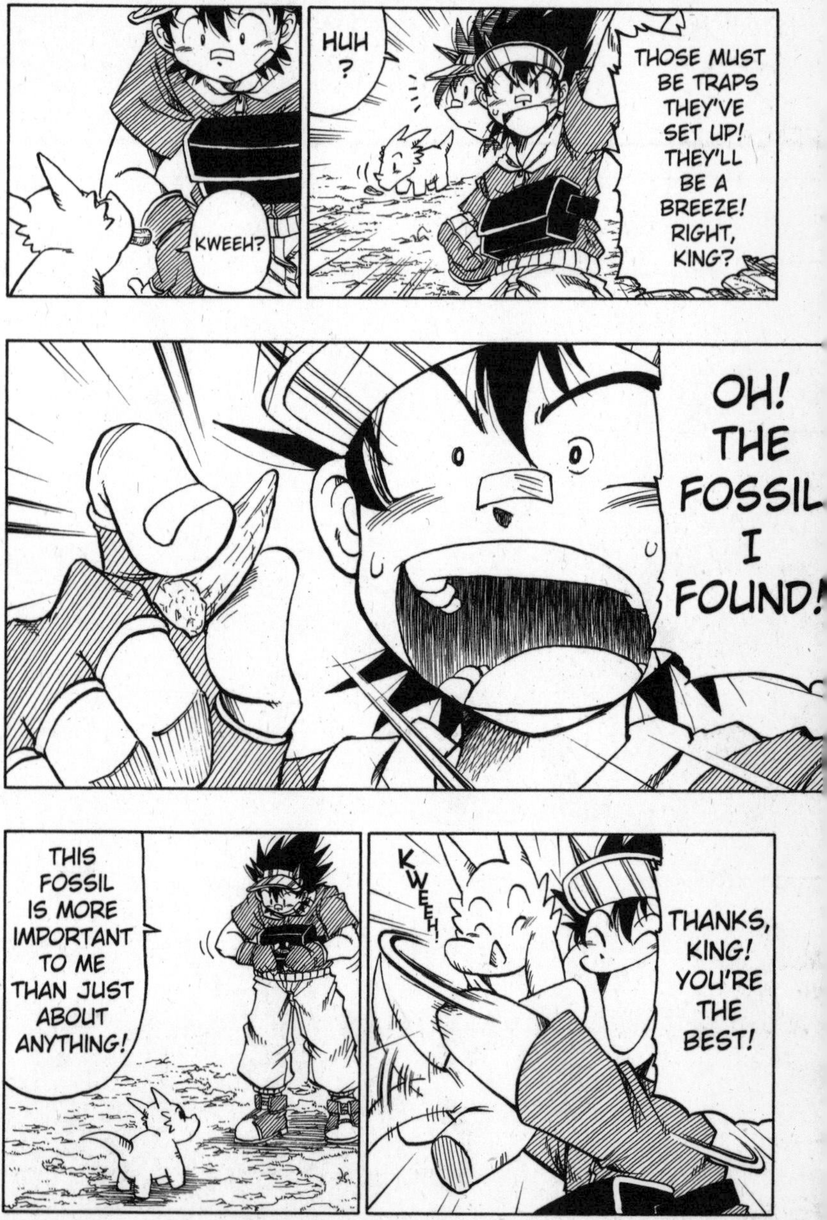
THOSE MUST BE TRAPS THEY'VE SET UP! THEY'LL BE A BREEZE! RIGHT, KING?
HUH?
KWEEH?
OH! THE FOSSIL I FOUND!
THANKS, KING! YOU'RE THE BEST!
KWEEH!
THIS FOSSIL IS MORE IMPORTANT TO ME THAN JUST ABOUT ANYTHING!

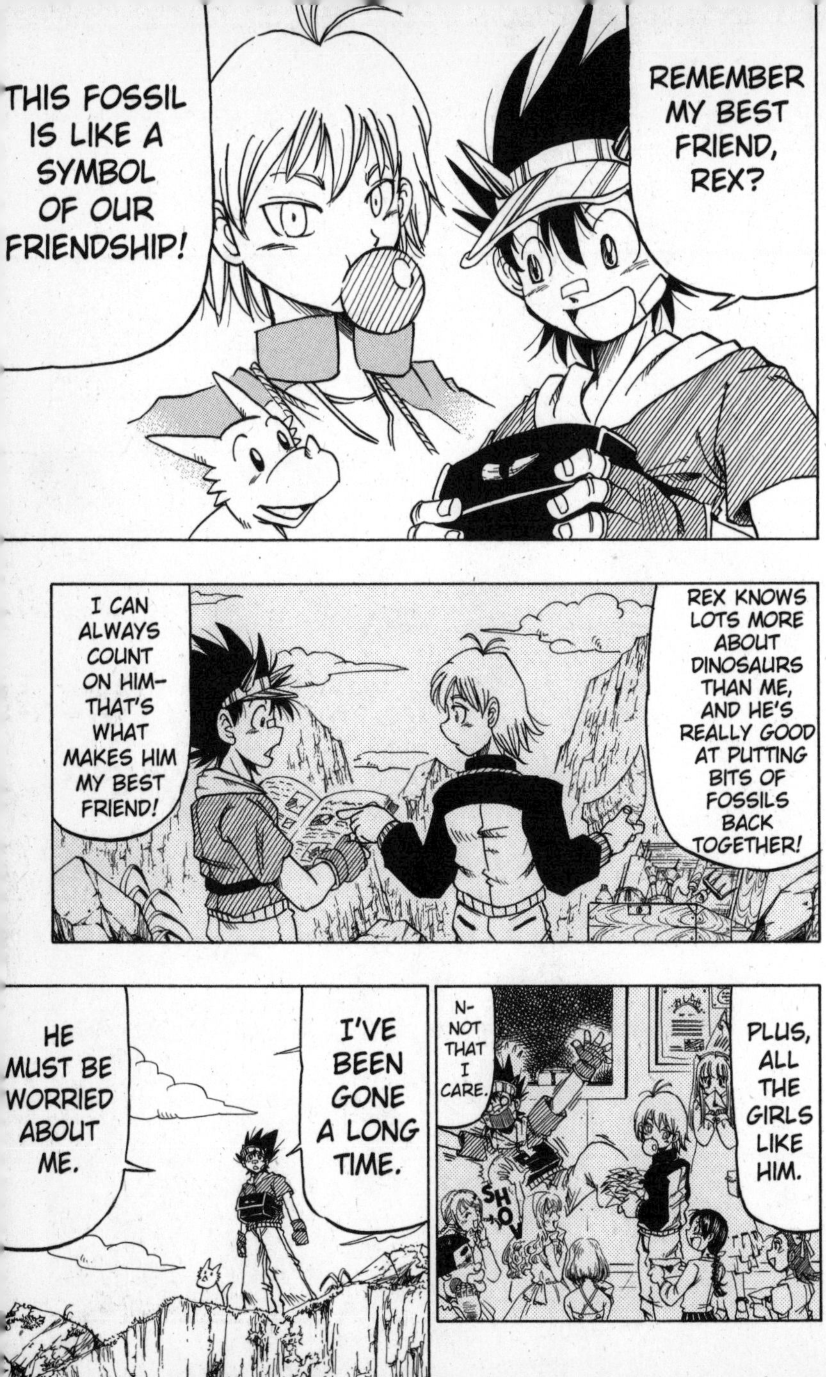
REMEMBER MY BEST FRIEND, REX?
THIS FOSSIL IS LIKE A SYMBOL OF OUR FRIENDSHIP!
REX KNOWS LOTS MORE ABOUT DINOSAURS THAN ME, AND HE'S REALLY GOOD AT PUTTING BITS OF FOSSILS BACK TOGETHER!
I CAN ALWAYS COUNT ON HIM–THAT'S WHAT MAKES HIM MY BEST FRIEND!
PLUS, ALL THE GIRLS LIKE HIM.
N-NOT THAT I CARE.
SHOV
I'VE BEEN GONE A LONG TIME.
HE MUST BE WORRIED ABOUT ME.

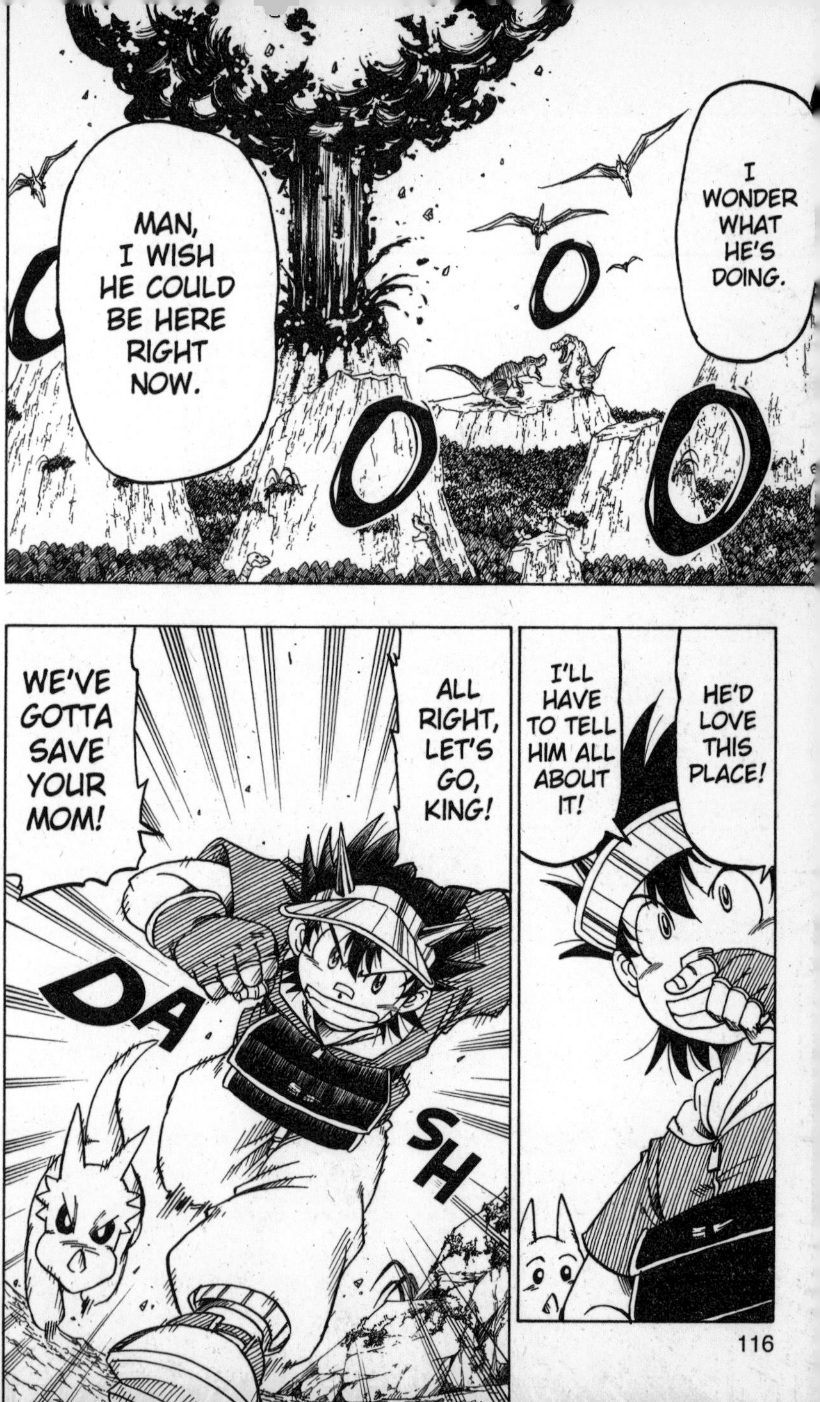
I WONDER WHAT HE'S DOING.
MAN, I WISH HE COULD BE HERE RIGHT NOW.
HE'D LOVE THIS PLACE!
I'LL HAVE TO TELL HIM ALL ABOUT IT!
ALL RIGHT, LET'S GO, KING!
WE'VE GOTTA SAVE YOUR MOM!
DASH

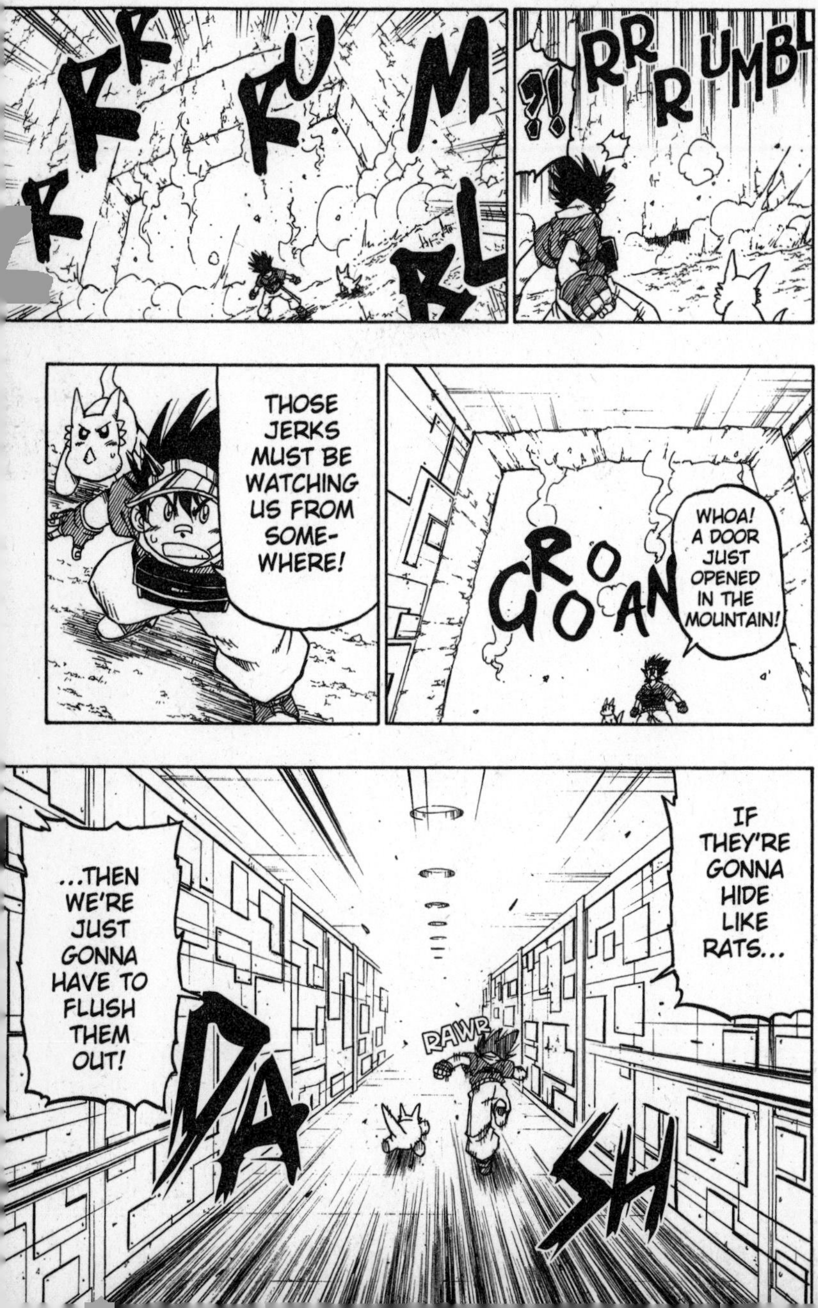
?!
RRRUMBL
RRRRUMBL
WHOA! A DOOR JUST OPENED IN THE MOUNTAIN!
THOSE JERKS MUST BE WATCHING US FROM SOME-WHERE!
IF THEY'RE GONNA HIDE LIKE RATS...
...THEN WE'RE JUST GONNA HAVE TO FLUSH THEM OUT!
RAWR
DASH

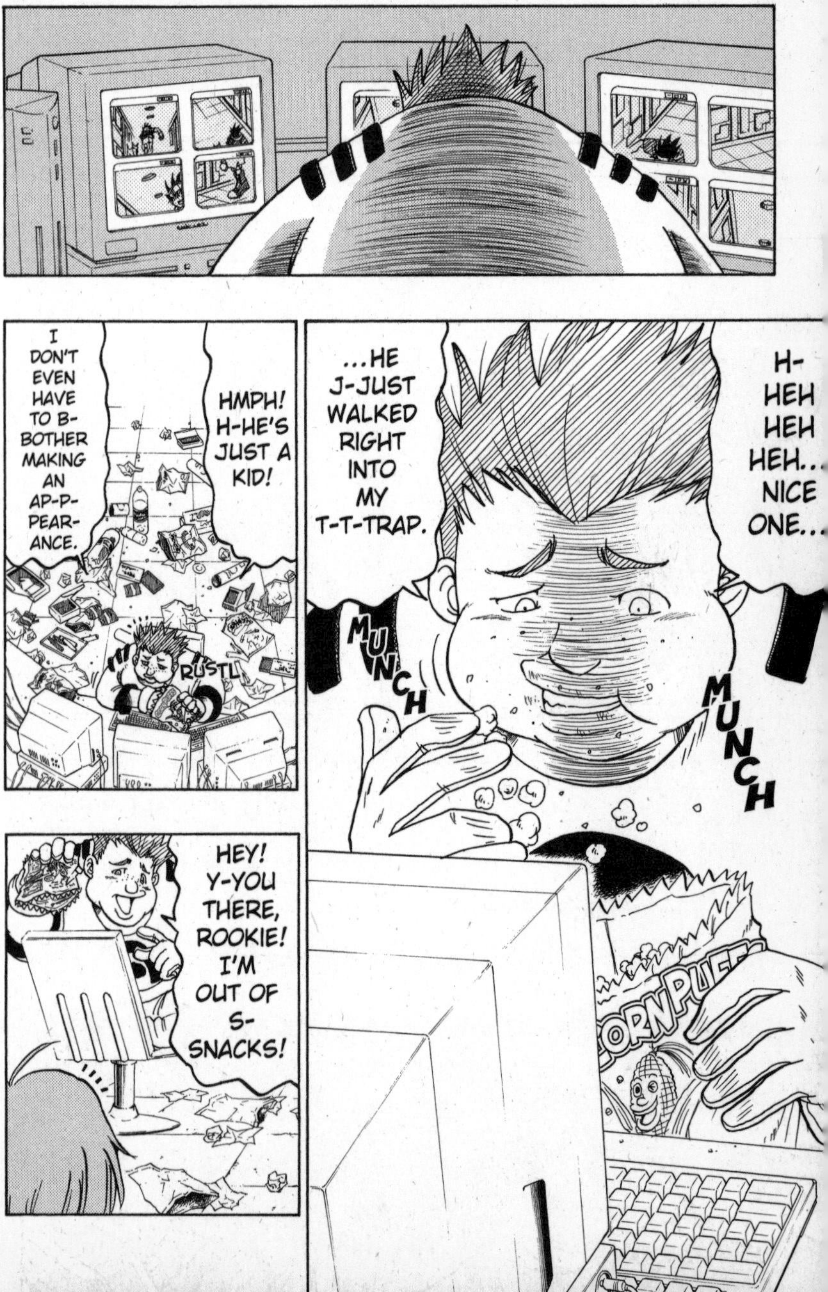
H-HEH HEH HEH... NICE ONE...
...HE J-JUST WALKED RIGHT INTO MY T-T-TRAP.
MUNCH
MUNCH
HMPH! H-HE'S JUST A KID!
I DON'T EVEN HAVE TO B-BOTHER MAKING AN AP-P-PEARANCE.
RUSTL
HEY! Y-YOU THERE, ROOKIE! I'M OUT OF S-SNACKS!

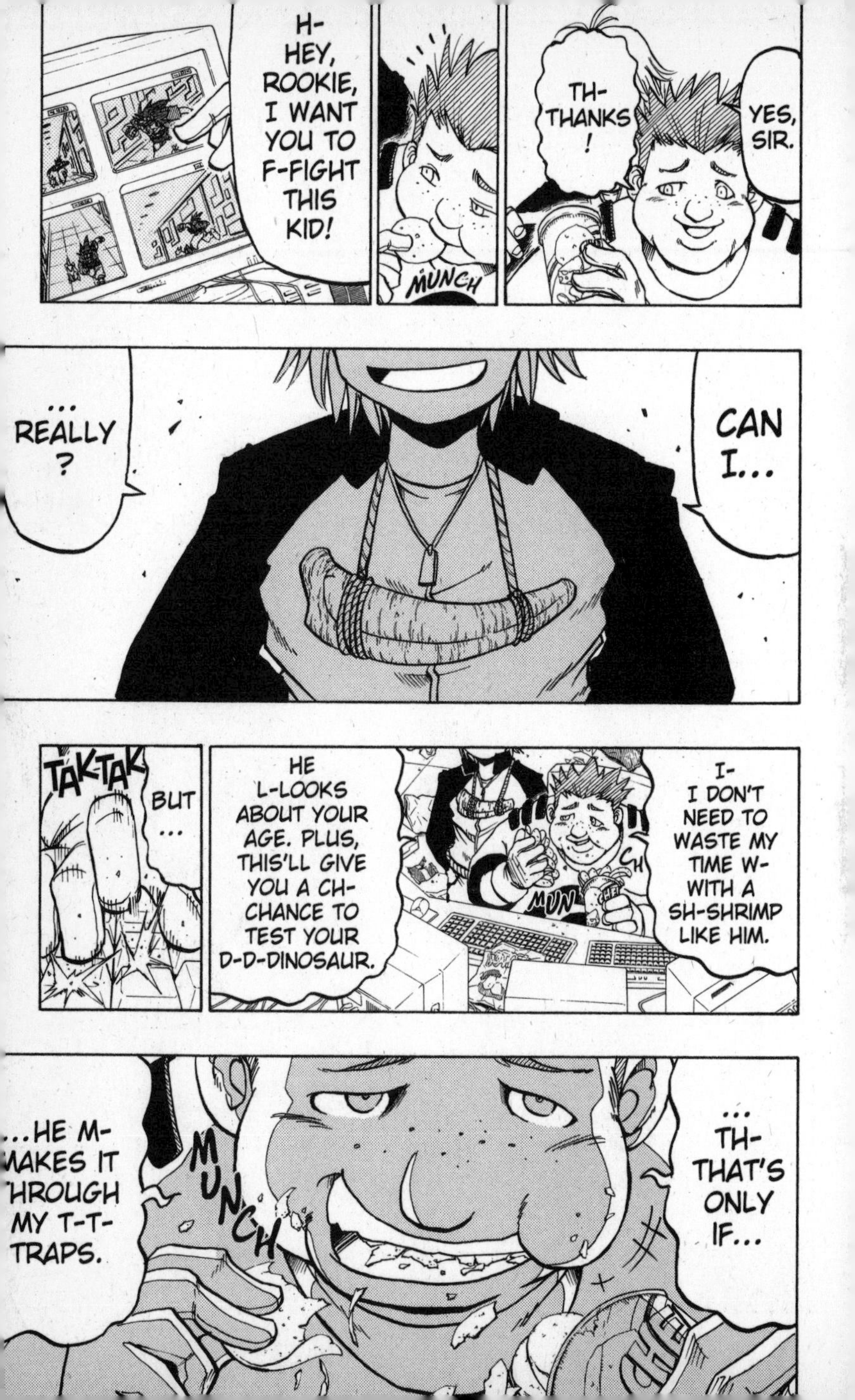
YES, SIR.
TH-THANKS!
MUNCH
H-HEY, ROOKIE, I WANT YOU TO F-FIGHT THIS KID!
CAN I...
...REALLY?
I-I DON'T NEED TO WASTE MY TIME W-WITH A SH-SHRIMP LIKE HIM.
HE L-LOOKS ABOUT YOUR AGE. PLUS, THIS'LL GIVE YOU A CH-CHANCE TO TEST YOUR D-D-DINOSAUR.
TAK-TAK
BUT...
...TH-THAT'S ONLY IF...
MUNCH
...HE M-MAKES IT THROUGH MY T-T-TRAPS.

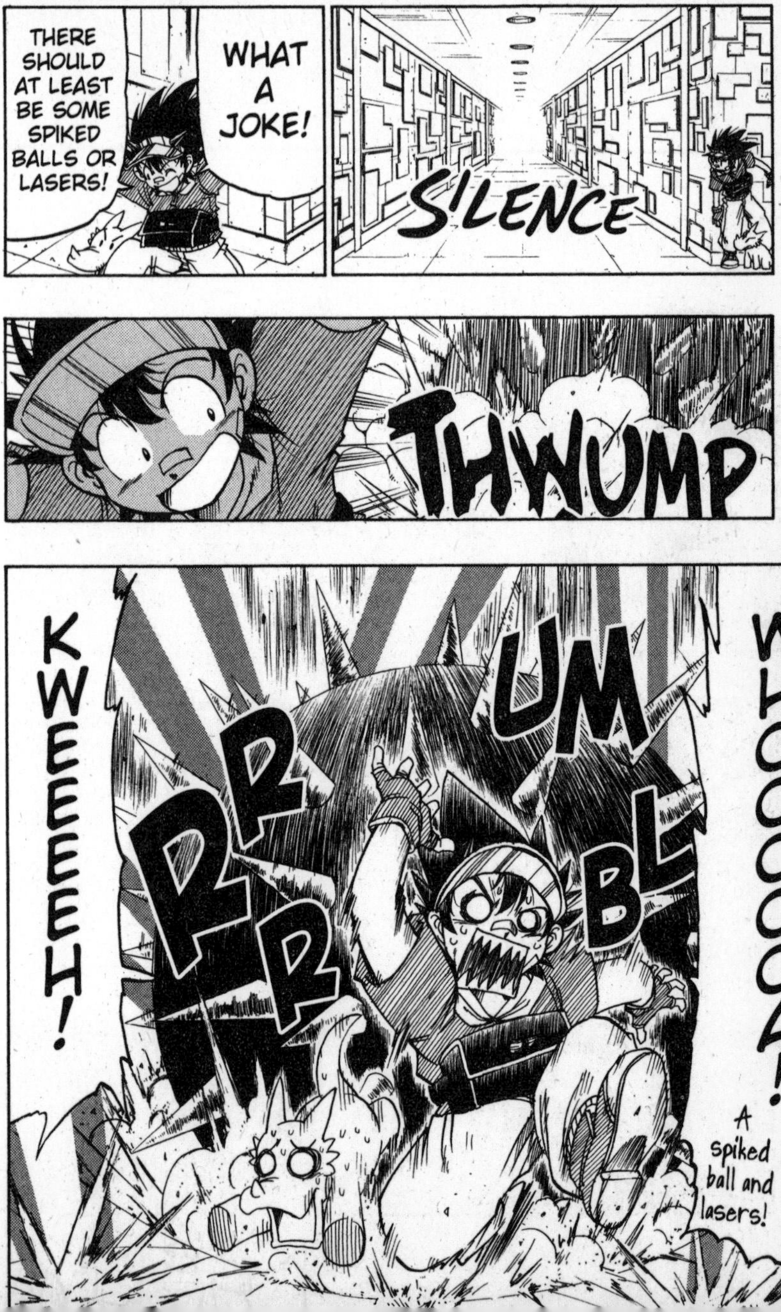

SILENCE
WHAT A JOKE!
THERE SHOULD AT LEAST BE SOME SPIKED BALLS OR LASERS!
THWUMP
WHOOOOA!
A spiked ball and lasers!
PRRUMBL
KWEEEEH!

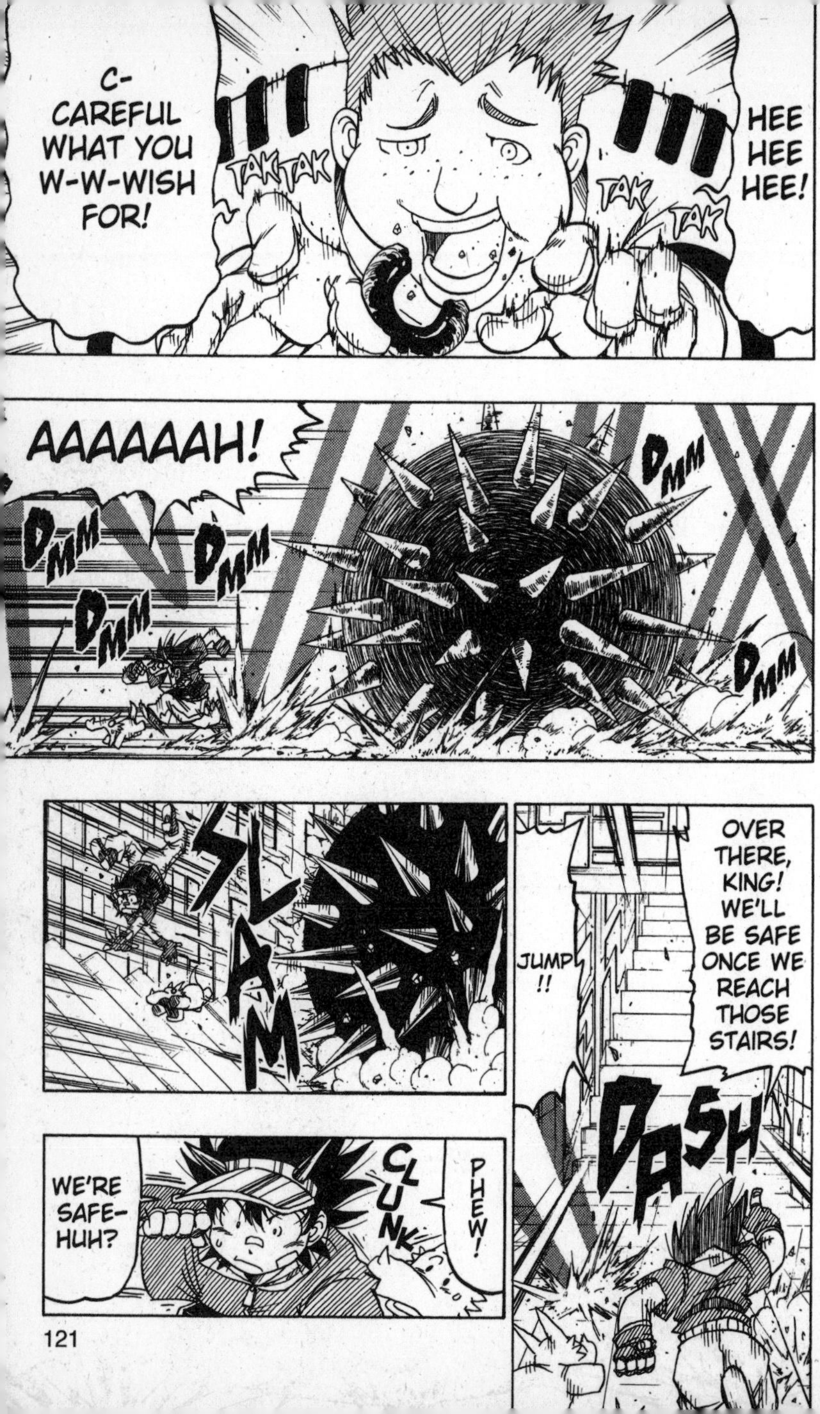
HEE HEE HEE!
TAK
TAK
TAKTAK
C- CAREFUL WHAT YOU W-W-WISH FOR!
DMM
AAAAAAH!
DMM
DMM
DMM
DMM
OVER THERE, KING! WE'LL BE SAFE ONCE WE REACH THOSE STAIRS!
JUMP !!
DASH
SLAM
PHEW!
CLUNK
WE'RE SAFE-HUH?

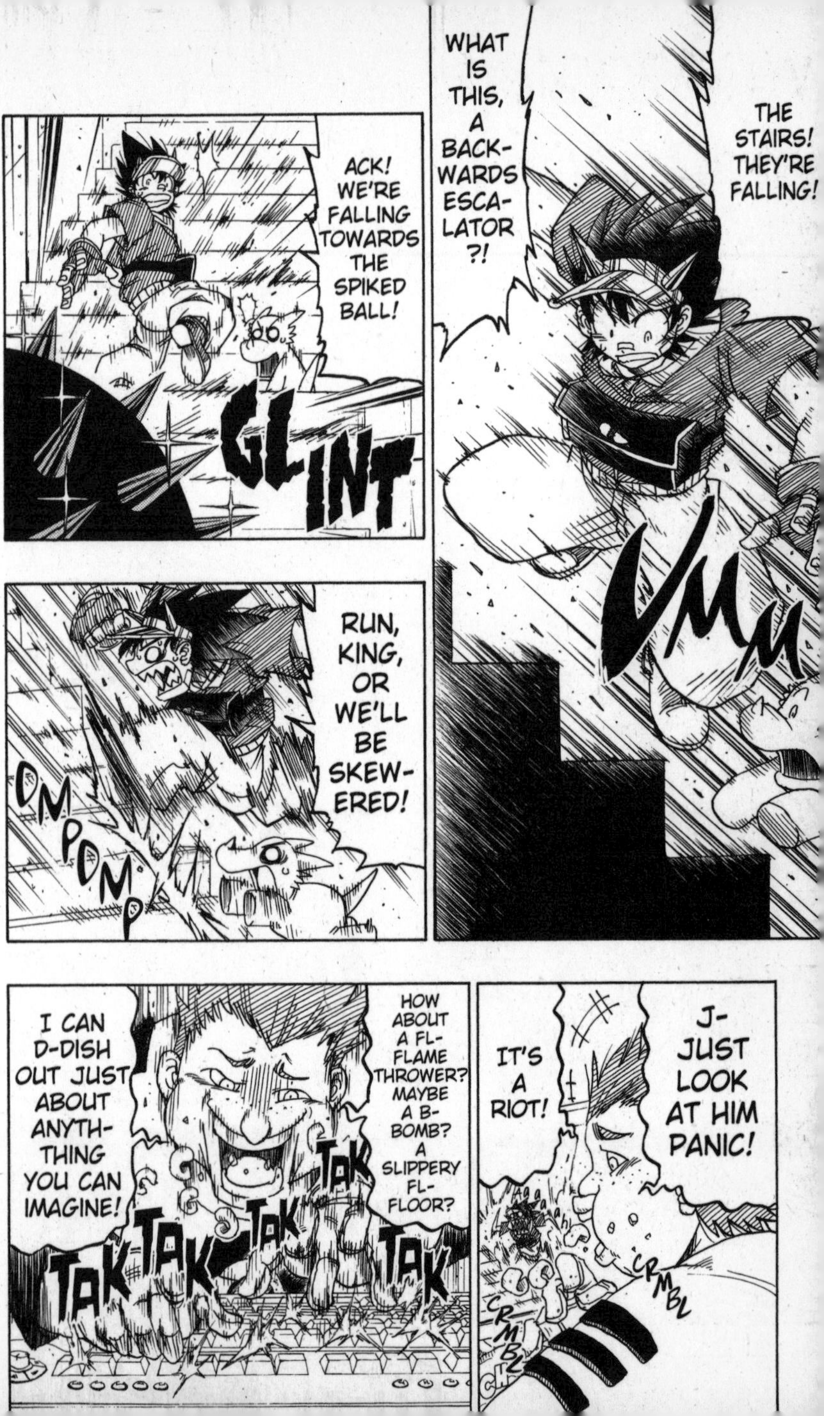
THE STAIRS! THEY'RE FALLING!
WHAT IS THIS, A BACKWARDS ESCALATOR?!
VMM
ACK! WE'RE FALLING TOWARDS THE SPIKED BALL!
GLINT
RUN, KING, OR WE'LL BE SKEWERED!
POMPOMP
J-JUST LOOK AT HIM PANIC!
IT'S A RIOT!
CRMBL
CRMBL
HOW ABOUT A FL-FLAME THROWER? MAYBE A B-BOMB? A SLIPPERY FL-FLOOR?
I CAN D-DISH OUT JUST ABOUT ANYTHING YOU CAN IMAGINE!
TAK TAK TAK TAK TAK

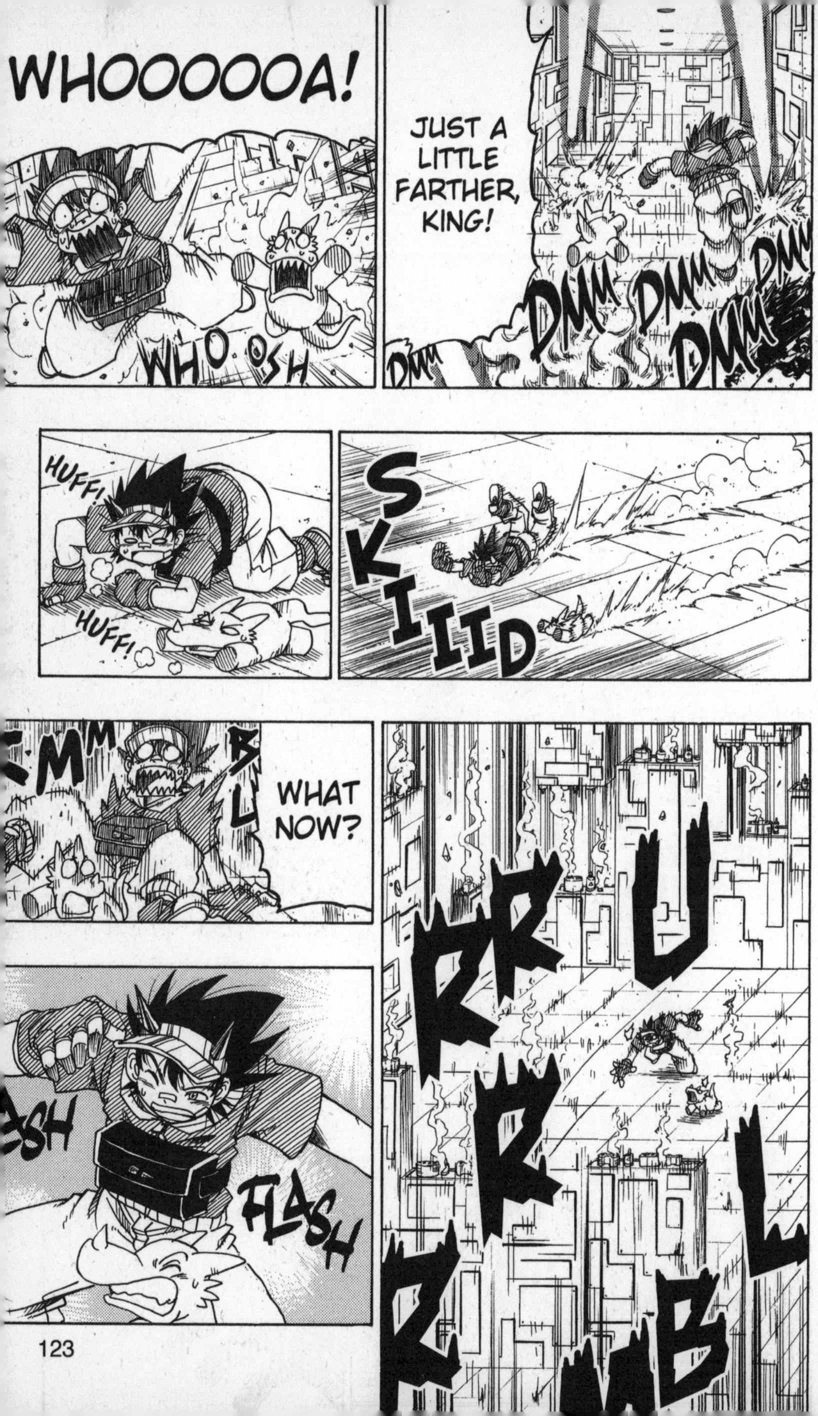
JUST A LITTLE FARTHER, KING!
DMM DMM DMM DMM DMM
WHOOOOOA!
WHOOSH
SKIIID
HUFF!
HUFF!
WHAT NOW?
FLASH

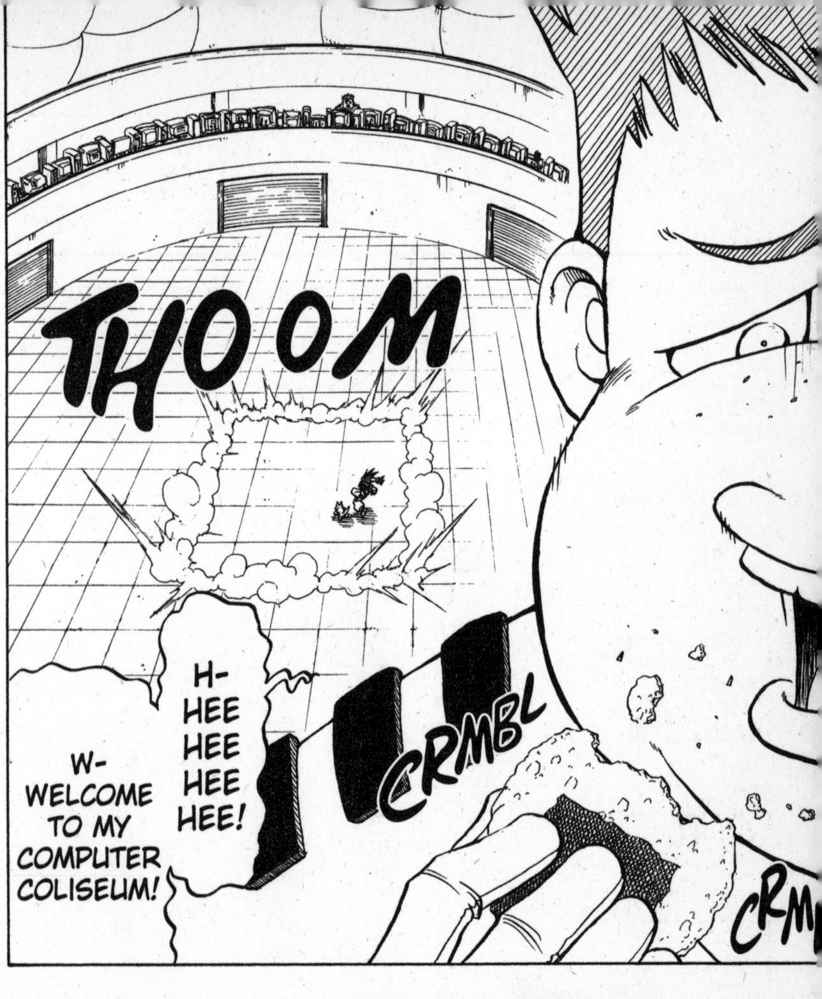
THOOM
H-HEE HEE HEE HEE!
W-WELCOME TO MY COMPUTER COLISEUM!
CRMBL
CRM

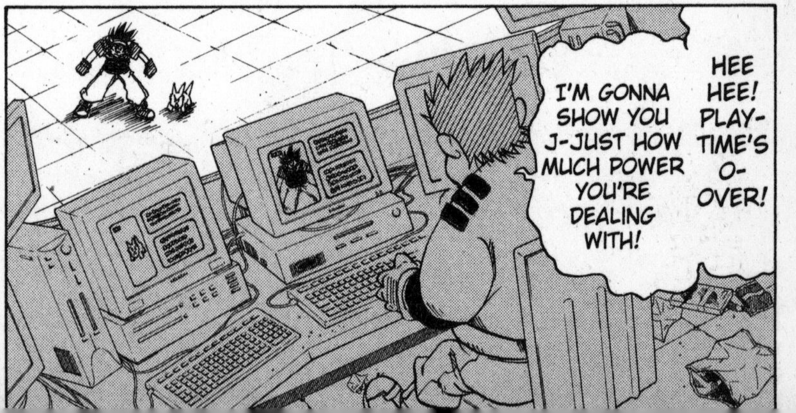
HEE HEE! PLAY-TIME'S O-OVER!
I'M GONNA SHOW YOU J-JUST HOW MUCH POWER YOU'RE DEALING WITH!

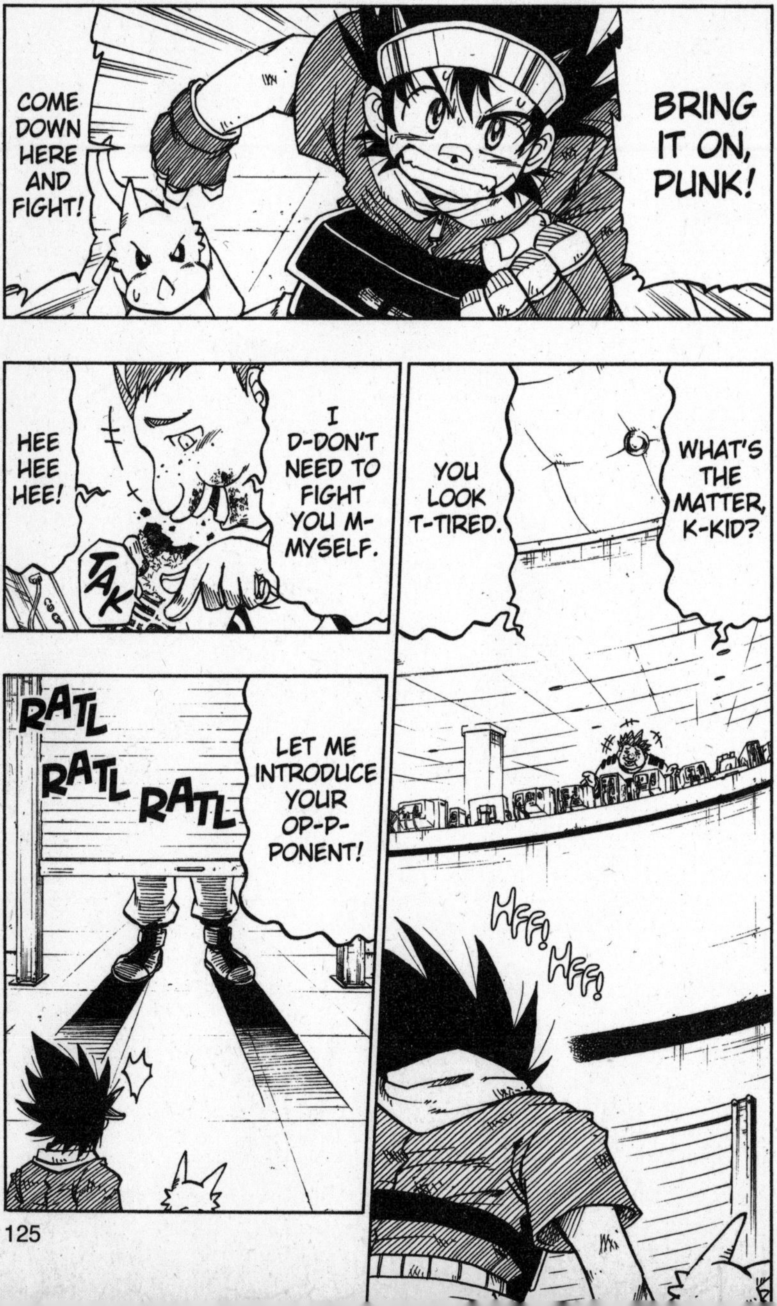
BRING IT ON, PUNK!
COME DOWN HERE AND FIGHT!
WHAT'S THE MATTER, K-KID?
YOU LOOK T-TIRED.
HFF! HFF!
I D-DON'T NEED TO FIGHT YOU M-MYSELF.
HEE HEE HEE!
TAK
RATL RATL RATL
LET ME INTRODUCE YOUR OP-P-PONENT!

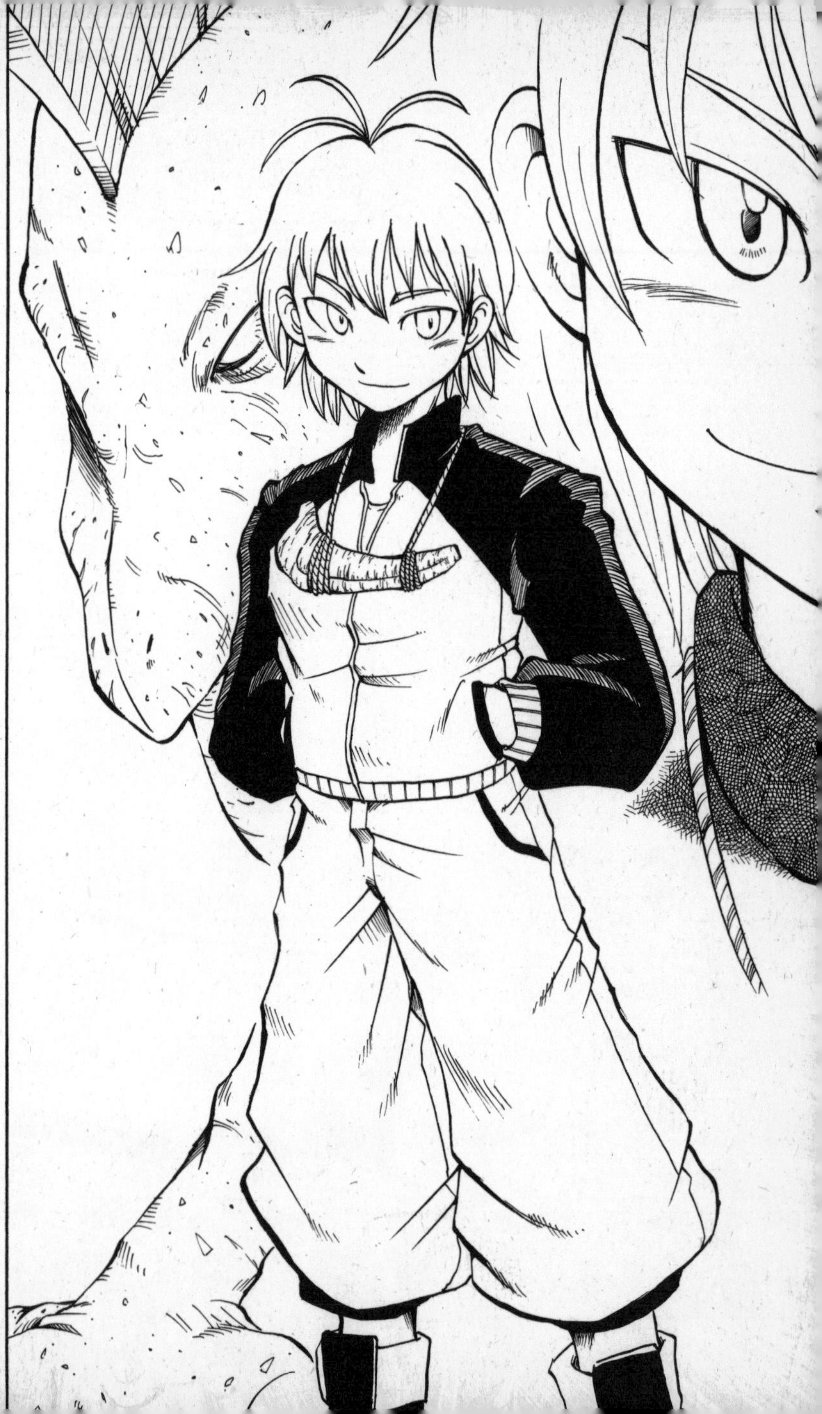

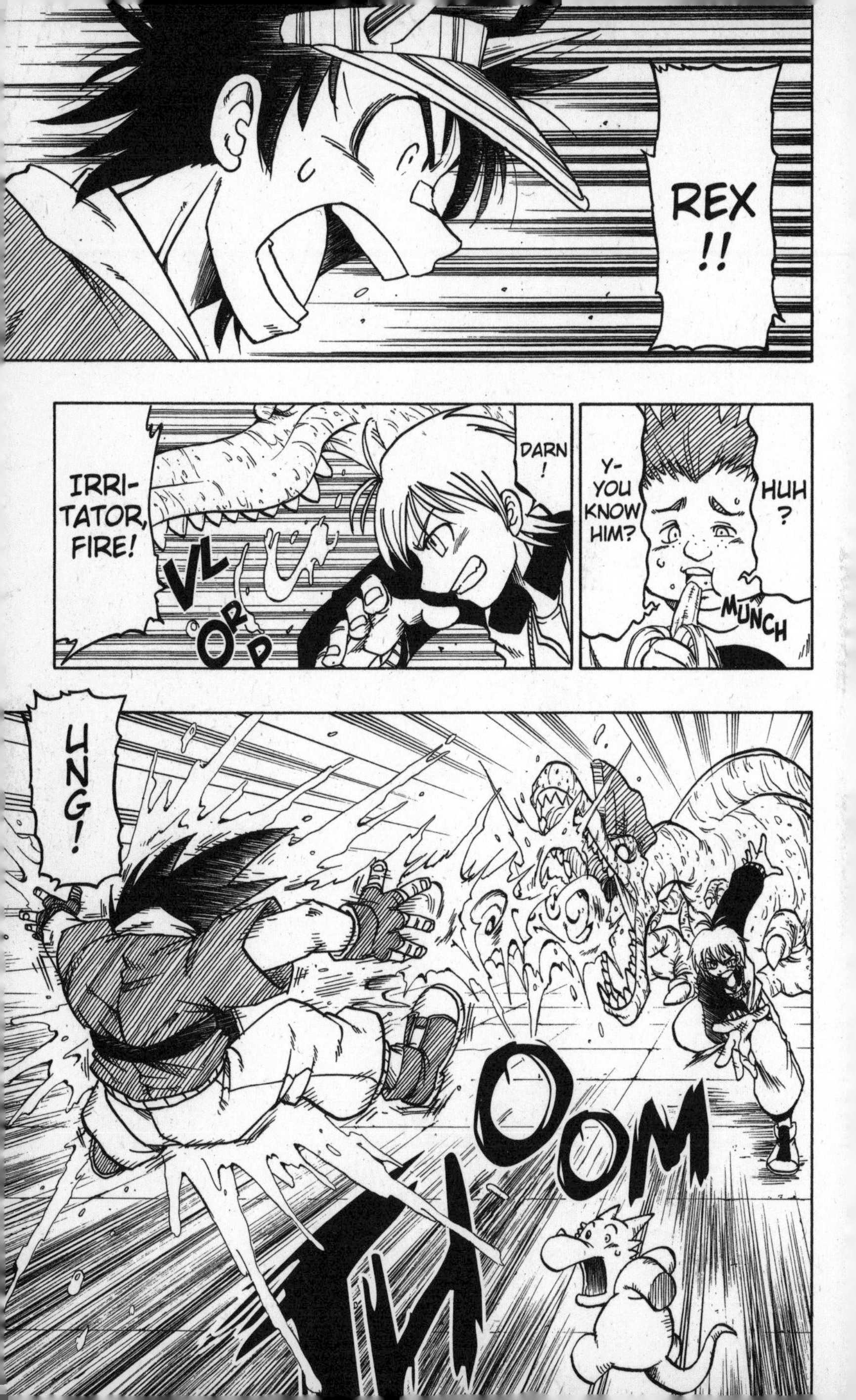
REX !!
HUH ?
Y-YOU KNOW HIM?
MUNCH
DARN !
IRRITATOR, FIRE!
VLORP
UNG!
OOM

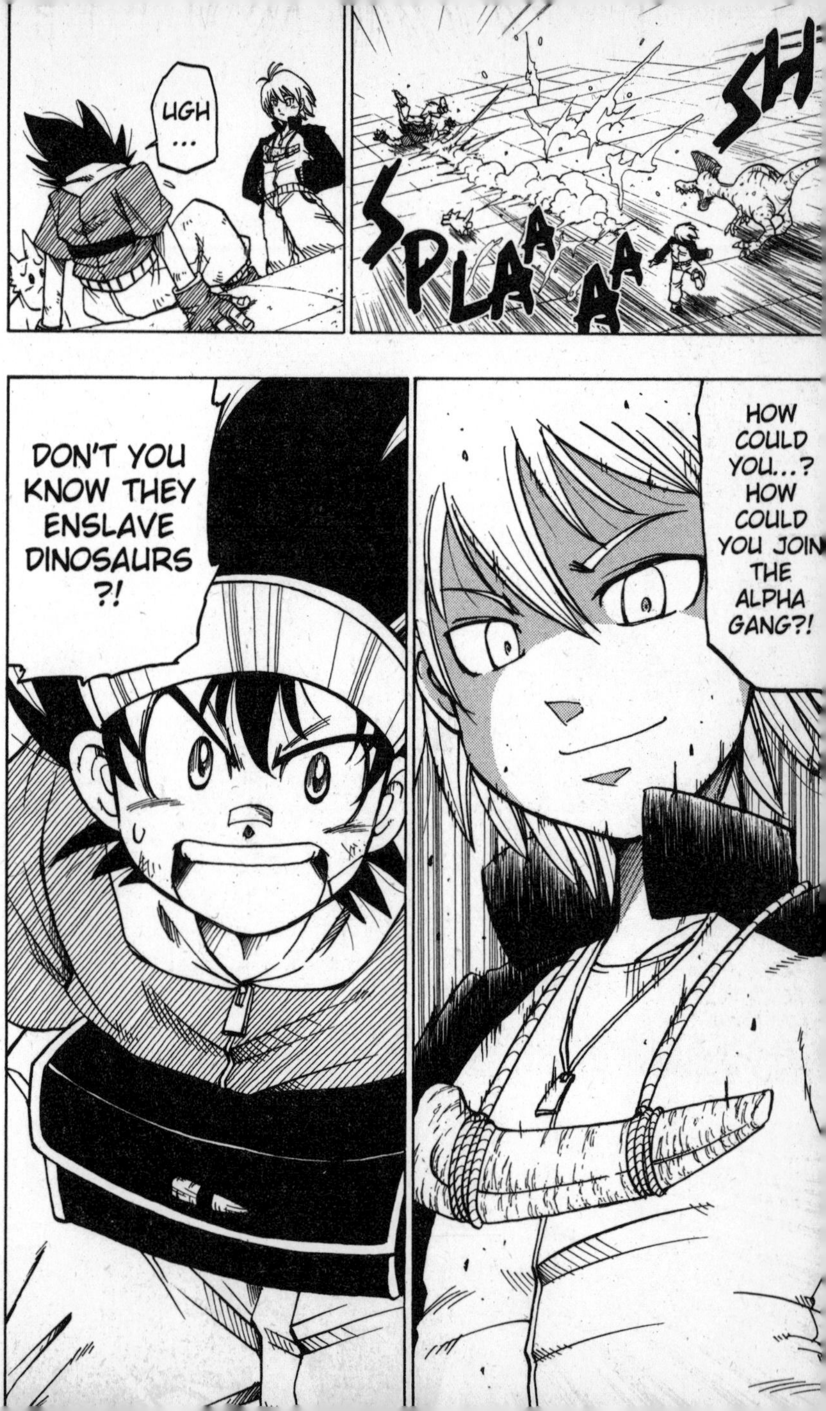
SH
SPLAAAA
UGH ...
HOW COULD YOU...? HOW COULD YOU JOIN THE ALPHA GANG?!
DON'T YOU KNOW THEY ENSLAVE DINOSAURS?!

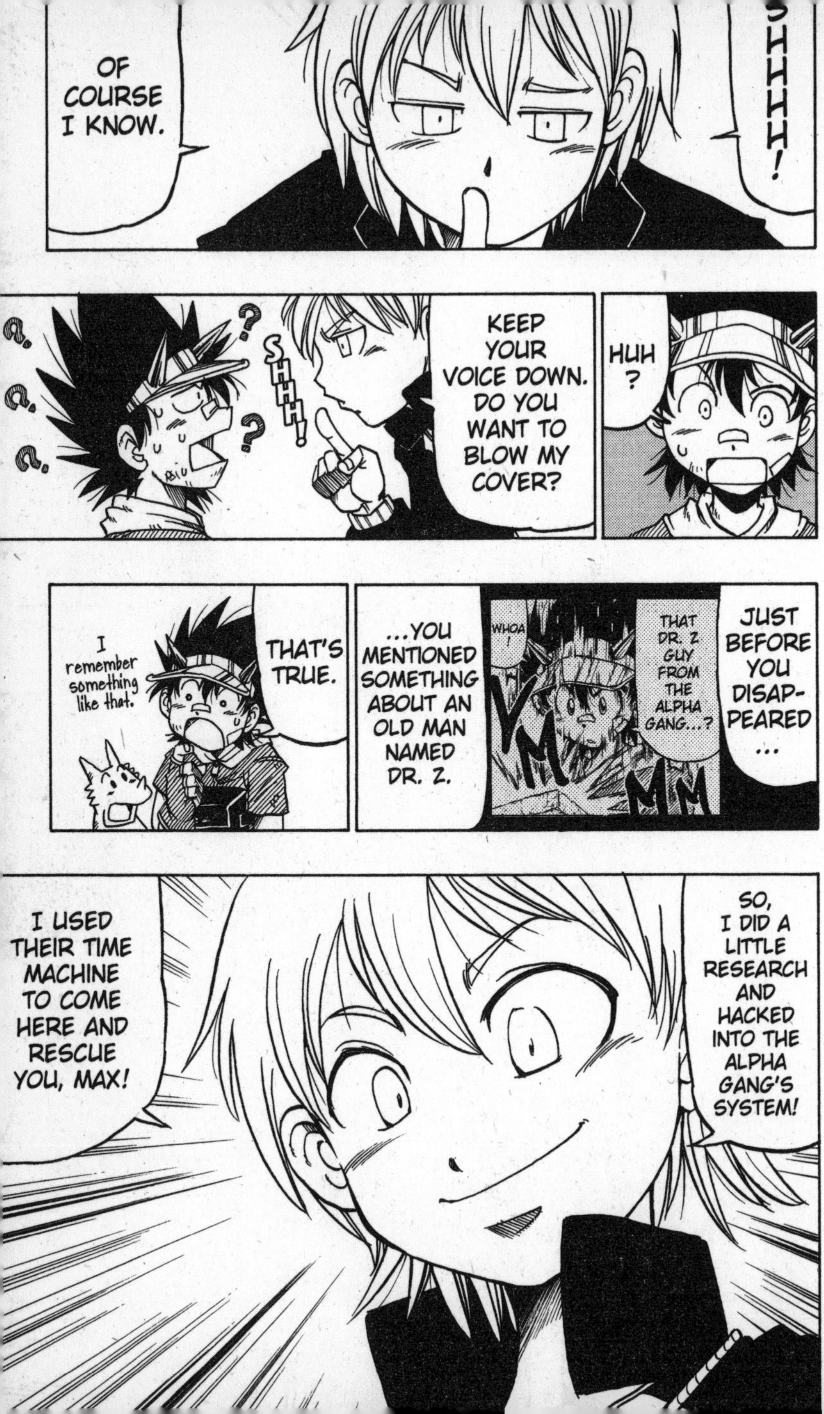
SHHHH!
OF COURSE I KNOW.
HUH?
KEEP YOUR VOICE DOWN. DO YOU WANT TO BLOW MY COVER?
SHHH!
JUST BEFORE YOU DISAP-PEARED...
THAT DR. Z GUY FROM THE ALPHA GANG...?
WHOA!
...YOU MENTIONED SOMETHING ABOUT AN OLD MAN NAMED DR. Z.
THAT'S TRUE.
I remember something like that.
SO, I DID A LITTLE RESEARCH AND HACKED INTO THE ALPHA GANG'S SYSTEM!
I USED THEIR TIME MACHINE TO COME HERE AND RESCUE YOU, MAX!

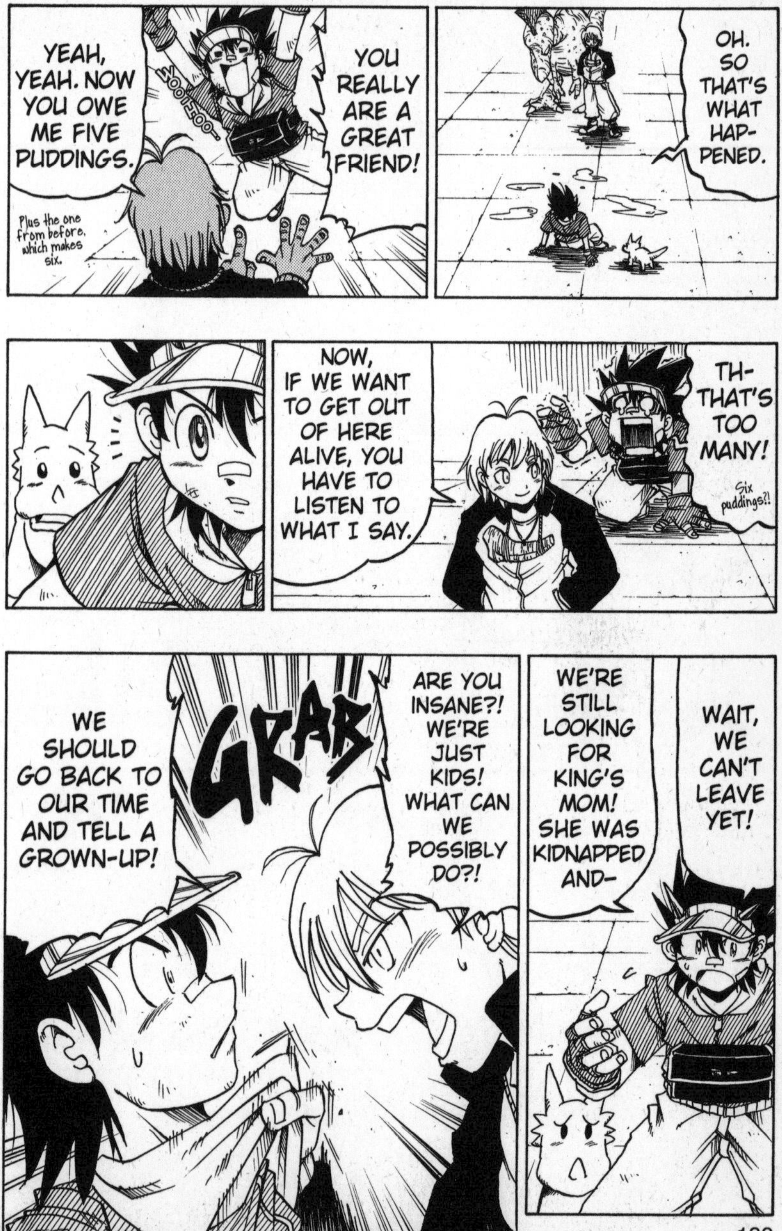
OH. SO THAT'S WHAT HAP-PENED.
YOU REALLY ARE A GREAT FRIEND!
YEAH, YEAH. NOW YOU OWE ME FIVE PUDDINGS.
Plus the one from before, which makes six.
TH-THAT'S TOO MANY!
Six puddings?!
NOW, IF WE WANT TO GET OUT OF HERE ALIVE, YOU HAVE TO LISTEN TO WHAT I SAY.
WAIT, WE CAN'T LEAVE YET!
WE'RE STILL LOOKING FOR KING'S MOM! SHE WAS KIDNAPPED AND-
ARE YOU INSANE?! WE'RE JUST KIDS! WHAT CAN WE POSSIBLY DO?!
GRAB
WE SHOULD GO BACK TO OUR TIME AND TELL A GROWN-UP!

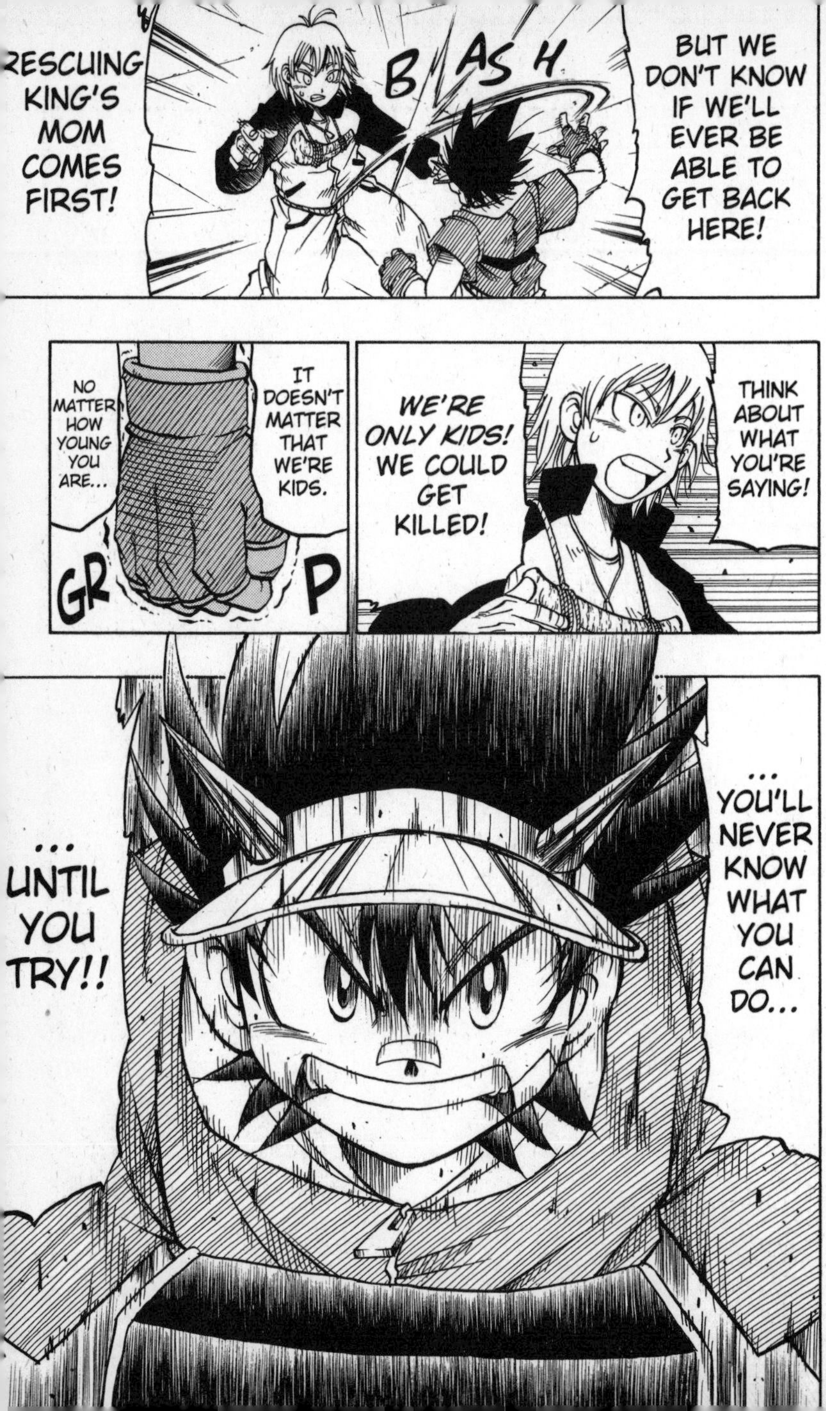
BUT WE DON'T KNOW IF WE'LL EVER BE ABLE TO GET BACK HERE!
BASH
RESCUING KING'S MOM COMES FIRST!
THINK ABOUT WHAT YOU'RE SAYING!
WE'RE ONLY KIDS! WE COULD GET KILLED!
IT DOESN'T MATTER THAT WE'RE KIDS.
NO MATTER HOW YOUNG YOU ARE...
GR P
...YOU'LL NEVER KNOW WHAT YOU CAN DO...
...UNTIL YOU TRY!!

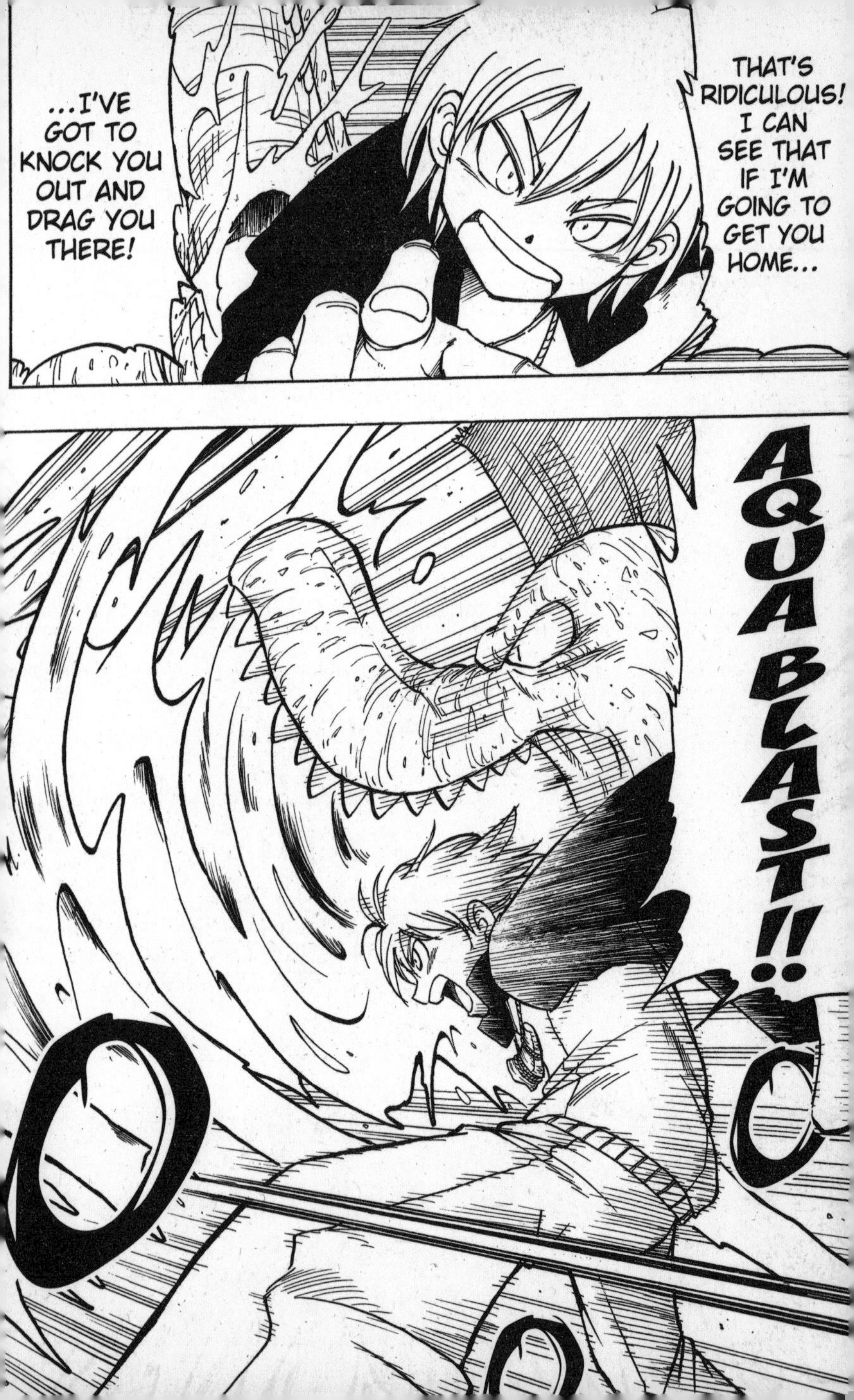
THAT'S RIDICULOUS! I CAN SEE THAT IF I'M GOING TO GET YOU HOME...
...I'VE GOT TO KNOCK YOU OUT AND DRAG YOU THERE!
AQUA BLAST!!

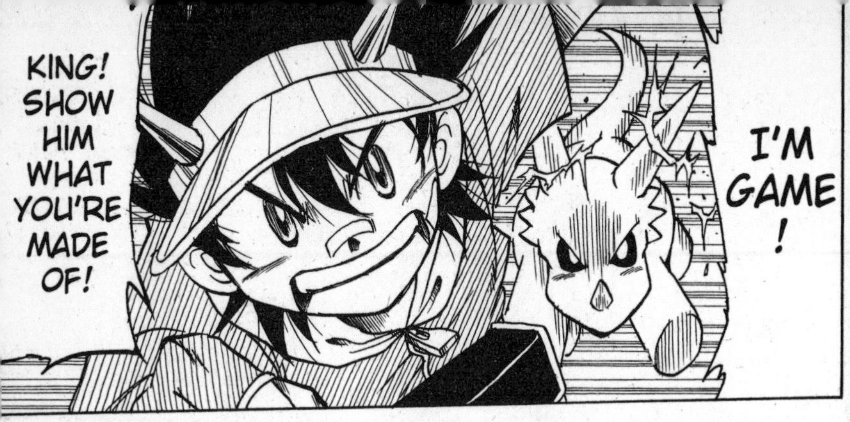
KING! SHOW HIM WHAT YOU'RE MADE OF!
I'M GAME!

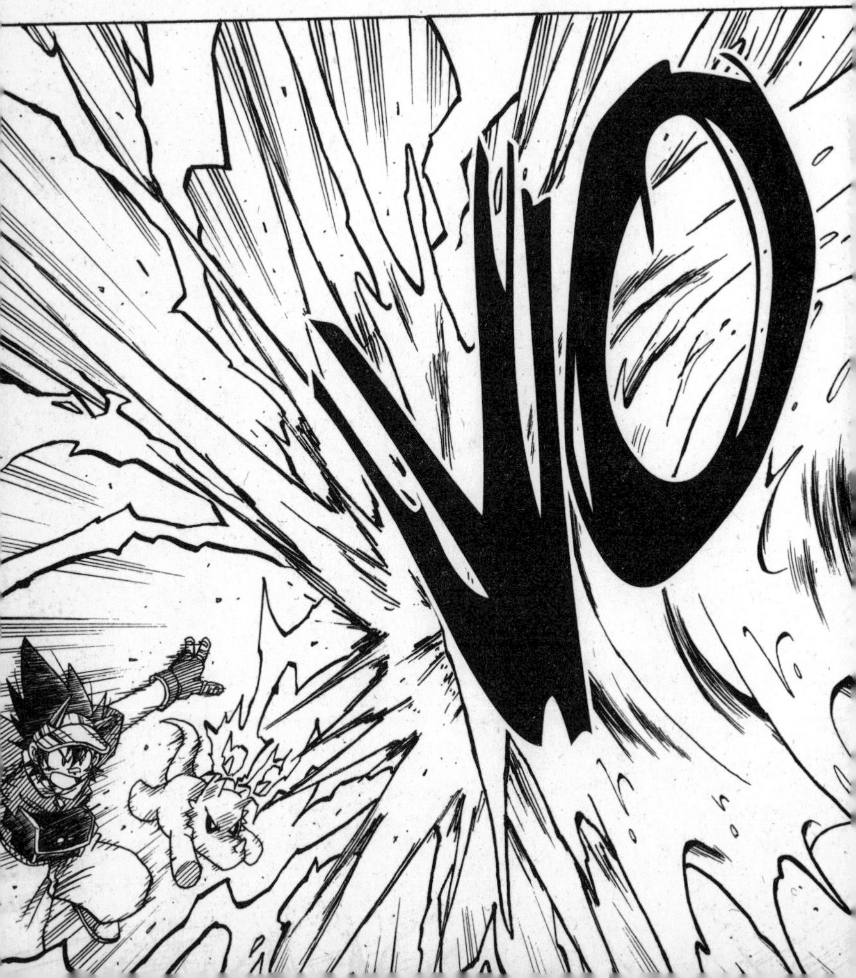

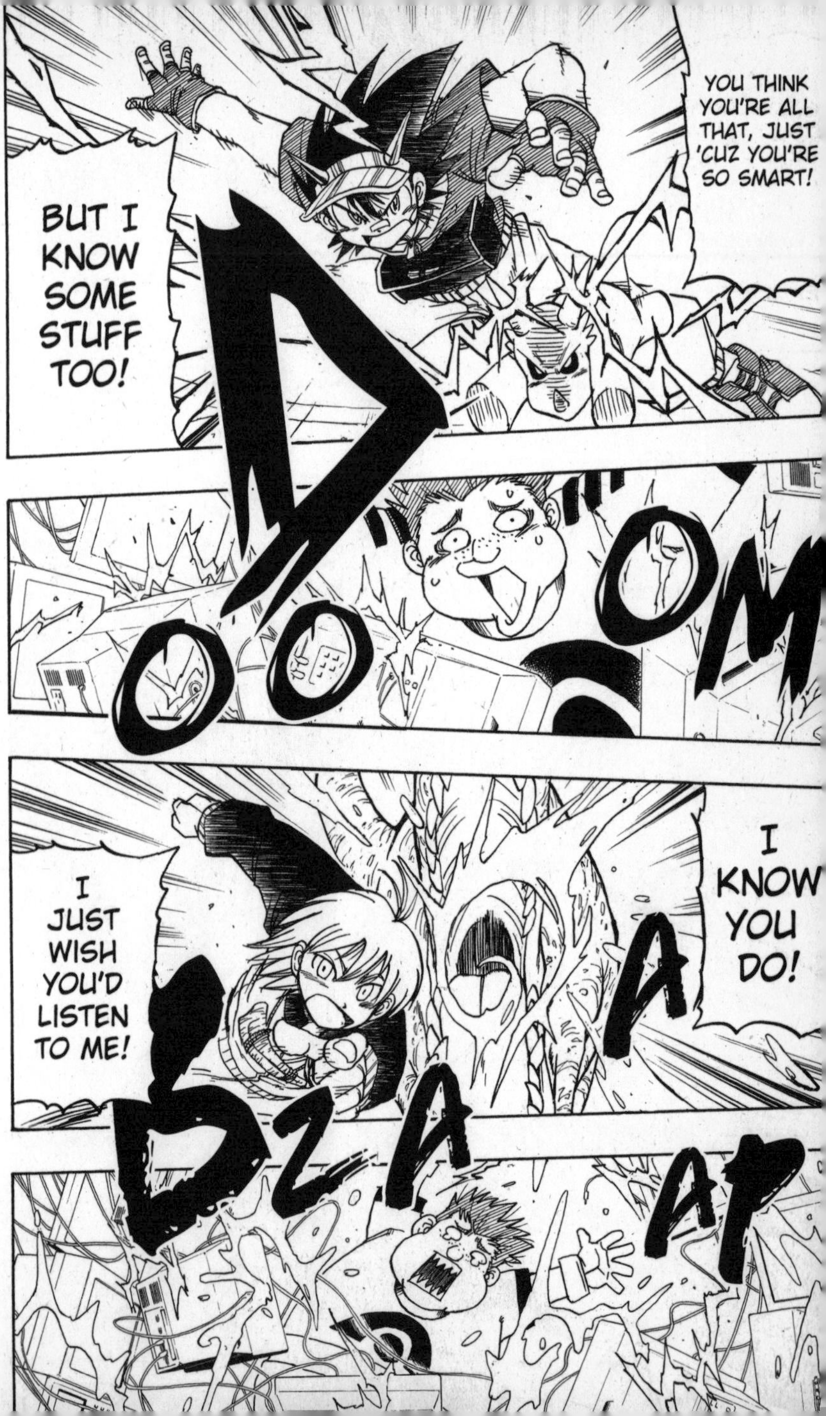
YOU THINK YOU'RE ALL THAT, JUST 'CUZ YOU'RE SO SMART!
BUT I KNOW SOME STUFF TOO!
DOOOOM
I KNOW YOU DO!
I JUST WISH YOU'D LISTEN TO ME!
DZAAAP

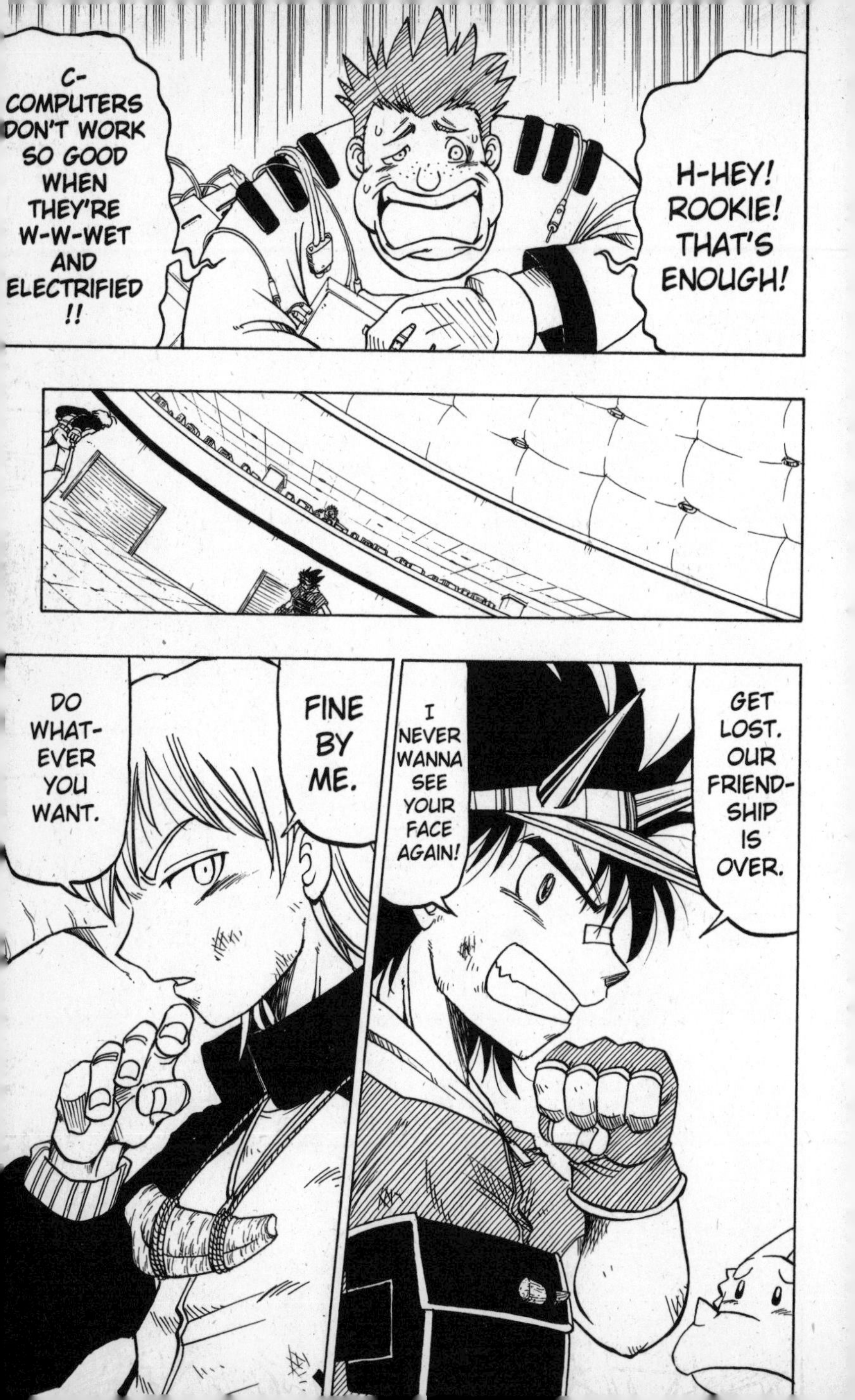
H-HEY! ROOKIE! THAT'S ENOUGH!
C-COMPUTERS DON'T WORK SO GOOD WHEN THEY'RE W-W-WET AND ELECTRIFIED !!
GET LOST. OUR FRIEND-SHIP IS OVER.
I NEVER WANNA SEE YOUR FACE AGAIN!
FINE BY ME.
DO WHAT-EVER YOU WANT.

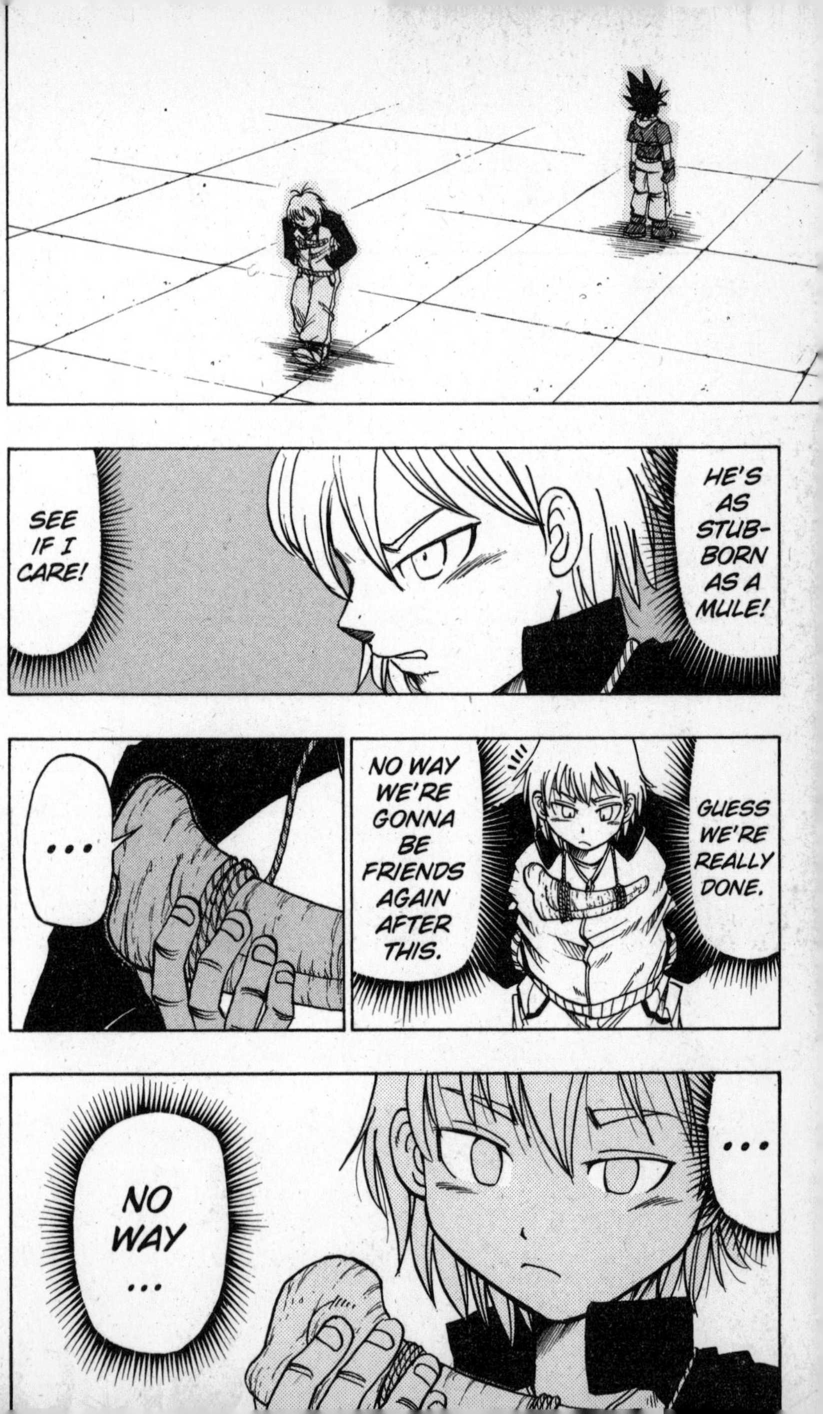
HE'S AS STUB-BORN AS A MULE!
SEE IF I CARE!
GUESS WE'RE REALLY DONE.
NO WAY WE'RE GONNA BE FRIENDS AGAIN AFTER THIS.
...
...
NO WAY ...

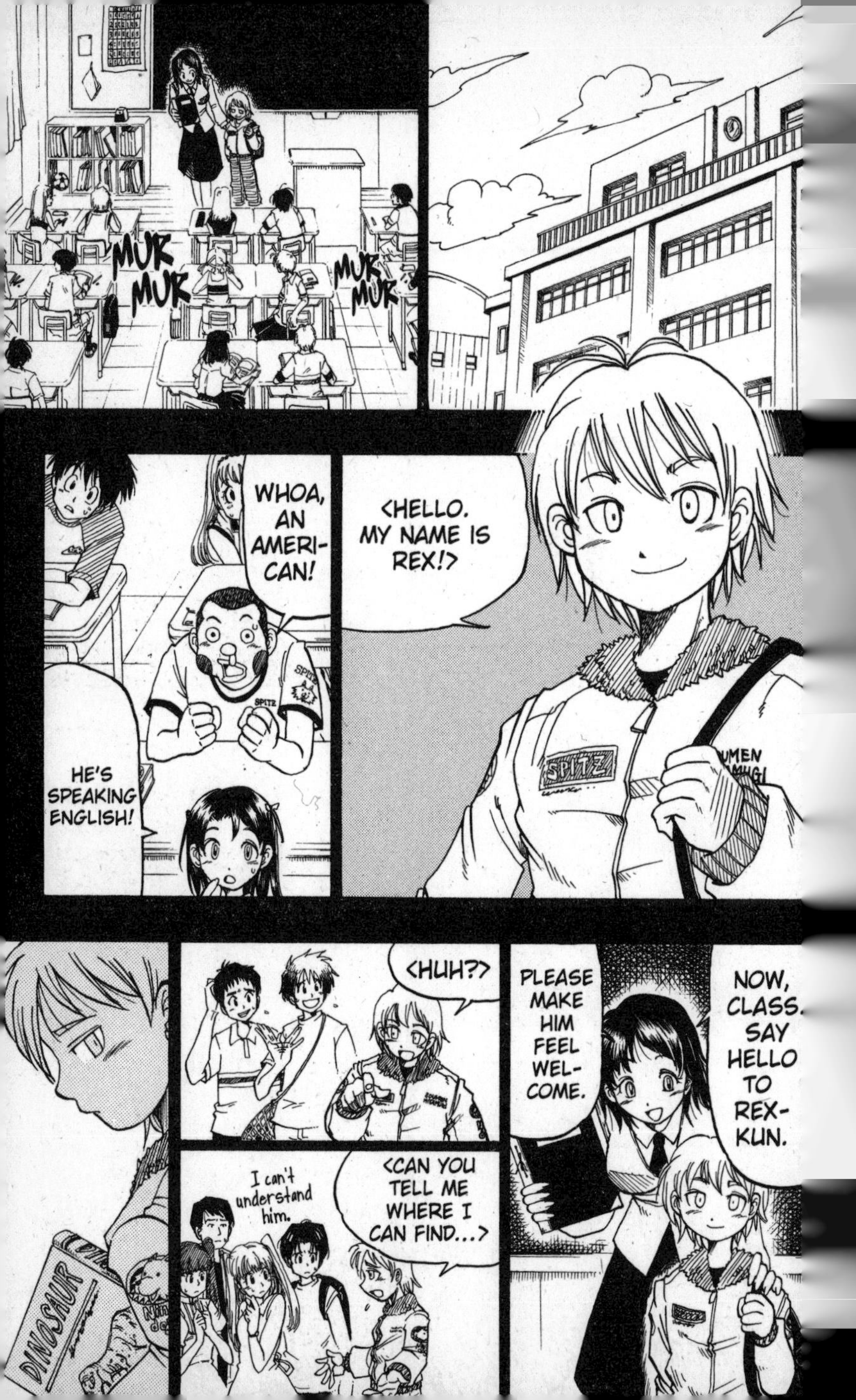
MUR MUR
MUR MUR
<HELLO. MY NAME IS REX!>
WHOA, AN AMERI-CAN!
HE'S SPEAKING ENGLISH!
NOW, CLASS. SAY HELLO TO REX-KUN.
PLEASE MAKE HIM FEEL WEL-COME.
<HUH?>
<CAN YOU TELL ME WHERE I CAN FIND...>
I can't understand him.
DINOSAUR

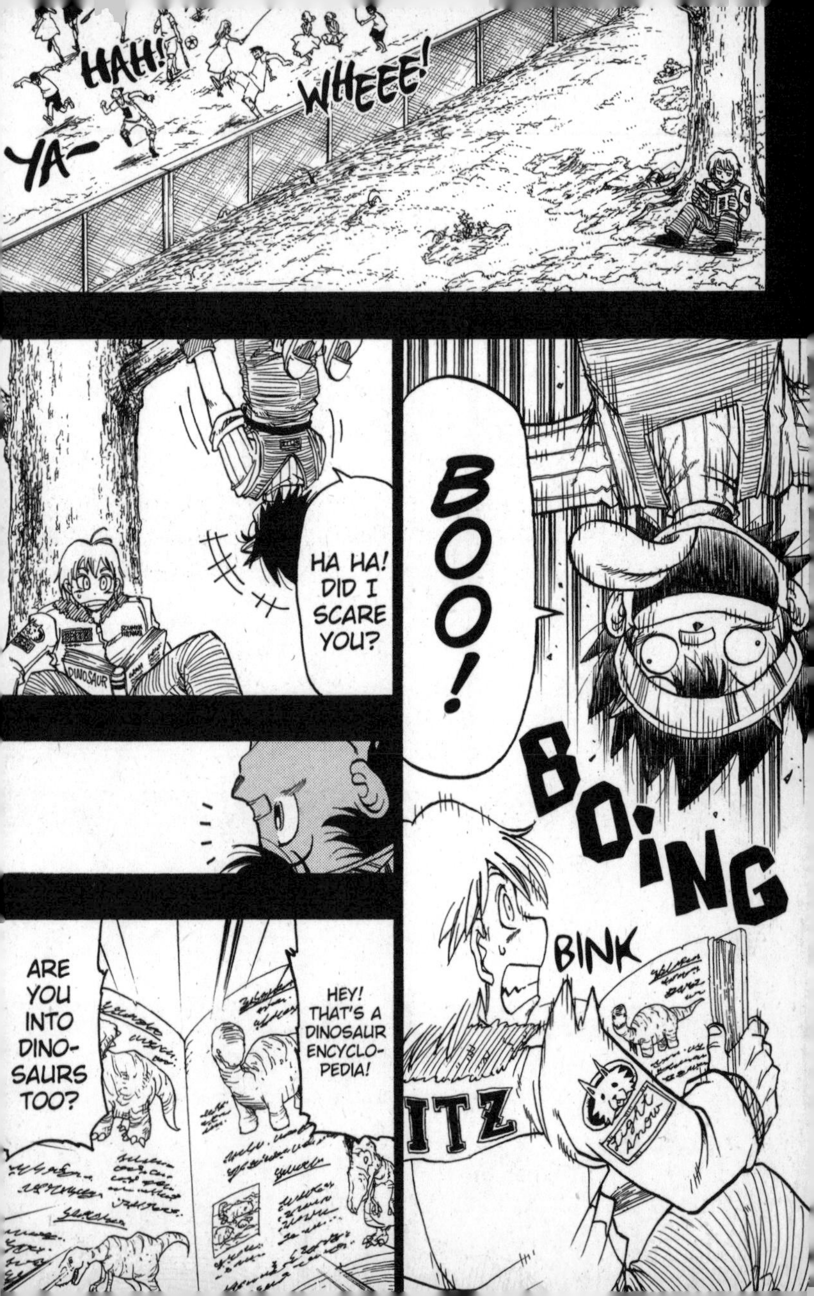

WHEEE!
HAH!
YA-
BOO!
BOING
BINK
HA HA! DID I SCARE YOU?
DINOSAUR
HEY! THAT'S A DINOSAUR ENCYCLO-PEDIA!
ARE YOU INTO DINO-SAURS TOO?

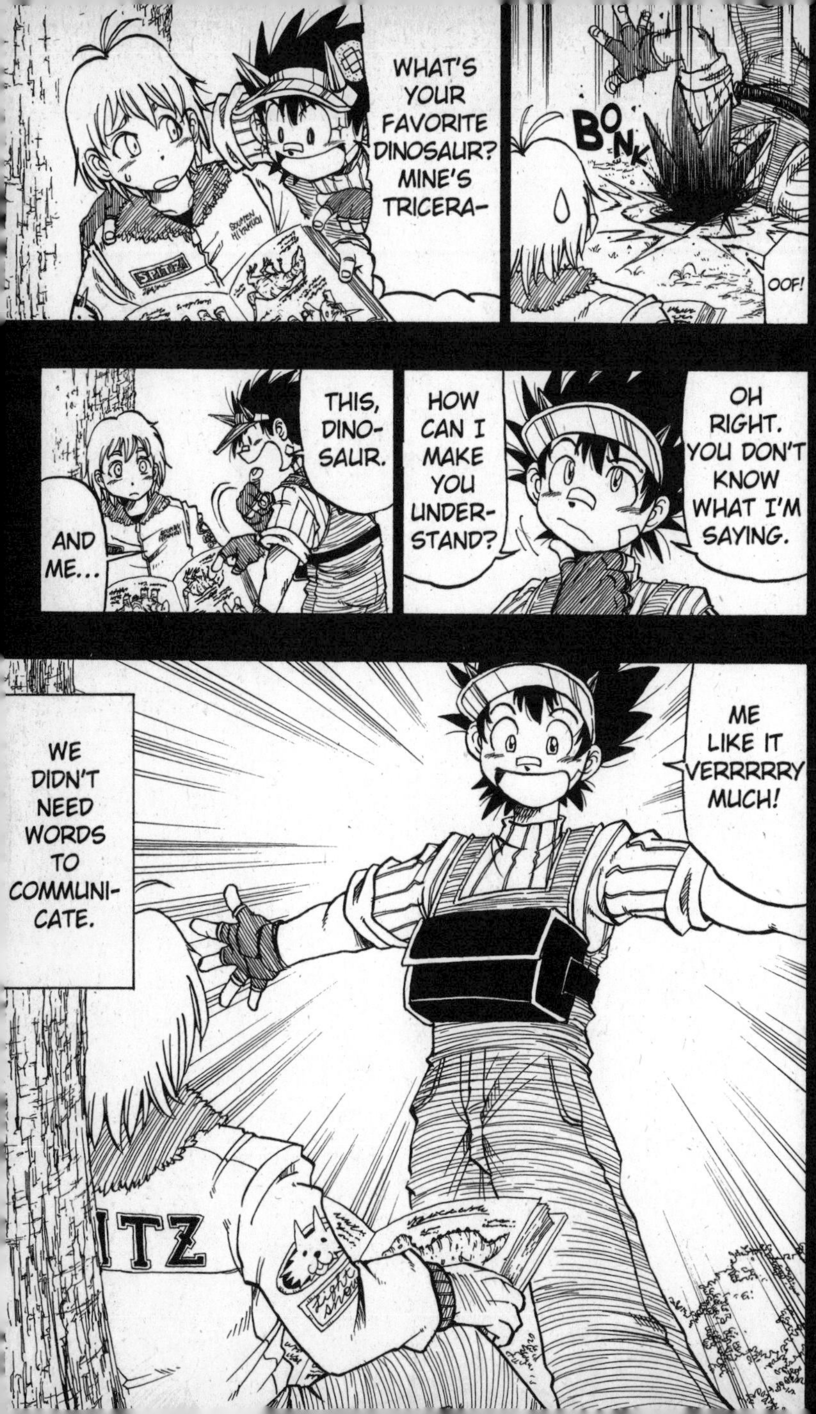
BONK
OOF!
WHAT'S YOUR FAVORITE DINOSAUR? MINE'S TRICERA-
OH RIGHT. YOU DON'T KNOW WHAT I'M SAYING.
HOW CAN I MAKE YOU UNDERSTAND?
THIS, DINOSAUR.
AND ME...
ME LIKE IT VERRRRRY MUCH!
WE DIDN'T NEED WORDS TO COMMUNICATE.

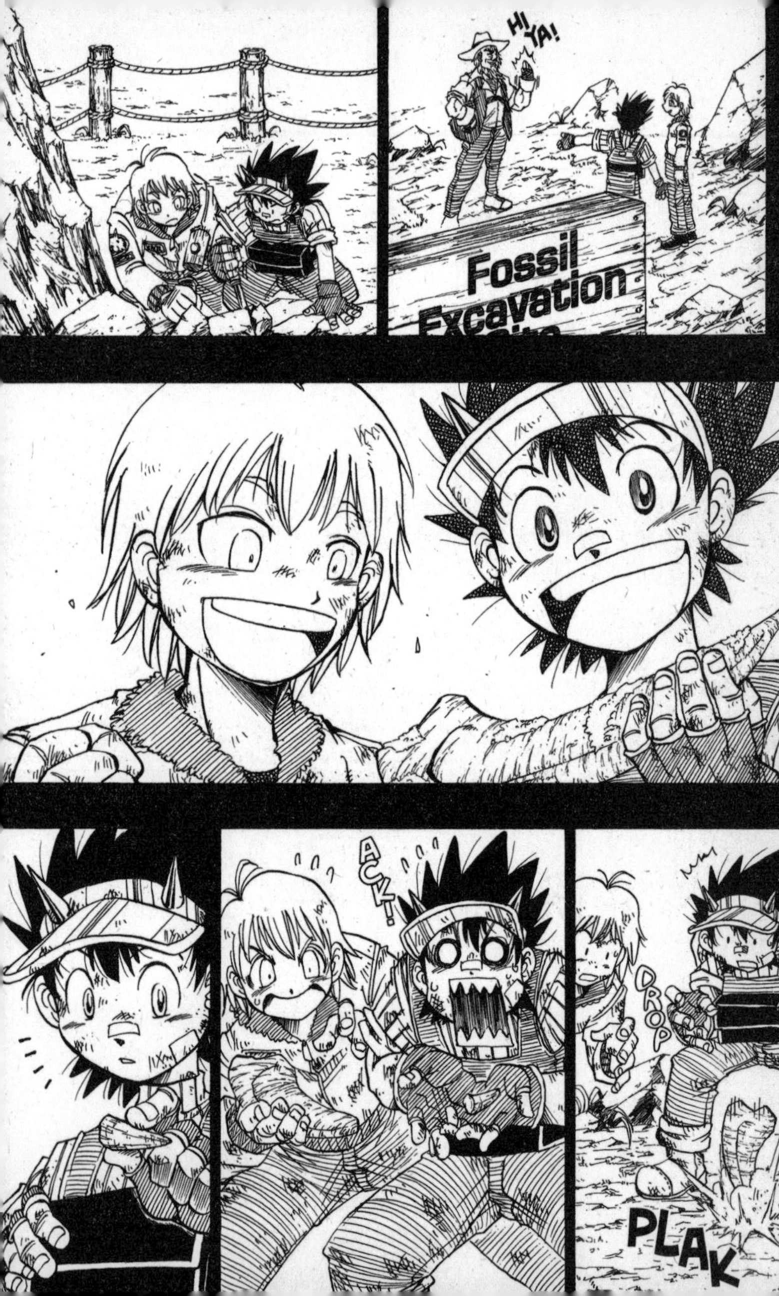
HI YA!
Fossil Excavation
DROP
PLAK
ACK!

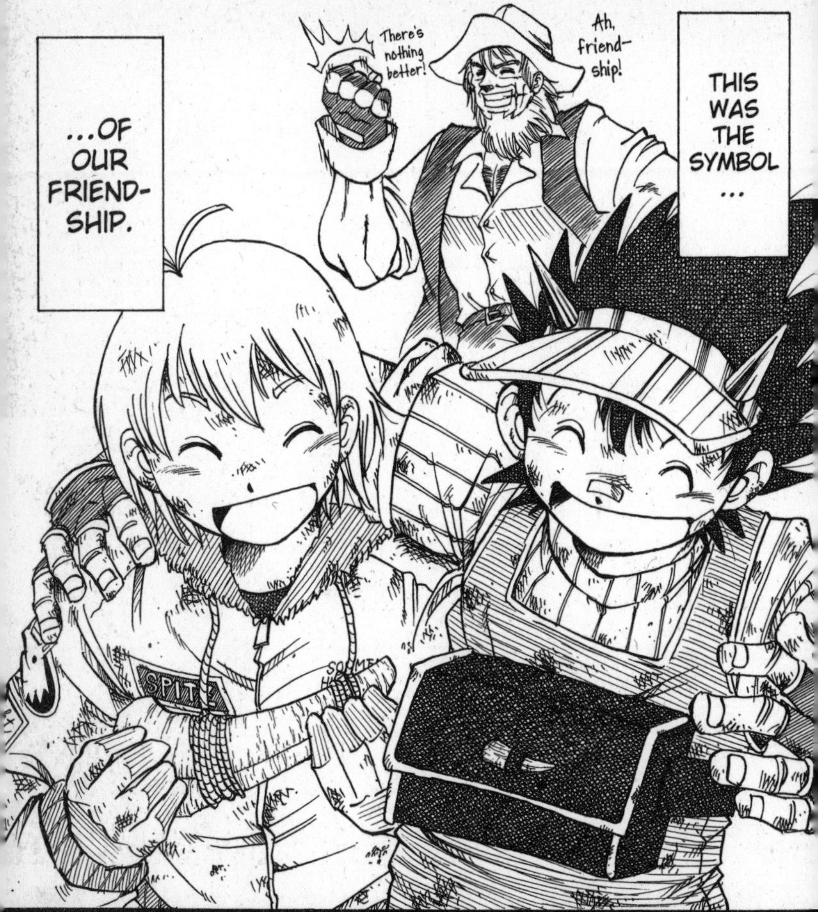
THIS WAS THE SYMBOL...
Ah, friend-ship!
There's nothing better!
...OF OUR FRIEND-SHIP.
SPITE

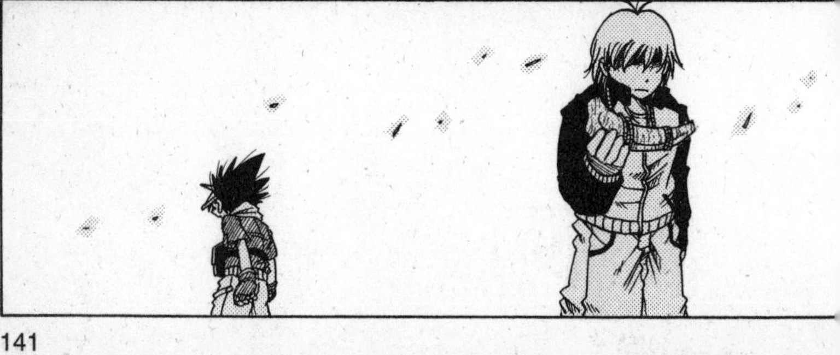

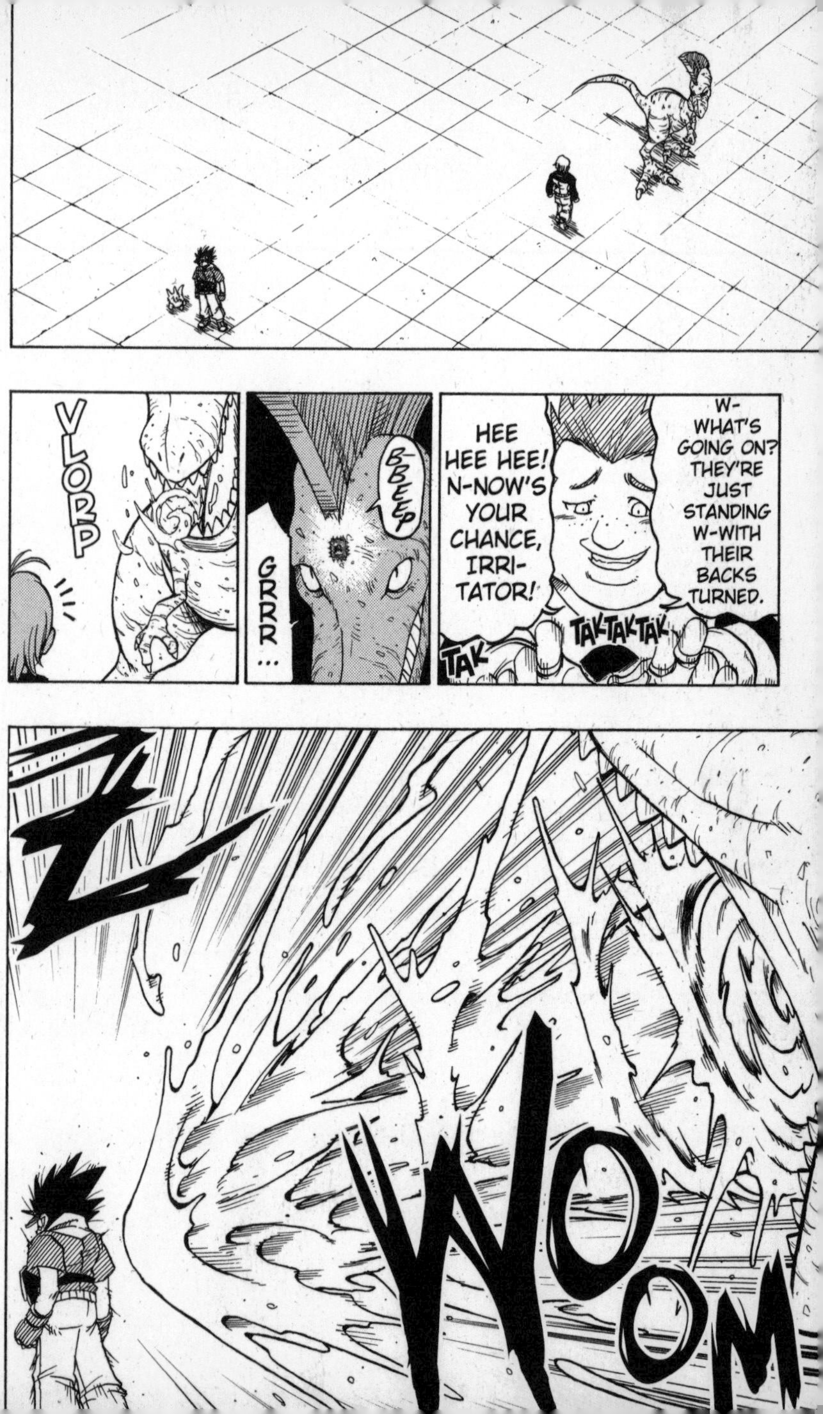
W- WHAT'S GOING ON? THEY'RE JUST STANDING W-WITH THEIR BACKS TURNED.
HEE HEE HEE! N-NOW'S YOUR CHANCE, IRRI-TATOR!
TAKTAKTAK
TAK
B-BBEEP
GRRR...
VLORP
WOOM

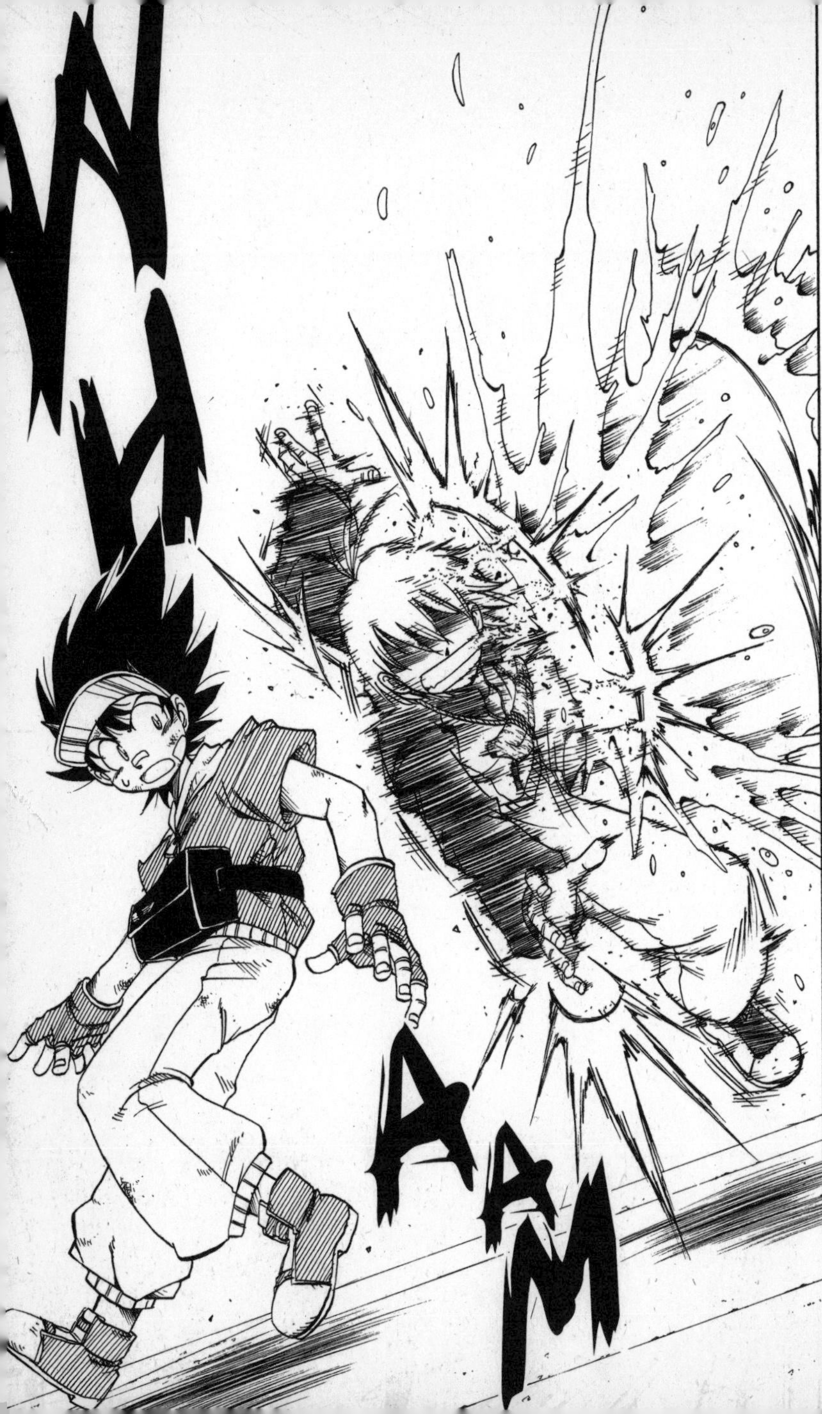
WHAAM

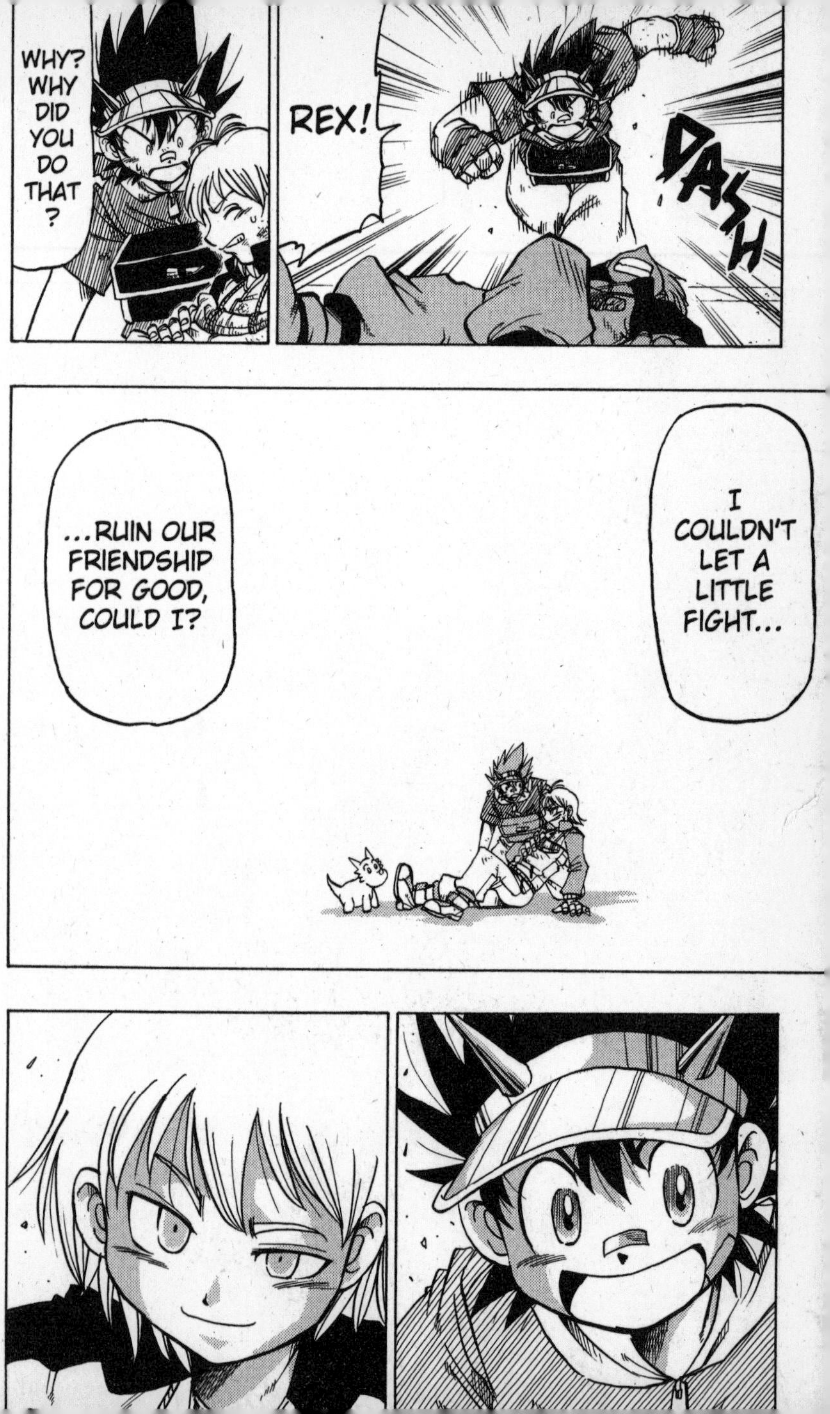
DASH
REX!
WHY? WHY DID YOU DO THAT?
I COULDN'T LET A LITTLE FIGHT...
...RUIN OUR FRIENDSHIP FOR GOOD, COULD I?

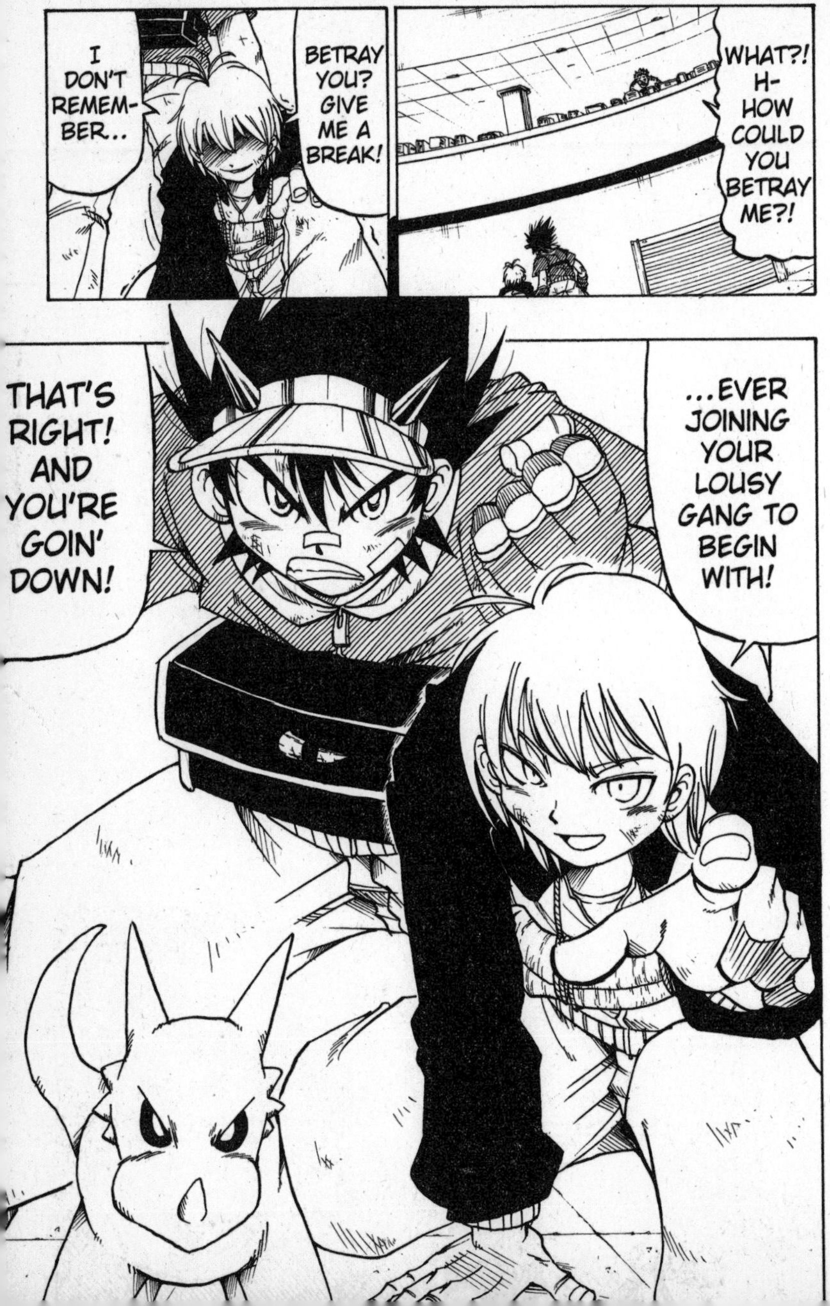
WHAT?! H-HOW COULD YOU BETRAY ME?!
BETRAY YOU? GIVE ME A BREAK!
I DON'T REMEMBER...
...EVER JOINING YOUR LOUSY GANG TO BEGIN WITH!
THAT'S RIGHT! AND YOU'RE GOIN' DOWN!

DIG IT!

Uncover facts about dinosaurs, their super moves and their trading card stats!

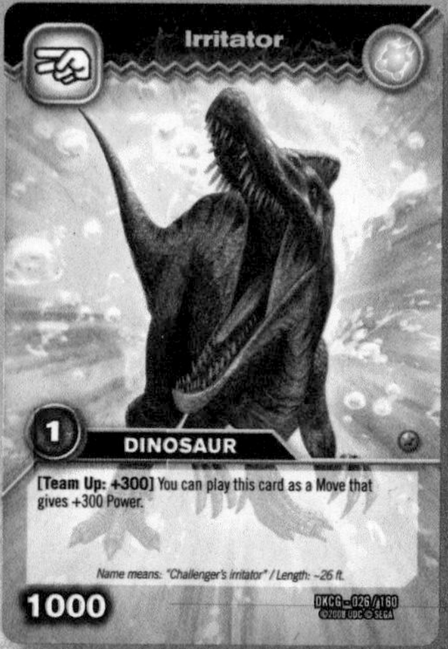
Irritator
1
DINOSAUR
[Team Up: +300] You can play this card as a Move that gives +300 Power.
Name means: "Challenger's irritator" / Length: ~26 ft.
1000
DKCG-026/160
©2008 UDC © SEGA

IRRITATOR

Irritator means "Challenger's irritator"
Length: approx. 26 ft.
Lived in: Cretaceous Period
Discovered in: Brazil
The Irritator was related to the Spinosaurus, and it had a large crest on its head.
Card Rarity: Gold Rare
This **Water** Dinosaur is doubly deadly—you can use it like a regular Dinosaur card or play it as a Move card to help one of your other Dinosaurs.

SPIKE ARROWS

Spike Arrows isn't mentioned in this chapter, but this Super Move does show up later in the book!
Card Rarity: Common
Dinosaurs like Stegosaurus and Ankylosaurus were covered in sharp spikes for defense. With this Super Move, they can shoot them out in a fierce attack! Spike Arrows gives a +1000 power boost, but only for an **Earth** Dinosaur with the **Paper** icon.

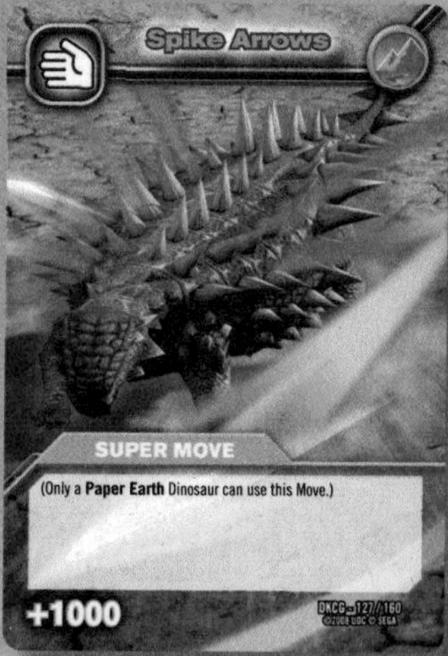
Spike Arrows
SUPER MOVE
(Only a Paper Earth Dinosaur can use this Move.)
+1000
DKCG-127/160
©2008 UDC © SEGA

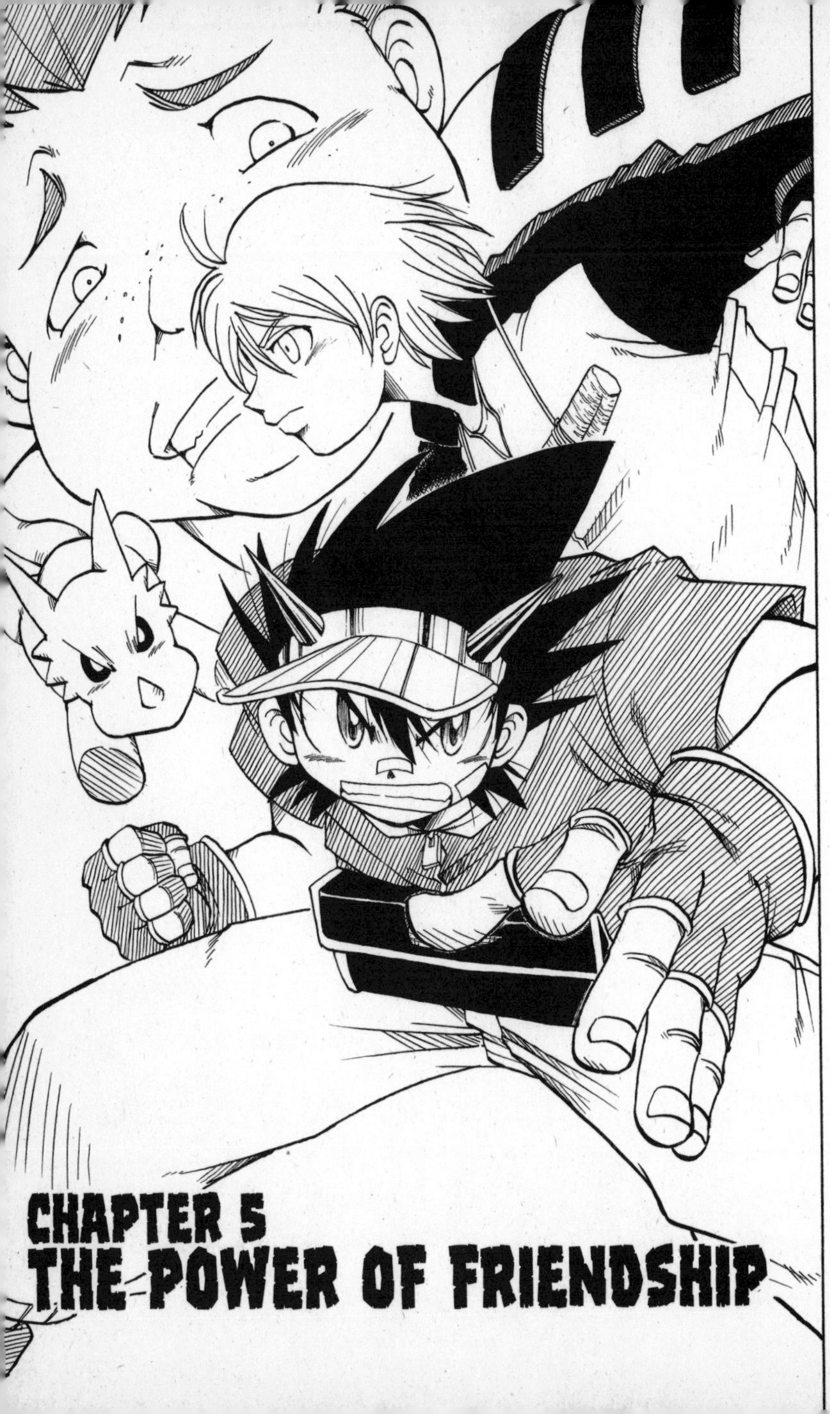
CHAPTER 5
THE POWER OF FRIENDSHIP

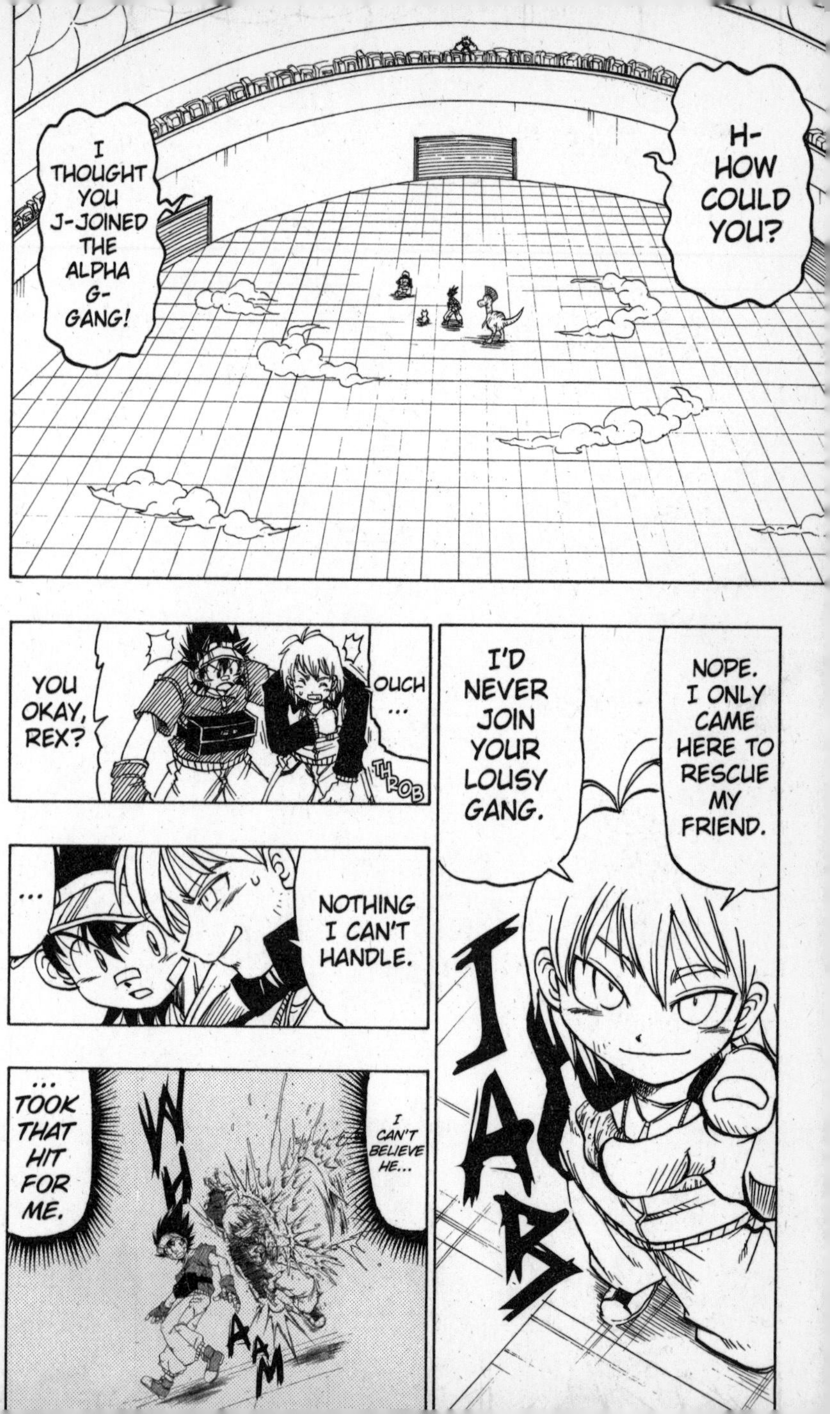
H-HOW COULD YOU?
I THOUGHT YOU J-JOINED THE ALPHA G-GANG!
NOPE. I ONLY CAME HERE TO RESCUE MY FRIEND.
I'D NEVER JOIN YOUR LOUSY GANG.
JAB
OUCH...
THROB
YOU OKAY, REX?
NOTHING I CAN'T HANDLE.
...
I CAN'T BELIEVE HE...
...TOOK THAT HIT FOR ME.
WHAAM

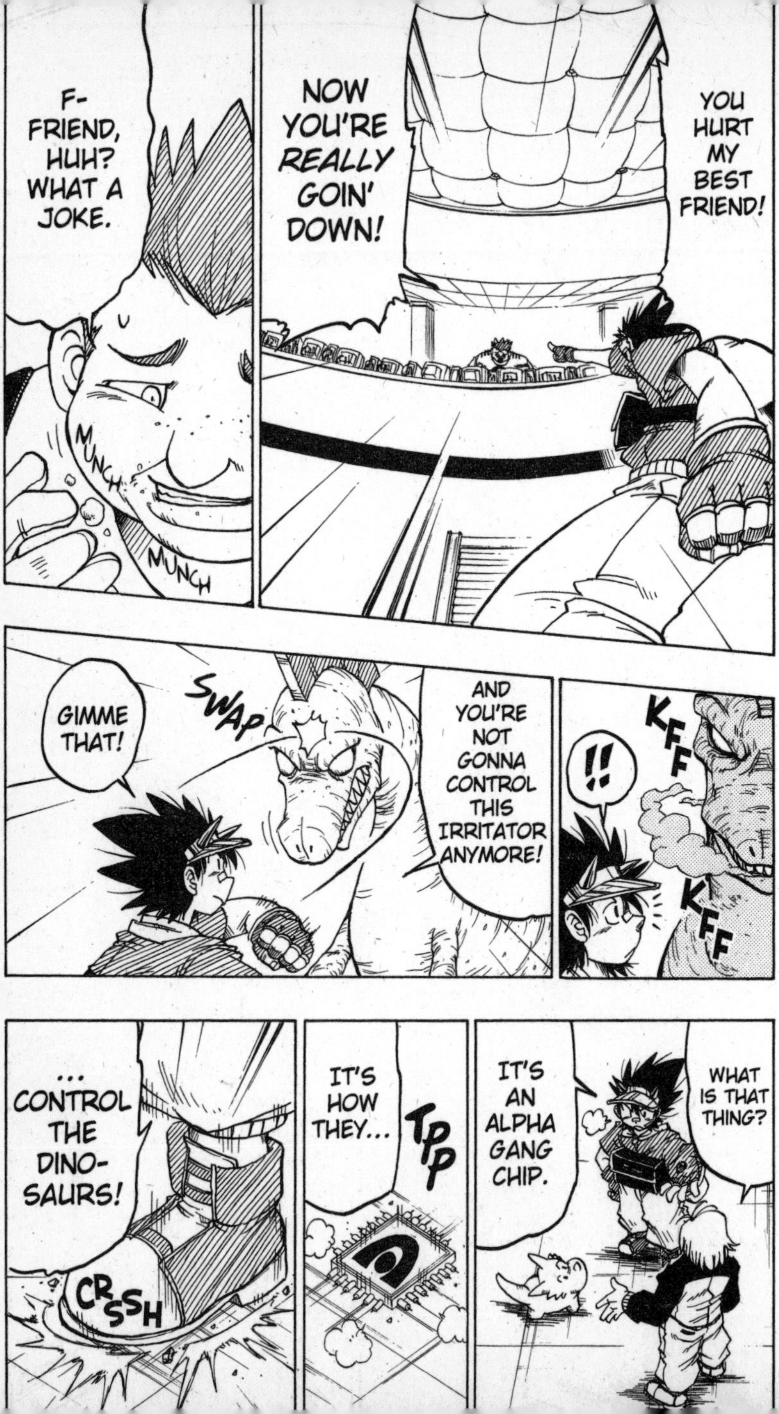
YOU HURT MY BEST FRIEND!
NOW YOU'RE *REALLY* GOIN' DOWN!
F-FRIEND, HUH? WHAT A JOKE.
MUNCH
MUNCH
KFF
KFF
!!
AND YOU'RE NOT GONNA CONTROL THIS IRRITATOR ANYMORE!
SWAP
GIMME THAT!
WHAT IS THAT THING?
IT'S AN ALPHA GANG CHIP.
TPP
IT'S HOW THEY...
...CONTROL THE DINO-SAURS!
CRSSH

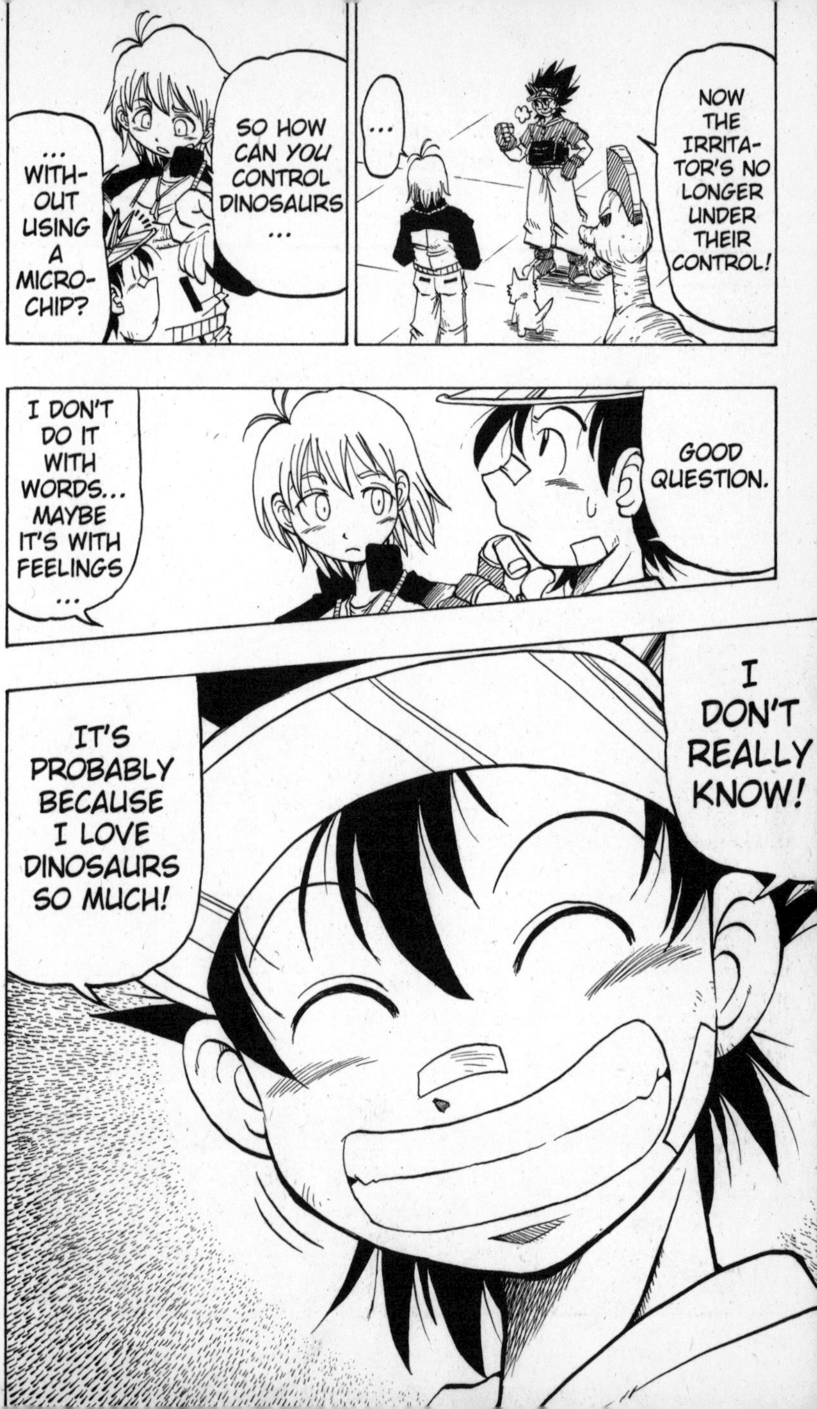
NOW THE IRRITATOR'S NO LONGER UNDER THEIR CONTROL!
...
SO HOW CAN YOU CONTROL DINOSAURS ...
... WITHOUT USING A MICROCHIP?
GOOD QUESTION.
I DON'T DO IT WITH WORDS... MAYBE IT'S WITH FEELINGS ...
I DON'T REALLY KNOW!
IT'S PROBABLY BECAUSE I LOVE DINOSAURS SO MUCH!

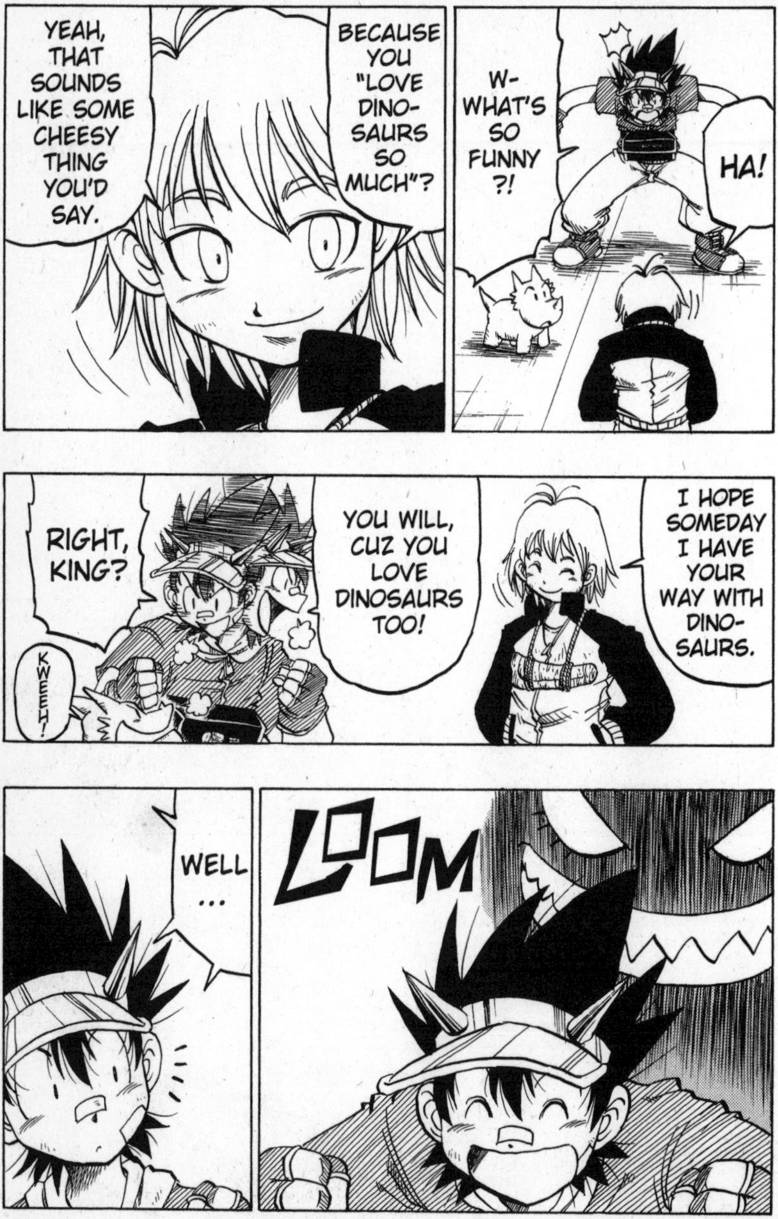
HA!
W-WHAT'S SO FUNNY ?!
BECAUSE YOU "LOVE DINO-SAURS SO MUCH"?
YEAH, THAT SOUNDS LIKE SOME CHEESY THING YOU'D SAY.
I HOPE SOMEDAY I HAVE YOUR WAY WITH DINO-SAURS.
YOU WILL, CUZ YOU LOVE DINOSAURS TOO!
RIGHT, KING?
KWEEH!
LOOM
WELL ...

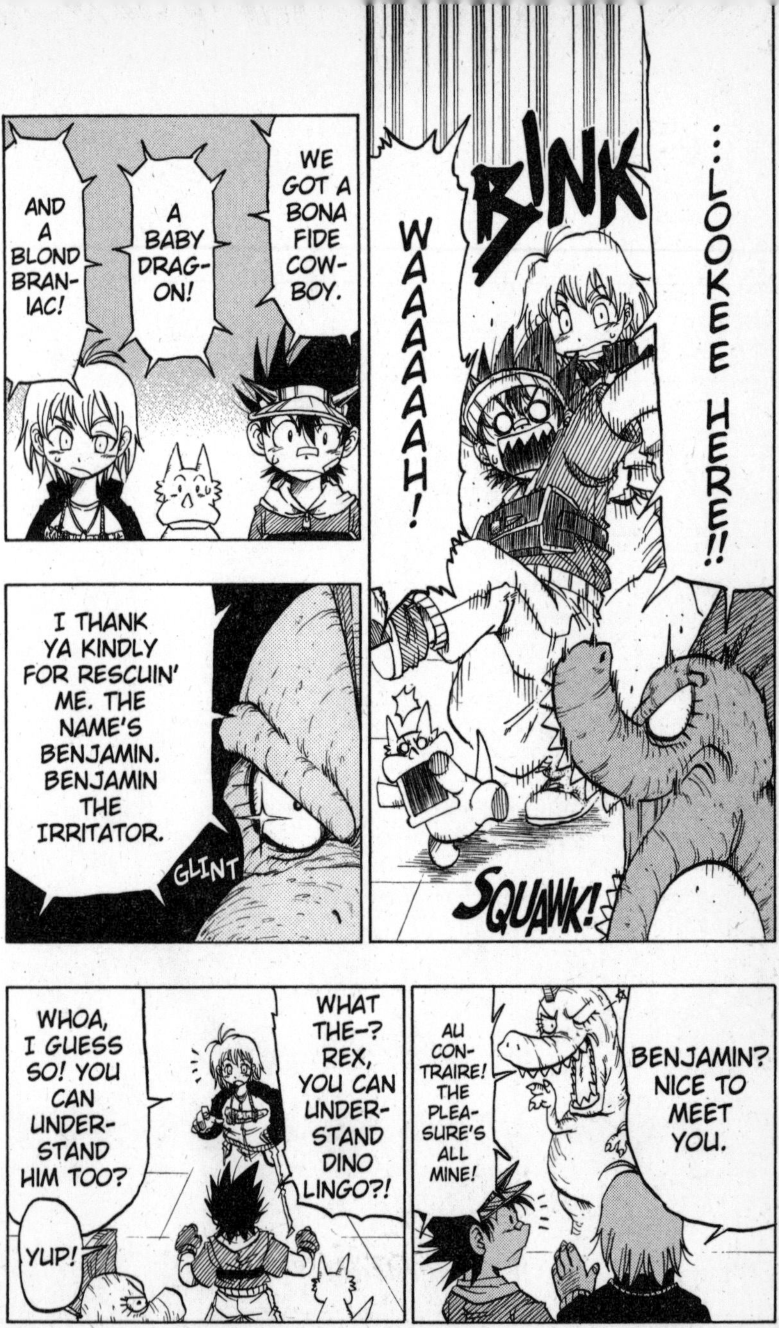
...LOOKEE HERE!!
BINK
WAAAAAAAH!
SQUAWK!
WE GOT A BONA FIDE COW-BOY.
A BABY DRAG-ON!
AND A BLOND BRAN-IAC!
I THANK YA KINDLY FOR RESCUIN' ME. THE NAME'S BENJAMIN. BENJAMIN THE IRRITATOR.
GLINT
BENJAMIN? NICE TO MEET YOU.
AU CON-TRAIRE! THE PLEA-SURE'S ALL MINE!
WHAT THE-? REX, YOU CAN UNDER-STAND DINO LINGO?!
WHOA, I GUESS SO! YOU CAN UNDER-STAND HIM TOO?
YUP!

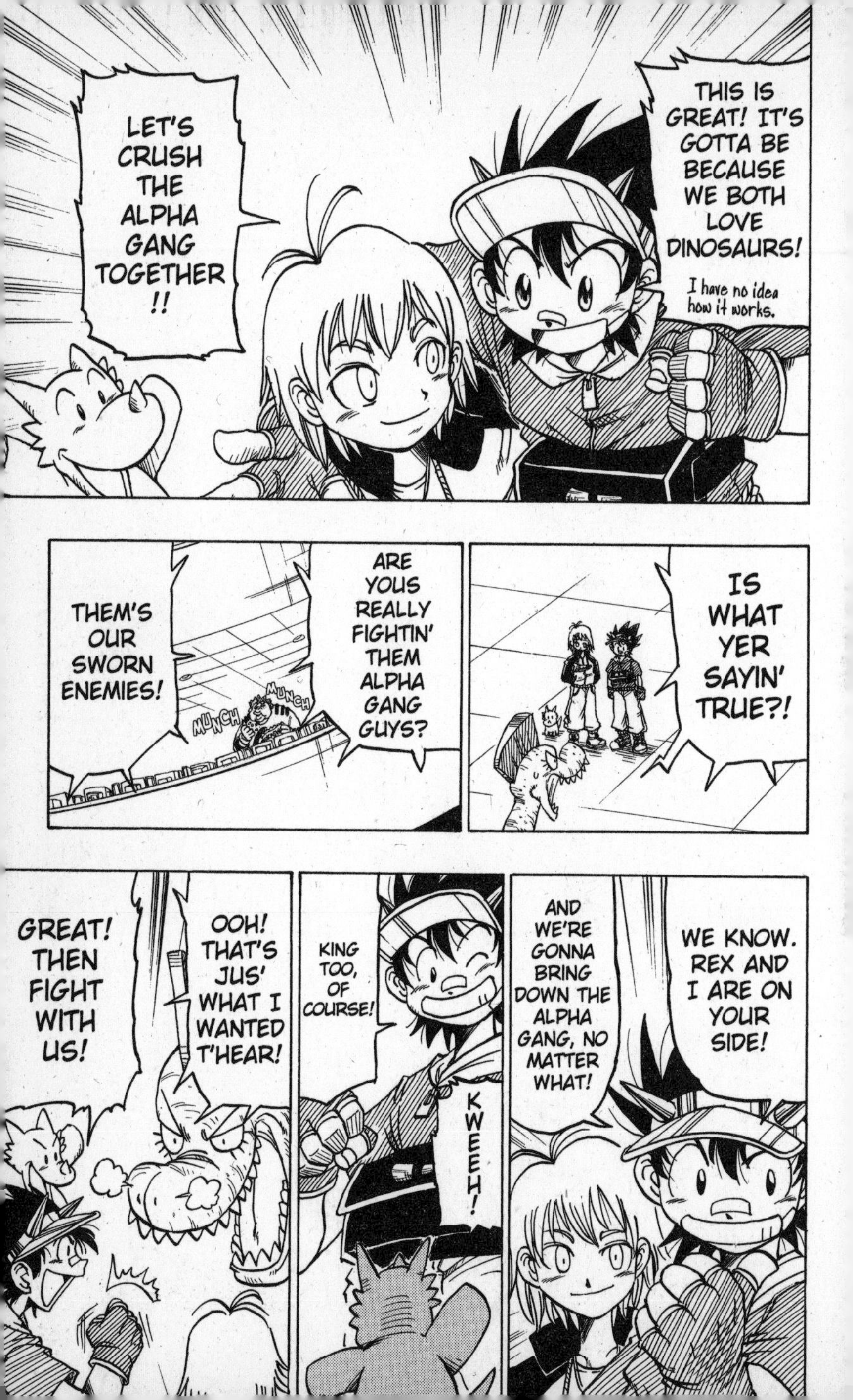
THIS IS GREAT! IT'S GOTTA BE BECAUSE WE BOTH LOVE DINOSAURS!
I have no idea how it works.
LET'S CRUSH THE ALPHA GANG TOGETHER!!
IS WHAT YER SAYIN' TRUE?!
ARE YOUS REALLY FIGHTIN' THEM ALPHA GANG GUYS?
MUNCH
MUNCH
THEM'S OUR SWORN ENEMIES!
WE KNOW. REX AND I ARE ON YOUR SIDE!
AND WE'RE GONNA BRING DOWN THE ALPHA GANG, NO MATTER WHAT!
KING TOO, OF COURSE!
KWEEH!
OOH! THAT'S JUS' WHAT I WANTED T'HEAR!
GREAT! THEN FIGHT WITH US!

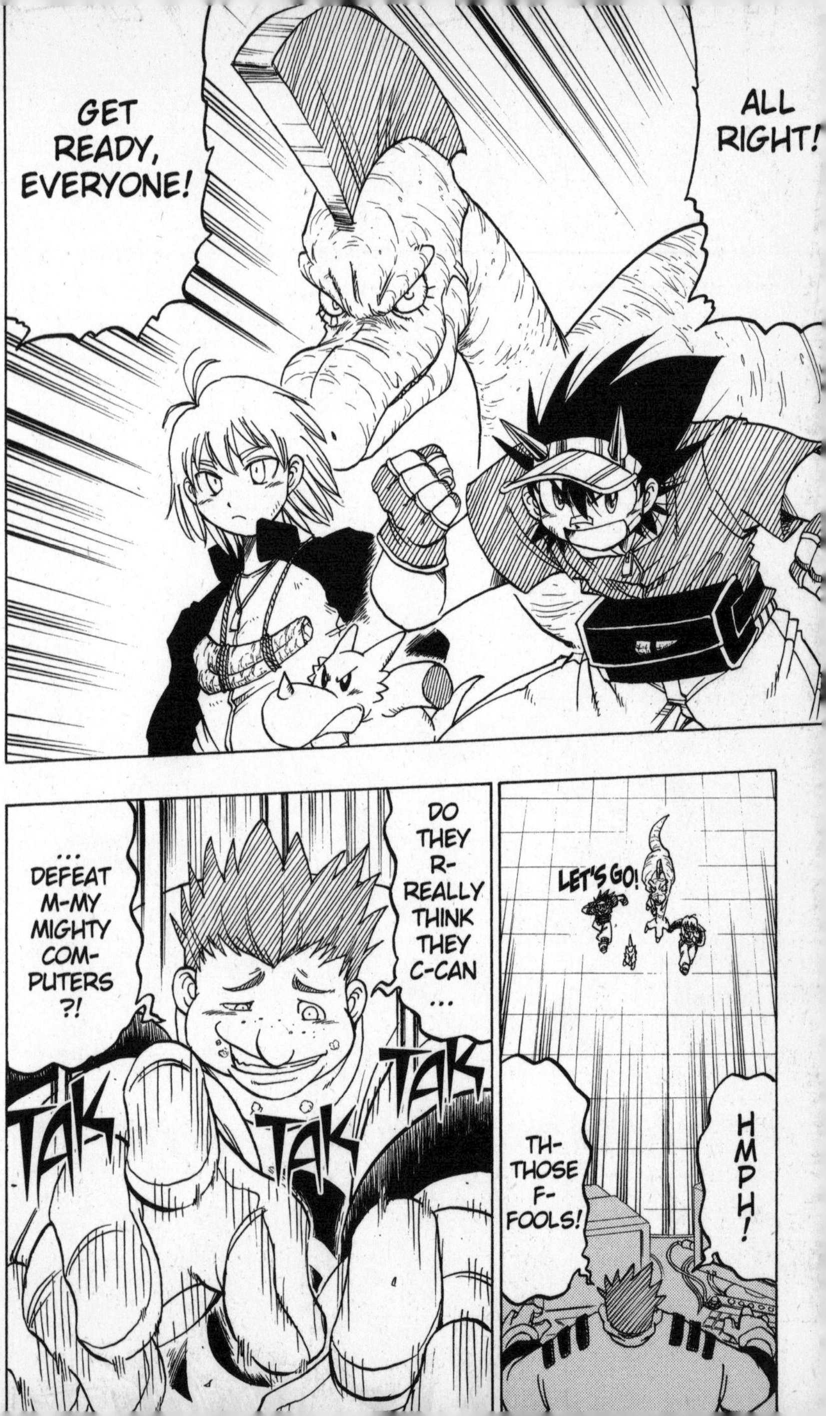
ALL RIGHT!
GET READY, EVERYONE!
LET'S GO!
HMPH!
TH-THOSE F-FOOLS!
DO THEY R-REALLY THINK THEY C-CAN ...
... DEFEAT M-MY MIGHTY COMPUTERS ?!
TAK
TAK
TAK
TAK

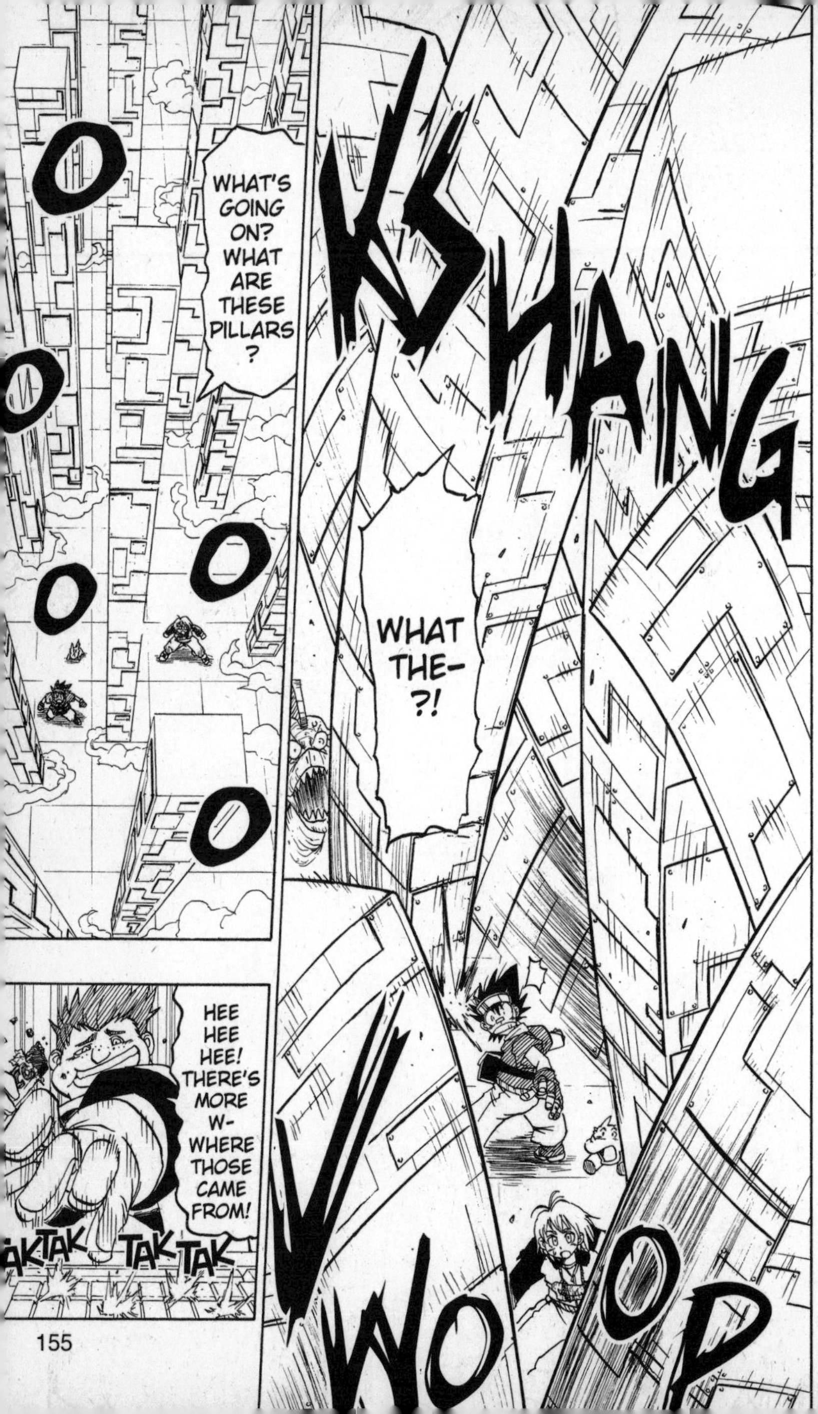
KSHANG
WHAT THE-?!
VWOOP
OOOOO
WHAT'S GOING ON? WHAT ARE THESE PILLARS?
HEE HEE HEE! THERE'S MORE W- WHERE THOSE CAME FROM!
TAK TAK TAK TAK

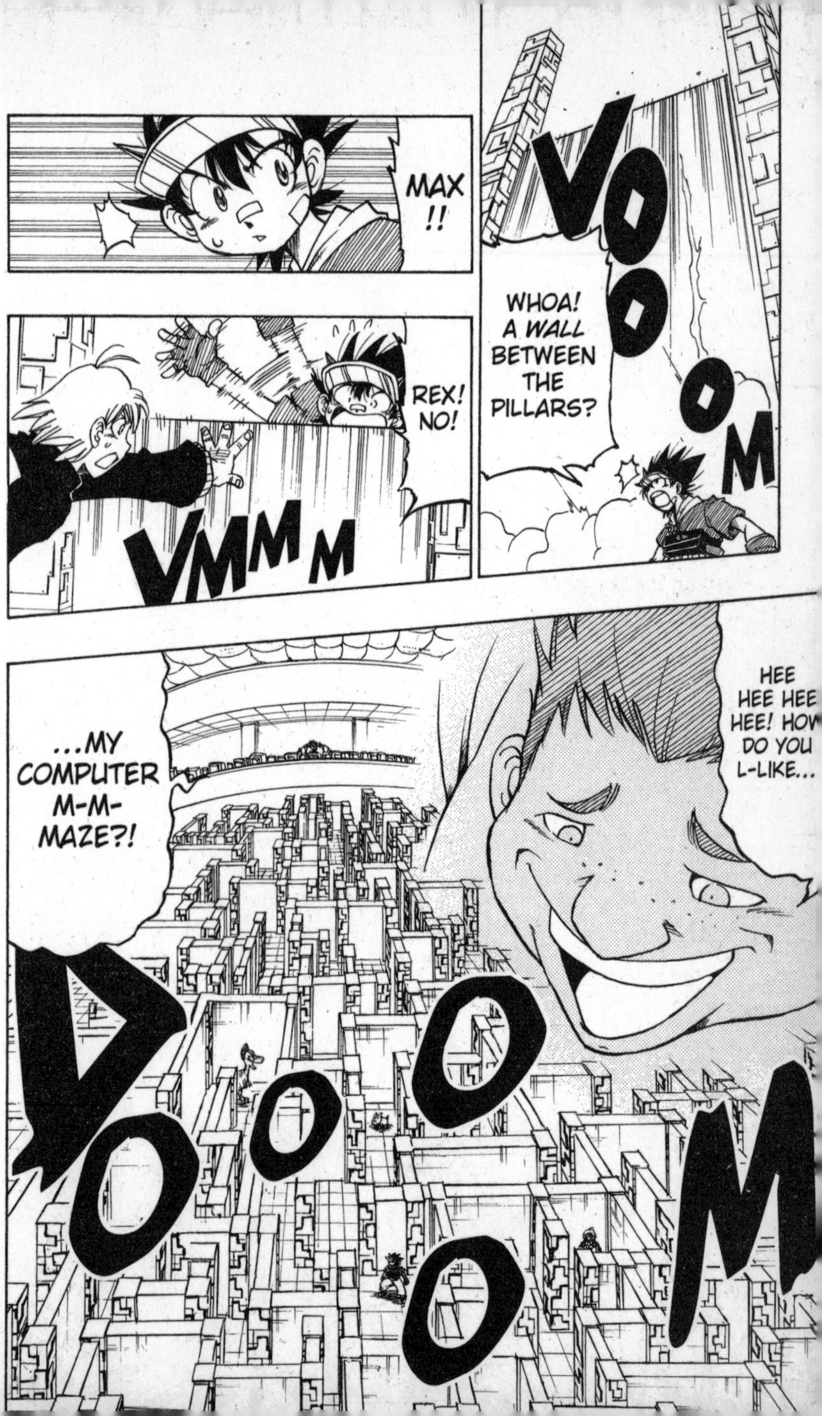
VOOOOM
WHOA! A WALL BETWEEN THE PILLARS?
MAX !!
REX! NO!
VMMMM
HEE HEE HEE HEE! HOW DO YOU L-LIKE...
...MY COMPUTER M-M-MAZE?!
VOOOOOM

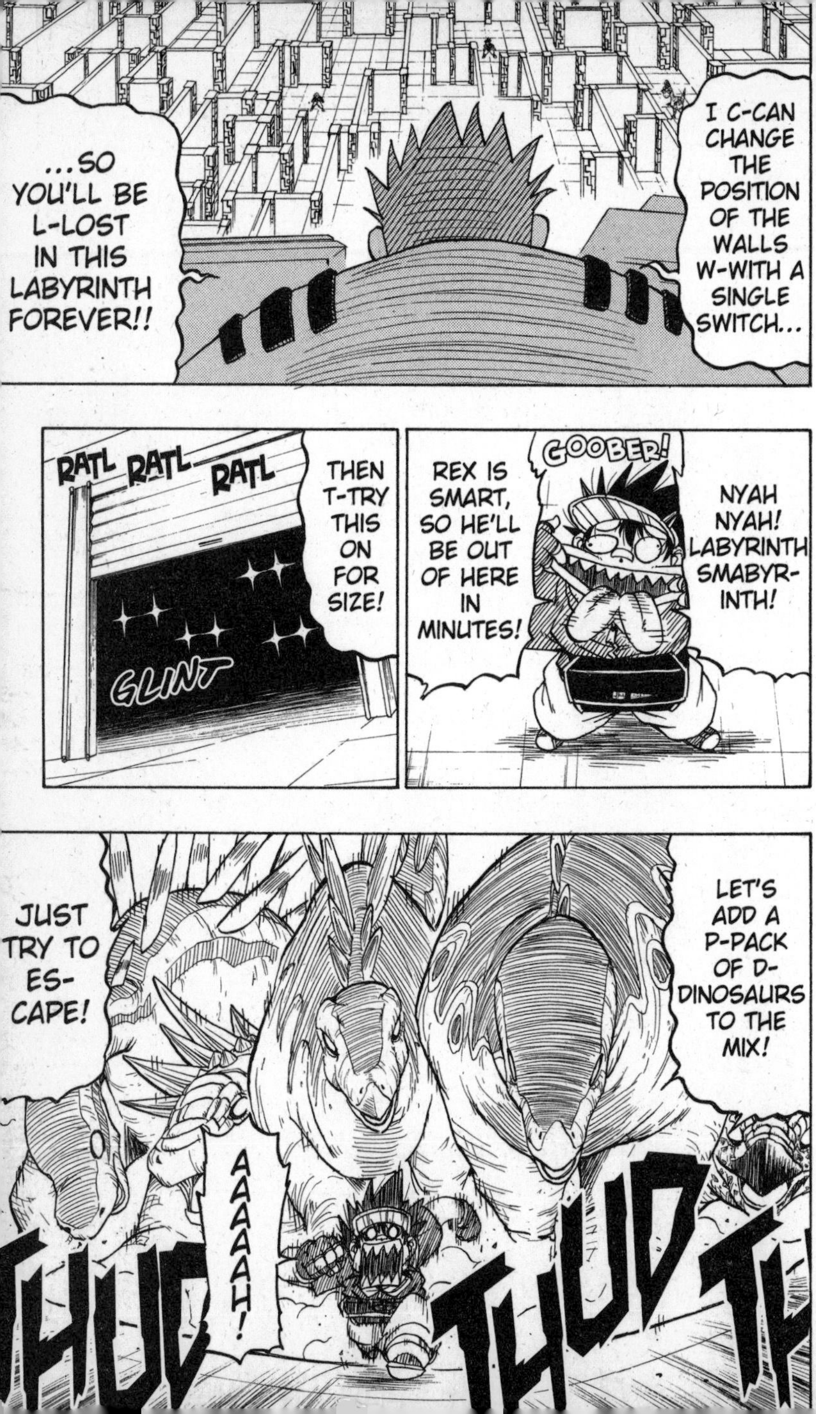
I C-CAN CHANGE THE POSITION OF THE WALLS W-WITH A SINGLE SWITCH...
...SO YOU'LL BE L-LOST IN THIS LABYRINTH FOREVER!!
GOOBER!
NYAH NYAH! LABYRINTH SMABYRINTH!
REX IS SMART, SO HE'LL BE OUT OF HERE IN MINUTES!
THEN T-TRY THIS ON FOR SIZE!
RATL RATL RATL
GLINT
LET'S ADD A P-PACK OF D-DINOSAURS TO THE MIX!
JUST TRY TO ES-CAPE!
AAAAAAH!
THUD THUD

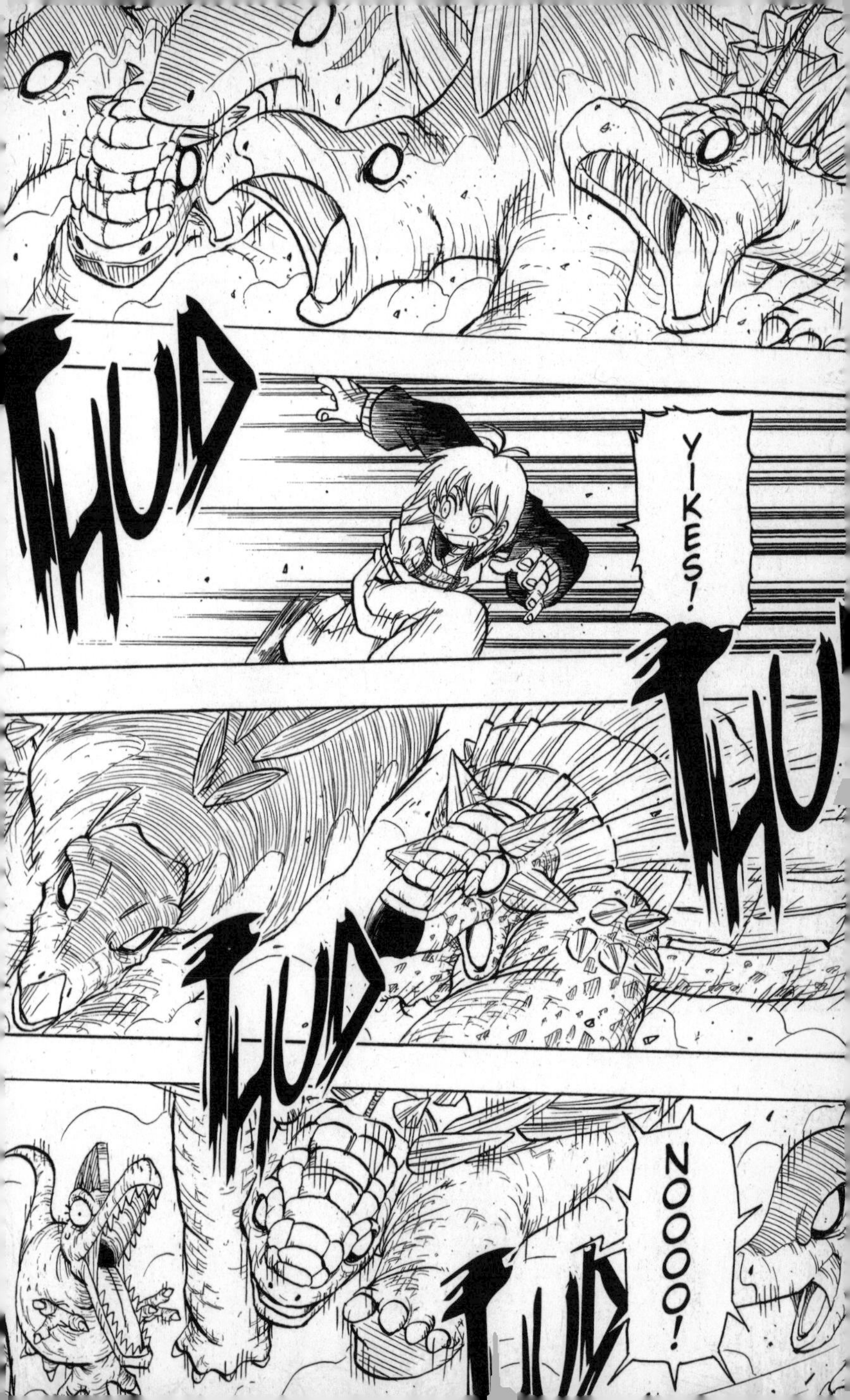
YIKES!
THUD
THU
THUD
NOOOO!
THUD

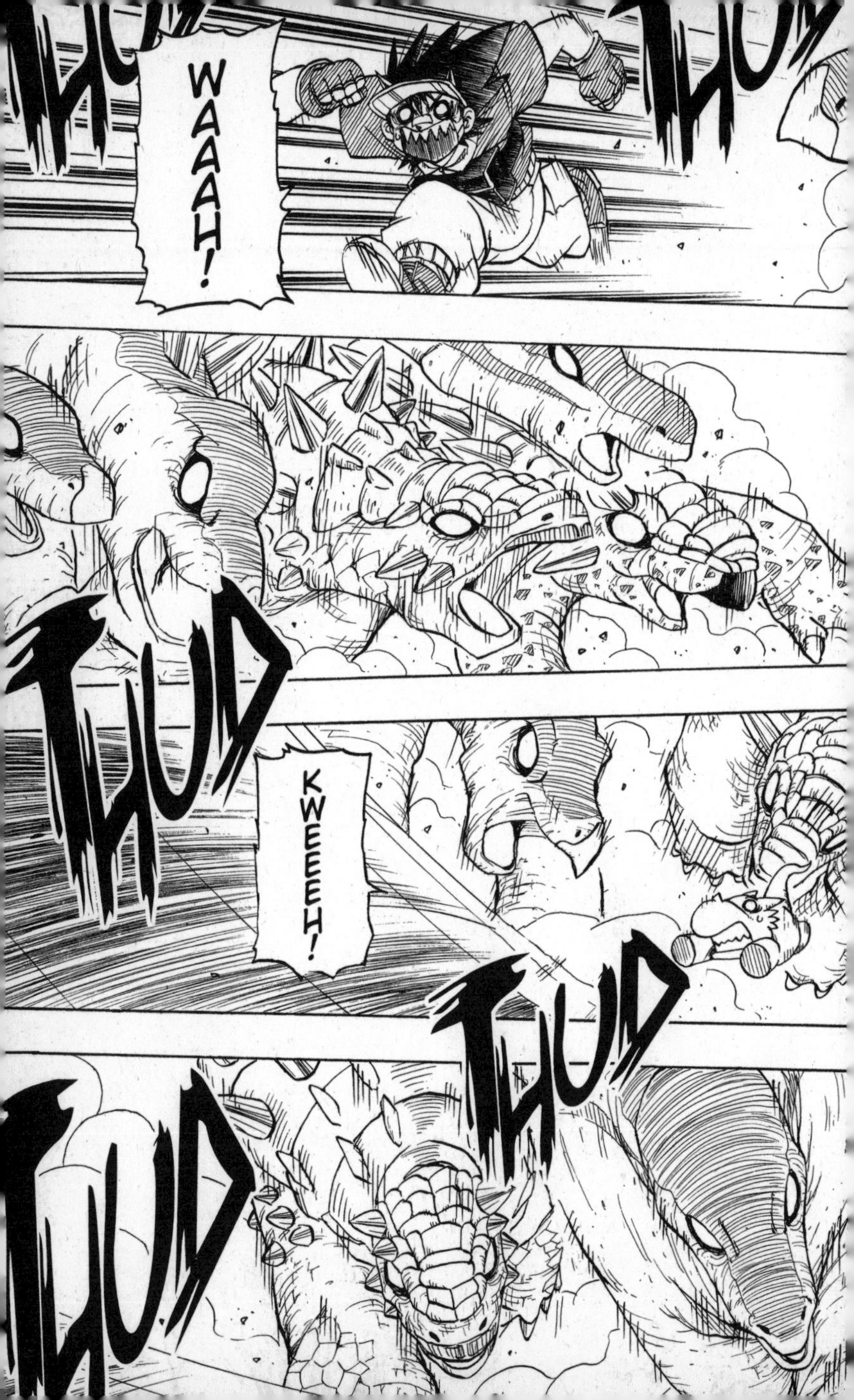
WAAAAH!
THUD
KWEEEEH!
THUD
THUD
THUD

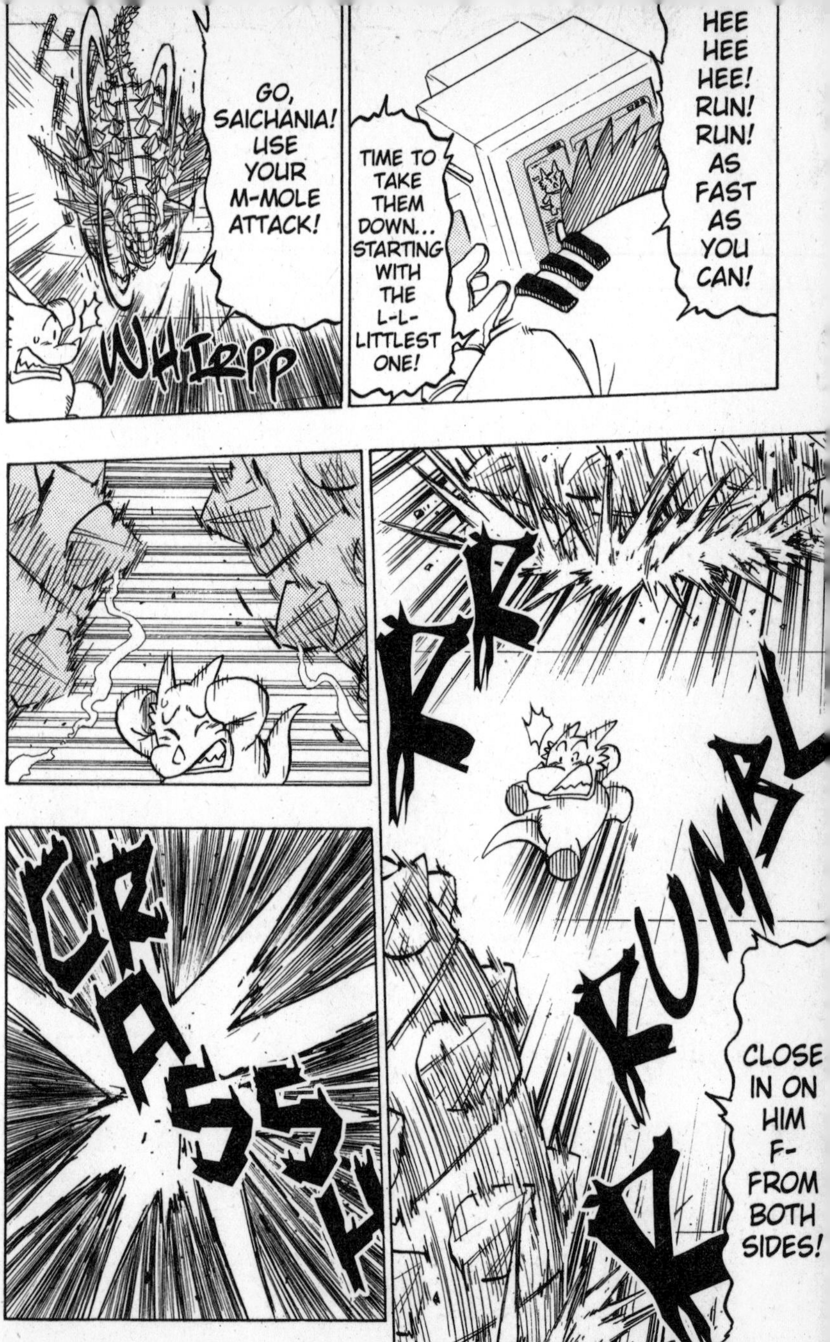
HEE HEE HEE! RUN! RUN! AS FAST AS YOU CAN!
TIME TO TAKE THEM DOWN... STARTING WITH THE L-L-LITTLEST ONE!
GO, SAICHANIA! USE YOUR M-MOLE ATTACK!
WHIRPP
RUMBL
CLOSE IN ON HIM F-FROM BOTH SIDES!
CRASSH

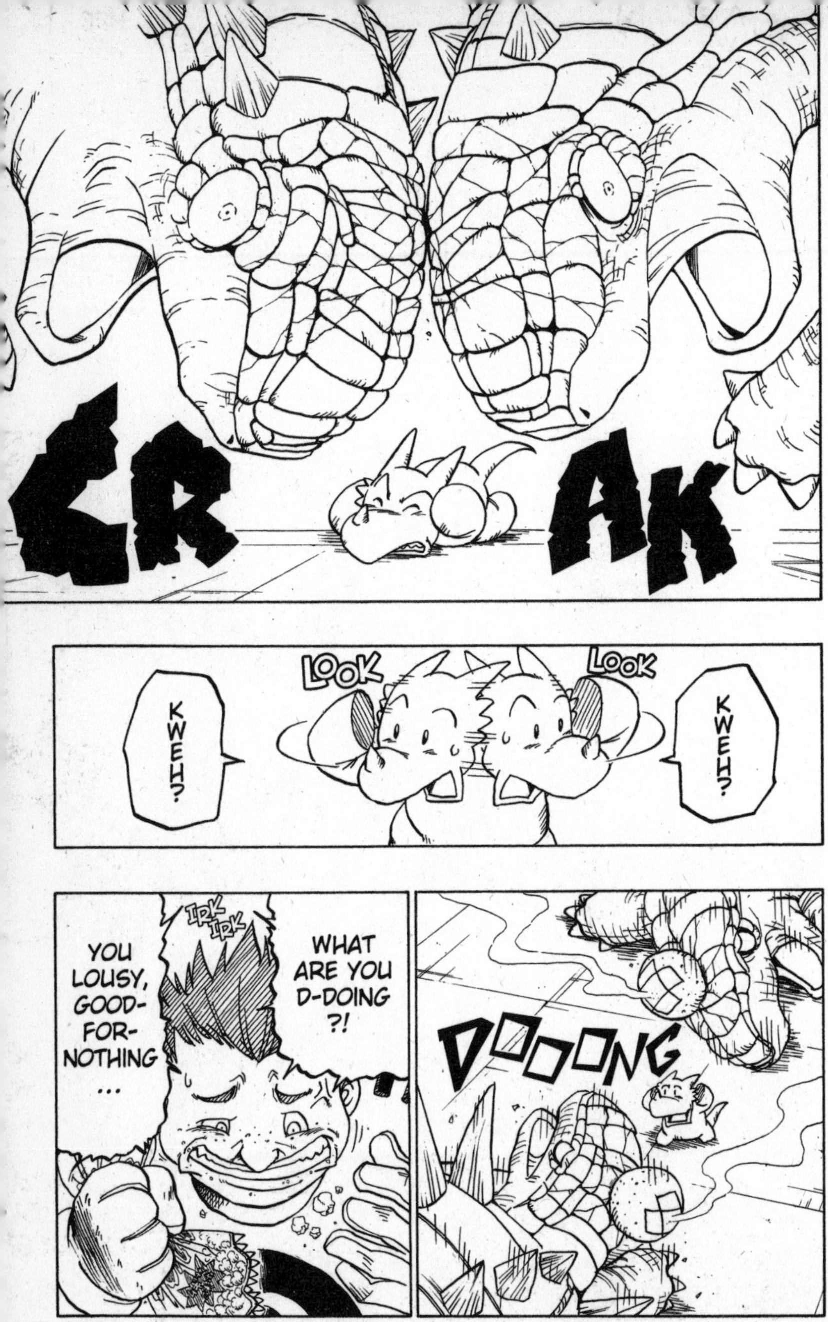
CR
AK
LOOK
KWEH?
LOOK
KWEH?
DOOONG
WHAT ARE YOU D-DOING ?!
IRK IRK
YOU LOUSY, GOOD-FOR-NOTHING ...

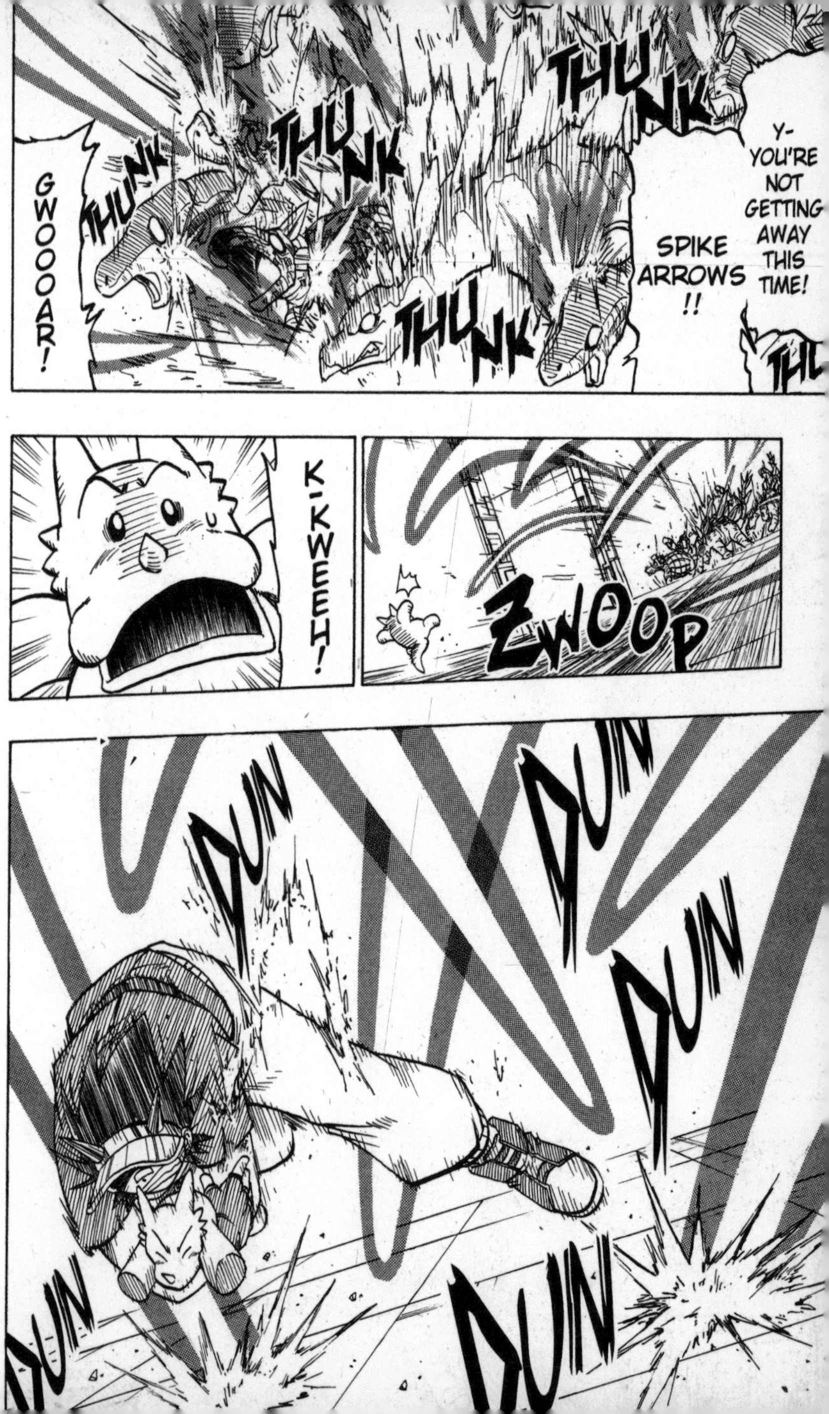
THU
Y- YOU'RE NOT GETTING AWAY THIS TIME!
SPIKE ARROWS !!
THUNK
THUNK
THUNK
THUNK
GWOOOOAR!
ZWOOP
K-KWEEEH!
DUN
DUN
DUN
DUN
DUN
DUN

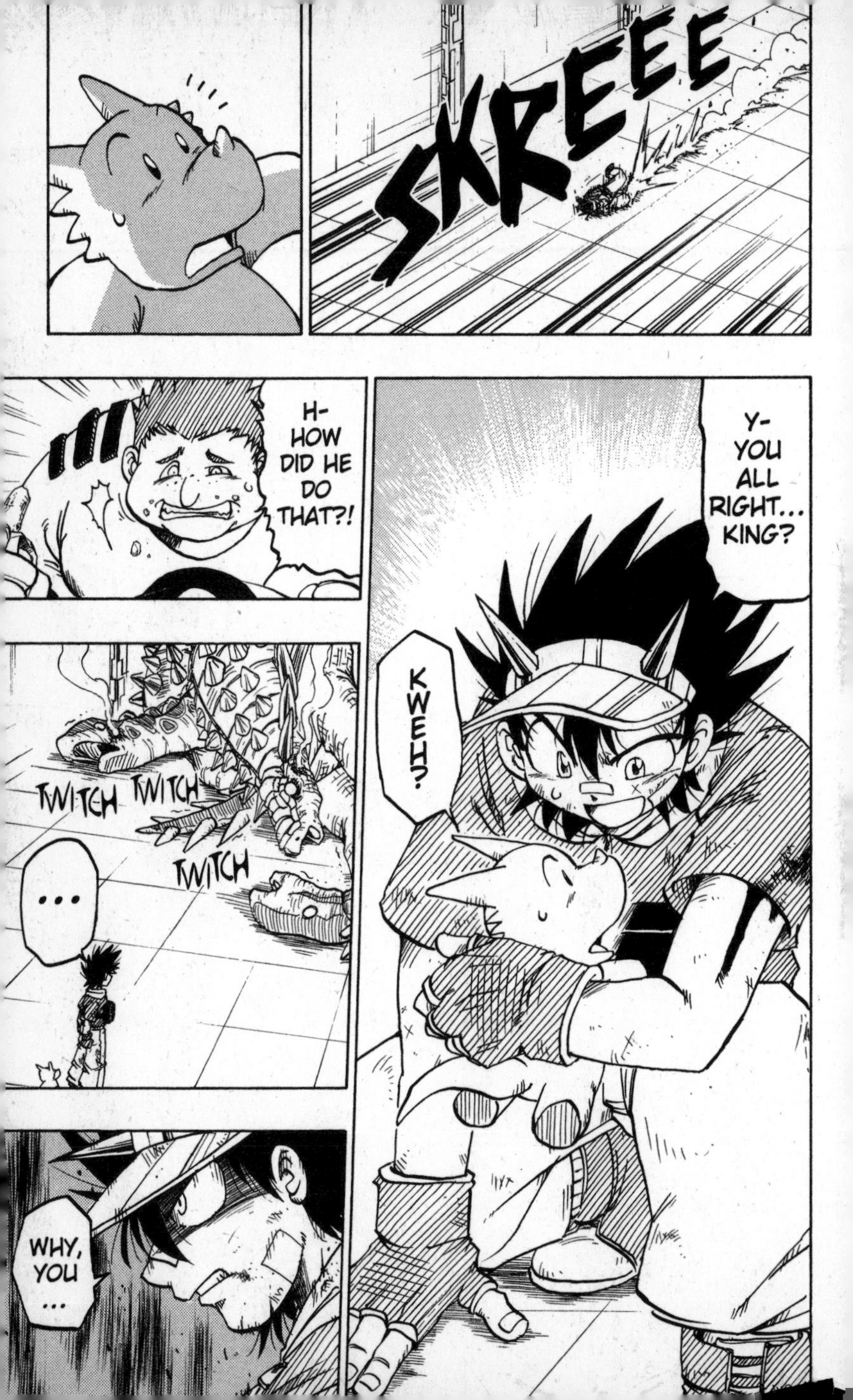
SKREEE
Y-YOU ALL RIGHT... KING?
KWEH?
H-HOW DID HE DO THAT?!
TWITCH TWITCH
TWITCH
...
WHY, YOU ...

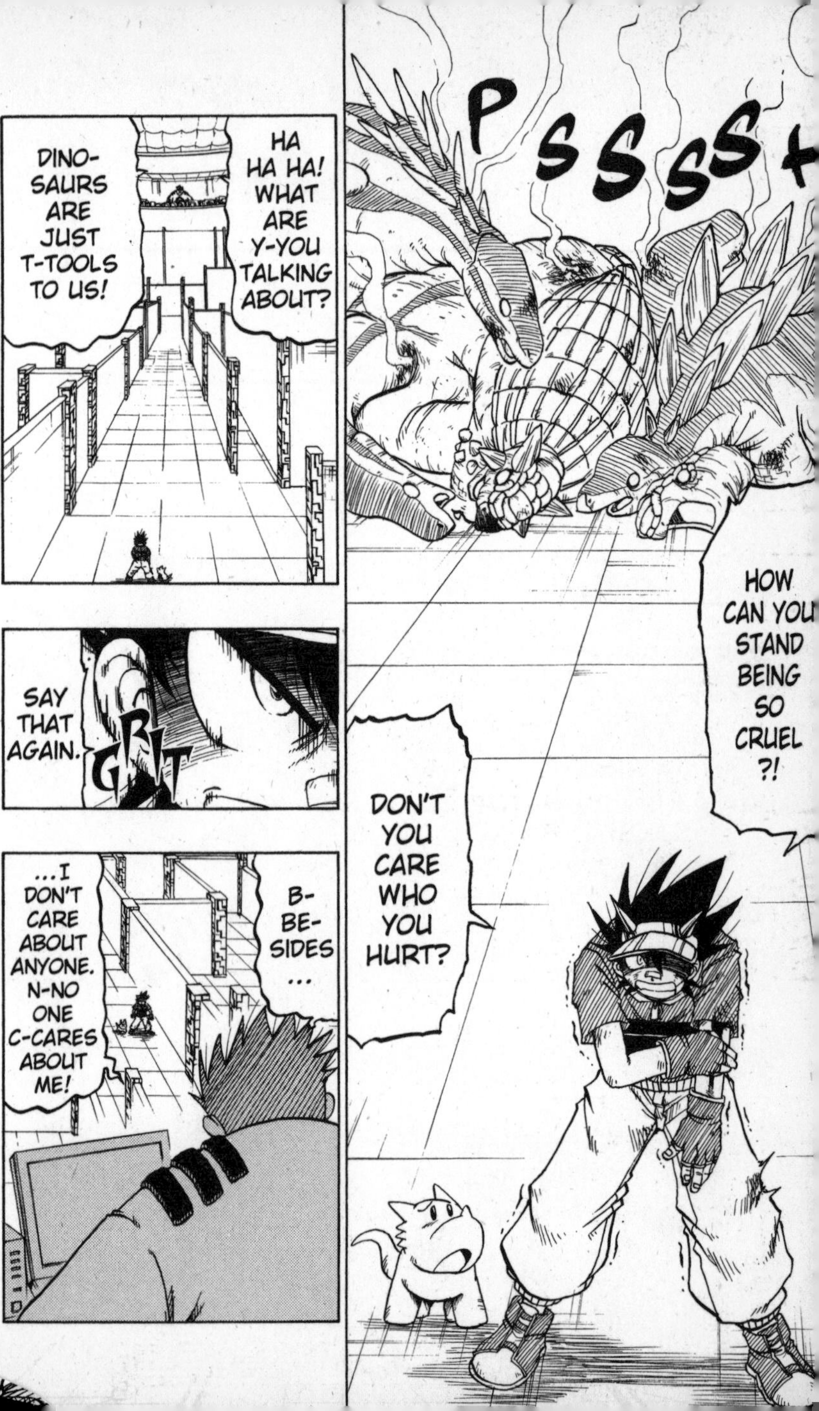
PSSSSS
HOW CAN YOU STAND BEING SO CRUEL?!
DON'T YOU CARE WHO YOU HURT?
HA HA HA! WHAT ARE Y-YOU TALKING ABOUT?
DINOSAURS ARE JUST T-TOOLS TO US!
SAY THAT AGAIN.
GRIT
B-BESIDES...
...I DON'T CARE ABOUT ANYONE. N-NO ONE C-CARES ABOUT ME!

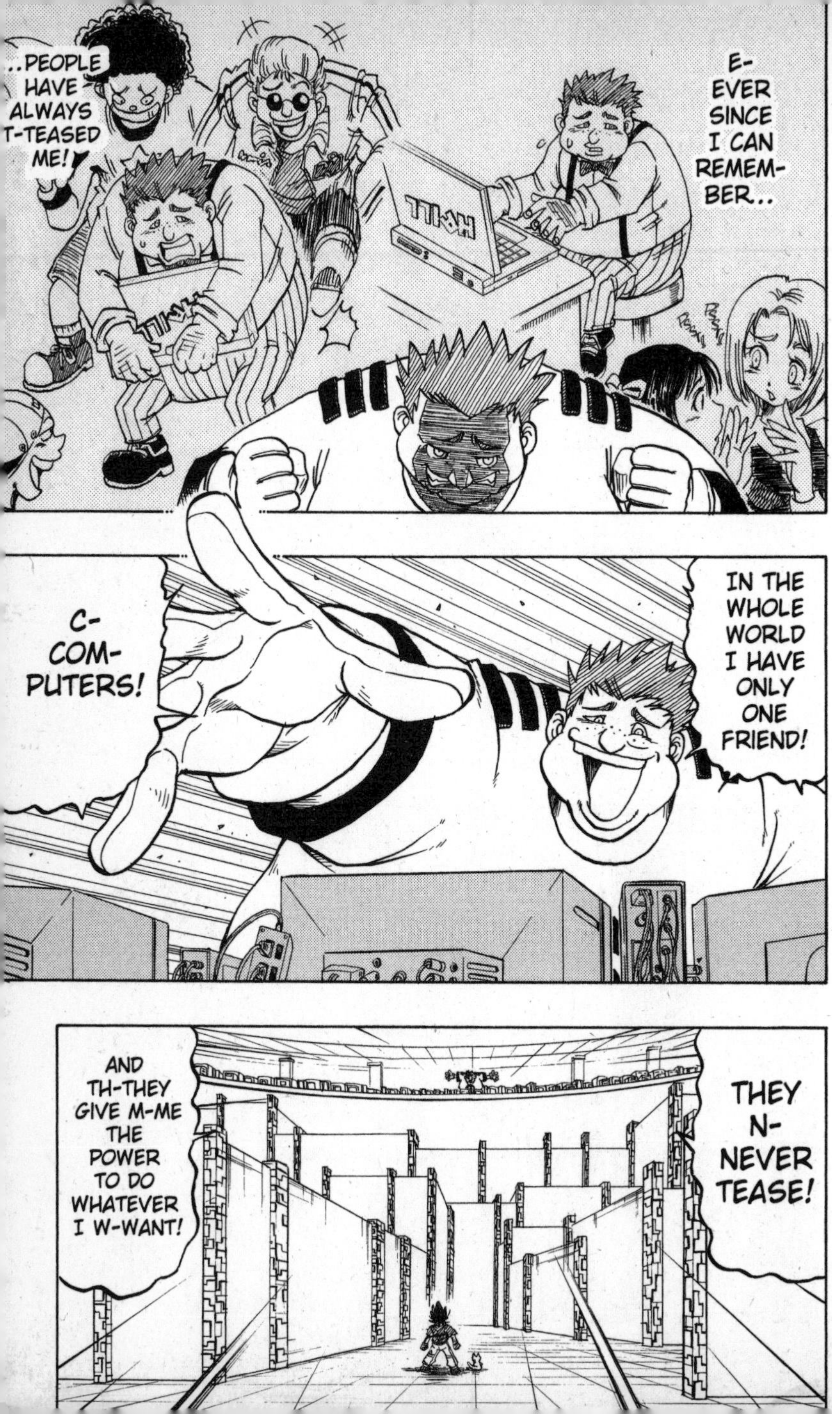
E- EVER SINCE I CAN REMEMBER...
...PEOPLE HAVE ALWAYS T-TEASED ME!
IN THE WHOLE WORLD I HAVE ONLY ONE FRIEND!
C- COMPUTERS!
THEY N- NEVER TEASE!
AND TH-THEY GIVE M-ME THE POWER TO DO WHATEVER I W-WANT!

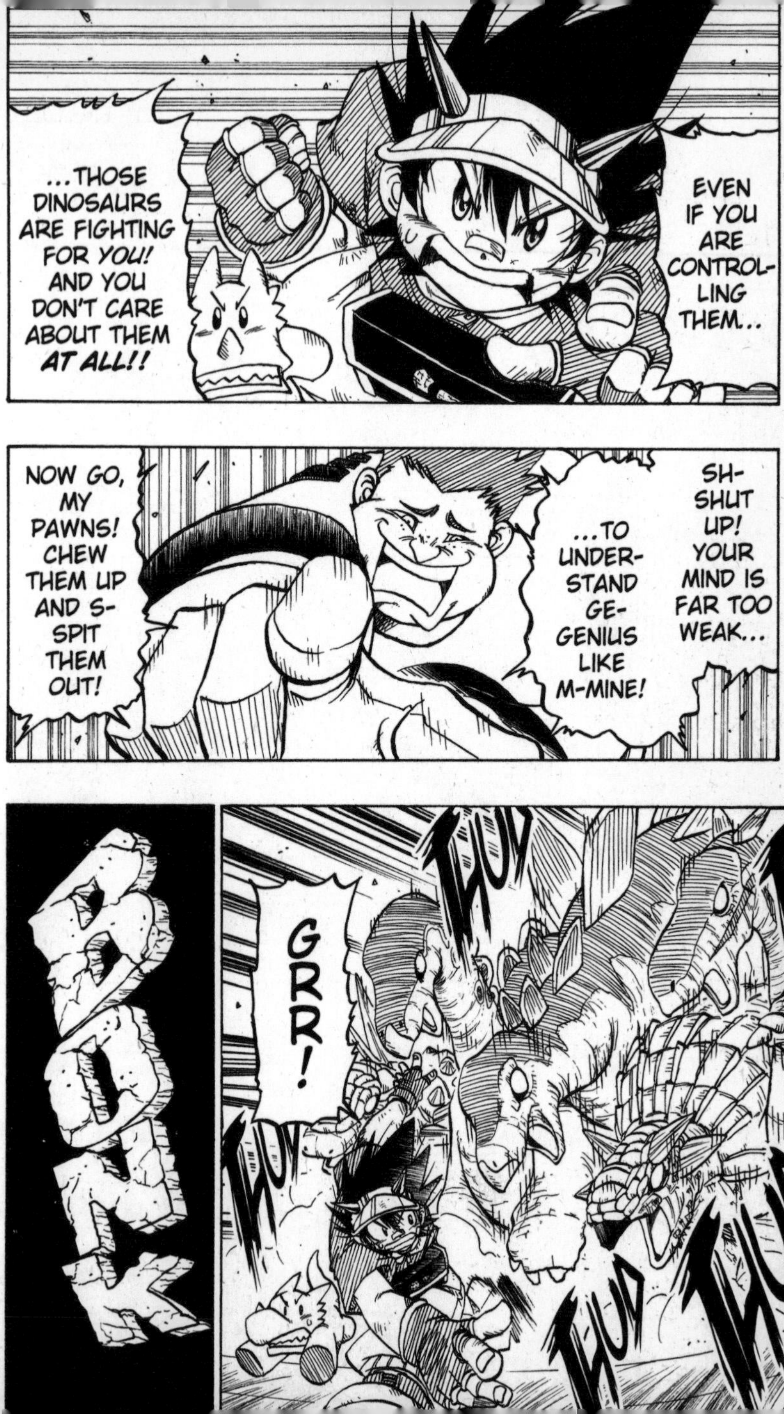
EVEN IF YOU ARE CONTROL-LING THEM...
...THOSE DINOSAURS ARE FIGHTING FOR YOU! AND YOU DON'T CARE ABOUT THEM AT ALL!!
SH-SHUT UP! YOUR MIND IS FAR TOO WEAK...
...TO UNDER-STAND GE-GENIUS LIKE M-MINE!
NOW GO, MY PAWNS! CHEW THEM UP AND S-SPIT THEM OUT!
THUD
GRR!
THUD

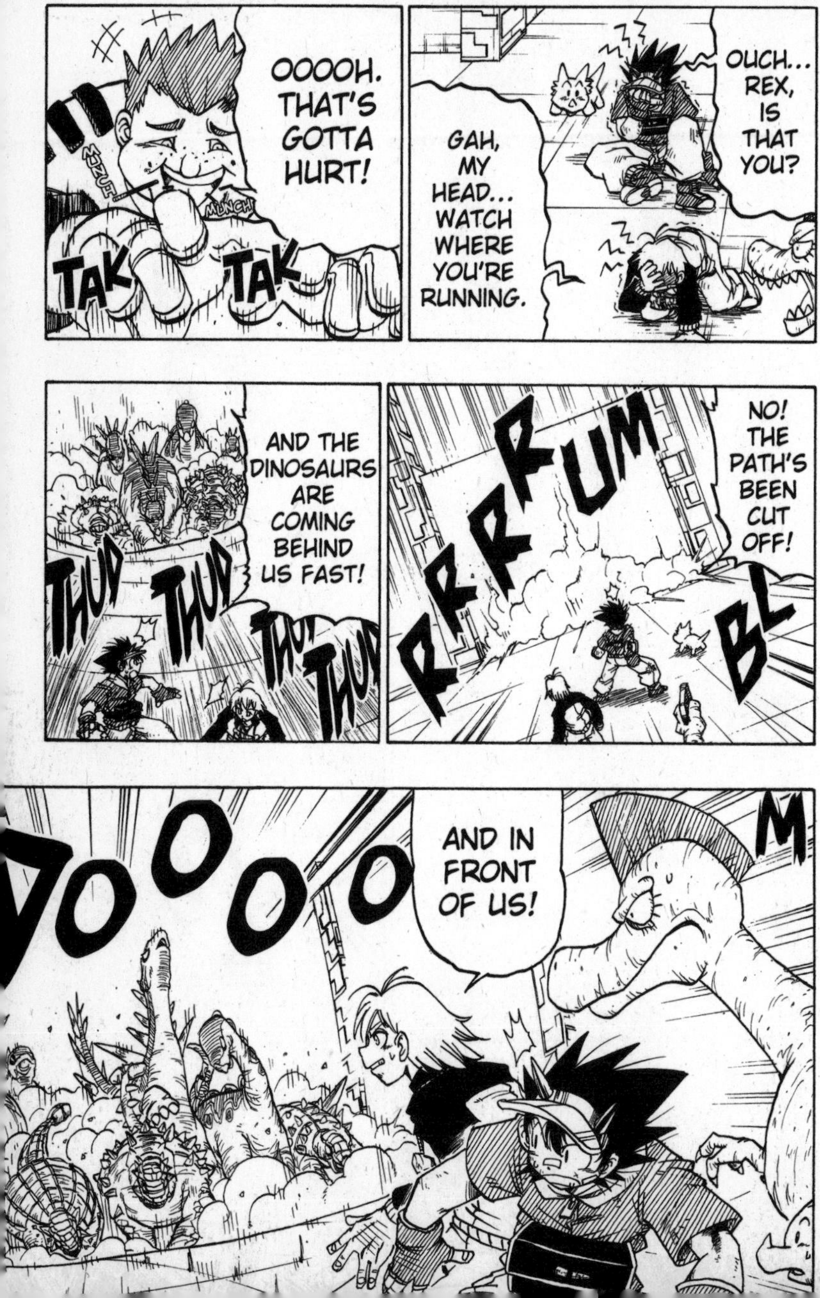
OUCH... REX, IS THAT YOU?
GAH, MY HEAD... WATCH WHERE YOU'RE RUNNING.
OOOOH. THAT'S GOTTA HURT!
MUNCH
MUNCH
TAK TAK
NO! THE PATH'S BEEN CUT OFF!
RRRRUM
BL
AND THE DINOSAURS ARE COMING BEHIND US FAST!
THUD THUD THUD THUD
M
AND IN FRONT OF US!
DOOOO

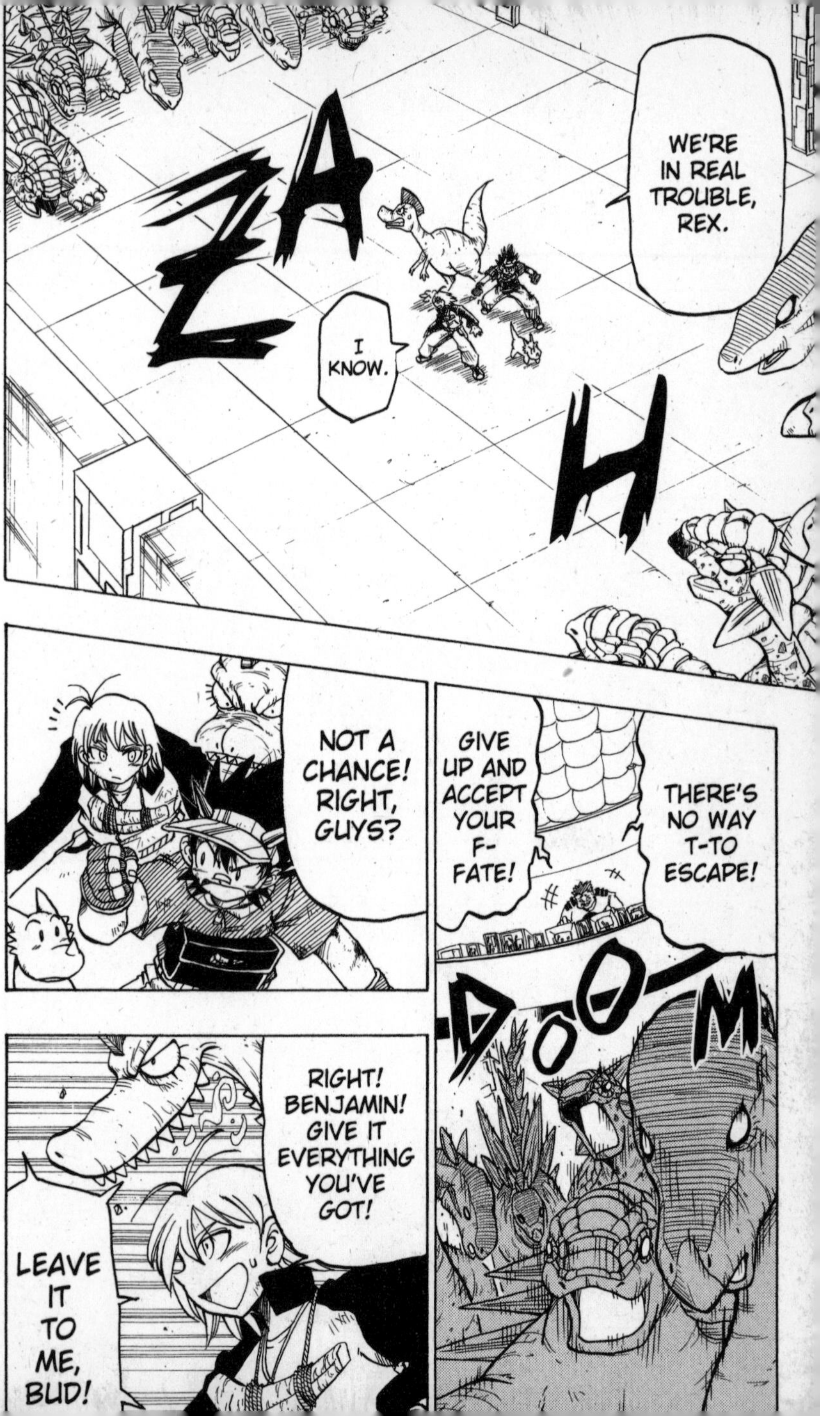
WE'RE IN REAL TROUBLE, REX.
I KNOW.
THERE'S NO WAY T-TO ESCAPE!
GIVE UP AND ACCEPT YOUR F-FATE!
NOT A CHANCE! RIGHT, GUYS?
D-O-O-M
RIGHT! BENJAMIN! GIVE IT EVERYTHING YOU'VE GOT!
LEAVE IT TO ME, BUD!

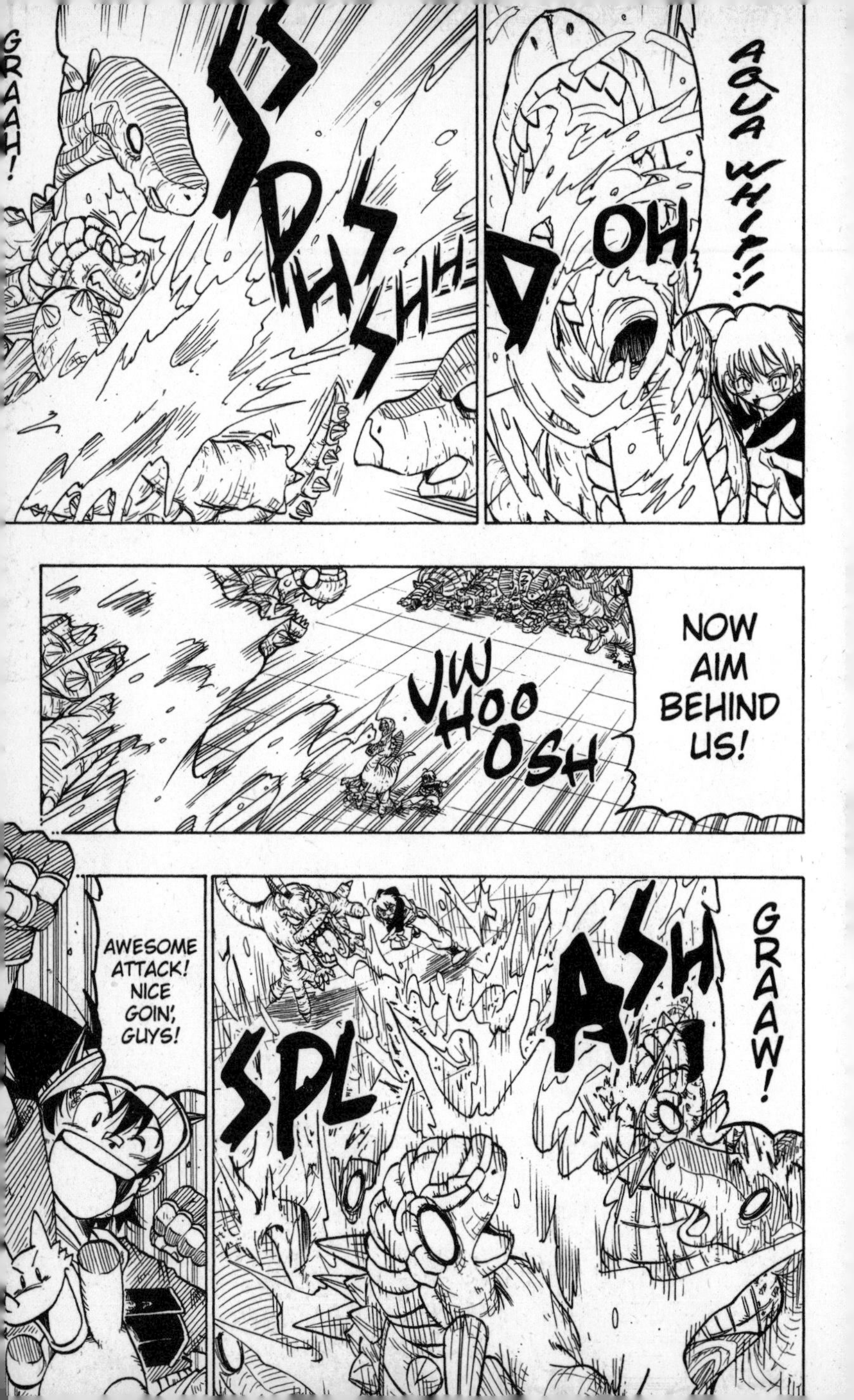
AQUA WHIP!!!
DOH
SPHSHHH
GRAAAH!
NOW AIM BEHIND US!
JWHOOOSH
GRAAW!
SPLASH
AWESOME ATTACK! NICE GOIN', GUYS!

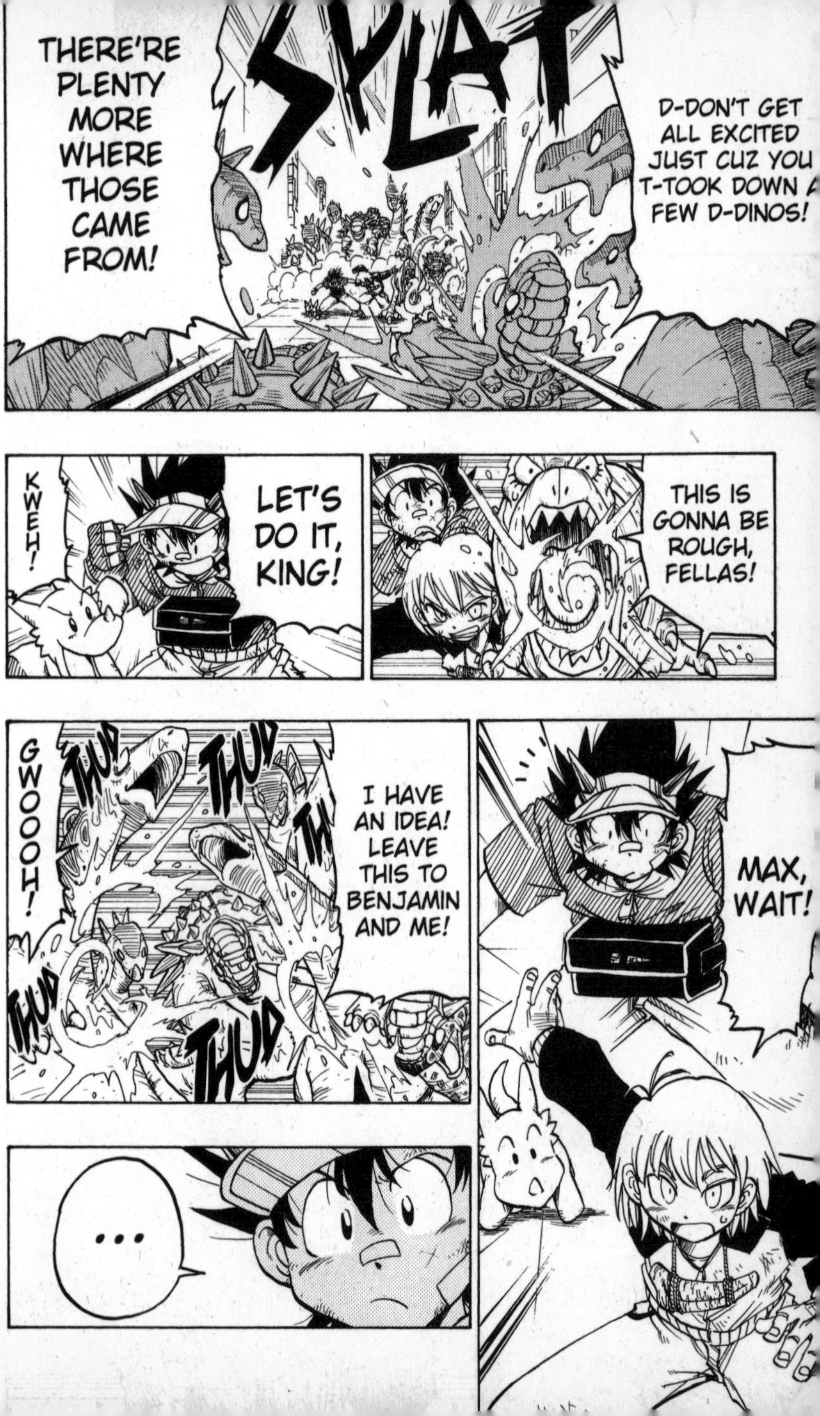
D-DON'T GET ALL EXCITED JUST CUZ YOU T-TOOK DOWN A FEW D-DINOS!
SPLAT
THERE'RE PLENTY MORE WHERE THOSE CAME FROM!
THIS IS GONNA BE ROUGH, FELLAS!
LET'S DO IT, KING!
KWEH!
MAX, WAIT!
I HAVE AN IDEA! LEAVE THIS TO BENJAMIN AND ME!
THUD
THUD
TH
GWOOOOH!
THUD
THUD
...

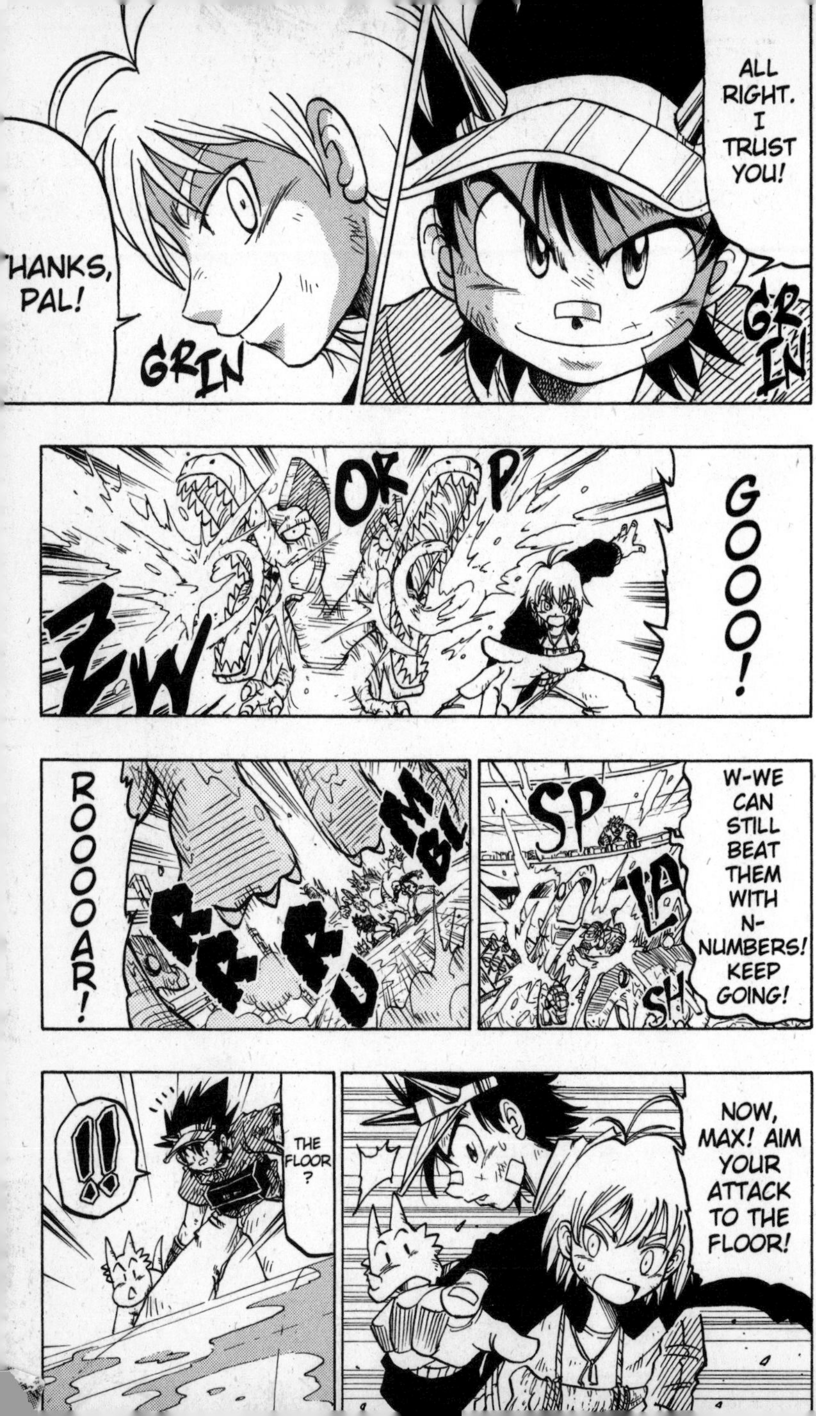
ALL RIGHT. I TRUST YOU!
GRIN
THANKS, PAL!
GRIN
GOOOO!
W-WE CAN STILL BEAT THEM WITH N-NUMBERS! KEEP GOING!
ROOOOOAR!
NOW, MAX! AIM YOUR ATTACK TO THE FLOOR!
THE FLOOR?
!!

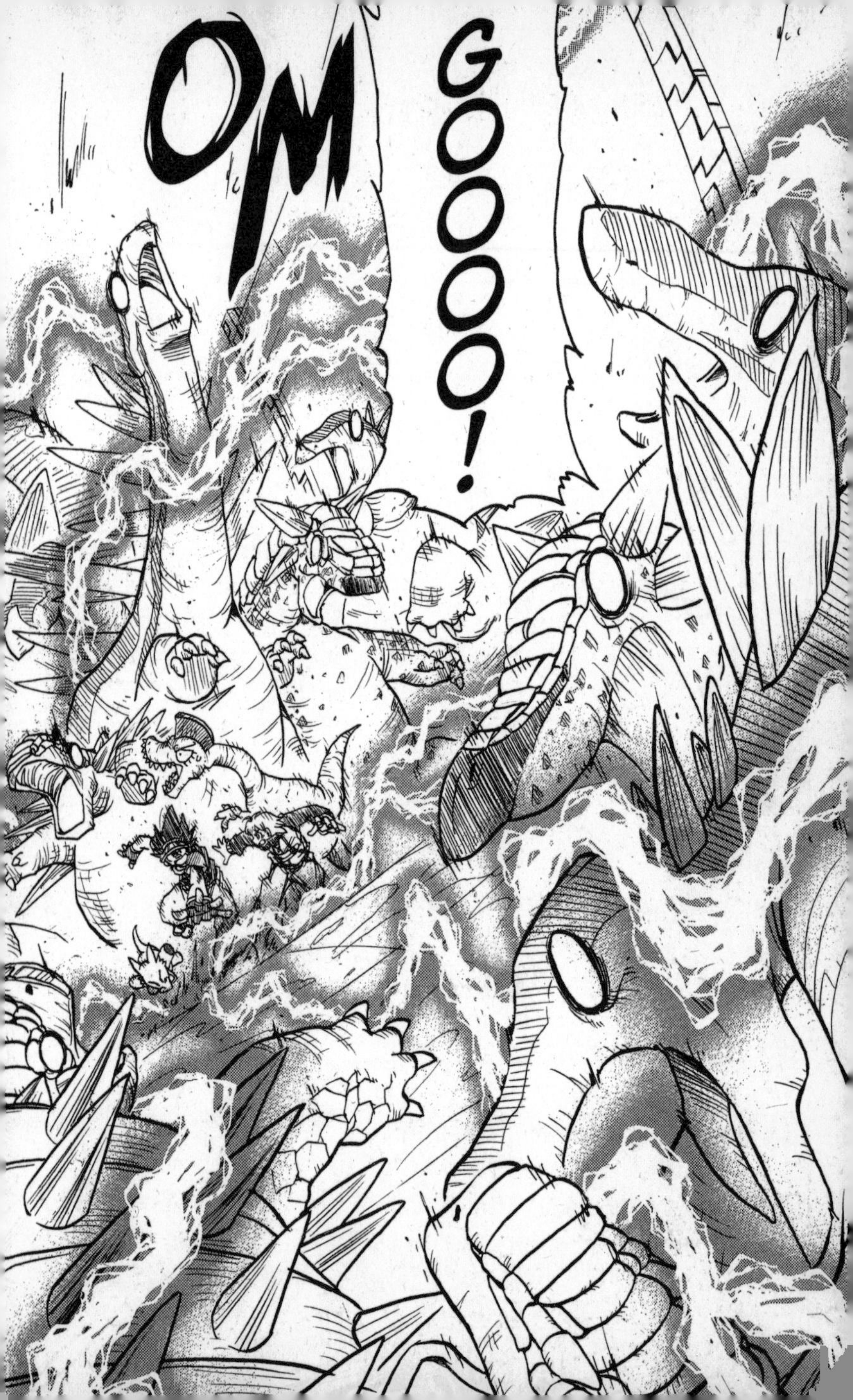
OM
GOOOOO!

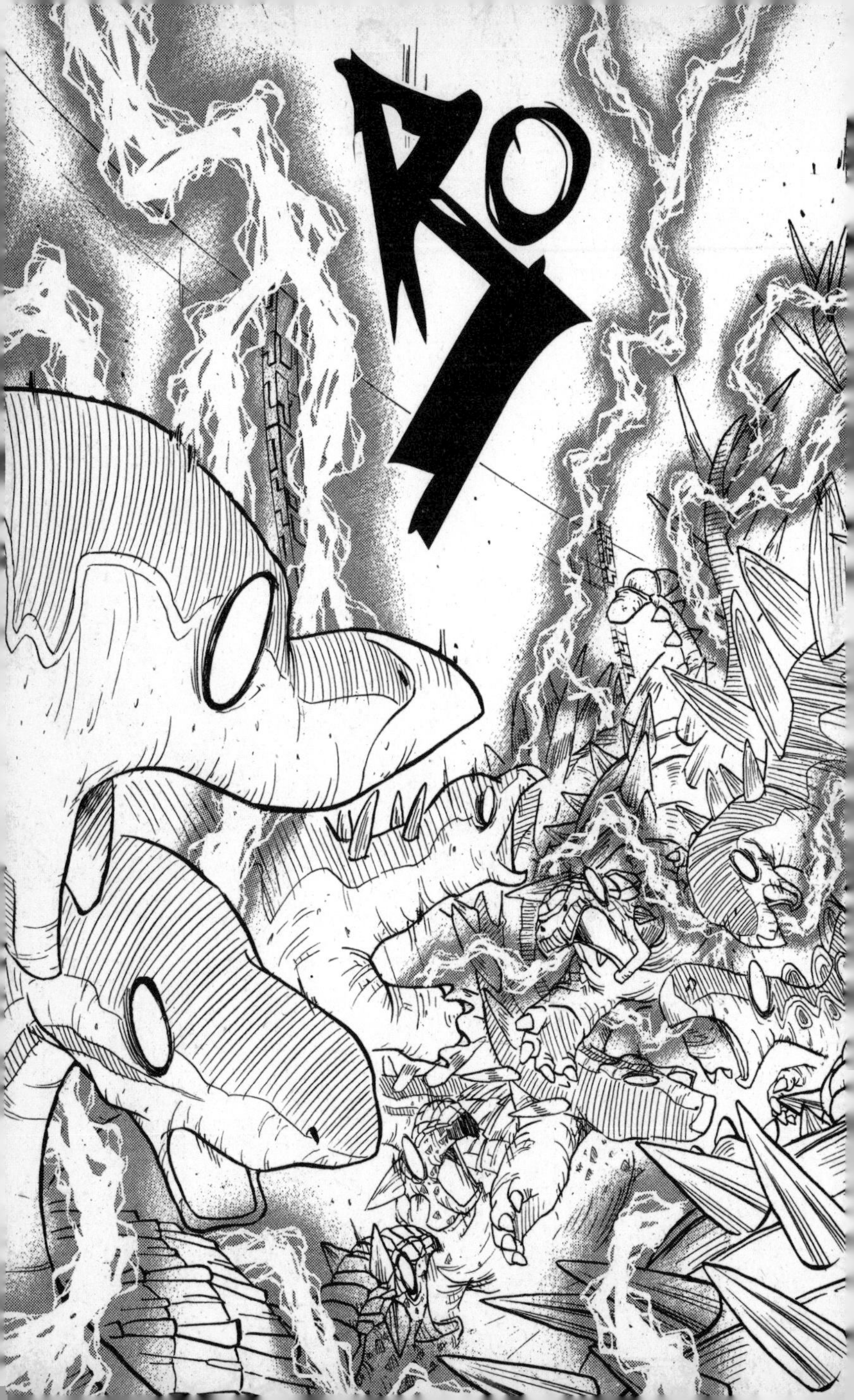
ROT

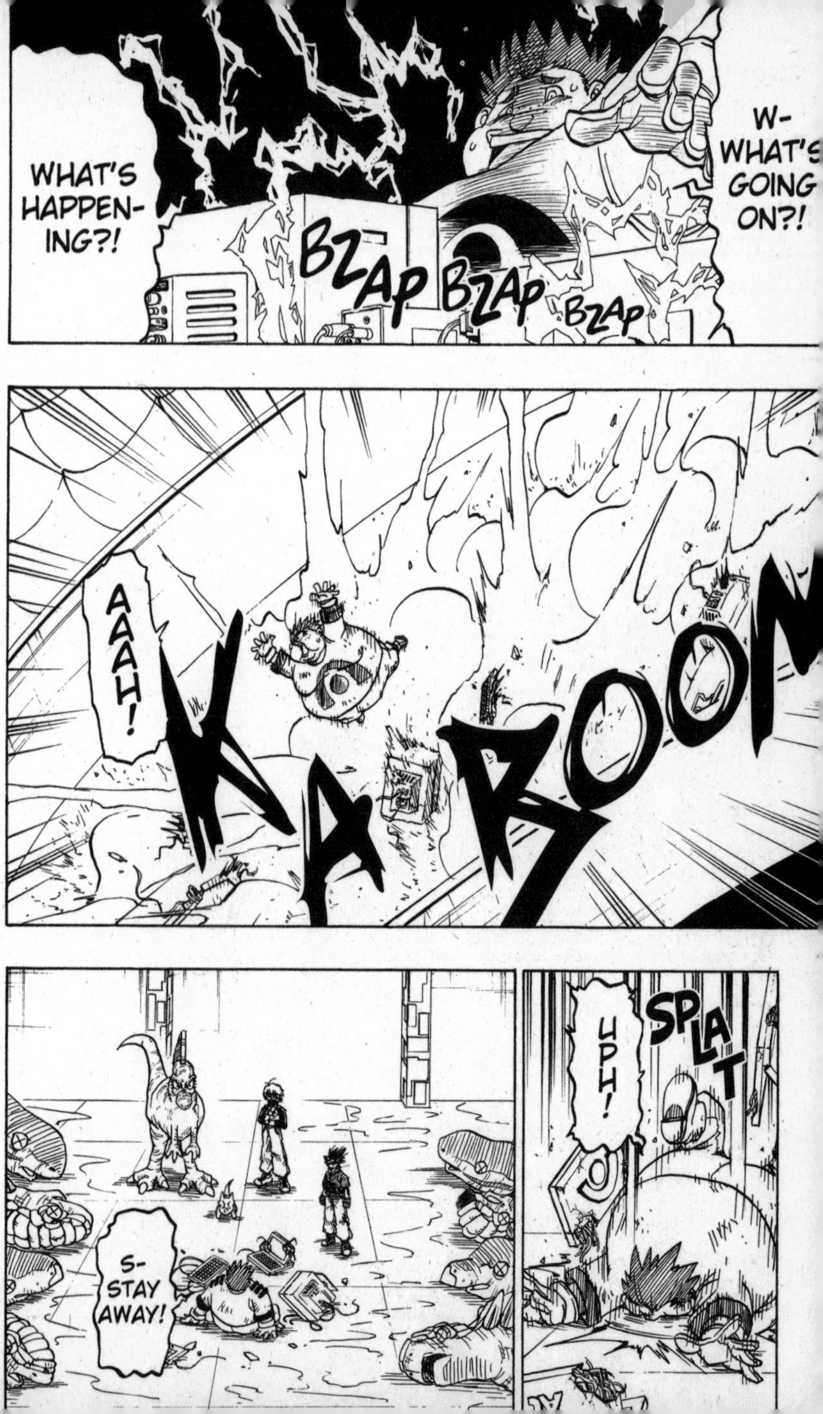
W-WHAT'S GOING ON?!
BZAP BZAP BZAP
WHAT'S HAPPEN-ING?!
KABOOM
AAAH!
SPLAT
UPH!
S-STAY AWAY!

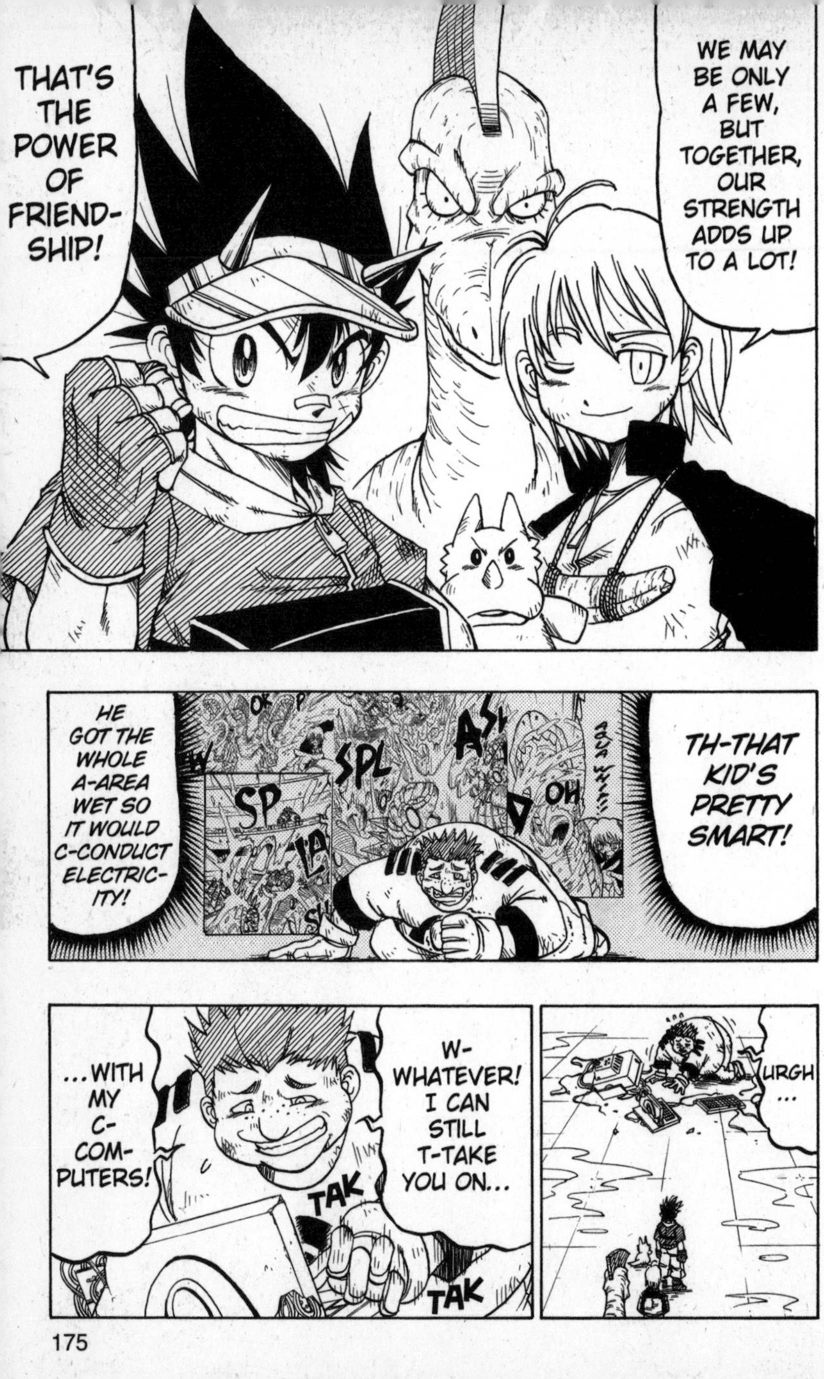
WE MAY BE ONLY A FEW, BUT TOGETHER, OUR STRENGTH ADDS UP TO A LOT!
THAT'S THE POWER OF FRIENDSHIP!
TH-THAT KID'S PRETTY SMART!
HE GOT THE WHOLE A-AREA WET SO IT WOULD C-CONDUCT ELECTRICITY!
URGH...
W-WHATEVER! I CAN STILL T-TAKE YOU ON...
...WITH MY C-COMPUTERS!
TAK
TAK

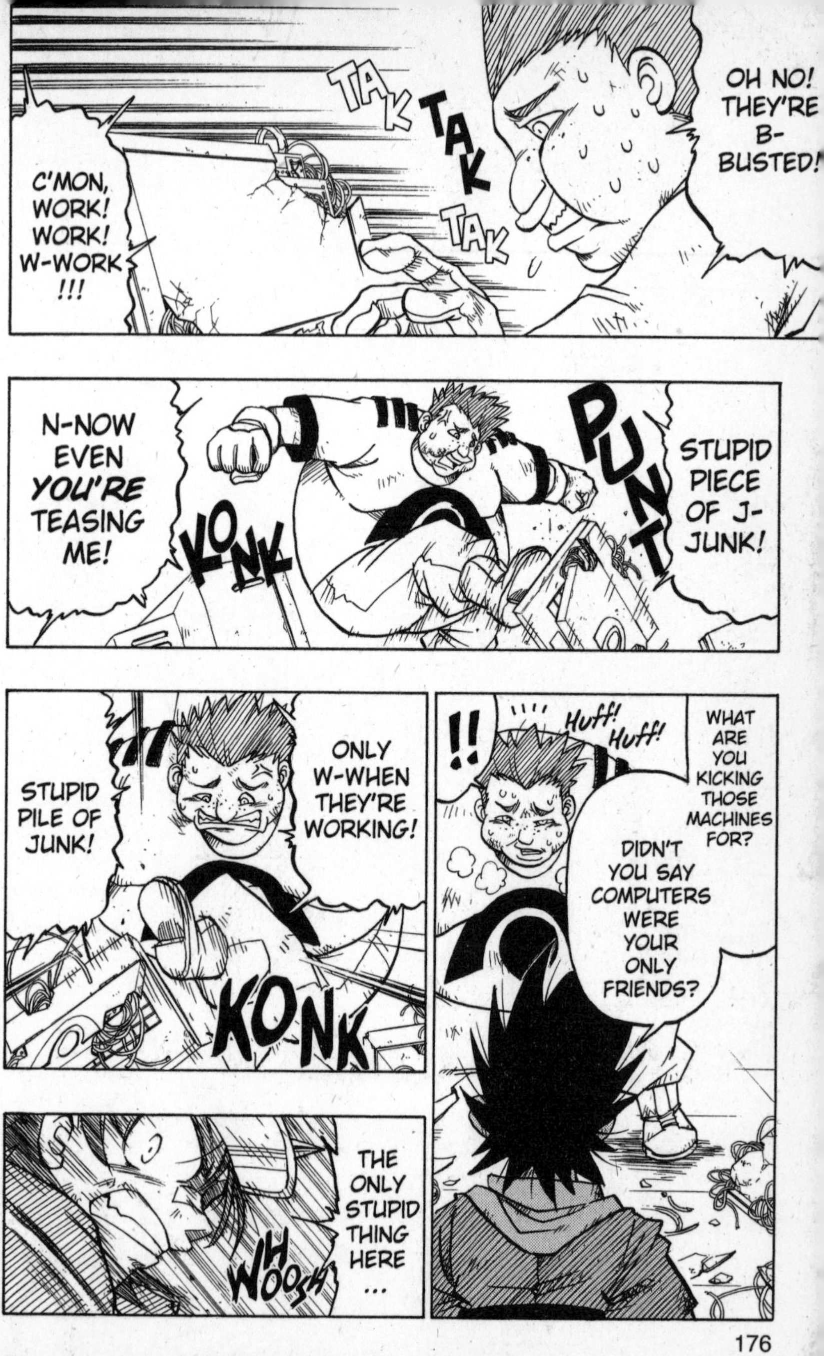
OH NO! THEY'RE B-BUSTED!
TAK TAK TAK TAK
C'MON, WORK! WORK! W-WORK!!!
STUPID PIECE OF J-JUNK!
PUNT
KONK
N-NOW EVEN YOU'RE TEASING ME!
WHAT ARE YOU KICKING THOSE MACHINES FOR?
Huff! Huff!
!!
DIDN'T YOU SAY COMPUTERS WERE YOUR ONLY FRIENDS?
ONLY W-WHEN THEY'RE WORKING!
STUPID PILE OF JUNK!
KONK
THE ONLY STUPID THING HERE...
WHOOSH

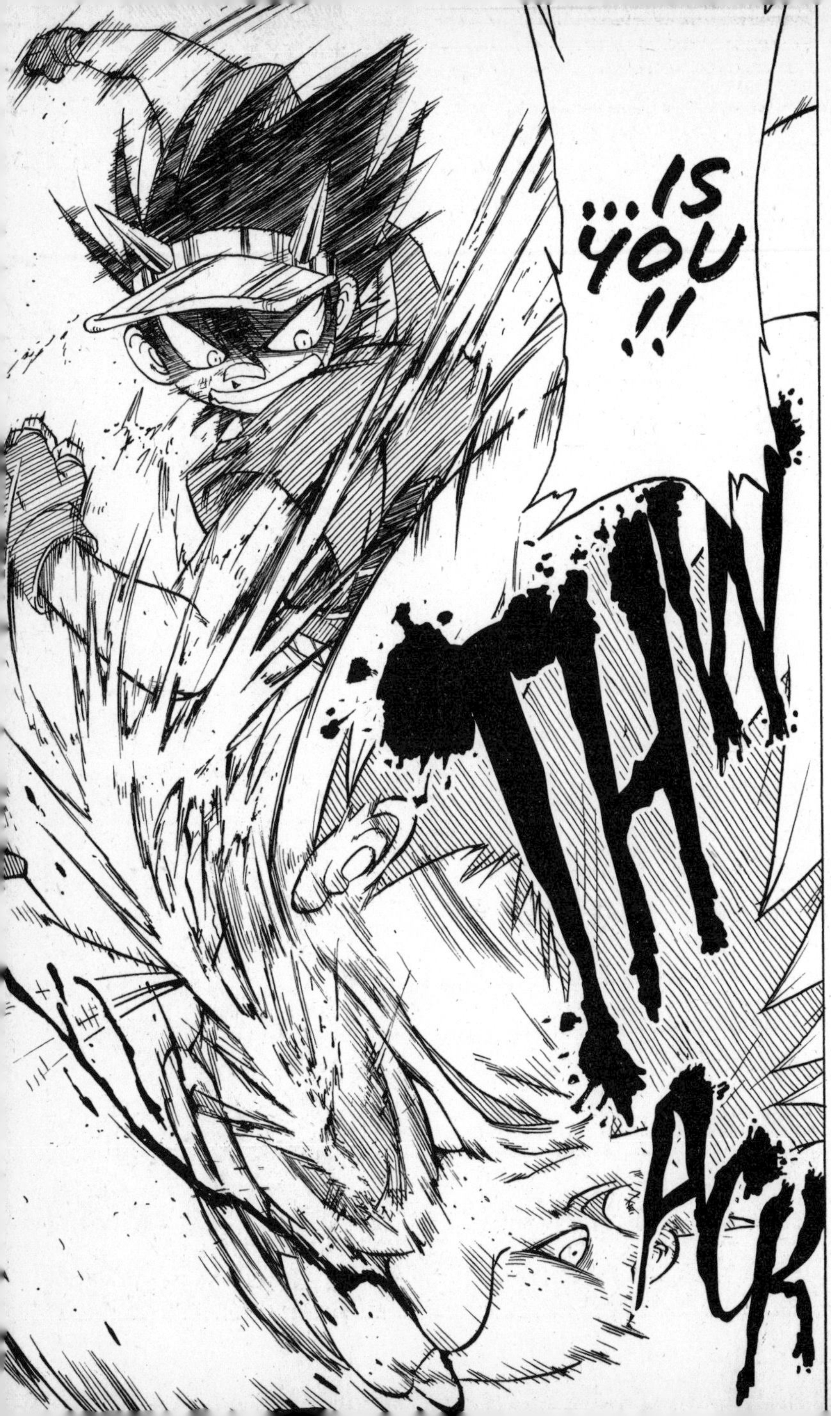
...IS YOU!!
THWACK

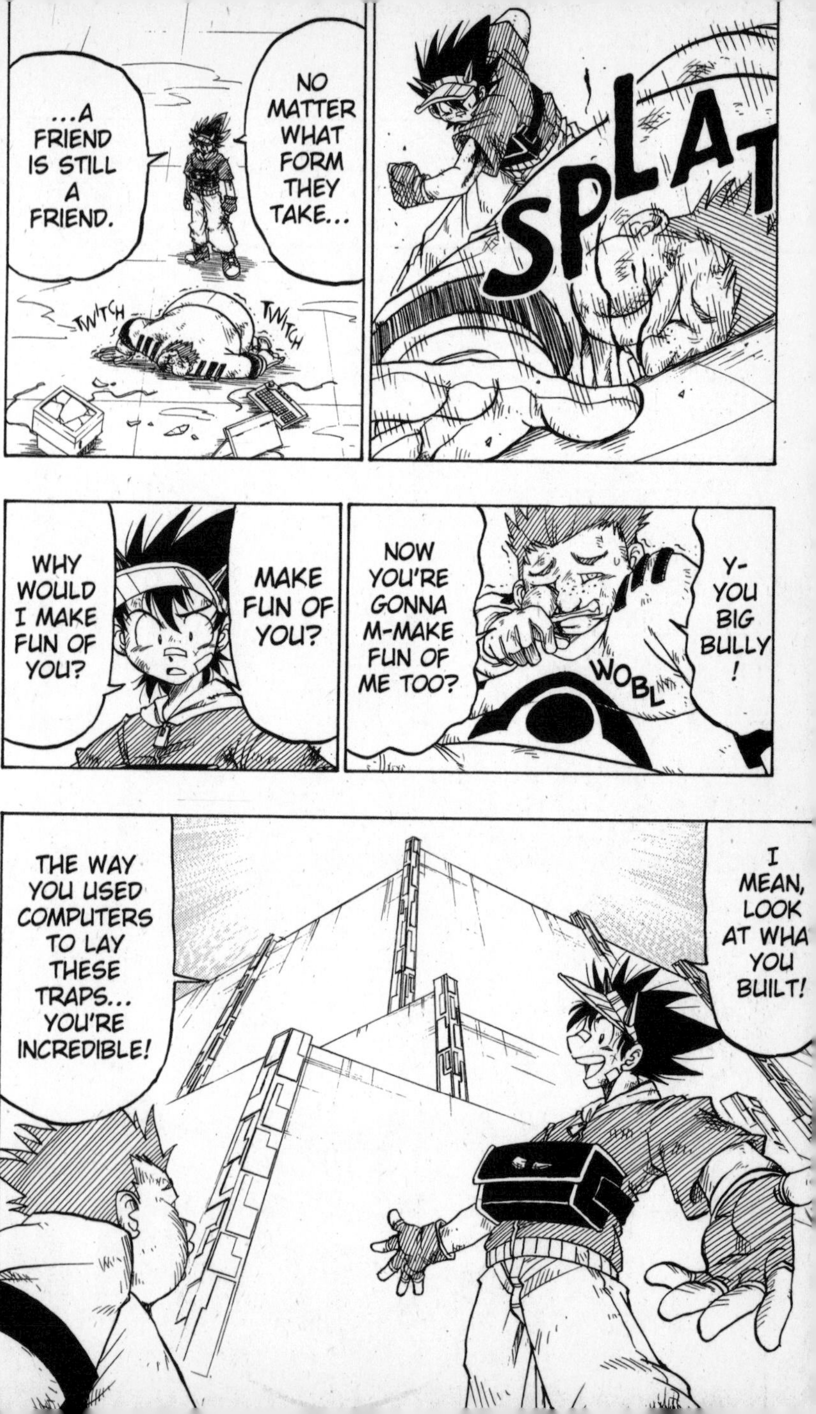
SPLAT
NO MATTER WHAT FORM THEY TAKE...
...A FRIEND IS STILL A FRIEND.
TWITCH
TWITCH
Y-YOU BIG BULLY!
NOW YOU'RE GONNA M-MAKE FUN OF ME TOO?
WOBL
MAKE FUN OF YOU?
WHY WOULD I MAKE FUN OF YOU?
I MEAN, LOOK AT WHA YOU BUILT!
THE WAY YOU USED COMPUTERS TO LAY THESE TRAPS... YOU'RE INCREDIBLE!

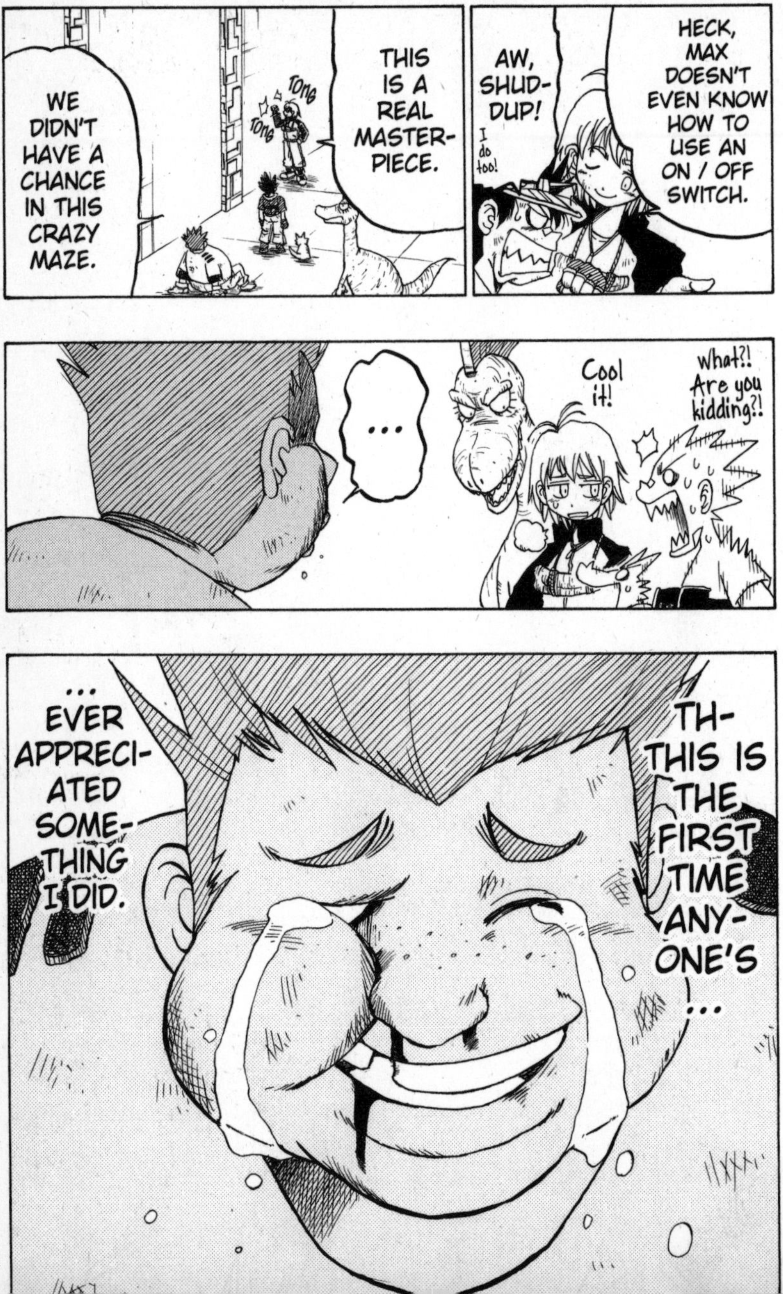
HECK, MAX DOESN'T EVEN KNOW HOW TO USE AN ON / OFF SWITCH.
AW, SHUD-DUP!
I do too!
THIS IS A REAL MASTER-PIECE.
TONG
TONG
WE DIDN'T HAVE A CHANCE IN THIS CRAZY MAZE.
What?! Are you kidding?!
Cool it!
...
TH-THIS IS THE FIRST TIME ANY-ONE'S...
...EVER APPRECI-ATED SOME-THING I DID.

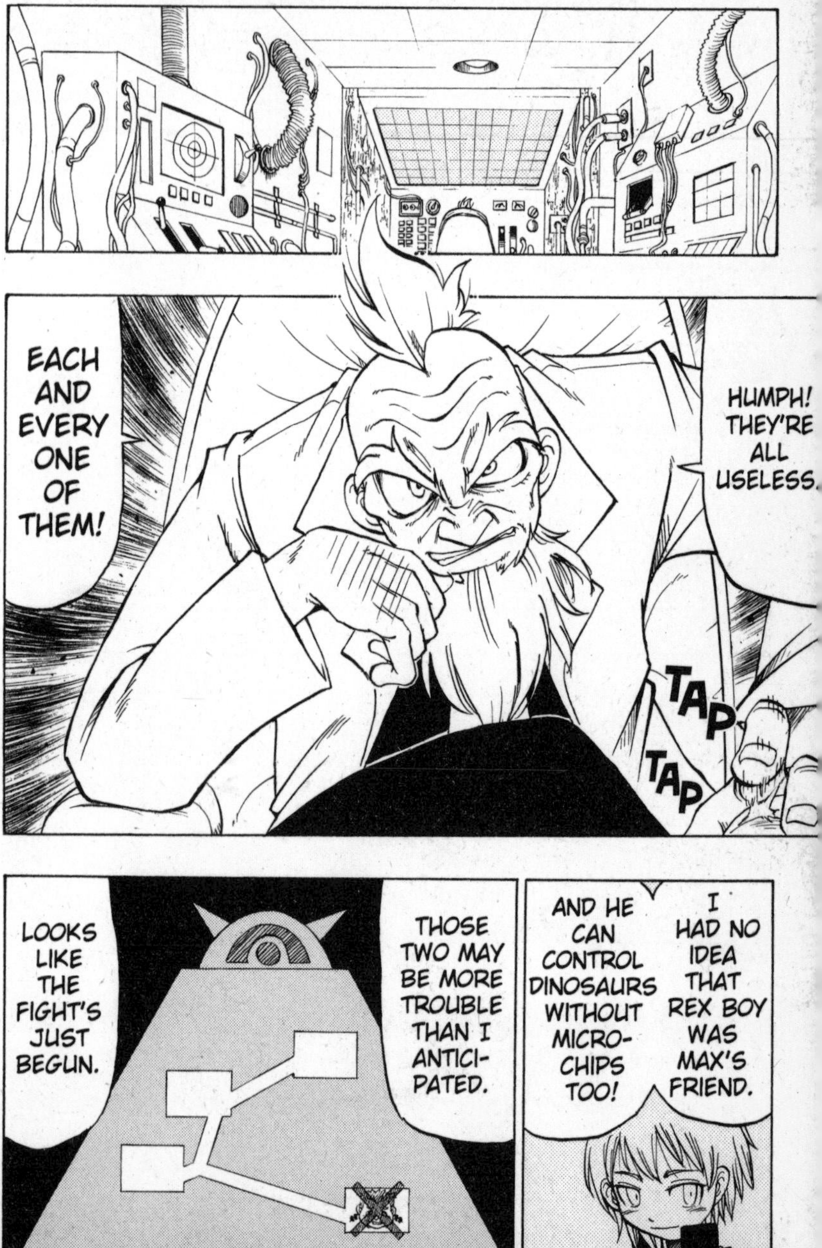
HUMPH! THEY'RE ALL USELESS.
EACH AND EVERY ONE OF THEM!
TAP TAP
I HAD NO IDEA THAT REX BOY WAS MAX'S FRIEND.
AND HE CAN CONTROL DINOSAURS WITHOUT MICRO-CHIPS TOO!
THOSE TWO MAY BE MORE TROUBLE THAN I ANTICIPATED.
LOOKS LIKE THE FIGHT'S JUST BEGUN.

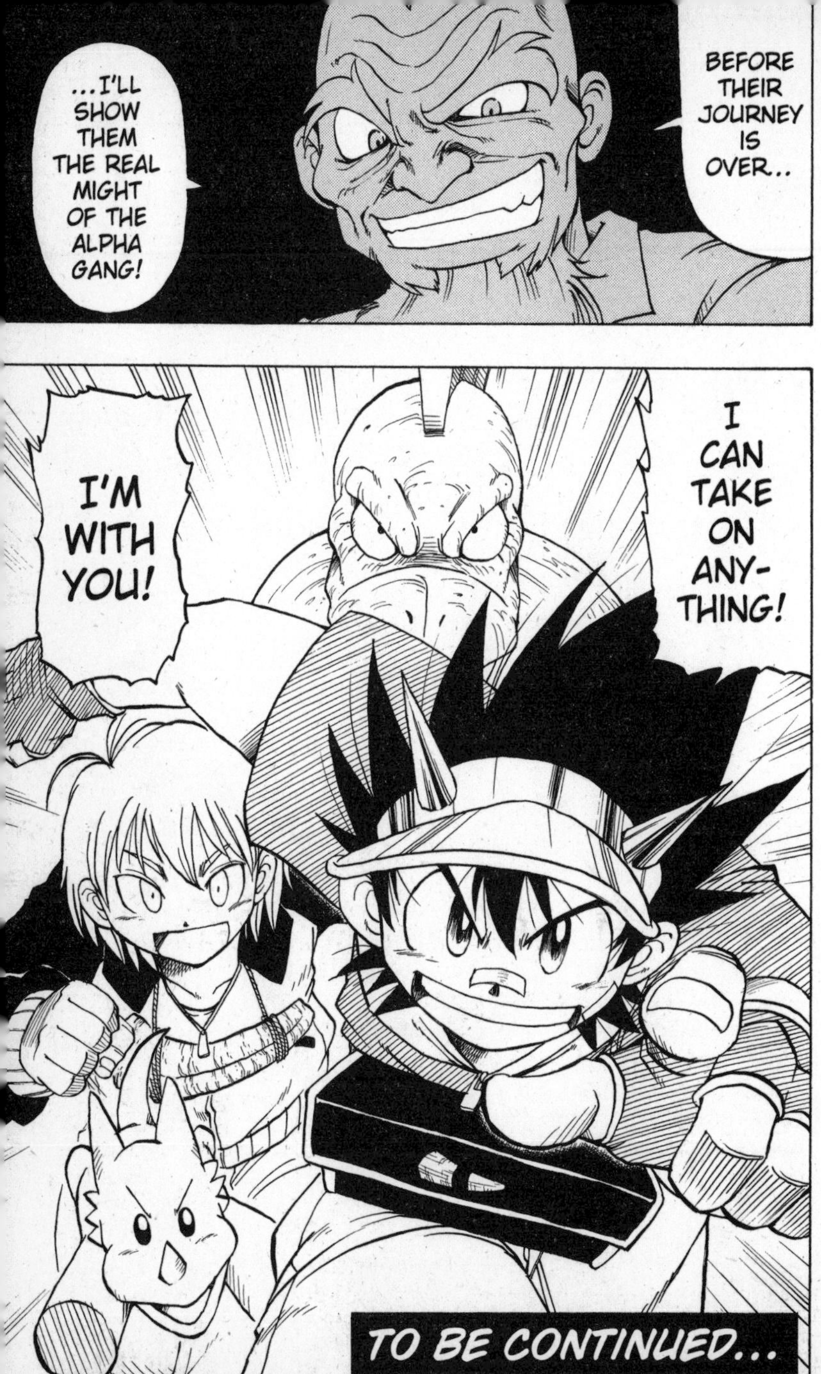
BEFORE THEIR JOURNEY IS OVER..
...I'LL SHOW THEM THE REAL MIGHT OF THE ALPHA GANG!
I CAN TAKE ON ANY-THING!
I'M WITH YOU!
TO BE CONTINUED...

DIG IT!

Uncover facts about dinosaurs, their super moves and their trading card stats!

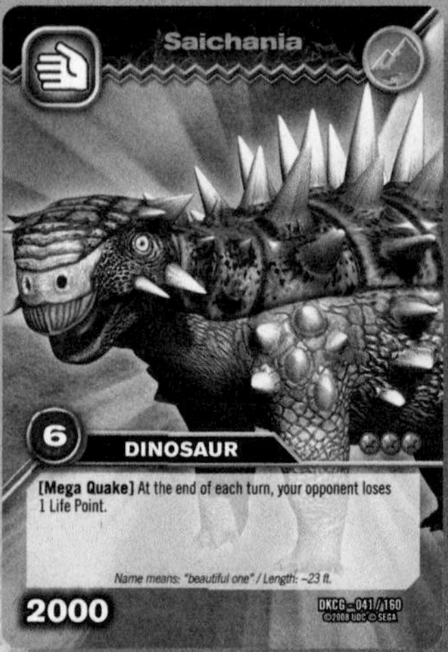
Saichania
6
DINOSAUR
[Mega Quake] At the end of each turn, your opponent loses 1 Life Point.
Name means: "beautiful one" / Length: ~23 ft.
2000
DKCG - 041/160
©2008 UDC © SEGA

SAICHANIA

Saichania means "beautiful one"
Length: approx. 23 ft.
Lived in: Cretaceous Period
Discovered in: Mongolia
One of the most powerful **Earth** Dinosaurs, Saichania's thick armor plates protected it from attacks.
Card Rarity: Silver Rare and Colossal Rare
Saichania's **Mega Quake** ability lets it deal damage without even attacking. Use it with the Super Move Spike Arrows for maximum power.

MOLE ATTACK

Card Rarity: Common
Smash your opponent with a rolling attack! This **Earth** Super Move can be used by any Earth Dinosaur that has a **Scissors** icon. Like Spike Arrows, Mole Attack gives a Dinosaur +1000 power for battle–the maximum you can get from a Super Move!

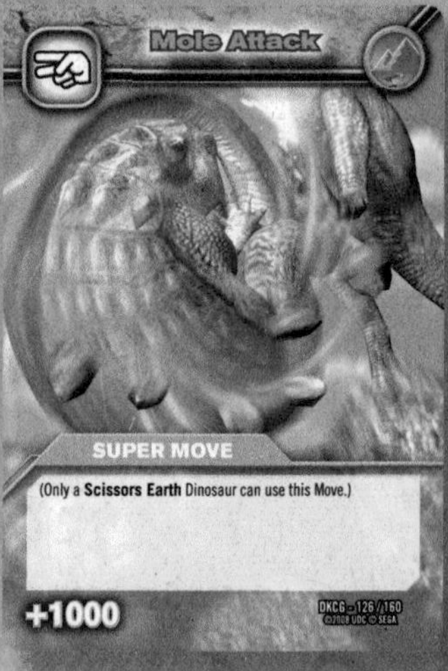
Mole Attack
SUPER MOVE
(Only a Scissors Earth Dinosaur can use this Move.)
+1000
DKCG - 126/160
©2008 UDC © SEGA

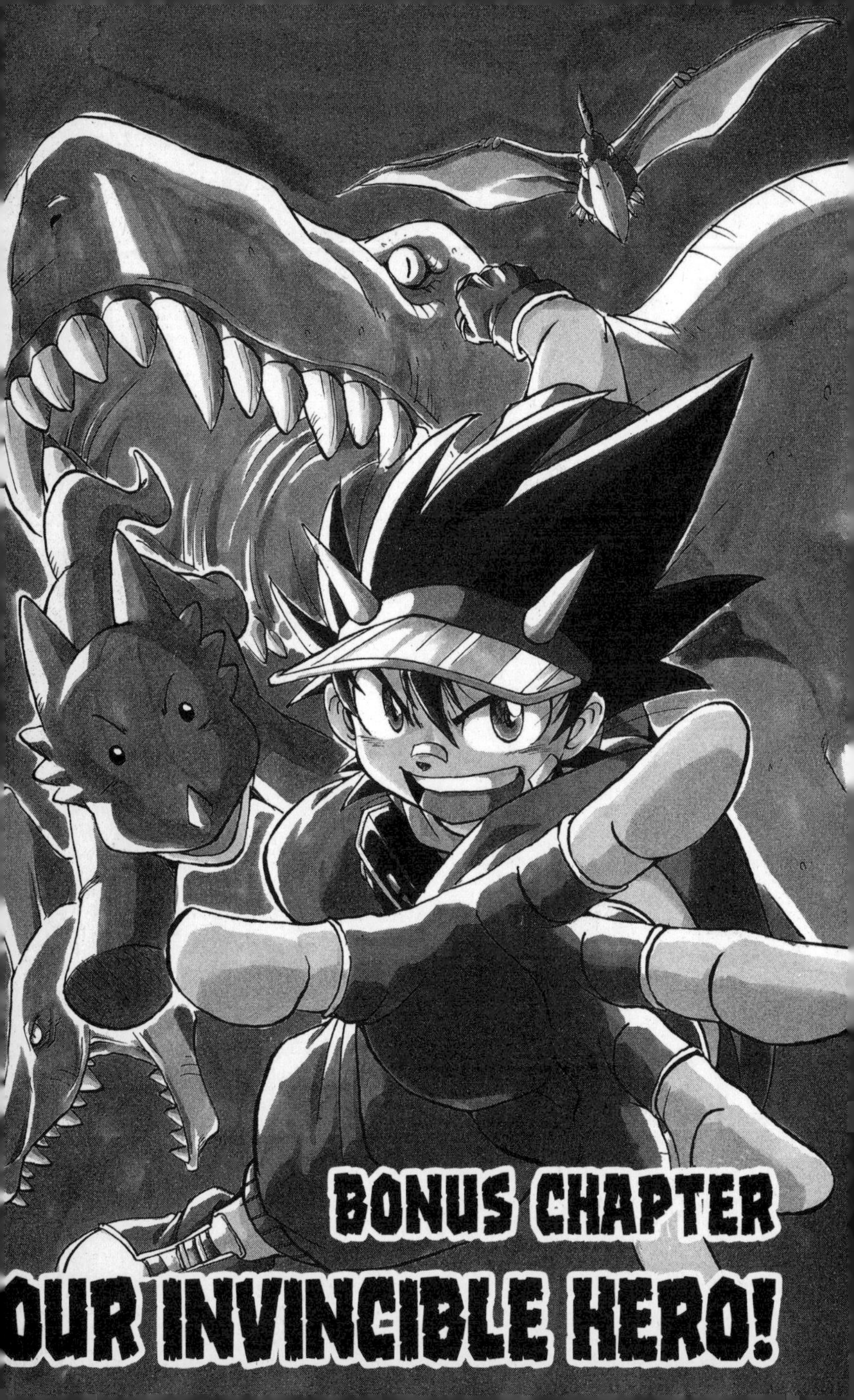
BONUS CHAPTER
OUR INVINCIBLE HERO!

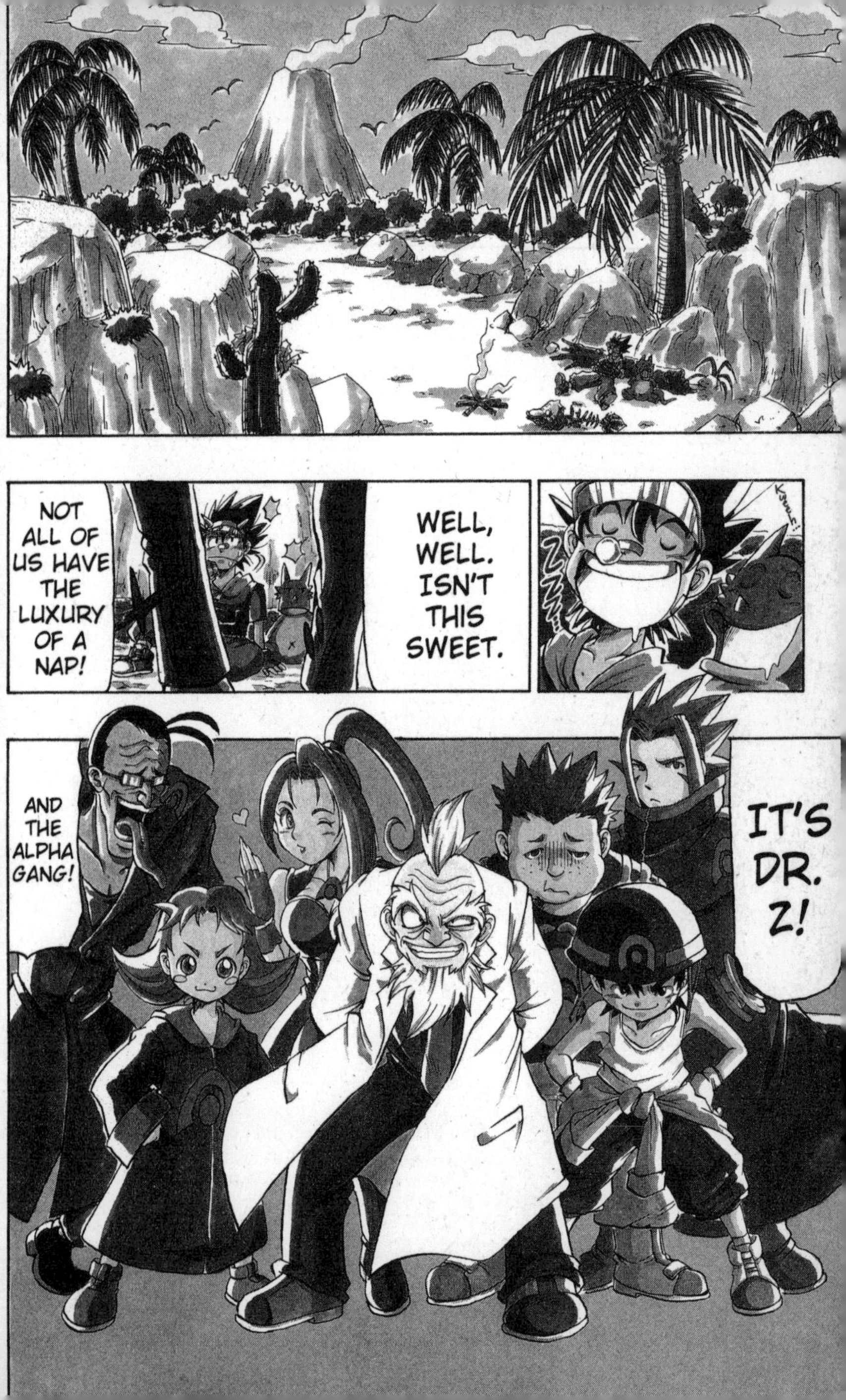
Kweeh!!
WELL, WELL. ISN'T THIS SWEET.
NOT ALL OF US HAVE THE LUXURY OF A NAP!
IT'S DR. Z!
AND THE ALPHA GANG!

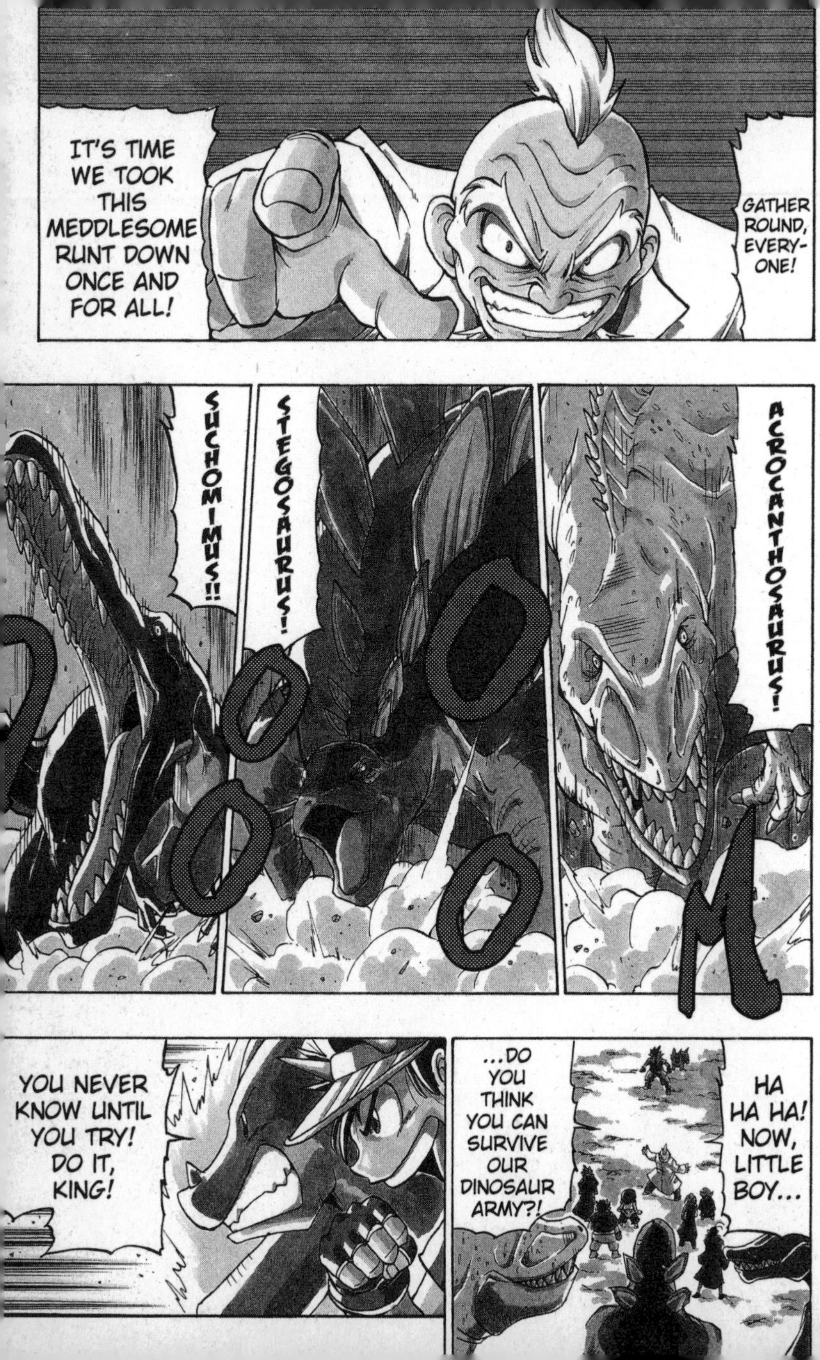
GATHER ROUND, EVERY-ONE!
IT'S TIME WE TOOK THIS MEDDLESOME RUNT DOWN ONCE AND FOR ALL!
ACROCANTHOSAURUS!
STEGOSAURUS!
SUCHOMIMUS!!
OOOOOM
HA HA HA! NOW, LITTLE BOY...
...DO YOU THINK YOU CAN SURVIVE OUR DINOSAUR ARMY?!
YOU NEVER KNOW UNTIL YOU TRY! DO IT, KING!

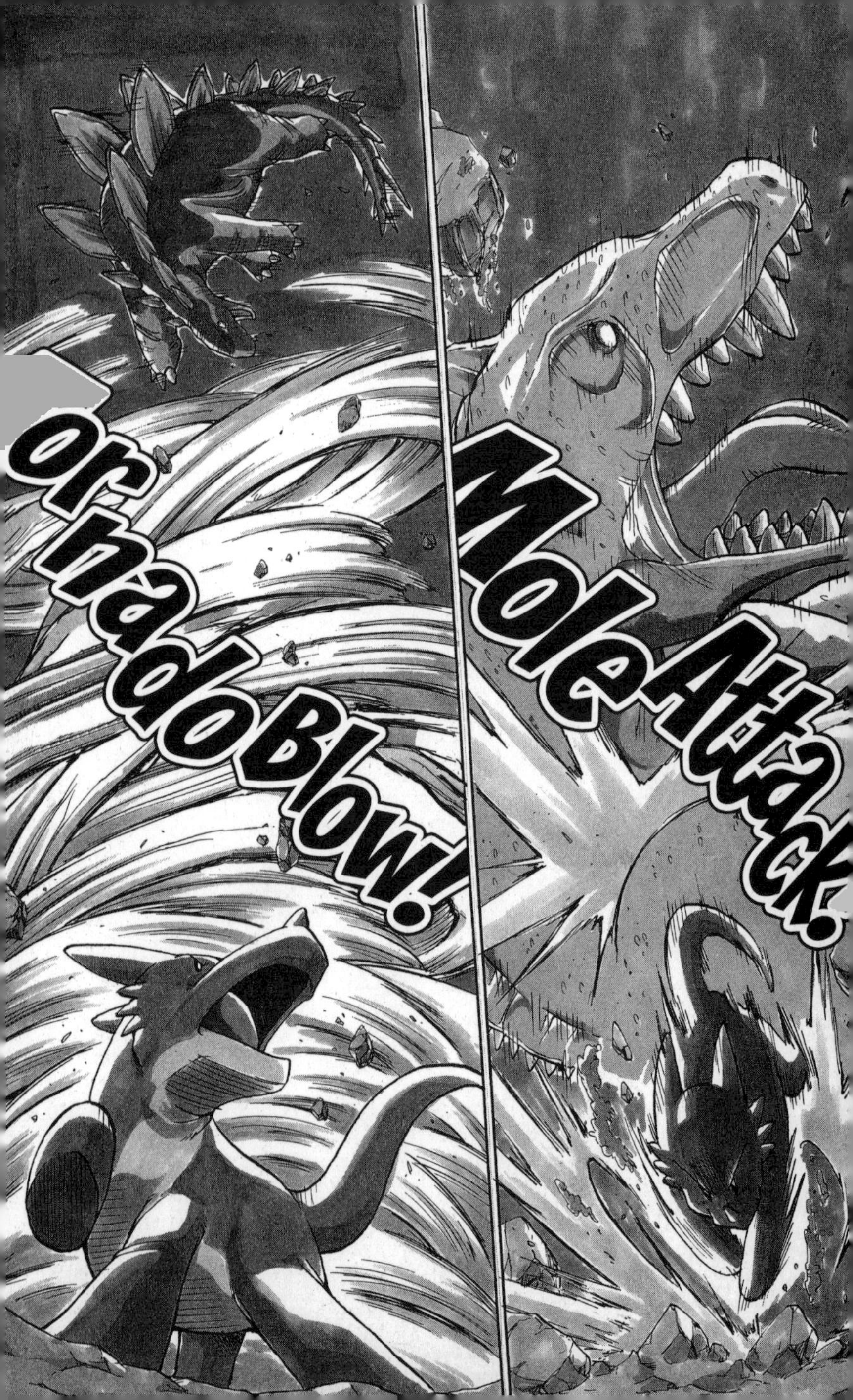
Mole Attack!
ornado Blow!

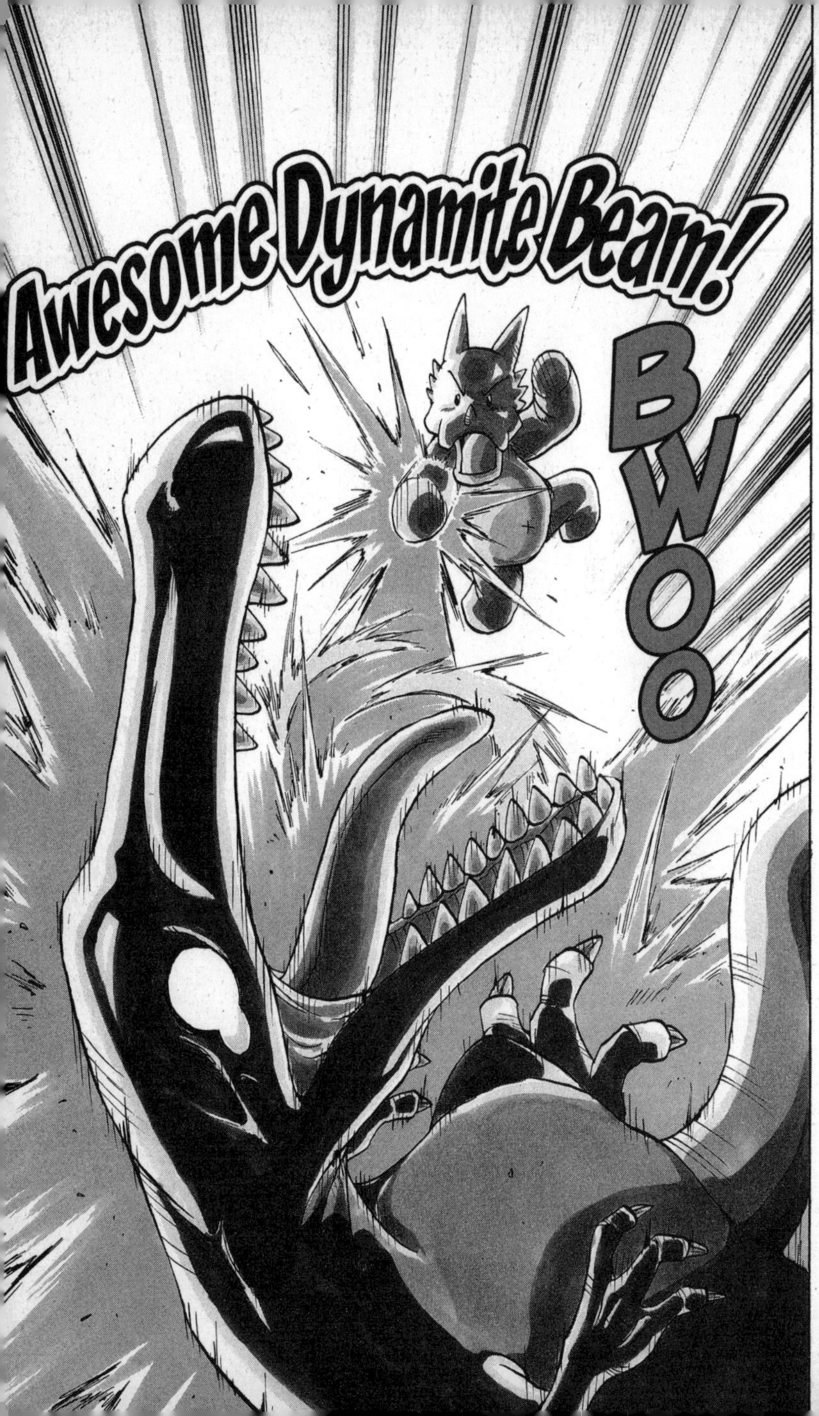
Awesome Dynamite Beam!
BWOO

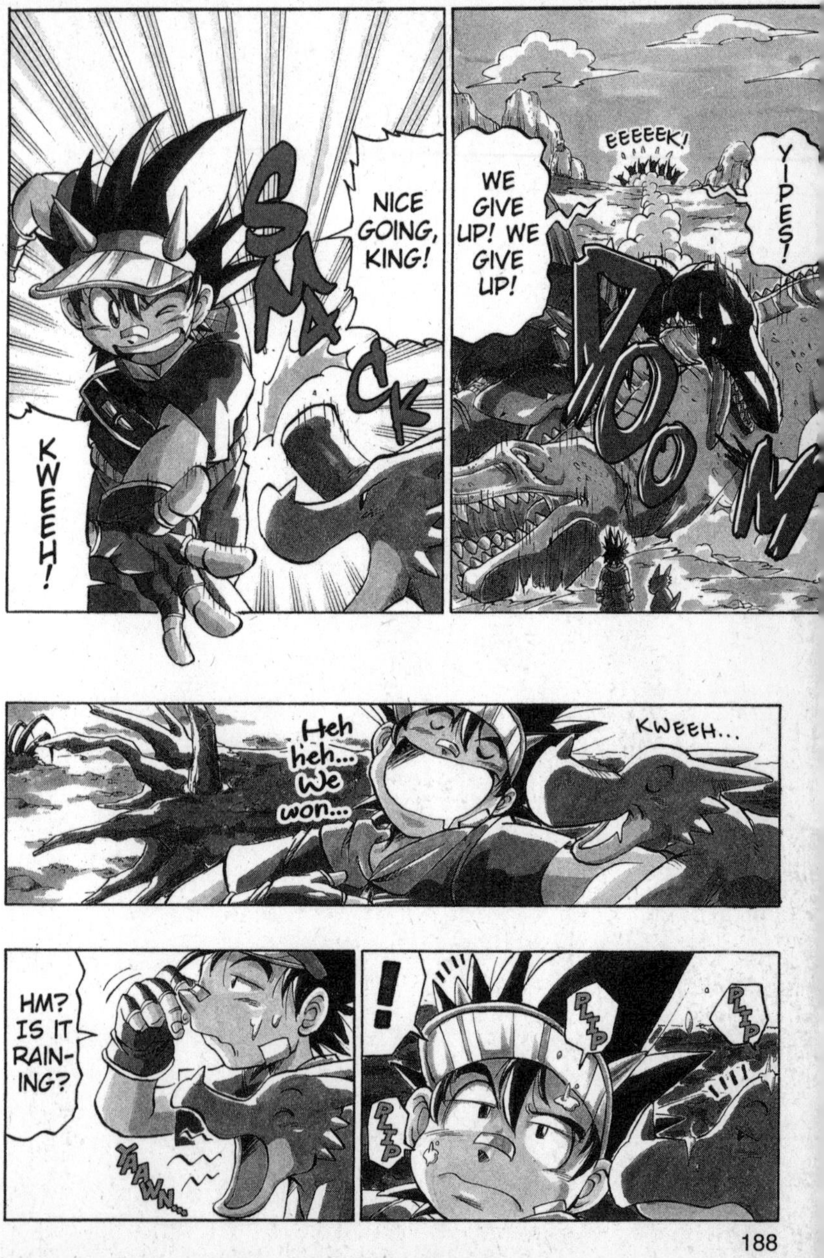
YIPES!
EEEEEK!
WE GIVE UP! WE GIVE UP!
DOOOM
NICE GOING, KING!
SMACK
KWEEEH!
KWEEH...
Heh heh... We won...
!
PLIP
PLIP
PLIP
HM? IS IT RAINING?
YAAWN...

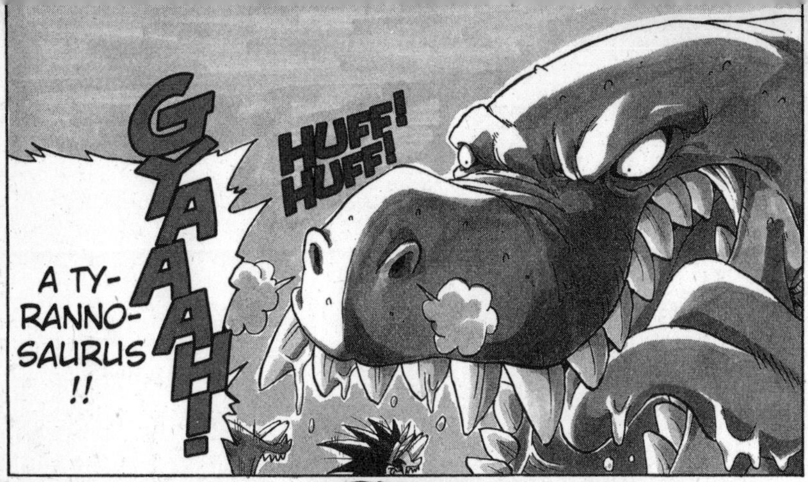
HUFF! HUFF!
GYAAAH!
A TY-RANNO-SAURUS !!
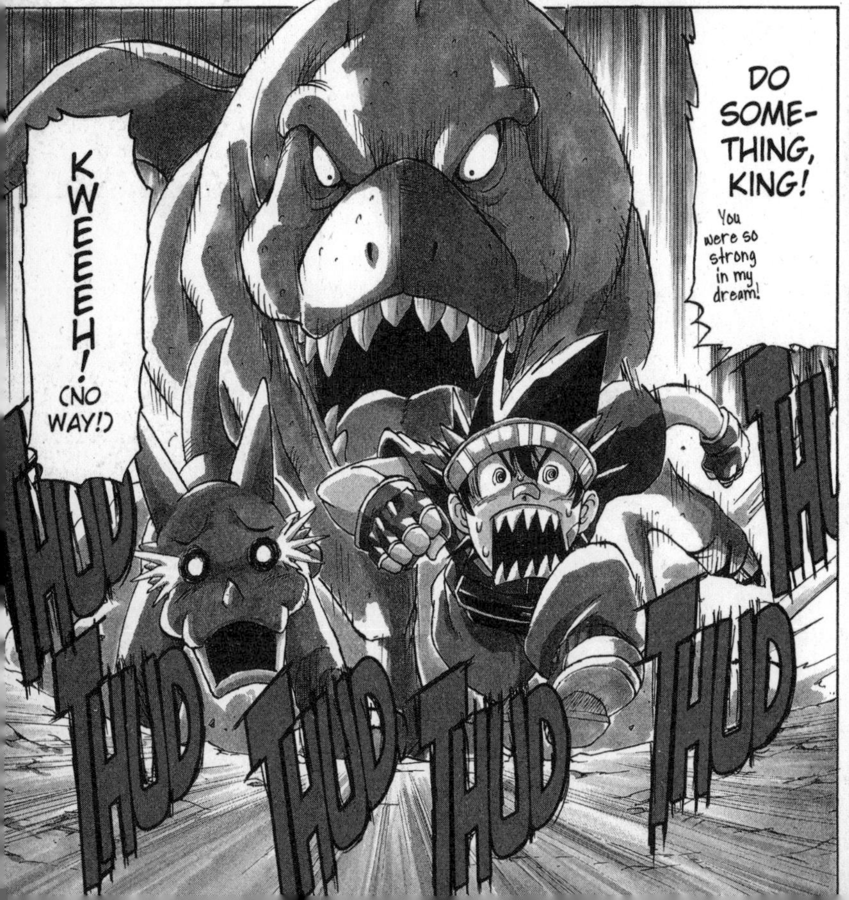
DO SOME-THING, KING!
You were so strong in my dream!
KWEEEEH! (NO WAY!)
THUD
THUD
THUD
THUD
THUD
THUD
THUD

IN THE NEXT VOLUME

Max, King, Rex and Benjamin seem like an unstoppable team, but are they ready for what the Alpha Gang has in store? Find out in volume 2 of *Dinosaur King*!

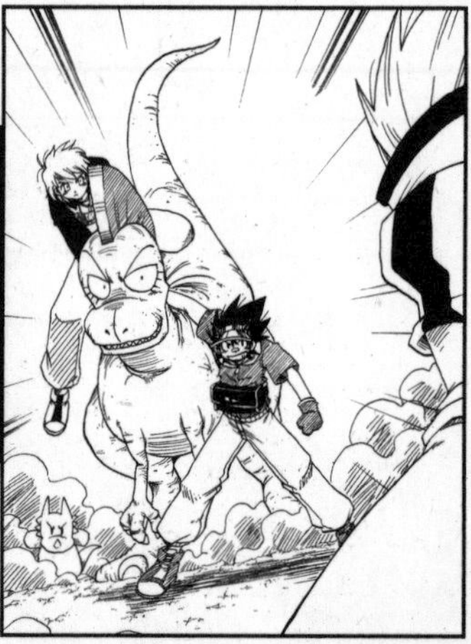

ABOUT THE AUTHOR

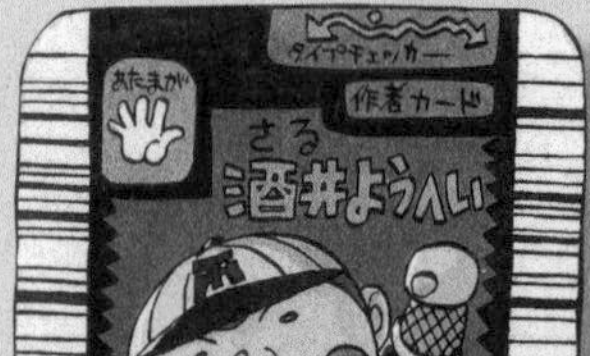
作者カード
酒井ようへい
0.5
20

Card text:
Yohei "Saru" ("Monkey") Sakai
(His full name is Yohei Sakai, but his nickname is "Saru".)
-Author card -Technique: 0.5 -Power: 20

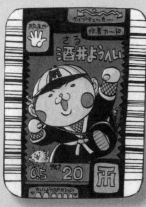

Yohei "Saru" Sakai, creator

Lived in: He is barely living in the present.

Discovered in: Yamaguchi Prefecture

Yohei Sakai is the author and illustrator of this manga.

Favorite Thing: The Hanshin Tigers baseball team from Osaka

DINOSAUR KING
VOLUME 1
VIZ KIDS EDITION

STORY AND ART BY
YOHEI SAKAI

© 2006 Yohei SAKAI/Shogakukan
© SEGA/Sunrise, Nagoya Broadcasting Network
© SEGA
All rights reserved.
Dinosaur King is a registered trademark of Sega Corporation.
Dinosaur King Trading Card Game cards produced
by The Upper Deck Company, Inc.
Original Japanese edition "KODAI OUJA KYOURYU KING"
published by SHOGAKUKAN Inc.

Translation/Katherine Schilling
Touch-up Art & Lettering/Annaliese Christman
Graphics & Cover Design/Yukiko Whitley
Editor/Traci N. Todd

VP, Production/Alvin Lu
VP, Sales & Product Marketing/Gonzalo Ferreyra
VP, Creative/Linda Espinosa
Publisher/Hyoe Narita

Dinosaur King Trading Card Game cards produced
by The Upper Deck Company, Inc.

Printed in the U.S.A.

Published by VIZ Media, LLC
P.O. Box 77010
San Francisco, CA 94107

10 9 8 7 6 5 4 3 2 1
First printing, February 2010